CONTENTS

creating murder   1

CREATING MURDER

David Nightingale

Chapter 1 – The journey to a new home

Within the South east of England, a little over 10 miles from Reading, there lies a peaceful village called Crowthorne. Set deep within the lush Berkshire countryside. Perhaps a quiet jewel; easily missed within the crown of this busy world. This village milieu provides stark contrast to the almost frenzied hustle and bustle of Great Britain's capital, which sits a solitary hours drive away.

Perhaps akin to a land where time seems to stand still. Yet, beware an irony barb; settle here at your peril. For in your slumber and before your very shut eyes, something invisible lies in wait; ready to ensnare. For this humble Crowthorne can surely stealthily pounce, devouring the once plentiful morsels of your very life.

Life here is like a well-worn journey, executed on constant repeat. Lulled into travelling as an automaton with threads of consciousness slipping between every finger; we arrive at a destination as if teleported across the sands of time. Stay long enough to hear the hypnotic lullaby; awareness suspended, the decades tick merrily by. Time does its work; a terminator, for sure.

The Crowthorne village offers few modern shops. The three local pubs yield a night life that can have changed little, over the last several decades. A tranquil façade apathetically emanates; seemingly incongruous with the twenty first century pace of life. The calm is only intermittently broken by the various vehicles that meander through; rarely stopping, just passing through.

At the end of this sleepy village stands a late night supermarket, representing a rare and ill-fitting intrusion upon traditional Crowthorne life. If one crosses over a road and walks a little to the left, then lying in wait is a large sign post stipulating directions to numerous destinations. Amidst the various names, there is a small rather humble looking pointer, pointing up a winding road, with the information, *'Broadmoor ½'*. This winding road leads to a notorious habitat. A habitat which is perhaps even more shielded than this quiet country village, which lies as it's host.

Towards the end of a very early morning journey, Jim Butler is still and in motion; seated in the back of a black Audi. He finds his attention very briefly lassoed by this same pointer, *'Broadmoor ½'*. Very nearly half a century into his life, it is this sign that beckons Jim towards his new destiny.

Handcuffed to a host on either side, Jim is occasionally brought back to the present moment from the uncomfortable pinch of metal against skin. The power differential not lost on Jim, albeit experientially and below the level of conscious analysis. For the first time in many decades, Jim feels akin to a child surrounded by parental figures. More than a small part of our Jim is warm to this dynamic.

The ambience inside the vehicle is relatively tranquil. Heaters not needed, but turned up full. Occasional relaxed conversation, mixed with middle-of-the-road sixties music playing at a relatively low volume. The Audi shows off an impeccable interior and exterior façade; enough to leave the most officious valet adrift, without purpose.

Jim's nasal cavity could never sidestep the fragrance from not one, but two separate air fresheners. Unbeknownst to our Jim, he is exposed to 'Apple Green Cider' and 'Evergreen Forest' fragrances. The latter duo thoroughly elbowing out their only competitors, in the form of the residue of car cleaning products and country smells from intermittently ajar windows.

Jim notes the vehicle smoothly transitioning up the winding road. Passing houses on both sides, alongside the odd tree twisting teasingly amidst the hypnotic Berkshire breeze. Other than a deafening silence outside the vehicle, this part of the journey is initially unremarkable. Yet, as one negotiates the second winding bend, to one's left appears a large sign. In bold red ink, it proclaims the implicit notoriety of this small Berkshire village:

SPECIAL HOSPITAL
SERVICES AUTHORITY
BROADMOOR HOSPITAL

Just before one reaches the sign there are two white pillars at either side; these bare testimony that one has entered the Broadmoor estate. Further up on the opposite side of the road there is a smaller sign, far less bold and containing a much lengthier script:

PRIVATE. NO THROUGH ROAD.
SPEED LIMIT 20MPH. HIGHWAYS ACT 1980 – SECTION 31
THIS IS NOT A PUBLIC RIGHT OF WAY AND IS SUBJECT
TO THE PROVISIONS OF THE ROAD TRAFFICS ACT

By this stage, having reached "Upper Broadmoor Road", one is becoming increasingly engulfed by a vast array of tall outreaching pines. To the left emerge two large estates, providing shelter for the Broadmoor staff. The white exterior of these abodes provides harsh contrast to the red brick context, which dominates their surrounds. Recent constructions, daring to rudely trespass upon scenes which never jaded of being frozen.

Further up the left, the trees stand even taller. These leafy offerings beyond shielding the road; prone to intimidate all that lies so far beneath their peak. This lofty greenery gives one side of the guiding funnel, leading inexorably to the Broadmoor institution.

On the right side, there is some grass land and an ever nearing line of densely packed pines. The latter aligned congregation provides the other side of the encroaching funnel. Our Jim travelling within this outer stricture; set to deliver him to his new beginning, perhaps akin to a friendly fallopian tube.

Difficult not to be humbled by the vastness of the natural barriers, yielding an inevitability to the path. Submission surely follows, perhaps without choice. If one is not wholly over-awed by the vast size of this shielding, then follow the road up through another bend. Then, an ambiguous red brick totem gradually starts to emerge.

Near the top of this notorious hill, the towering upright trees sway knowingly amidst the circulating Berkshire winds. Tall trees that have seen many come and some surely go. Yet feel the warmth of the silence from these great trees, as they knowingly witness the entirety. Their being wholly unpolluted by the toxic pong of fickle judgements. Standing tall and free from the most foul distillations of a cesspit bubbling with language. Futility not needed.

As one emerges at the pinnacle of this assent to Broadmoor Special Hospital, a section of this vast Victorian effigy leaps out and imprints upon the innocence of any newcomer. Yet, the continuing consistency of this nineteenth century asylum typically finds a path to calming even the most anxious of its visitors. Set within beautifully rich Berkshire countryside, the general aura of the asylum echoes the peaceful harmony of the natural surrounds.

Scattered around the top of the upper Broadmoor road, one sees many a new seedling apparently thriving amidst this soothing country retreat. Perhaps mirroring the patients of this special hospital, blanketed and nurtured by more than this backdrop. Planted in a soil that can render a rush of stability, deep within.

The Audi gently pulls up only several parking spots from the main entrance; our Jim arrives at unfamiliar surrounds. He notices the car's digital clock revealing a green representation of:

8:43am.

Mists of societal stigma may cloud new arrivals. Yet, beyond the vast red brick Victorian wall, the institutional network appears to emanate a distant glow. Jim, moments away from entering. He arrives, at a beginning.

Readied or not, much awaits him. Momentarily, on the outside, looking in. The latter perhaps an ironic echo of our Jim's very life?

Chapter 2 - Sentenced and judged

Following the very recent courtroom verdict, Jim ready to amble at the consequent starting blocks. Arriving at Broadmoor Special Hospital, poised to serve the first morning of an indeterminate sentence. Within the press, Jim's major crimes are described; not unhindered by opinion.

Whatever Jim's crimes, the few who vaguely knew him suggest it was 'totally out of character'. Yet, the courtroom psychiatric expert witness begs to differ. By virtue of his actions and the twisting turns of his court case, Jim may well spend the rest of his life within his newly found asylum.

Yet before Jim's life unfolds before us, the story takes a brief detour to an inconsequential residence. A residence unconnected to Jim in any way. Yet, perhaps a relentless echo of the planet he inhabits.

In this house, a couple play out a not untypical scene over breakfast. Their kitchen clock showing 8:43am. As we have seen, Jim simultaneously arrives at the outer limits of his new home, well over a hundred miles away from this middle class residence.

This distant family, surrounded by the aura of strong filter coffee and burnt toast. The pulp newspaper front page graces the table, amidst this feast of toast, coffee, and cereal. The bold and cowardly headline *'Monster gets Justice'* provides the digestible simplicity that the audience need. The masses tend to fiercely cling on to the illusory moral high ground.

"He had a choice, and he chose to do what he did – it's that simple. Jim Butler is pure evil" Jane says to her husband Sam,

Sam had previously dared to float the question *'I wonder why he did it ?'.*

Sam raised his eyebrows slightly in response to Jane's conclusions, as if still ponderous. Jane wanted to close this case.

'HAVE YOU READ WHAT HE'S DONE?' Jane asked incredulously, with raised voice.

'YOU CAN'T DO THAT AND NOT BE EVIL SCUM' she declared with volume still up several notches; the prosecution resting briefly.

Jane seems angered by Sam's questioning *'why ?'.* Silence prizes out a continuation, from Jane, in the form of: "*I know about bad times and hardship, but I don't go around doing things like that*".

Jane's bottled up anger is freed up by a marked lack of insight and understanding. You could say she is blessed. Alternatively, maybe she is better described as achieving the largely durable defence of being *'normal'?*

On goes the agitated racket against Jim's core. The masses magnetically drawn to look the other way as complexity walks by, unnoticed. The societal lenses see our Jim so clearly; a vision of Jim immersed wholly in a vacuum of nothing but pure 'free will'.

If you can hold up a most opaque template, then the most appealing shapes can be carved from this gunk known as language. Black and white if you please, no need to get painfully caught on the jagged grey areas. Of course, spare a thought; nature's claws hold the broad heaps of society just as tight.

Jane and Sam's children are still vaguely present. They manifest partly in the form of a mischievous ten year old boy Tom, with red curly hair. Tom sits an arms length from his more reserved and slightly older brother Josh. Young Tom briefly notices the headline and asks *'Who's the monster?'*, as he munches enthusiastically on a piece of slightly burnt toast.

Jane steps in and quickly retorts, ' *he is a very, very bad man and he will be in prison for the rest of his life'*. Tom's questions continue, and Jane relentlessly places her rusty template over the eyes of this young fellow. The lessons endlessly unfold, shadowing a childhood. Tom is being readied for the world in which Jane and the masses live.

Philosophers might contemplate the well-worn path of pontificating over issues such as, *'if a tree falls in a forest and no one is around to hear, does it make a sound?'*. Reality weeps, but hushed and still so imperceptibly quiet. A journey awaits.

Chapter 3 - Entrance to incarceration.

A car pulled up at a huge wooden door, marking part of the perimeter of Broadmoor Special Hospital. Jim seated in the Audi; awaiting his life's latest offering. It remains 8:43am.

To fully land in Broadmoor requires both criminality and what used to be termed 'madness'. So, typically the patients within Broadmoor have committed a most serious crime; often murder. However, these patients are deemed to have been not been criminally responsible at the time of committing the offence, by virtue of suffering with clinically significant mental health problems.

Aged nearly fifty, Jim arrives at the gates that mark the new confines of his existence. Being trapped speaks loudly to him of a lovely freedom. Freedom from a world he has long since grown weary of.

Freedom from a society riddled with hypocrisy and facade. Jim has spent worthless decades relentlessly floundering to win at this video game called 'life'. Finally, he can see the beautiful vision of 'Game Over'.

Many years as an adult; finally, no longer burdened by the prevalent pressure to sustain a social illusion of being normal, successful and decent. He has the blessing of a new identity, which is so much easier to sustain. He feels himself already settling into labels of: 'criminal', 'insane' and a 'failure'. Labels which release him from the chains of pretense.

A heavy weight of expectations slip off him. Like an over-used work horse, finally put out to pasture. He reaches the prison of a High Security Special Hospital and this prison seems to reach out to him. Emotionally beckoned in by the arms of every element of this Victorian symbol of compassion: the bricks, the doors, the windows, and the walls.

'*Come in, Jim, Cooommme in*'. Jim's soul could almost hear the institution willing him to its bosom, resonating at a level more true than language and awareness. He feels sucked in, through the very gates. Unbeknownst to this Jim, those same gates had fixed it for namesakes to take cover here. Trying to remain graceful, but a sense that our Jim was running from a world outside these gates.

Many years ago: Jim's birth marked something being pushed and squeezed from a maternal vessel into a waiting world. A world which was ripe with perversity; surely, readied for his arrival. Many years later, Jim has washed up here, at Broadmoor; after being wholly battered by an endless futile struggle to solve unfolding riddles.

Perhaps the world had lay in wait and ready to pounce, at his birth? The world that sprung out on him had pushed him through the harsh strictures of its architecture, for year after year after year. Only now, had he seemingly emerged into a new arena. Yet this re-birth was not accompanied with the same yelling and crying.

It is Jim's first time incarcerated, though perhaps he is merely beginning another sentence? On arriving at the Special Hospital, Jim is taken by a burly man calling himself a '*nurse*' and a hesitant lady. '*I am nurse McCarron*' the burly man gently announces, '*and this is my colleague nurse Stevens*'. He paused, and then declared, '*we are going to take you to your room*'.

'*How are you ?*' he asks.

'*I'm fine*' Jim retorts.

Indeed, despite being a man having just been convicted of

what we understand to be a most heinous crime and sentenced to an indeterminate sentence, 'he feels fine'. It seems a new chapter has perhaps begun.

'Do you prefer Jim, or Mr Butler?', nurse McCarron enquires.

"Jim", he replies almost reflexively. Mentally, he quickly leaves the scene of his response. A soothing departure from a life dominated by personal acts or utterances being an overture to over-thinking, drenched with negative self-evaluation.

When Jim is clearly within the confines of the special hospital, his handcuffs are taken off. This surprises him. Nurse McCarron briefly gives Jim direction, in the form of *'We are here to help you. If you are good with us, then we will be good with you'*.

The guidance is mixed with Nurse McCarron's lingering eye contact, but it seems to hurt less than in the outside world. The greying beard of this nurse seems to suggest intelligence and compassion, with a strikingly over-sized belly perhaps reflecting over indulgence. McCarron dons thick arms like tree trunks, but still there are perceptible muscular bulges.

Both Nurse McCarron and Nurse Stevens are dressed in a blue uniform, with a large bunch of metal keys attached to their belt via a chain. They regularly take the keys out of a leather pocket threaded onto their belt, to open large metal doors. Jim is drawn to the jangling of the keys and the loud clank from the closing of the metal doors.

Each clank from a new metal door feels like another barrier between him and the harshness of the outside world, increased cushioning at every portal. A tiny specimen; gleefully stuck fast in this vast Victorian web, with a myriad of nooks and crannies. The environment seems to be a mix of prison and hospital.

The hospital elements of this milieu resonate with Jim's meaning system as a sense of 'being cared for'. At this stage, reality remained a largely uninvolved spectator. We might wonder, could this setting offer a type of re-parenting; perhaps even healing some of the faulty circuity within Jim's brain?

Nurse Stevens is present, but easily missed. She is of average build and her face seems worn down by several decades of life. Her eye contact is fleeting and accompanied by a brief forced smile. She seems exposed by her short brown hair, which appears to fit uneasily with her evasion. Akin to a rabbit in headlights: it is as if she is constantly unsettled in the present moment.

In the outside world, Jim would personalize nurse Stevens's demeanour. Her lack of warmth would typically unleash a swarm of wasps in his mind, buzzing aggressively in all the ways that she could think badly of him. It would hit him, like a careless arrow burrowing through the heart. Within Jim's new home, he manages to internally float the idea that nurse Stevens is perhaps battling with her own demons, rather than judging him and his.

After walking across a couple of yard areas, they arrive at what looks like a new one-storey building. After Nurse Stevens opens and closes an external and internal door, they land in a communal area with a large TV set upon the wall. Jim's eyes meet a group of inmates, or 'patients' as they are more usually called.

The patients appear randomly spaced out, across this lounge area. They are dressed in normal everyday clothes. This mixed group seem sufficiently at ease that they are able to gently and calmly take an interest in this new arrival. More lazy-Sunday-afternoon type glances, rather than cat-on-a-hot-tin-roof hypervigilance.

At the near end of the room, Jim is struck by a semi-circular room with large glass windows overlooking the communal area. As two males in blue uniforms exit this room to greet them, Jim realises that the semi-circular room is the Nurses office. The Nurses introduce themselves and shake his hand.

Next, Jim is shown to a small bedroom. Just prior to entering, Nurse McCarron introduces the room to him with an enthusiastic, 'this is your bedroom, Jim'. Jim notes the en suite facilities. Broadmoor Hospital already seeming to Jim to be a gift, that keeps on giving.

The room is neat, but small. Jim views the comfort of a single bed. Close by, there is a plastic looking surface jutting out from the wall representing a table. Jim also has a carefully designed chair, made with material which seems to match his makeshift table. The room is finished off with a couple of shelves, elevated above the table.

The colours are light throughout the room. Jim is settled by the nature of the pink hue of the walls, which surrounds him. It seems quite gentle. All surfaces have rounded corners. Nothing sharp. Nothing harsh.

'*Evening meal is served in three hours, Jim*' nurse McCarron announces, '*I'll get you a menu*'. After briefly departing, he returns with a menu and a crayon.

'*Just put your name at the top, shade in the boxes for what you want, and hand it in to one of the nurses on the ward*' nurse McCarron advises. He then follows this with a jokey, '*great service here – it's like a hotel!*'. He accompanies the line with a gentle smile, which cleanses and leaves no trace of his bulky and muscular presence.

'*Are you OK with us leaving you here, Jim?*' nurse McCarron asks, '*You can wander out to the TV room whenever you want*'.

'*That's great. Thanks for your help?*' Jim replied.

Jim is left alone. He glances at the menu and notices that the evening meal consists of: starter, main meal, and desert. Three choices for each. He shades: 'soup of the day', 'fish and chips', and 'apple pie'. After handing the form to a nurse, he returns to his room.

It seems strange to say, but Jim feels at home. After navigating a life-long journey of feeling like he has been trying to fit a square peg into a round hole, he truly *feels* at home. Then, a gentle knock at the door. A man in jeans and a striped shirt greets Jim.

'*Hiya mate, my name is David. I have been here for eight years. Don't worry, you'll be fine here*', this new character asserts re-assuringly.

After briefly chatting with this fellow patient, David asks rather pointedly '*what is your story, mate?*'. Over the coming years, Jim addresses this question extensively within therapy and within his head. He tries to make some sense of his life journey. I guess to address Jim's 'story', it is useful to go back into the shadows of his history; many years before he plunged to depths of notorious indecency.

Chapter 4 – An overview of Jim's late teens and early adulthood: the Golden years?

Before the cloak is removed on specific events in Jim's life, an overview meanders. Scattered elements of a childhood could be under our very nose, but perhaps no smoking gun. How do these elements of childhood coalesce with each other and with a myriad of unknowns; what do they ultimately shape and forge? The proof of the pudding may lie best in the eating; beyond childhood, an adulthood awaits. For now, a childhood left hidden.

Perhaps the path that a man will tred, often firmly layed down long before the wee boy reaches an adult form. In his late teens and early twenties, Jim experienced various life events. That said, to borrow from Beveridge: even by the age of eighteen, he was far more prone to see what lay behind his eyes, rather than what appeared before them.

Jim's experiences were coloured more by what went on in his mind, rather than the situations which truly played out in external reality. Jim experienced *his* world. His being more than impacted by anxiety and autistic threads.

Jim arrived in the embryonic stage of adulthood, fixed with a set of behavioural patterns which saw him relentlessly trying to fit himself into a slot called 'life'. He kept trying to fit this mould with a breath-taking relentlessness, which for so long was not greatly dimmed by an unerring consistency of failure. Sinking; unable to see life rafts.

How many times do we try to push a square peg into a round hole? Perseverating like an individual carrying a brain whose frontal lobe had been mauled by a hungry tiger. Jim kept using similar short-term strategies which unerringly hit the bulls-eye of unfulfillment, without markedly changing himself or his situational context. An emotional pain inside him steadily grew, accumulated, and festered.

Nowhere was the ill-fit more striking than Jim's approach to using toilets within public; extreme and impactful avoidance. An avoidance of urinating in public toilets from early childhood, and a sense that bodily functions were in some way wrong and shameful. Gods watched on, and an environment had worked hard on crafting the architecture of Jim's mind. Or, if you prefer, Jim was making choices.

As the sands of time elapsed in Jim's childhood, he acquired a set of tools for dealing with his world. He learnt an imperative of almost complete avoidance of using toilets outside the home. By the time his age reached double figures, he was struck down by an inability to say to people whom he knew outside the family that he was going to the toilet.

In time, Jim developed a physiological response whereby he felt less of an urge to urinate when he was in public or in the presence of others. When he wished to urinate but perceived that another person was in ear shot, he was joined by his regular companion anxiety and found himself simply unable to release excess fluid. A most irksome handicap within a social world; our Jim increasingly fleeing to avoidance, denial, and more than a heap of shame.

On the outside; Jim's persona relentlessly strives to give off a scent of normality. On his inside; Jim is stunned by the rotting stench of shame and self-hatred. Why can he not do what everyone else does, and simply use public toilets? Shame fuels both avoidance and silence, which breeds more shame.

Jim's main tool was toxic avoidance and he clung to this with all his being. Too scared to down tools. This agonising bop is sustained for Jim's teens and young adulthood, not really even beginning to let go until into his thirties.

The tighter he clung to avoidance, the tighter and tighter it clung to him. His longevity of pursuit woven of a type of reality well learned. His being and his soul were worn down further and further and further, with each drip, drip, drip of every passing second.

The golden years of Jim's life passed by. The photographs reflected a young life of socialising, working within an office job, and being active. They seemed to represent a normal life. Akin to a poker player that constantly bluffs that they have a good hand; yet breaching etiquette by never showing their cards. Jim's secrecy cultivated shame, denial, and unhelpful delusion.

Relentlessly Jim entered normal situations, which mixed terribly with his learnings. He had a companion with him throughout, who he simply could not shake off. Every situation he went into, he unfortunately had to take himself along.

After entering adulthood, Jim strives for solutions to a deeply personal and unsolvable enigma. Succeed in a social world, and never use a toilet in the presence of people outside his family. Jim, within a vicious cycle which he comes to know as life.

Flailing, coming up short, drenched with failure, and tortured internally. Yet, too scared to vary strategy. Not putting the puzzle down for so many years, until significant criminal offending steps in.

Well over one hundred thousand hours elapse. Millions of minutes stumble by. Several hundred million seconds cruelly slip through Jim's fingers, as he scrambled and yearned to solve this perverse conundrum. Our Jim yearning for an escape hatch, but never looking to change fundamental unworkable rules for living. Perhaps no mental re-route for this terminator?

Chapter 5 – Early adulthood socialising

In life, it is said that often 'you get what you focus on'. By the time that Jim had reached adulthood, it seemed that 99% of his attention was firmly focussed on 'possible doom' rather than 'possible glory'. The praise for the latter lay not purely at the feet of an in-built emotional propensity.

Clearly, the genetic fabric behind this emotional leaning deserves great credit. The genetics on his mother's side unerringly blighting several generations with what was coined as 'nerves' back in the day. That said, surely, Jim's childhood environment also contributed massively? If Jim's genetics got the award for always focussing on what might go wrong, then it would be beyond rude if the influence of Jim's learning in childhood did not get mention in the acceptance speech.

Diligent coaching tracked Jim throughout the childhood years. Jim had learnt to flee from joy whenever it seemed near, to the familiar surroundings of contemplating 'how it all could go so horribly wrong'. The rare arrival of any grain of joy was almost a gateway to heightened anxiety. Some might call it guilt, but its subtleties were probably a bit more complex. Childhood saw Jim's mother Kath constantly jigging to themes of 'what will they think?' and 'what could go wrong'. Jim learned to see the world largely through Kath's eyes; they grew to share a sullied lens.

Right at the heart of teenage Jim's afflictions was often overvaluing (caring too much about) what other people thought of him. Or to be more technically precise and given that mind-reading is not possible, he cared too much about *'what he thought other people thought about him'*. This latter data was corrupt and tainted by Jim's internal shame and low self-esteem.

Jim's over-valuing of 'what he thought other people thought of him' translated into a constellation of poisonous ingredients. The bubbling toxins included: maladaptive avoidance, shame-based secrecy, and wasting much of his attention within his own mind. Our Jim landed in adulthood, with painfully high levels of self-consciousness and never far from niggling worries about how others were judging him.

The formula for Jim was straightforward: social situations = high anxiety, and an orientation to social situations as contexts in which he needed to perform and convince others of his value. To those not pocked by excessive worries about what other might think of them, social situations can maybe represent exciting opportunities and not intimidating sources of threat. Oh for our Jim to borrow such eyes, just for one solitary evening.

Jim tried to socialise and fit in on the outside. He began to try to uneasily squeeze himself into life, like a fully grown elephant relentlessly flailing to fit into a human wet-suit. He formed friendships with three similar aged local lads, namely: Spider, Yatesy, and Fraz.

For Jim in his early adulthood, there was very little about himself he was comfortable with. His shame made him feel small. In actual fact, the body which Jim transported himself around in was a reasonable frame, to the outside world. In young adulthood, Jim stood at around six foot three inches tall and was slightly thinner than average. He wished to be smaller, partly because it would make it easier to blend in and not stick out.

Moreover, Jim's attitude towards himself was such that anything about himself was automatically a negative characteristic in his mind. Along the lines of the Groucho Marks assertion

21

that, 'I refuse to join any club that would have me as a member'. Jim knew what was truly great and magnificent, namely: everything that was diametrically opposite to himself.

Whilst his core burden remained mainly invisible, the repercussions and manifestations were ever present for Jim. It crystallised with an impressive and tragic solidity. Jim had learned so well from his mother that ultimately the mention of toilets or the sight of friends going to the toilet yielded an emotional eruption to be masked. On some deeper level, it released torturous cries from his core, about: what he couldn't do and that others might notice the invisible truth about a predisposition which seemed drenched with illogicality. In his mind, he was far worse than weird.

Shame roared inside. Simultaneously, an outside persona strained to sustain something which was not, with the depths often creaking with despair. Much was masked on the outside. Inside, self-hatred blossomed and saturated every aspect of his being.

Jim retained his problems with going to the toilet in public. The parameters firmly crystallised into a pattern in which he was often able to use public toilets when he was out on his own in public, albeit uneasily. There was the odd occasion after trying to keep up with Fraz's drinking and after about twelve pints of lager that bodily sensations broke through which pushed him into the toilet, even though friends were out with him.

The process was elaborate. Jim would initially look to extricate himself from his friend's eye gaze, before movement. Ideally, he would also look for a moment when his friends had perhaps recently visited the toilet such that he could feel more assured that they would not accompany him. Even then, his terror and his over-filled bladder meant that he was typically unable to urinate within public toilets.

This led to a type of performance anxiety, whereby he would be afraid that he would not be able to urinate when he entered a public toilet. His mind never tired of shaming him internally by emphasising that he could not perform this simple task that ever other human being seemed to execute effortlessly and almost unthinkingly. In Jim's mind, the worth of his soul depended on his ability to complete; so much on the line. Jim, shy to the irony that his effort and his thinking were integral to the problem.

For Jim: entering a public toilet when he was out with friends became like going *'over the top'* in the trenches of World War One. Only very rarely, he would venture. Anxiety levels were instantly at a seven or eight out of ten, where ten is the most fear the human body can create and zero is relaxed. There were many false starts, where he willed his body to move towards the toilet, but it remained paralysed with fear.

Even the picture of the figure on the sign that signified the male toilet sat uneasily with him. A totem deeply smeared with danger and unwelcome meaning for Jim. If he found the courage to move towards a toilet, his fear quickly danced to the uncertainty of 'will there be anyone in there?'.

Experience had taught him that the presence of another person would mean he physically could not urinate during that visit. The inducement of a billion pounds would not alter this; he simply did not operate the levers any more. An impenetrable barrier was formed by the synergy of physiological learning, negative expectancies, the glare of a thousand invisible eyes, and deep seated fear. A sphincter winced.

Opening a public toilet door to enter was like cutting the wires to de-activate a bomb. Do I cut the red wire or the blue wire? As he pushed the toilet door, time briefly stood still.

Jim waited for the doom of another person being present, with his senses on high alert. Throughout the night out, he reflexively monitored movement near the toilet. Particularly in the minutes before exceptionally rare use of the toilet, he sought to wait until a minute or two had passed since anyone entered the toilet. Still, there were many times when his surreptitious due diligence was insufficient.

A heart sink worthy of stopping an army would follow if his movement to the toilet was met with another set of eyes making similarly oriented bodily movements, simultaneously or just after. He was then akin to a condemned man walking from his prison cell, to the electric chair. Like a passenger in a plane, peering out of the window and powerlessly watching an inevitable path to a high speed collision with the ground.

Of course, he flinched inside. On the outside, he strove with all his senses to appear the cool and normal guy that he knew he simply wasn't. Again, this cheap salesman trying to peddle an insincere and misleading version of reality; Jim never bought the pitch.

On the inside, his mind created the most shameful, anxious, and distorted image of himself that it could muster; he could mind read the mind reader. The audience could see inside his soul and he could see what they were seeing; his mind galloped to threat and worst case scenarios, and this became his reality. He lived firmly within his own injured mind.

Sometimes, Jim would avert his walk to a public toilet early on in its initiation, perhaps sensing footsteps behind him or movement at the side. The flashing lights of a nearby fruit machine might provide a beacon of distraction for a re-route, but inside he knew that his false start had been judged by many eyes. As if they knew the all-encompassing fear which felt to stain the entirety of his contorted soul.

Sometimes, if Jim did continue his trip to the toilet with other eyes also en-route, then he needed an 'out'. Often, he would enter the toilet, grab a piece of toilet roll from inside a cubicle, and make a gesture of blowing his nose on the way out; his being flimsily justified. Posturing that he merely had wanted to blow his nose, so as to avoid the inevitable anxiety-soaked failure to urinate. He struggled to squeeze any product from his nose, but managed to crush out more shame from his core.

The capitulation sounded deep echoes of the feelings which accompanied Jim in his eleven year old form, when he made his tearful utterance of *'I don't want to fight'* to an eager South-worth, with crowds gathered on the school field to judge the spectacle. Long before adulthood: Jim was programmed to never venture out without his close companion fear. Neural pathways also colluded to render a hypersensitive hair trigger, that activated him hiding and avoiding. Jim, surely a born coward?

If Jim made the walk alone to the public toilet and there was someone there when he arrived inside a toilet, his internal thoughts would hit him with *'you won't be able to urinate – you are so shamefully weird'*. Striking like a wrecking ball. He would also have the challenge of acting *'not nervous'*. He was terrified that the person would notice his fear and see inside his soul.

A tsunami inside his body had to not even betray a ripple at the surface. He was then like an individual subjected to headphones intermittently dispensing randomly-spaced brief pulses of 130 decibels of white noise, yet required to sustain a constant unchanging facial expression. Powerful electric shocks inside his shell, with an imperative to avoid conduct-ance to the audience; no outlet; smoking his insides.

Regardless of what Jim's face really looked like in that moment, he created an internal image of his face having a million signs of 'what he felt' and 'who he was'. His emotion strove fervently to create an internal representation of how this other individual saw him and what they thought and felt about him. Internally generated conceptions of *'What's the worst that I could look like'*, taken by Jim as a clean window onto reality. Not knowing that the window was a fun house mirror reflecting back purely what was within the depths of his troubled mind. He felt beyond humiliated by the reflection of himself that stared back at him, deep within his own mind.

Within a public toilet, Jim always used the cubicle. He could not just stand at the urinals for the eternity that it might take for the golden product to emerge. However, if someone came into the toilet, then Jim's senses would pick up the noise. In his mind, a mix of anxiety and shame instantly heightened, and he simply could not urinate. Jim became conscious of cogs turning in the brain of the person who had entered the toilet. These foreign cogs must surely be turning awkwardly with judgement, *'there is no noise coming from that toilet, what is he doing in there?'*; grinding out emotional intensity and disapproval within his audience.

Jim's mind also flicked through the catalogue of *'who that might be that had entered the toilet?'* and *'what they might think?'*. He tried to internally appease and justify himself to each one of his internal representations of others, but the emotion stood firm between them. It prevented communication.

In the context of his shame, Jim's mind inadvertently began to define an ability to consistently use public toilets as the diagnostic test of whether a person had value or was worthless. Jim knew that for him, by far the most difficult thing was *initiating* urination in public toilets. On the rare occasions he could initiate, he could typically continue.

Pathetically, on several occasions, Jim had started to urinate in the private cubicles in an empty toilet and then he gambled. The toilet was empty and so he ceased the flow for a couple of moments, quickly exited the cubicle, and continued in the urinal. In Jim's mind: this meant that if anyone came in, he could demonstrate that he was 'normal' and was able to urinate in the urinal, like a 'man'.

In his mind, he was striving to sell what he thought was a better version of himself. Like that old poker player holding simply Jack high and striving to represent an unbeatable hand. Jim never lost sight of the fact that he was holding Jack high. Behind the defensive fog in his mind, it never stopped stinging. He might weakly and very slightly appease the audience in a moment, but he never began to satisfy the inner critic.

Now, to the vast bulk of people, Jim's thoughts around toilets may seem unfathomable and at best bordering on crazy. Indeed, why would he 'choose' to think that way. The reality was that Jim had high levels of toxic negative emotion in this area. In a sense, Jim was not 'thinking', but rather he was feeling and the thoughts were close to mere side-effects.

When the emotion that a modern human feels is so strongly polluted with fear and shame, it is that primeval emotion that pushes so hard to drive the logic and the thinking. His ability to think logically was a passenger in this specific area, with his emotional feelings firmly having both hands on the steering wheel. Jim's logic little more than a passenger, travelling helplessly towards the relentless crashing of his potential.

Occasionally, logic tried to prudently tap emotion on the shoulder and advise, but this merely irked emotion and it remained steadfast in retaining complete dominance. Still, Jim's logical mind did criticise himself so heavily, as if it was truly driving. An irony lost on Jim.

On Masolw's hierarchy and to the masses, using the toilet is very basic and not especially noteworthy. However, when it meshed with Jim's psyche, it was bordering on an insurmountable block to progressing up Maslow's pyramid. The base of the pyramid mocked his attempts to scramble up, again and again and again. His shame-driven secrecy lubricated every side of the pyramid; he just kept slipping back down.

Strange to say: but until well into his thirties, Jim did not really look closely at himself or his problems. What drew together Jim and his three friends, Spider, Yatesy, and Fraz? One thing may have been that they did not seem to scrutinise him and they did not question him. It perhaps takes unusual material, to craft out the construction of a most rare life path.

Jim's own lack of insight was such that he would readily agree to have drinking contests with Fraz in the pub, almost as if drinking a double-figure number of pints of beer was straightforward to him and his shy bladder. Then, early on during the competition with toilet neurosis firmly in hand, reality would set in. It was unclear whether Jim's mind or his bladder were under the most pressure, but his attempts to fit in would fuel the charade of these drinking contests.

Similarly, Jim agreed to venture on a one week holiday to Blackpool with his three friends. They shared bunks in the same room. Much to the displeasure of his bladder, Jim had limited alone time. Whilst Plato's assertions that necessity is the mother of invention may have value, Jim's definition of what was necessary placed him on the rack. He was worshipping a false God, but with the insight of a religious zealot.

For many years, the battle continued between Jim's drive to

meaningfully connect with others juxtaposed gratingly with his mind's insistence that he fell so woefully short and needed to mask much of himself and his problems. He had specific mental issues blocking the validation and social success that his mind craved. Still, year after year, he rallied and sought to live off the unclean crumbs which he encountered.

Jim went through the motions. He played pool; even joining the pool team of the local pub. He played cards with his friends, typically for small sums of money.

Jim played golf with Spider. During the eighteen hole experience, the toilet neurosis did not significantly come into play. He chatted about sport and he sought to appear normal. Hell, there were even a few moments when he very briefly lost himself and experienced pleasure.

Activity could sometimes be a pleasant distraction. He might even briefly take an eye off liberally scattered landmines of other's negative judgements of him; triggered by everything and nothing. Few and far between, Jim briefly laughed. If one looked even closer at Jim's history and like a child tirelessly looking for a four leaf clover, then there were probably slightly more than one occasion when Jim's laughs were not wholly feigned.

Considering his internal reality in his own head, Jim often blended in reasonably well. I guess the external reality (i.e., what others saw) reflected a quality of life which was light years above the quality of life which he truly lived, in his own mind. Often able to sell the notion that he was a reasonably normal and acceptable human being, but he certainly did not buy this vision within his own inners. His striving to be seen as 'normal' mixed uneasily with an inward proneness to define everything about himself as 'not normal'. A grating cacophony, within his own mind.

Jim undoubtedly got some limited social validation from friends. That said, his shame-based secret regarding his difficulties using public toilets stood out; internally diluting this validation by several oceans. His friends seemed to partly accept him. However, in his mind, this did not really count. Other people did not truly know him and his shameful problems. He knew that if they did, then they would view him with that same horror and disgust that he felt towards himself. He arrived in adulthood, long since stuck.

Chapter 6 – Jim's link with his mum deepens

With Jim' aged twenty, his parents split up. His father Patrick had been having a secret affair for more than a few years. On May 23rd 1988, Patrick suddenly announced that he was leaving Kath (Jim's mother).

'There is nobody else, but this is just not working' Patrick declared.

Patrick's tone and demeanour betrayed his attempts to portray being emotionally unconnected to his divergence. He appeared genuinely saddened by something about the end of this era. That said, Patrick's upset was truly dwarfed by desperate wails of pain emanating from a Kath that lay prostrate.

'I'll never leave you, mum' Jim said to Kath, as she kneeled crying on the lounge floor.

'Promise me you won't do anything daft?' Jim asked Kath. She just continued sobbing.

....

Jim's concerns were partly fuelled by his maternal grandmother (Freda) having walked out from a psychiatric ward when he was aged about fifteen. She was missing for several weeks over a bitterly cold Christmas. The family searches yielded nothing.

Ultimately Freda was found floating within a local canal, with her soul having long since departed. Patrick identified her, to protect Kath from the ordeal. The coroner recorded an open verdict, but some suspected that mental torment may have driven Freda to take her own life.

Freda had eight siblings and it transpired that each of them had problems with their 'nerves'. Each had suffered with a condition termed 'irritable bowel syndrome', alongside a proneness to depression and anxiety. The dice of genetics seemed mockingly loaded.

At the end of her life, Freda's anxiety was largely a type of obsessive compulsive disorder. This included feeling guilty about her own thoughts. Thoughts without action seemingly inconsequential, certainly within a land rich with a drought of neurosis. Sadly, Freda mentally lived far from this latter haven.

Many things mean, simply what we make them mean. Lingual babbling so often bafflingly barbed. Freda developed thoughts of killing family members, and made the illogical leap that *'having the thought means I might likely carry out the action'* and *'having the thought means I am a terrible person'*.

As Freda was such a kind and sensitive person, she was horrified by this possibility. She then got trapped in a relentless vicious circle of *'trying not to have a thought'*. As is often illustrated by asking a person to try hard to not get an image of a pink elephant, it transpires that: if a human soul tries very hard not to have a thought then it tends to keep popping into their head.

Hence, recurrent thoughts which so appalled Freda were in many ways merely a sign of a normal human brain; so tormentingly misinterpreted by poor Freda. Haunted by doubts that her thoughts might translate into action. Freda perhaps taking a stand to protect her loved ones; an icy submersion evaporating doubt.

It was as if Freda's mind thought '*what is the worst thing I could think*' and then having identified it, her mind spent years trying not to think it. Like a container full of water with holes in, the water seems to just find a way out. The thoughts Freda feared just kept leaking from her brain. A brain that never tired of torturing her.

Kath's specific concerns were not a perfect replica of Freda's. However, as the saying goes: the apple perhaps did not fall too far from its tree. Our Jim's reflexes inbuilt; perhaps insufficient to dodge the falling fruit?

....

If we switch back to the reality of our twenty year old Jim, the home was quieter and more predictable after Patrick left. Fairly soon after leaving the family, it emerged that Patrick had moved straight in with another woman (Lacey). He had been having an affair with Lacey on and off for nearly a decade prior to his departure.

Kath was met with the trauma of Patrick's departure and his affair. It left her in huge turmoil and Jim remained living at home with Kath. He felt her post-Patrick vulnerability scratching at him within his mind; he attempted to protect her. Kath needed Jim, even before Patrick left. After Patrick left, Jim would get even more of his mother's attention.

They generally got on well. However, if Jim's path did not suit Kath and an argument ensued, Kath would readily raise the stakes. On one occasion when Jim stuck to his guns and vocally disagreed with Kath, she was taking her nightly medication. Kath grasped the opportunity by declaring, '*I might as well just take all my tablets, as I am always in the wrong*'. Jim quickly came back onside. He learnt to align his position even better with Kath's world view.

After he left, Patrick was requiring Jim to meet up with him around once a month. Patrick would occasionally render the catch up even more awkward by bringing his new partner, Lacey. Lacey's nervousness perhaps pushed vexatious levels of extraversion out of her.

It seemed that Lacey had perhaps seized Patrick's attention by unwearied over-sexualised overtures. She moved, dressed, and spoke beneath her years. As if, she was convincing herself that the sands of time had been on strike. Beyond the clothes, the bleached blond hair, the sun bed tan, and several layers of make-up, there surreptitiously lay a woman who had already seen over five decades of existence.

Patrick and Lacey were undoubtedly a couple, performing in unison. Collectively striving to paper over a reality that time and experience had inevitably done its work. Maybe denying that the grim reaper may well now lay in wait, not far down their road. Travelling a path which probably enhanced their journey; forever young. Each to their own. If they could dodge the type of mirrors whose reflection might sting them, then perhaps, why not?

After his parents break-up, meeting Patrick seemed to more than anger his mother. Jim found himself within what might be described as a recurrent double-bind or somewhat of a 'Catch 22'. Whilst Jim's main support went towards Kath, he felt some weight of obligation to keep some contact with Patrick. So, he would ask Kath, *'is it OK if I meet with dad?'*.

Kath would verbally reassure him with something like, *'of course, Jim. Even though your dad and I have split up, he is still your dad. It is important that you keep contact with him'*. However, when he returned home after meeting his father, Kath had the manner of a disgruntled teenager. She seemed to be wilfully 'pretending to pretend' that there was nothing wrong. Jim was wrapped in knots. The icy conditions at home could take days to thaw, with guilt following Jim like a ball and chain.

Chapter 7 – Jim's love life in early adulthood; a new possibility?

Jim's love life was stuck on the runway throughout his teens and twenties. He had a strong sexual drive, but an absence of a vessel on which it might crystallise. A toilet-related neurosis presented obstacles.

Beyond that, relationships entail letting another person close to ourselves. The close gaze of another augmented self-consciousness. In his own mind: the self that our Jim was conscious of reflected a most foul specimen. He was more than drizzled in a sauce of self-hatred and shame. His emotion was very conscientious in seeking to hide himself; certainly keen not increase the focus on himself, through the warped mirror of another's eyes.

Aged twenty one and Jim had still not had a partner. He was attracted to women. That said, his burgeoning and unfulfilled sexual drive was such that he might have been attracted to a frog, if it had dared to stay close to him for a few lazy seconds. Frustration and unease leaked from Jim's every pore.

Aged twenty one, and along came what the outside world might label as 'an opportunity' . For Jim, a better phrase may have been 'an ordeal'. Soon after Patrick left Kath, he would ask to meet with Jim in one of the nearby pubs. This enabled Patrick to dispense his fatherly duties, around once each month.

One particular Monday night at a pub called the 'Golden Fleece', Patrick had arrived to accompany Jim and Jim's friend Yatesy. Jim unable to avoid noticing that Patrick had started to dress differently since he left Kath. He seemed drawn to clothes which would perhaps be more fitting if he had been able to shed at least a couple of decades. By that point, Patrick was a man that had already travelled past the 'fifty' marker.

Patrick arrived at the pub wearing: a white jacket, a bright blue Lacoste polo shirt, faded jeans, and casual shoes. There was also an absence of socks, as if Patrick was doing a lame audition for 'Miami Vice'. His demeanour within his attire offered clues, suggesting that this players self-concept was bulging with how it was beyond cool. Perhaps like a novice Omaha player convinced that he is revealing a hand as powerful as a royal flush at show-down, when the veteran players can see nowt but a pair of jacks. Still, Patrick basking in the delusion.

Patrick was also showing off a different shade to his skin. It fell somewhere between a tan and the redness of an embarrassed man, suspected of wearing a red all-in-one cat suit underneath his clothes. He had recently returned from a two week holiday in Skegness with Lacey, and his glow suggested that he had spent most of his waking hours on the beach.

The combination of a summer heatwave and his desire to burn beauty into his skin seemed to have come together, like the perfect storm. Surely only a whisker away from troubling the specialist burns unit in the local hospital? That said, Jim had learnt that Lacey worked part-time as a beauty therapist and he felt unable to rule out some presence of crudely applied fake tan or make-up.

Jim's friend (Yatesy) was around six foot. Conspicuously, he always smelt like he had recently bathed in a vat full of pungent aftershave. The aroma of Yatesy not just accompanying his presence, but often signalling it well ahead of the arrival of his physical frame. Like a dinner bell, indicating a meal likely to soon land. An odour travelling through the hooter, often ahead of Yatesy's shape beginning to trouble the back of any associated retina.

Yatesy also invested plentiful energy into striving to fit snugly with the fashion of that era. The latter seeming to carefully choose his clothes. Careful attention invested in his presentation; striving to cater for both the visual and the olfactory senses of any audience. Not done there, he began increasingly talking in such a way as to mirror his favourite pop star, Morrissey. Vocally affected, tick.

Despite all this impression management, Yatesy's romantic success was marginally better than the vacuum which Jim had dutifully sustained. Posturing and hot air replaced any real substance, for Jim and all his friends. On this specific Monday, it would be Jim's own propensity to social bluffs which would draw him into a trap, after following crumbs which Patrick's whims so blatantly scattered.

'*Eeeh Jim, Lacey's daughter's friend, Tracy, is a real belter*' Patrick announced.

'*Oh Yes*' Jim said, not quite knowing where to take this conversation.

'*She comes round to the house a lot and I could fix you up with a date*' Patrick declared.

Yatesy had been listening intently and felt comfortable enough to forward his encouragement, '*hmmm, get in there Jim*' he advised.

Jim felt fenced in. '*Yes that's great dad, I'd be happy to go on a date with this Tracy*' Jim offered.

Jim often appeased in the moment, in a way that seemed to reflect that his brain did not fully grasp that tomorrow does tend to arrive. As it happens: it tends to arrive even more predictably than say, the 8:32am to Waterloo. The timely arrival of the latter can be impacted by a range of factors, whereas the arrival of tomorrow for any given individual seems to be only deterred by a state known as death.

Later that week, on a Wednesday, the phone rang. By that point, Jim had largely forgotten about his verbal contract. As agreed, Patrick had arranged for Jim to have a date with a young lady named Tracey. Jim was to meet Tracey at 8pm on Saturday in a pub called the Wagon and Horses, in the local town. It was agreed. His fate was sealed.

Jim's anticipatory anxiety started to grow. Alongside this, his brain briefly let in thoughts of a young lady with model-like good looks developing an instant and unshakeable attraction towards him. For a brief moment within Jim's mind, his mental representation of 'Tracey' could neither keep her hands off him and nor could she keep her clothes on. 'Ooooh, Tracey'. Marvellous that the power of the human imagination knows few bounds.

Catastrophising quickly pushed fantasising aside. Jim's mind raced with a myriad of negative evaluations of himself. Riding on a horse named negativity, he rode off from the present moment to a plethora of negative outcomes which stretched into a future not yet lived. That said, Jim lived mostly in his mind.

Jim tried to distract himself over the next couple of days. Yet partly through the moments that had rained down on him and accumulated in his life, reality had perhaps slightly worn down denial in him. He was beginning to realise that he could not indefinitely hold off the future.

It perhaps had echoes of an eleven year old Jim. In particular, that period between a lightbulb moment of learning that his foe Southworth was stronger than him and the approach of the deferred fight. That long night at the age of eleven, fruitlessly: willing a different reality, willing himself to be able to turn back time, and willing that tomorrow never greeted him.

With his anxiety, meeting Tracey would perhaps feel a bit like walking onto the field to fight Southworth, amidst a sea of judgement-drenched expectant eyes. Ultimately, tears and submission squeezed from his frightened frame, a decade earlier. Even his adult negativity could not drum up expectations that Tracey would fight and physically attack him. Yet he was again trudging, like a man who deep down in his soul knew that he was ill-equipped and inadequate.

On that day of reckoning when he faced Southworth, the mixture of elements elicited molecules of two hydrogen atoms bonded with an oxygen atom. Or more precisely: water, in the form of tears. The inner turmoil remained. But by adulthood, Jim's emotion was pushed deeper into his soul. Manifestations on this latest day of reckoning would likely be different, but certainly no less ugly.

Chapter 8 – The day of the blind date arrives, with Jim shuffling off to meet his fate.

The red lights of a digital clock stare out at Jim, in the form of 6:31pm. Jim is readying himself. His mind strains to see the future.

Unable to release the crystal ball within his mind, he stares into it and a vision clears at 6:32pm. A mirror awaits him. The same faded jeans and faithful white tee-shirt which sometimes felt so good, standing now as shining symbols of his inadequacy. He could see an elongated head, which had once appeared in proportion. Attempts to hide in Brut aftershave wholly fail to dissolve Jim's sense of self; emotional valence unchanged.

Jim sensed his boring conversation, though he had not actually uttered a word. Maybe he did not have to hear? He just knew.

Although several miles still separated them, Jim could feel Tracey's valuation of him. He felt a painful sense that Tracy had a myriad of choices in this world.

'Why would she ever choose me?' he asked himself. He had not the answers. Surely easier to sell anything else on this planet, rather than this Jim. Any attempts to trap Tracey's affections were surely futile? Hemmed in, he kept moving forwards.

Jim decided to arrive at the wagon and horses pub at 7:30pm. He was planning to try to use the toilet straight away, which would allow him and his bladder more time. He would try to relax himself during the thirty minutes before Tracey arrived. Reality knew that the chances of achieving this latter target of a relaxed state were probably slightly less than, say, the likelihood of him learning to fly by flapping his arms.

Jim felt invisible eyes and judgements with his every move. Even on the taxi journey to the pub, his emotions jigged like he was the star in the Truman show. Our Jim constantly appeasing the hidden cameras; whilst simultaneously looking at their monitors, deep within his troubled mind.

Jim paid the taxi with a generous tip. This behaviour was likely fuelled partly by a child-like inner wish to mend a self-esteem which had been battered by a lifetime of onslaughts. Taking a teaspoon of water out of the sea, and hoping to change the water levels of a vast ocean.

Jim moved towards the door of the wagon and horses. Adrenaline was pinging round his body at breakneck speed; virtually bursting the pipes. A hand reached out to push open the black door; ready to unwrap what fate had in store.

Fast forward about a decade: our Jim would read a research study using physiological measures of anxiety which indicated that when a skydiver is jumping from an aeroplane, the period of maximum anxiety is just *before* they jump out of the plane. When they actually commit and jump from the plane, they: leave behind the weight of *'will I, won't I?'* uncertainty, are propelled from their mind into the present moment, and their anxiety tends to lessen. Jim opened the wagon and horses door, and entered. Whilst he had committed and jumped into his new reality, he did not notice any anxiety exiting past him as he made his entrance. Here, perhaps no sense of a parachute?

Jim felt the gaze of many patrons, without even needing to look up. He strained to survey the room, praying that a 'Tracey' had not landed ahead of schedule. He could not find a searching or interested look from any female in the room. A reality that he had come to know, only too well.

Jim's anxious mind scanned like Arnold Schwarzneger's character in the terminator, looking for a 'match' to his self-generated internal representation of 'Tracey'. Slumped at the bar, there was a large lady with short spiky hair. She looked to be coming up to retirement age.

Not even Jim's anxiety could convince him that this specimen might be the match. Yet, a part of Jim yearned that she was 'Tracey'. A contrast less harsh than the beautiful avatar that Jim had internally created for our Tracey, sat alongside his sorry ass. As if, the pressure boring down from the hand of a whimsical God would be lifted; team Jim facing Accrington Stanley, rather than Barcelona in their prime.

Jim continued scanning and observed a sign that said 'toilets'. His anxiety instantly changed up a few gears, and he progressed towards it. He opened the door and there was a man at the urinals and his only cubicle was locked; presumably occupied by some unknown.

Jim had to wait for the cubicle to be released. He felt himself lingering uneasily in the toilet, ineffectively striving to justify himself to judgements in his head. Hit by a barrage of thoughts so quickly that one just blended into another: they'll think you are weird, they will wonder what you are doing just waiting, should I wait outside?, they'll think I am a loitering with sexual intent, etc., etc.,. Each thought mixed in a boiling flask, heated by an underlying anxiety.

A reality of around ninety seconds was lived as many hours, within the internal circuitry of Jim's neural architecture. The cubicle door opened, Jim entered. On passing the prior occupant, he reflexively strained to avoid the emotional landmine of firm eye contact. Dodging a reflection from the mirror of a foreign retina, buried deep inside his own skull.

Jim initially tore off toilet tissue, blew a nose which knew it did not need blowing, and then flushed the toilet to create noise. The audience which had emerged from the cubicle might then perceive that he was in there legitimately. With the noise of the flush, they might not notice if his blushing bladder could not achieve the normality of his peers. An absence of the tinkle of normality, perhaps imperceptible. But, perhaps not?

Each noise from the nearby limits of the toilet was surely a prick to our Jim's inners; lanced by this other perspective, deep within his mind. With his senses on high alert, the brief flushing noise and the refilling of the cistern did not come close to masking the noise from the individual that was still within the toilet area. His attitude to Jim was so abhorrently tangible to Jim, his senses could touch and taste it.

A sense of worthlessness filled up in Jim, with a speed that dwarfed and embarrassed a plodding toilet cistern. Emotion drowned out clear thought. But again a cocktail of vague thoughts ran into each other, 'what if I can't urinate?', 'how long can I stay in here before people think it's weird?', 'will people in the bar area be wondering why I have been in here so long?', 'I know I am not going to be able to urinate, I am too anxious', etc., etc.,.

Jim's thoughts and concerns had travelled a long distance since the beginnings of a toilet neurosis in childhood. Within their travels, they had changed in different ways. However, their transformation had not diluted their toxicity.

At last, Jim could hear the noise of the stray individual exiting the toilet. Sometimes in his past, he would pathetically peer out to make sure he was alone; very occasionally startled by a noiseless form. His anxiety did not want to make this move today. He tried to reassure himself.

Whilst he did not explicitly think it, it was as if: 'they're gone', 'you are in the toilet on your own', 'the pressure is partly off', 'nobody is listening and judging', and 'nobody will know if you are unable to urinate'. Anxiety dropped from being a deafeningly loud scream within Jim's soul, to merely being a very unpleasant rumbling roar. However, Jim was pretty sure that he would be unable to urinate.

Moments later, the door to the toilet opened again and Jim had the noise of another audience. Emotion ratcheted up again. That sealed it. He felt that he could stay here the rest of the day and would still not be able to urinate. A white flag had to be raised, with Jim again choosing a sickening surrender.

Jim took on the challenge of simply exiting the cubicle, washing his hands, and returning to the bar area. Compassion might suggest that Jim could have praised himself for the 'process' (the bravery of taking on something he was anxious about and trying), rather than getting bogged down on the outcome (not being able to urinate). In Jim's mind, self-hatred filled up every crevice; there was no room for an ally such as compassion. For this Jim, the latter rarely welcomed in.

Blinding neon signs lit up in Jim's soul: 'you are a failure', 'you can't do what everyone else can', 'you are weird', etc., etc.,. Alongside this, most of his senses were filled up with pre-verbal intense emotional aching and throbbing. His being strained and pulsed.

Catastrophising that he had learnt in childhood joined in, with themes such as: 'this will completely spoil the date', and 'you need to get home as quick as possible so that you can urinate'. The soothsayer has spoken. She always did.

Jim exited the toilet, feeling several feet shorter. Shame surrounded him. He sat at the bar and ordered a pint of lager. He glanced at his watch and noted '7:35pm'.

Every movement behind him was followed by a furtive glance. Jim's self-consciousness was such that when Tracey appeared, he would be looking more at 'what his mind told him she saw of him' rather than her actual manifestation. The technical term for Jim's tendency was 'processing the self as a social object', through the biased lens that a shame tarnished self-esteem provides.

Jim waited, but not wholly alone. No trace of 'anticipation of opportunity', but conjoined with a sense of pressure to perform. Jim wanted to please and impress the unknown Tracey. He still craved being a winner. Desire, not fully shooed off by a sense of knowing it's futility.

Alas, particularly within Jim's mind: the presence of another person yields a knee-jerk press of the switch for heightened self-consciousness. The person in front of him becomes like a mirror through which Jim sees himself. This latter vision not formed from the veridical snatch of an external world, but based on a reflection of the toxic self-hate that pollutes his inner mind. A mirror pointing inwards, into the tortured depths of his mind.

To an extreme level, Jim had evolved to a point that he rarely saw outside his head. Hopelessly flawed in perceiving interpersonal reality. He relentlessly reads the mind of his audience, but unbeknownst to him with the proficiency of a backstreet charlatan.

Minutes stutter and stagger by, in slow motion. Jim feels frozen. He checks his watch again, 7:53pm. Bruce Springstein blares out throughout the pub:

'....*You can't start a fire, you can't start a fire without a spark. This guns for hire, even if we're just dancing in the dark'.*

Our Jim needs a spark; yet surely no small fiery particles here, just cold dull ashes. A gun not so much for hire, as locked safely and securely in a cabinet. Defensive and avoidant to his core; Jim could not remember a time that he had possessed the requisite key or combination.

The song that surrounded him perhaps speaking of: expressing, taking risks, and stepping out. The words reverberate around a forlorn character. A character not versed in grabbing fate by the throat and squeezing out what is required to fulfil his needs. A mantra of: sit passively, hide yourself, pretend you don't want what you truly desire, and let your 'fate' run round unchecked.

The words of Bruce's song just bounce off Jim, with a fit which is the antithesis of resonance. Less than a crumb of his attention is free to make out the specifics of the ambience. His focus already marching to a different tune, fully inwards. Perhaps, '*Born to run*'.

After several further intermittent glances at the watch. He is met with the vision of '7:59pm and 43 seconds', with anxiety reaching fever pitch. Many more seconds elapse, without major shifts in the external world. Will Tracey turn up at all?

Chapter 9 – Holding out for a Tracey

By 8:25pm; still no appearance from Tracey and Jim had made nearly three pints of lager disappear. He remained at the bar, though more company had anchored themselves to him. He was increasingly joined by the companions of a distended bladder and the anxious tummy that had blighted generations of his familial kin on his mother's side. Holding back the tide, on both fronts.

Jim glanced again, and was met with a vision of '8:27pm'. Jim's stage fright dwindled slightly, as he began to allow the hope that the show had been called off. Seconds later, the doors swung open and a figure walked in.

Jim's scanning eyes bravely settled on the figure. The gender was right. The age seemed somewhere around the mark. The figure also appeared to be glancing round the room, as if searching for something. Jim's body got up, while he disappeared further into himself.

'Tracey?' he asked, his frowning soul creating a most discomforting smile.

She smiled nervously, and uttered, *'Yes....Jim?'.*

Tracey held the demeanour of a conscientious student opening an envelope that revealed an examinations results card showing straight 'fails'. Unbeknownst to Jim, much of this was simply that Tracey had landed outside her main comfort zone.

'Yes, can I get you a drink Tracey?' Jim asked, reaching for the only part of the script which his mind had managed to muster.

'Ok. I'll have a Southern Comfort and lemonade', Tracey replied.

Tracey, perhaps still lacking full awareness that the nomenclature of the latter beverage would likely be the only comfort that this evening would offer. What impression would the nib of Jim's soul make on the new moments they would share? Well, it seemed close to pre-set.

As he ordered the drinks, Tracey's perfume collected under Jim's nose. A pungent smell of roses, with some citrus elements. Jim's lack of positive romantic experiences in his history meant that the aromatic emanations from Tracey would not carve a path in Jim's mind to echoes of previously lived ecstasy.

Drinks purchased. The two victims of Patrick's whims sat on bar stools, close together and yet several worlds apart. Shifty eye contact passes between them. Tracey was a bit nervous, but her life raft of coping skills and defences stretched well beyond the self-defeating avoidant tricks that Jim had up his sleeve.

Jim occasionally pointed his eyes towards his transient audience. She was around six inches smaller than the six foot three inches of Jim, with a medium to slender build. Her breasts were perky and not yet succumbed to the sands of time. Long auburn hair, which was carefully coiffured to leave gentle curls at its tips. Clothing was very much smart casual. A woman clearly magnetically drawn to over-priced brands.

'Great to meet you' Jim said

'I really did not want to come today and I nearly didn't turn up' Tracey vented, with strings perhaps being pulled by nervousness and striving to protect an ego within.

'Your dad' she continued whilst raising her eye brows, 'relentlessly badgered me into coming' Tracey's agenda continued.

'*Haaa Ha...Sorry about that*' Jim offered, conjuring up a most off-putting fake laugh. The bulk of what Jim communicates to Tracey does not travel on the wings of his words, but rather his non-verbals uncloak him at every turn. Beyond the awkwardness, he pushes down a small up-rising of anger feelings towards his father.

A brief silence follows, which crow bars further words from Jim's inner vault.

'*Have you ever been on a blind date before?*' Jim asks.

'*No. You?*' Tracey replies, drawing on her vocabulary somewhat thriftily.

'*No, it's the first time*' Jim said, perhaps identifying a crumb of common ground.

'*What are your work or hobbies?*' Jim asked.

'*I work as an artist and make money selling my work*' Tracey expressed, with a tone that seemed to convey pride.

Jim very briefly allowed himself to wonder if male buyers of her art may be buying a fantasy of getting closer to this youthful beauty, rather than a tangible product. An uncharacteristic thought which was initially not part of his dominant self-consciousness, prior to feeling slight guilt. The guilt, born partly of an emotional sense that Tracey could hear his thoughts.

'*I am an administrative assistant*' Jim replied. He was pleased to reveal what felt to be the respectability of having a job, even though the job fitted him about as well as a giants foot trying to squeeze into a baby's mitten.

The conversation crawled back and forth for around fifteen minutes. Typically, with Jim serving and Tracey providing no more than a half-hearted perfunctory return.

Then, Tracey began talking about having been in a relationship with Rick for three years, which ended around two months ago. She seemed to be idealising this ex-partner and their three year relationship. She expressed that she was not ready for another relationship. Apparently, 'the breakup had hurt too much'.

The Gods perhaps mocking Jim, yet again? There's always a flaming Rick type character in the background. The bastard, clearly raising the bar to levels that are out of sight. Tracey's portrayal of this 'Rick' character arrived like a crowbar, cranking open a leaky inner vault within Jim; allowing yet more inadequacy and shame to ooze out, polluting his being.

Jim instantly knew that what he had to offer was worse than a cheap flat Pomagne, sat so pathetically next to the Dom Perignon Rose Gold Champagne that Tracey had bathed in for three whole years. He had never met Tracey's ex-boyfriend. But within the cesspit of his own mind: our Jim absolutely knew that he fell so gratingly short, when compared to Rick the great, or anyone else come to think of it. Yet, maybe in some ways Jim's sense of self was closer to Rick than he knew; perhaps typically only separated from 'Rick' by a leading 'p'.

Jim's unease also grew with Tracey mentioning an ex. Most worryingly, it felt that the microscope could come dangerously close to looking at his ex's. His early hair trigger 'what if' warning system had unfortunately not given a false positive on this occasion. The microscope homed in; Jim squirmed uneasily beneath the lenses.

'You had any painful break ups?' Tracey asked, perhaps looking for validation or balanced disclosures after opening up slightly. Maybe very loosely akin to Dr Hannibal Lecter requesting *'Quid pro quo'* from Agent Clarice Starling, though Jim felt the dynamics at play placed him more in the character of Dr Lecter.

During his childhood, Jim's mother had repeatedly conveyed that lying was just about the worst crime on the planet. Not surprisingly in this context, Jim was not blessed with great fabricating skills. He still strove to dodge bullets, either ineffectively or through evading issues.

'No, Tracey.....Nothing too painful' Jim opened up, pausing slightly before delivery; with eyebrows slightly raised, as if to flick through a thick catalogue of all his ex-partners.

The PR department in Jim's head preferring this statement to the more accurate and complete response of, *'No Tracey. In the whole of my life, I have never had a partner or come close to having a partner. I am inadequate and clueless'.* For Jim, no matter how hard he ran, shame was never far away; irony missed. His shame, akin to a paralysed limb: without apparent useful function, but it still stuck to him and he brought it everywhere.

'Tell me about Rick, what was he like?' Jim asked, seeking to subtly nudge the microscope away from the non-existence of his romantic history. There was also a part of him that perhaps wanted ideas about what he 'would have to be', in order to have a partner for more than the brief speck of time that he anticipated that Tracey would begrudgingly donate to him.

'I'd rather not, it's too painful' Tracey quickly retorted, with obvious irritation.

Jim sensed that Tracey's upset likely partly fuelled by her sense of loss mushroomed in an instant. In particular, the loss grossly bloated by memories of the great Rick being juxtaposed with the hopeless specimen that greeted her on this fatuous blind date. Tracey's experience with Jim thus far, seemingly akin to pulling teeth.

'I'm not staying out late, but we can have one quick drink at a pub in the town centre' she stated assertively, already apparently planning her exit.

'Shall I order a taxi?' Jim asked.

'No, my car is outside' Tracey replied.

Tracey exited first, with Jim close behind. He had survived round fifteen or twenty minutes with his date; perhaps another badge for his measly collection. A companion to sit with the sticker he received at the age of nine, for his third place in the potato and spoon race. Though Tracey's non-verbal output was prone to sting, Jim had mentally shifted to a point that he was not putting many words or labels onto the unfolding events or his feelings.

Somewhat depersonalised; increasingly feeling as if he was not as firmly located within his body. What magic tricks or witchcraft had rendered him 'disappeared'; a soul exiting its frame. Jim's magic: a resistant bladder and a reflexive party trick of dissociation in public. No Ketamine required.

Anxiety had carried off most of Jim's attention. Amidst the expanding detachment, there were blessedly insufficient remnants left to fuel much thinking. Though numbed, he still felt.

Tracey's car was parked just outside the pub. A two seater classic sports car, appearing in pristine condition and yet perhaps older than it's driver. A vehicle, likely not wholly unconnected to Tracey's sense of self.

'Wow, nice car' Jim said.

Whilst Jim felt that Tracey was oriented to him like he was perhaps unworthy to breathe the same air, his appeasement and attempted flattery probably sprung out of a strong craving to fit with another person.

Jim had still not fully given up on wanting to be liked. As if some part of him felt like the hounds that pursued him in his own mind might be called off, if only he could only find the holy grail of connection with a soul that he felt had affinity for him. Tracey's apparent dislike of Jim mirrored Jim's negative feelings towards himself; not surprising as they were both firmly anchored deep in Jim's mind. Perhaps they had something in common, after all?

With Jim complementing the car, Tracey forced out what was possibly a slight smile. After a quick journey to the local Town Centre, Tracey states 'We will go to Pilkington's wine bar'. The wine bar is full to bursting.

The Universe does not yield reward for Jim's flimsy attempts to get served amidst the crowds. Eventually, Tracey takes control herself and achieves the acquisition of their order. Jim's form stands, with Tracey. With his failed attempts as the hunter gatherer still fresh, Jim's tail has gone back even further between his legs. An orange juice for Tracey and another pint of lager for Jim.

Jim's nerves join forces with the several pints he has drunk, and he picks up signs that his bladder is creaking at the seams. Awkwardness appears on his face, as if he had just unexpectedly received the nip of a stray lobster. Jim pushes internal unrest deeper inwards and unconsciously dials down the sensitivity on his bodily sensations.

With the crowds in the bar, both Jim and Tracey struggle to be heard by each other above the vexatious cacophony of noise. Tracey looks increasingly frustrated. Then Tracey's word count more than doubles in their last couple of minutes together. She refers to having suffered a tough childhood, but having worked hard to enable herself to rent her own flat and buy her sports car. Tracey then moves onto aspects of her political views.

'We are too soft with people in this country, giving out welfare and benefits to lots of lazy people' Tracey expresses, perhaps somewhat harshly.

'I have had a tough childhood, but I have managed to make something of myself. Other people should do exactly the same. I have no time for people that play the victim and exploit the benefits system' Tracey stated.

Privately, Jim disagreed with aspects of Tracey's views. He felt her position uncompassionate and excessively opinionated about the journeys of people she did not truly know. So, one might expect that this would be Jim's focus and perhaps he would gently share his views. Yet, the architecture of Jim's mind did not allow such straightforward flow.

There were blockages from a shame-based sense that anything to do with himself (including his views) was axiomatically unworthy. This latter self-deprecating position was wired in Jim's mind as the simplest and most self-evident truth. Fundamental building blocks for him, in finding his path and making sense of his world.

Further, his core fears included contemplating and catastrophising that he could: be judged negatively, not liked, perhaps disappoint, or upset another person. He kept silent. However, Jim's anxiety settled on Tracey being able to pick up that he disagreed with specific notions which she held close and clearly valued. He felt both naked, transparent, and anxious that he had silently insulted Tracey by not suppressing sufficiently to blindfold her to his disapproval.

Our beginnings suggest crimes may be squeezed out of an older Jim. Yet this younger Jim seemingly oriented purely to committing crimes against himself; snuffing out his own potential and his life quality at every turn. Thoroughly fenced in by worries of negative judgement; nowhere for self-expression to go. Monstrous crimes, all against himself.

The audience left pondering, Jim maybe an innocent victim? Perhaps our Jim on the wrong end of a miscarriage of justice? Surely, far easier to get blood from a stone then squeeze a monstrous crime out of our this harmless ninny?

The evening ended, with Tracey transporting him home. Jim felt slightly triumphant that his cornered bladder had stood up to the onslaught of several pints and he had been on a date. Yes, he was handicapped. But just maybe, he had travelled a few steps closer to normality by being present (albeit barely) during this ordeal. He had experienced a blind date.

Jim's bladder perhaps started to celebrate that home was in sight and the pressure could soon be titrated down. Elsewhere inside, Jim knew most clearly that Tracey had experienced their time together as boring, irritating, and thoroughly unpleasant. In his heart, Jim knew that sadly he did not have a different 'Jim' to present to her.

As Jim got out of Tracey's sport car at the top of his street, he reflexively said to Tracey 'see you, *soon*'. His insight almost merged with the end of the word 'soon'. Instantly, Jim was left with what alien part of my being has pressed the switch for my vocal chords to release the word 'SOON'? As her car sped off into the distance, embarrassment fiercely grabbed him with both hands and shook him vigorously. Not completely unlike his primary school teacher, Mrs Yardley, after he screwed up his response to the register.

Jim knew and felt that his parting words to Tracey would be taken as him completely lacking insight. He would be seen as expecting and anticipating what the world would patently re-fuse to deliver, 'period' as the North Americans might say. He felt truly pathetic.

'SOON!'; it stung Jim. As if he believed that Tracey would want to answer the bell to round 2. He knew very well the white towel had been thrown in by Tracey, long before the end of their time together.

Jim worried about what the feedback from Tracey would be to his dad and his dad's new partner Lacey. He did not have to wait long, for these results to come in. Within two or three weeks, he visited his father at the home he shared with Lacey. When Jim arrived, Lacey's twenty three year old son (Simon) and his friend (Russell) were visiting as well.

Within minutes, Russell said 'tell me about the blind date with Tracey'. Jim knocked this back with a straight bat by saying something like 'yes, she was nice girl and I enjoyed having a drink with her'. Then, a mockery ensued.

'*Hmmm. Can't tell you how much she enjoyed it*' Russell said, respectfully trying to hold back or pretend to hold back, loud laughter. Simon joined in and they both laughed loudly and extensively, seemingly based on their ears still echoing with the feedback which Tracey had provided (about Jim).

It merely strengthened Jim's views that he fell massively short and nobody would want to commit to a relationship with him. He left his father's house soon after, feeling deflated and negatively judged. He would not have a relationship with a partner throughout his twenties.

Chapter 10 – Jim finds work
and a lust buried deep

In these late teens and early adulthood, Jim settled into an administrative office job in a Detention Centre. Unaware that what was loosely *'time behind bars'* would ultimately bookend much of his adulthood, at the beginning and the end. Jim would work in this early job from the age of nineteen up until an unceremonious departure at the age of twenty three.

In essence, this Detention Centre was a type of prison for young male offenders that were aged between seventeen and twenty one. They had typically committed petty crimes and were sentenced to a maximum of four months, with most released early provided they did not breach rules. The Detention Centre environment was suggested to be *'a short sharp shock'* aimed at diverting young offenders from criminal life paths.

The regime was harsh and strict. Many of the prison officers behaved such that they instilled fear into many of the young inmates. There were usually between around one hundred and one hundred and twenty young prisoners within the Centre, at any given time. Whilst Jim was a very similar age to the young offenders, he was a member of staff and not a prisoner.

This backdrop provided Jim's first infatuation, albeit defensively hidden. Sparks flew in Jim's neural synapses because he was afforded the chance to spend some time with Sharon Jones. Sharon was part of the education department, and was aged in her early thirties. The level of her flirtations and sexual innuendo were undoubtedly more than several standard deviations above the mean.

Whenever the opportunity arose, Sharon bent over desks in a way that rendered full-on X-rated porn movies subtle and under-stated. When Jim and Sharon were alone, she spoke of her sex life. She slipped out juicy details of her dalliances with the married governor of the Detention Centre (Carl Grant). Her sexual disclosures were unsolicited and delivered in the type of over-played sexual way that might characterise the expensive sex chat lines of that era. Jim transfixed, flustered, and unsure what to do with the receiver.

Sharon regularly provided Jim with longing eye contact, which he felt must be feigned. Still, passion raged inside him. His eyes could not bear the heat of this connection for a full second, constantly shifting around like an energised toddler being asked to sit still.

The level of disinhibition which Sharon displayed was at times on the verge of psychotic, albeit with the heat intensified by a young Jim's sexual starvation. She once spontaneously spoke in depth of an incident with a cucumber, along with intermittent sexual panting and loud breathing. On more than one occasion, she spoke of being about to meet the governor (Carl Grant) and sprayed perfume directly up her short skirt.

Unclear whether Sharon's brief laughter at such times was about her own behaviour. More likely, she sensed how easily she could render every part of Jim's body alight and yearning to passionately merge with her. Sharon, perhaps a bit like an enthusiastic rider with some new Ducati super bike between their legs. Thrilled, marvelling and maybe even overwhelmed with the sounds of immense power that accompany intense revving; a type of euphoric laughter breaking out.

In contrast, Jim felt overpowered and scared by the level of his cravings. He did not have that sense of the power he had over the world, but more the power that the world had over him. Sharon revved at will, wantonly.

Dragged by the damsel's Ducati; this way and that. Only Jim's extreme neuroses were able to clumsily apply the brakes. The inertia from the anxiety was strengthened by Jim's resounding sense that he was inadequate, unworthy, and pre-set to fall short. Whilst Jim defensively tried to appear disinterested, he was betrayed by the outrageously rouge blushing from indiscreet cheeks.

Sharon surely sensed a shy Jim's futile pretence, whilst all the time a volcano erupted inside him. Often Jim had the challenge of having to let the stirring in his trousers settle, before he could stand. Occasionally, a situation would dictate that he had to become upright at an inconvenient time. As he moved awkwardly around the desk, a pointed indicator seemed to shamefully betray his position. In young childhood, his grandmother Norma assured him that this was but 'the devil's work'.

Jim drew on a well-worn strategy that he invariably used when he was strongly attracted to a woman, he fought hard to give off the diametrically opposite impression of mere disinterest. Occasionally, an approach-avoidance conflict broke out; the latter always seeming to win the arm wrestle. Nevertheless, the attraction reached a crescendo when Sharon persuaded Jim to give her a game of table tennis, in a private room within the Detention Centre. Later that day, Jim awaited her arrival in the games room. He had sexual energy bursting from his every pore.

After Sharon had taken an age to get changed and readied, Jim heard the jangling of keys in a nearby outer door. Jim's body bursting with anticipation, with part of him wholly uneasy with its volume. Then, Sharon appeared, floating in on a cloud of the most intense of perfumes. She was wearing a short skirt over a skin tight leotard. Her breasts and nipples seemed pushed out that far that Jim could almost feel them reaching out to him.

Sharon graced the stage, with her body leaping and bouncing for each precious rally. Jim's mind was hypnotised, again and again. His brain felt pleasantly fluffy inside and less able to think in words. Alongside this, an uneasy stallion faced with his maiden outing.

Whenever the ball hit the floor on Sharon's side, it seemed that she bent over in a volitionally seductive way. When stooped, she held her position for more than an age; with part of our Jim drinking in every millisecond. Jim seeming to be repeatedly given the temporal space to fully complete his most sordid of fantasies.

Drawn in by a beacon that leaped out and imprinted on his mind; more than the reddening of a baboons rear. Jim's arousal firmed up and restricted his movement. Our Jim repeatedly trying to stealthily re-arrange his baggy shorts.

The best way to quell many an urge may often be to simply give in to it, but it seemed that Jim's foot always shadowed the brake pedal. Jim's cravings for Sharon remained, pushed down and unfulfilled. Sadly, Jim's inadequacies mean that this particular part of the tale does not become more juicy. Nevertheless, Jim continued in his employment in the Detention Centre, for around four years.

Aside from Jim, the next youngest staff member was aged in their early thirties. There were around a dozen administration workers, most of whom were females aged in their forties. Additionally, there were around twenty five prison officers and some support staff. For Jim at that time, there was only one Sharon Jones.

Chapter 11 – Jim's attempts to side-step the landmines within his work place

Within Jim's duties at the Detention Centre, he was required to assist with John Hart (a prison officer) in providing what was referred to as 'canteen' to the young prisoners. The prisoners did jobs of work within the prison or attended educational classes. For this, they were rewarded with a wage of maybe around £5 per week (back in the late eighties and early nineties), which they could spend at the weekly 'canteen'.

The money which they had accrued was written next to their name, in a logbook. On one occasion each week (Wednesday at 1pm, just after lunch), the prisoners would get the chance to spend some or all of their money in what was basically a small shop. The shop sold items such as: sweets, drinks, and toiletries.

Jim dreaded this aspect of the week, with a passion. Torment began with walking into a dining hall, filled with eyes. Typically there were around one hundred and twenty prisoners sat at various tables; about two hundred and forty eyes. For Jim, these eyes just sat in wait, readied to scrutinise and judge.

Mid-way along the dining hall was a small room, with a serving hatch. This was where the supplies were stored and it was essentially the place at which Jim and John provided the shop facility to the young inmates. The inmates were called up, one table at a time. Jim's difficulties with this task began with his very entry. He and John unlocked the outer door and walked into this vast dining hall. It felt to Jim that the eye balls of each of the prisoners turned and fixated on him, as he walked half the length of this grand dining hall.

Jim's mind wholly felt and knew that his every movement and facial expression was placed under the microscope; viewed by over a hundred sets of busy ocular receptors. Worsened im-measurably because when Jim made this walk and intermit-tently when he was visibly at the serving hatch, some of these young offenders took it upon themselves to surreptitiously wolf whistle. The whistles sat uneasily with Jim's history, which included: extensive exposure to the bigoted teachings of the homophobic Braithwaite family in childhood, low self-esteem, a strong tendency to focus on the negative, and over-concern for what other people think.

Jim's mind de-coded this wolf whistle as *'these people believe that I am homosexual'.* A needle pointer for belief strength that might have briefly hovered around 50% sure, simply magnet-ised to the extreme of the scale; he knew it. Like a jaded arm wrestler, holding the mid-point and suddenly overcome. Jim sensed that maybe these dozens of prisoners could look dir-ectly into his soul, seeing things that he himself could not yet 'see'. It would be a ridiculously under-stated euphemism to suggest that Jim was insecure with this internal situation, floating prominently within his mind.

Maybe not politically correct (PC) to refer to this uneasiness, but Jim grew up in the seventies and eighties; in a rough North-ern town where the sheriffs were sadly bigotry and venom. Perhaps easy to sit back feasting in an arm chair next to the log fire, and make judgements about how people behave within the rat-a-tat-tat of a war zone many hundreds of miles away. The sands of time can change much; several decades on when 'the force of the situation' switches from what had been hurricane forces in one direction to more than a breeze in the diametrically opposite position, a person's orientation may change. If it suits, then we could ignore the elements and greedily yank ourselves conveniently to the moral high ground.

At this time, Jim's reflexive knee-jerk defence was that it was imperative that he convinced these plethora of judgements that he was a strong macho heterosexual man. But how could he do that, walking across a dining hall and serving sweets from a hatch? Rest assured, he would try with all his being.

Unfortunately, the harder Jim tried to convince his audience of what they might see as masculinity, the less masculine he felt. His anxiety was such he tried to create an image of what these young offenders saw of him, when they looked at him. As if he could mind read, he knew what they saw. Problematically, the mental image of himself that Jim created in his threat-sensitive mind was somewhere between a mincing Larry Grayson and a softly spoken Julian Clary, of that era.

When Jim walked into the canteen, his lips seemed to quadruple in size. He fought hard to try to make his lips not protrude or push out. The more he fought the more conscious he was of them and the more they pushed out, in his mind. Jim was conscious of over two hundred individual eyes and frantically trying to avoid each and every one. With eye contact, their judgements weighed down on him even heavier.

When Jim had interchanges with each inmate at the counter, he strove to compensate by deepening his voice. He also ceased the polite pleasantries which were usually standard reflexes for him. For those couple of hours working the serving hatch, he was too macho for niceties. Striving with all his being to neutralise a million disgusted Braithwaites within his mind. The judgements weighed heavily on Jim throughout the weekly 'canteen' and he would carry them about dutifully in between canteens.

The challenges which Jim found were not merely from the inmates. Jim also had difficulties with some of the staff. Some of the prison officers were undoubtedly supportive of Jim, perhaps providing him with colourful guidance or engaging in friendly banter. Jim was able to enjoy aspects of this and he sometimes felt a friendliness which was behind what they said and did. One prison officer, whilst always warm would regularly tell Jim, 'you are dressed like a bag of shit'. However, his tone was so friendly that the words did not sting.

Alongside this, Jim did feel aggression from a small number of the staff. The prison officers would regularly shower the prison inmates with verbal aggression, threat, and intimidating demeanour. It is possible that partly because Jim was aged similar to the inmates, the prison officers may have sometimes slipped into some of that aggression with him.

There was an instance when Jim was mid-way photocopying as part of his job, when the small Scottish PE instructor (Pete Blake) arrived with photocopying in hand. For some reason, Jim was in a cheerful mood on that day and it is possible that Pete took this as him mocking his wait. Within seconds, Pete had dismissively yanked Jim's photocopying out of the copier, flung it on the floor, barged Jim aside, and begun completing his own photocopying. Jim sensed aggression within Pete and close to the surface and so he said nothing. In addition to fear, Jim felt slightly tearful.

Jim's esteem suffered onslaught from several of the prison officers, who would regularly ask him about his girlfriends. One day he felt so cornered by this that a dangerous joke became compressed out of him. It happened with one of the most butch and sexist prison officers in the unit, namely, Bob Holt. Jim was pouring himself a cup of coffee in a large common room, whilst Bob was sat alone in the room. The sequence went like this:

'Hey Jim lad, you out on the town last weekend? Did you get a shag' Bob enquired, rather directly.

Jim flicked through an inner catalogue of possible responses. He was generally conspicuously committed to truth, but he was not drawn to a response of, *'No Bob, to be honest I am in my twenties and I have not even had a passionate kiss, let alone a shag'*. Time ticked and he could not fathom an easy exit to this probe. Jim's responses were generally pretty uncontroversial and safe. However, from somewhere unbeknownst to him, he settled on saying:

'hey Bob, you know that you are the only man for me'.

Bob's face turned angry and he ran towards Jim. Jim had just squeezed round the door when he heard a metal chair thud against the back of it. Presumably the missile was launch from a Bob that Jim perceived had been at least fifteen yards away. He did not know if this show of anger was genuine or some high stakes charade; he would never find out.

An air of aggression did flow from a few of the prison officers. Indeed, aggression spilled over and led to the demise of one particular member of staff, Roy. Roy had always been pleasant to our Jim. However, on one fateful day, Roy would lose his temper with a prisoner that had forgotten his full 'kit' for a parade on the court yard.

A beating followed, which left the young outcast hospitalised. Jim did not witness this, but the prison buzzed with this intrusion to the humdrum; with the prison officer eventually getting sacked. A different governor and it would surely have been swept under an ample carpet, which at that stage was likely already outrageously cluttered below the underbelly.

Chapter 12 –Jim's competence
is questioned!

Within the Detention Centre, Jim's main duties were filing and photocopying. The latter required him to use only a very small sample of his potential; like a weight lifter tasked to lift a feather. Jim's brain was so under-used that he would often mentally switch off. Hence, he sometimes made very basic mistakes. This was to get Jim into trouble.

Files were very occasionally mis-filed, by Jim. Once, Jim was given the responsibility of sending out the daily postal items. Unfortunately, he forgot to put postage on several of the letters. This meant that some of the letters got returned, including the monthly expenses of the main boss (the 'Governor' of the prison).

Another occasion; he was asked to transfer some specific data from paper files to summary cards, for each of the one hundred and twenty prisoners. In order to ensure that he got everything right, he double-checked on the requirements of the task with the team leader Ms Jean Pascal. After four years in Jim's administrative assistant role, Jean then completed his annual performance appraisal later that week, with:

> *'Jim seems quite slow at learning new things and has to be told several times about how to follow fairly basic procedures'*

Alongside this, in this performance appraisal, Jim received *'unsatisfactory'* ratings from Pascal. The upshot was that at the end of the appraisal document, it was recommended that Jim be given six months to improve or his contract would be terminated. Now, in the grand scheme of issues like third world poverty or innocent victims in war zones, this may seem a relatively minor issue. For Jim, it felt to be more than everything.

One might wonder, how did Jim respond to the criticisms within his appraisal? Now, by this stage of his early twenties, Jim's character had developed in some interesting ways. In the context of the shame, low self-esteem, and doubt that merged with his soul: Jim felt hugely threatened by overt criticism. He was relentlessly bombarded by internal self-criticism within his own head, but for some reason he felt unable to carry the weight of actual criticism from others.

Criticism set off a very loud emotional false alarm within him, giving him an emotional signal which resonated as if something life-threatening had occurred. Like a faulty smoke alarm that keeps going off again and again, when there is no smoke and no fire. What Jim said and what he did in response to criticism often came on the crest of an emotional wave, rather than being built on sound and thought through logic.

Criticism seemed to yield an opportunity for Jim to do what his emotions were telling him, rather than doing what was most sensible and effective. It managed to funnel him into briefly letting go of some aspects of his regular inhibited approach to life. A safety valve opened; yet typically nothing good came out of it within Jim's external world.

Like a cornered animal, criticism left Jim feeling anger deep inside. Feelings of anger and aggression which were perhaps a welcome interlude from helplessness. A distraction from the brain teaser which life represented to him. He could simplify the world and temporarily make it all about this issue. Hence, his lens temporarily moved slightly off himself and away from his hopeless inability to fit fruitfully into the world; perhaps blessed external focus.

Jim's upset at the appraisal was compounded by his inner appraisal of Jean Pascal. Jean Pascal was a woman in her early forties. She was overweight, dressed as if she was two decades younger than she was, and seemed to perceive herself to be a sexual Goddess. He recalls her saying of a famous deep voiced singer of that era (Rick Astley) who was half of Pascal's age, '*he could sing to me, but I'd kick him out of bed – he's not attractive*'.

For Jim's fury, Pascal appeared as a mutton-faced hag; posturing that the world ought to view her as fresh and early on the incline, when she was patently stale and over the hill. Our Jim generally still held onto much kindness. Yet here, post-appraisal anger was the shepherd; skilfully leading his thoughts and attitudes. Maybe, a clue to the future lies herein; perhaps more than tea leaves cluelessly strewn at the lower reaches of a mug. Could anger compress deeds out of Jim's humble shape?

Jim sensed that Pascal had an ill-deserved grandiosity. None of this bothered Jim, particularly. What he did struggle with was what seemed, to him, as Pascal's hypocritical predisposition and blatant insincerity. The latter troubling him so much more since he had been heartlessly struck by those critical shots, fired by Mrs P.

Jim spent much of his day in an open plan office, with three other middle-aged women. Pascal was sweetness and light to the face of her colleague, Sarah. However, whenever Sarah was not in the office, it was a reliable predictor of Pascal being heavily critical of Sarah to the other colleague (Rachel). The criticism was interwoven with endless speculation about Sarah having an affair with one of the married prison officers.

When Sarah was back in the office; a switch was pressed such that Sarah remained none the wise about the frequent verbal clawing at her. It was all put on hold, until her back was again turned and she was not in earshot. In Jim's mind, Pascal was phoney.

Jim was evasive, strove for impression management, and dodged many an issue. However, he felt that somehow he danced between the raindrops and was perhaps generally a consistent and truthful soul. Or maybe more precisely, he hid mainly by what he did *not* say, rather than what he did say.

Jim did engage in much shame-based attempts at representing a picture that even he did not believe in. Yet, within his mind this was less outrageous than outright insincerity and wilfully using words which convey an untruth. Further, Jim's evasion was purely to appease his own shame, in an inner battle. An ineffective striving to make life more liveable, but not for venomous strikes aimed at other entities.

For Jim, sincerity and decency were 'oughts', as in a moral code that one should adhere to. Pascal did not fit this 'ought', particularly since the point that she criticised him within the appraisal. Rage, rising up.

Jim strove to cling onto the notion that the human species ought to be truthful, decent, and sincere. Possibly in this way, there were more holes for his anger to leak through. Or maybe, just maybe, he could even have the higher ground in just one area of his existence. A welcome sideshow to focus on, to provide respite from his awareness of: himself and the life that he and his past had created.

As Jim got to the end of his annual appraisal document, his head throbbed. Blood and adrenaline pumped impatiently round his frame, with every nerve and sinew heavily electrified. He felt threatened by being told that he fell short.

Our Jim knew he fell short, but strangely his frame could not cushion such views being explicitly stated by a separate specimen carrying human eyes. He was energised; such that he had inadequate resources to stay still or keep silent. On very rare occasions such as this: Jim's handbrake offered little resistance; his emotions pressed the accelerator pedal fully to the floor.

Right at the end of the appraisal document: he noticed that the appraisal was counter-signed by the main boss 'Carl Grant' (the governor of the Detention Centre), along with the words:

> *'I can confirm that the appraisal of Jim Butler by Jean Pascal represents a very fair and reasonable appraisal'.*

Jim's thoughts raced. *'How can this weasel Grant counter-sign my appraisal when I have not even seen him during all my employment at the Detention Centre?'.* His outrage probably mixed dangerously with his awareness that the married Grant was having a *'secret'* affair with a certain Sharon that so magnetically drew in our Jim's unexpressed passions.

Jim noticed that there was a section after Grant's signature, in which the person being appraised can make comments on their thoughts about the appraisal. He felt injured by the appraisal; he wanted to injure the injurers. His inner fury grabbed the nearest pen, and it wrote:

> *'I don't agree with the appraisal. The negative comments of Ms Jean Pascal are about me seeking confirmation before carrying out a specific procedure over one hundred times. I would suggest that it is better to be absolutely sure that I have understood instructions (by asking for confirmation), rather than repeating the same mistake over one hundred times. Hence, Ms Pascal's comments are ill-founded and really unfair. I think Ms Pascal is slapdash and has a tendency to jump to conclusions.*
>
> *Additionally, if a person is given a very simple and repetitive task, their mind begins to do it automatically and without thinking.*

This leads to more mistakes. The more clever the person, the more quickly a person is prone to switch to doing simple repetitive tasks automatically and without conscious thought. I want to contribute. I need more challenging tasks to get the best out of me. The work place is flawed, in that it is under-using my potential.

Finally, the governor has countersigned the appraisal, to say that he 'agrees in full' and believes that all Jean Pascal's comments are fair. This is ridiculous. In my four years, I have never seen the governor and nor has he been in the same room as me when I was working. Carl Grant cannot truthfully countersign, when he has no direct information about me.

Signed: Jim Butler (Administrative Assistant)

By young adulthood, Jim kept a naïve sense of entitlement to fairness close. When reality inevitably clashed intermittently with this latter sense of entitlement, it often permitted him distraction. This distraction would occasionally give him some limited respite from focussing on a 'self' which he truly hated.

Jim's words on the appraisal document were chosen by hurt and anger, with his logic and common sense having taken annual leave. Jim handed his appraisal to his boss, with the freshly made comments his pen had made. It would not take long for the fruits of his labour to come home to roost.

The very next day and soon after his arrival in work, Jean Pascal delighted in telling him that he had been summoned to attend the governor's office at 2pm on that day. She had no details, other than that he would be accompanied by Steve Williams (the administration boss). Uncertainty created ripples of worries and butterflies in his stomach.

A small part of Jim wondered if the comments he had written

on the appraisal might mean that he would be assigned more challenging tasks. A type of promotion, perhaps? Jim showing a positivity that was beyond unusual for him. Then there was also the uncharacteristic sticking his head above the parapet, with his comments on the appraisal document. There were signs that Jim was having a transient mental wobble, diverting himself well beyond what had become a well-worn script.

It was 1:57pm when Jim made the trek up a lengthy staircase, closing in on his fate. He was accompanied by Steve Williams (administration boss), who was very largely tight lipped. Within but a few second of arriving at the door of the grand office of the governor, Jim was able to fully release this unusual openness to a good development occurring in his life. There would be no promotion.

Jim entered the office accompanied by Steve, to be greeted by the governor and his stunningly beautiful young personal secretary. Jim observed the governor sat on a big leather chair, behind a large shiny wooden desk. The magnitude of the chair seemed such that it would allow ample comfort room for the likes of Robert Pershing Wadlow, the tallest man in the record books at that time. The governor's secretary hovered diligently and in silence, with the air of being in awe of her leader.

The governor (Mr Carl Grant) was the youngest person in the UK prison system to attain a governor post. He was aged in his forties. When erect, he was just under six foot. His physique and very rounded cheeks spoke persuasively of over-indulgence.

The accelerated rate of his career ascent was mirrored by what seemed to be accelerated hair loss. The few strands remaining were clearly grown long, likely bathed in thickening conditioner, and styled in a Bobby Charlton comb over. Maybe a suggestion that he had difficulties letting things go. He used a quantity of hair gel which might well have dissuaded a small hurricane from mockingly re-arranging his would-be thatch.

'Jim, I have read your comments on the D32 Appraisal document' the governor stated.

Jim was struck by the governor's aggressive body language, his red cheeks, and his loud and harsh tone. Jim felt that the governor had anger bouncing around inside him, sure to find a path out. It was as if Jim's mere arrival seemed to be an aggressive strike to this man. His anger like a greyhound in the traps, poised. Surely so close to that moment, when the rabbit passes and the starting stalls open up.

'I found your comments to be immature, rude and impertinent' the governor barked.

Jim felt himself shrinking. He had no idea what impertinent meant. Yet, he suspected it was not a compliment, from the words it was keeping company with.

'Yes governor, I am sorry. I was upset by the appraisal' Jim whispered. Without thought, he was wide eyed, anxious, and apologetic. Jim's anger was yanked from his grasp, by this man's power.

'You have a lot to learn about behaving with dignity, maturity, and respect', the cheating governor continued.

Jim remained silent, but hurting inside.

'Now, I was close to terminating your employment. Think yourself lucky to have another chance. Buck up your ideas from here. Now, get out of my sight before I change my mind' the governor provided, as his verbal parting shot.

Jim exited the room on command. His tail, again between his legs. He felt uneasy as he made the journey down the steps, almost like he had left something behind in the governor's office. There was clearly nothing physical that he had forgot. Maybe he was without the very marginal unattached thread of pride and self-respect, which had not fully been shed from his person before he entered the plush office.

Steve held onto his silence. That said, he found it within himself to squeeze his face together in a way that elevated a pair of taut cheeks. It seemed to convey that he too was perhaps hurting and unsettled by what had just befallen our Jim. Perhaps like a conflicted member of a drunken group gathering around a vicious assailant giving another person a kicking; not supporting the defeated; yet his demeanour did not fully rule out at least some minor disagreement with the proceedings.

As Jim finally stepped off the last stair, he was greeted by the sight of Jean Pascal. She gave a wholehearted 'Hi', alongside the most full smile that Jim had ever seen adorn her timeworn face. She positively beamed, with a smile like the proverbial Cheshire cat. Jim was on autopilot and slightly dissociated, but he reflexively returned the 'Hi'.

For the next two hours, Jim filed and photocopied. His attentional resources channelled heavily into brooding about both the 'unfair' appraisal and the roasting from governor. It burnt his mind over and over again, in an upwardly escalating cycle.

Jim left work and returned home. That evening, he was even closer to being wholly oblivious to the various verbal offerings that his mother Kath repeatedly dished up. His mind continued to beat him harshly, with the firm stick of yet another failure in his life.

Jim had kept his nose to the grindstone of adversity relentlessly, for so long. He was beyond weary with it. Alongside this, by the tender age of twenty three, Jim's personality was strongly woven with avoidant threads.

Like the battered and barely functional terminator: his neural circuitry had lit up and meandered down a plethora of routes, looking for the *'re-route'* to salvage something from this latest indignity. The elements came together and the next day, Jim's flimsy and maladaptive attempts at face-saving crystallised in phoning Steve Williams and resigning from his post.

Jim would jump first, perhaps trying hopelessly to convince himself that it was all wholly beneath him. Jim's mind had run from the alternative of possibly being pushed or catapulted from his role. This would have felt an even bigger failure; possibly leaving an unshakeable stain upon his being.

Jim more than sensed that he was not good enough. Hell, he absolutely knew it. His mind had pulsated with the notion that if he did not quit, then he would likely be sacked at some point. Surely, by quitting, he had thrown a ticking time bomb out of the window?

Yet again, the path of least resistance had welcomed him with both arms. Jim's work place did not resist and the deed was done. What was left was twenty three year old Jim; unemployed, ego further battered, and having left his last job under a cloud.

Chapter 13 – Rumours abound

After losing his job, Jim fell into the habits of over-sleeping and engaging in very little. He had oceans of free attention in his mind, which washed up into every crevice of self-hatred and worry. A small bastion of *'normality'* remained, in the form of his weekly trip to the 'White Hart Inn' public house.

With Jim's social anxiety and his neurotic bladder, this weekly outing to the local pub was most certainly not squarely within his comfort zone. If zero was relaxed and ten was the most anxious Jim had ever been in his life, he usually ran at about a six or a seven within this public setting. The other people within the pub were like mirrors through which he saw himself, albeit the image grossly negatively distorted by abundant self-hatred. The evening was consistently not comfortable and at times, even torturous.

So, how many times does someone need to place their hand deeply into a fire, to realise nothing satisfactory comes from that endeavour? In such an avoidant person that Jim undoubtedly was, one might wonder why would he continue to take these trips to the pub on? To begin to understand that, one would need to know that a part of Jim still yearned to fit in and be accepted. Not fully drained out of him by a quarter of a century which had been saturated with consistent and spectacular failure, at every turn. He beseeched the world to allow him to be a winner.

Inside Jim, there were desperate pleadings for warm human connection and respect from others. Perhaps willing a scene like the one that befell George Bailey at the end of 'It's a Wonderful Life', with people convincingly telling him how great he is and how his life is a success. Of course, Jim's mind would take some persuading to buy into this blissful vision. The best used car salesman in the world surely struggle to land that pitch to Jim.

For Jim, it was as if to retain a position of fully downing tools was akin to completely losing hope. For some unknown reason: at this stage, part of his inner workings lent heavily against that path of wholly giving up. A small part of him behaved as if his past had lied to him for twenty five years and miracles were still possible. Twenty five years of hopelessly trying to squeeze the square peg that was himself into the round holes that the world placed everywhere for him. He continued.

Aged twenty five, Jim makes the weekly trip to the White Hart Inn. Glancing at his digital watch, he notes: *'7:43pm'*, and one extra press od the lower button would allow a vision of: *'13/05/93'*. Jim moves towards the faded brown door, wedged ajar. His past watches on, working his remote control with unscrupulous precision.

A reflexive glance at the window, probably hoping that his existence would be affirmed in the form of a reassuring reflection. Instead, a bolt of fear strikes inside, finishing in his stomach. The glance merely seems to telegraph a very large gathering of people inside the venue.

Jim moves through the ajar outer door, and his hand pushes open the inner door. The whoosh inside him, as if he is part of the Sweeney Flying Squad bursting into the house of a dangerous criminal. Jim glanced quickly around the approaching room, implicitly avoiding all detail. Evading the present moment; constantly on the run.

Jim cannot see his friend Spider (or Archie Brice, as he is also known), whom he has arranged to meet at quarter to eight. In external reality, none of the people in the pub really notice Jim or his insecure strivings. Yet deep down, his insides compress out a wholly different inner truth. Something within Jim evaporates all doubt; enabling residue to crystallise into the rigid form of a compelling notion that everyone is watching him, intently.

Jim can feel people watching him. He can see the monstrosity that they are seeing; it is purely him. He can mind read, such that he feels and knows their negative judgements. Their judgement weighs heavily. It is as if Jim's core angrily accuses him of committing a thousand crimes, with a delay before it even names one.

As Jim walks towards the bar, he can feel the gaze of a couple that are sat smugly at the bar. Instantly lanced by the thrust of their perspective. Jim feels his face slipping for a second, turning over a card which shows fear.

Jim visualises his horrific contorted fear soaked expression, which has left him exposed in front of the whole pub. Feeling like he is marked out; as if he could never fully remove this stain that he had just created. Eternity might engulf him, like it's never going to leave.

A young pretty barmaid makes movements behind the bar which seem to gravitate to Jim's direction. Her look conveys that she will have the grace to look past Jim's inadequacy and engage in a practiced ritual of providing a drink.

'Ppplease could I have a pint of lager?' Jim asks, internally stung by his imperfect verbal execution of the request.

'Is that all?' she replies,

'Yes, thanks' Jim offers, with his neurons not able to fully avoid the path that the barmaid felt his order was in some way not enough.

On receiving his pint, Jim instantly takes several large gulps. Imbibing analgesia or perhaps trying to begin the process of dissolving himself. He then walks towards the small and somewhat tatty pool room.

On entering, he is pleased to observe the sight of his friend Spider. Spider is sat on the old wooden benches attached to the wall. Anxiety drops from an eight to a seven for Jim, as if Spider's presence has somehow legitimised him slightly.

The night then unfolds like many others. Jim's awkwardness waxing and waning, consumption of around four pints, a few games of pool. There were also some words exchanged with Spider about pretty safe and uncontroversial topics.

Jim never tried to use the toilet in the White Hart Inn. He knew his blushing bladder would not facilitate the process. Alongside this, there were a specific group that got together and consistently blocked him from using the toilet, specific-ally: intense fear, uncertainty, worries about negative judge-ments from others, negative expectancies, and that heart sink feeling that he knew would be coming when he was unable to demonstrate being *'normal'* by releasing surplus liquid.

Perhaps only once in several years did he nervously enter the toilet in the White Hart Inn, pushed firmly by a bad cold and a nose that kept running. He simply grabbed some toilet paper from within one of the cubicles, and fled. Jim managed this complete avoidance of using the toilets in the 'White Hart Inn' by tending to only venture out for a couple of hours and re-stricting himself to around four pints.

Like Cinderella when the clock struck twelve; there was an imperative to leave after the regular time period had elapsed, as the bladder struck more than full. As he aged, he perhaps began to show more compassion for a bladder which had likely already ballooned out to leave little comfort room for his other organs. No longer the drinking competitions with Fraz, necking a dozen pints and some chasers. No longer such wanton disregard for a disloyal bladder.

If he was offered a billion pounds to hang with his friend for twenty four hours or the most beautiful potential partner in the universe revealed a yearning to spend more time with him, then his bladder would have to politely decline. Jim having lost whatever tenuous influence he had ever enjoyed on a key controller module, within his brain. Something alien and unerring pushed buttons on this controller, to fully orchestrate our Jim's orientation to use a public toilet when people he knew were around.

Or maybe certain buttons were just no longer functional, burnt out by Jim's life of avoidance? Either way, Jim long since ceased pulling the strings. The paths in his mind were so well trodden that they showed up as the deepest of furrows; he could no longer even peer over the edges.

So, this night at the White Hart Inn initially felt like any other. The usual angst and unease, flowing through Jim's every vein. But then, for some unknown reason, it seemed the Gods that looked over Jim perhaps grew impatient with his path? Or maybe Jim had inadvertently mis-stepped and incurred their wrath? Either way, theirs whims decided to unleash another growth opportunity upon his being.

Jim and Spider had gathered on one of the two fruit machines. The latter distraction taking Jim's anxiety down to the nirvana of perhaps only a five or a six out of ten. Whilst gambling was a partial relief, his money typically dissipated far more quickly than his tension.

As Jim and Spider interacted with what used to be called a one-armed bandit (before buttons, all but took over), Jim sensed movement nearby. He became aware of an individual named Conrad Mathews moving out of the door of the pool room, which left him only a couple of yards away. Spider vaguely knew Conrad and just gave a greeting and was about to exchange a small amount of what may have been relatively meaningless small talk. However, Conrad had other ideas.

Now, Jim was aware that Conrad had spent time in prison for physically assaulting somebody, but he knew little else about him. Conrad was aged in his late twenties. He was about six foot four inches and relatively slim. He had straight black hair, which almost reached his shoulders. His eyes were very narrow, with dark shark like inners.

On this night, Conrad took it upon himself to walk right up to Jim; closing the distance such that his head was literally about an inch or two from Jim's. Jim reflexively tried to move his own head back, but somewhat tardily as he was somewhat in shock. It was as if Conrad wanted their eyeballs to touch. Then, in perhaps the most aggressive and disgusted tone that Conrad could find, he shouted loudly at Jim:

'QUEER'.

The venom was unmistakeable. Conrad's body language and his voice teamed up; both straining every sinew and pushing together, wholly against our Jim. Spider sensed the direction, and said something like: 'hey, come on Conrad. What's up'. Conrad stopped for an instant and then repeated his process, pushing his face to Jim's so they were almost touching and shouting:

'QUEER'.

Jim was wide-eyed, in shock, out of his depth, and tongue-tied. He was without having any kind of scripted response for this aggressively delivered broadside. Conrad then walked away towards the bar, with withering and aggressive looks in Jim's direction as he went. He then sat at the bar, looking over the bar and perhaps into the mirror on the wall; continuing to drink further pints.

In looking over the bar, Conrad's eyes were blessedly pointed in the opposite direction to Jim. Amidst the loud background noise of 'Ghostbusters' and noisy chatter from around the pub, Spider tried to reassure Jim:

'ignore him, he's just had too much to drink' Spider suggested gently, concern etched over his face.

Conrad loose, dangerous; Jim beyond uneasy. Conrad's path not just a man seeking any spittoon for his bile. Surely, a man who plays the numbers and likes an easy victim. Conrad was close with several like-minded regulars, in this drinking hole. Maybe as Connor McGregor might enlighten, Conrad perhaps 'a strong man in groups'? Our Jim, certainly not oriented to test or expose him.

Reportedly, the bulk of people heterosexual. Many diverting from this latter path not able to show their hand amongst the bigotry of the seventies, eighties, and early nineties. In those days, perhaps only a minority of a minority stepping forward and owning a homosexual path. Conrad so ready to pick them off, that he's doing the outing. Conrad looked strong to our Jim, with venom which could surely fuel many a dubious deed.

Several minutes later, and another issue emerged. A man called Mick Thorsky had decided to throw his hat in the ring. After Jim had been in the pub many dozens of times without incident, coincidence would have it that another regular in the form of Mick Thorsky would approach Jim and say: *'you and me are having a fight outside'*. Again, aggressiveness and seriousness in tone and body language; it simply could not be missed.

Jim reeling in shock, offered *'no, I don't want to fight you'*.

Mick then went back into the nearby pool room and Jim would hear the farce. *'I'm taking my chain off before the fight'* Mick's determined voice uttered to his audience. He was announcing that he was readying himself.

'someone look after my chain, I am fighting that faggot outside' Mick continued.

Mick a wiry, unattractive man of average height. Nothing exceptional about him, but maybe he was seizing his vision of a chance to shine. In this sense, maybe not wholly dissimilar to an aspect of Jim: they shared the common human plight of wanting to feel good about themselves. A shared drive, but disparate modus operandi.

Jim recalled Mick's flimsy attempts to gain respect several months earlier. That time, the stage of the pool room: Mick, *'I won the jackpot on the slot machine last week'* – no response from his audience, pause *'and it repeated'* – tumbleweed blowing, no response from his audience, pause, *'and it repeated again'*. Jim lost count of how many times the Jackpot repeated, but eventually Mick left that stage unfulfilled. Heavens to Betsy, how many imaginary repeats of the Jackpot before his audience bow down?

Maybe God loves a trier. Returning from our digression; Mick perhaps felt that he had stumbled on a chance to demonstrate his manhood to an audience eager for stimulation. Jim, a convenient podium which he could stand on, elevated.

Perhaps in his mind, Mick was the ultimate man, and he could show that best by juxtaposing himself with what he packaged as his diametric opposite, conquering his opposite, and standing against all that it was. Or maybe his mind had skilfully sniffed out a convenient vessel, into which he could displace all his anger and frustration. A live specimen perhaps so much more cathartic than an inanimate punch bag. Either way, Mick certainly did not need Don King to encourage and promote this fight.

Mick was clearly winding himself up in a self-serving spiral of fury. At this point, Spider went in and tried to defuse things. Mick's voice quietened down for several seconds. Jim was not going to wait for Mick to find that voice again, or Conrad to raise the stakes further, or somebody else to step forward to take him on.

As Spider came out of the pool room, Jim uttered *'I'm off mate, see you soon'.* The fact that Jim was rife with sadness and devastation was transparent; for once too troubled to even put energy into the invariable emotional cover up routines.

'OK mate, catch up soon' Spider said. Even with all Jim's negative biases, he could not help but see that Spider seemed deeply saddened by events. Maybe the silver lining, Spider had shown decency, loyalty, and his expression exuded compassion for Jim's obvious upset.

Jim was on high alert when he exited the White Hart Inn. He was looking round consistently, on his return home. The events of the evening spun round his head, growing more foul with each rotation. Jim knew that within this rough, bigoted, unforgiving Northern village which was his home, there was clearly a rumour that he was homosexual. If he had ever had any suspicions that sense and decency prevailed in his home village, then he could now shed them.

How had this rumour started? Randomly? Based on him never having a girlfriend? Based on him never using male toilets? Based on manifestations of his anxiety? Based on an ex-prisoner at the place that he worked being discharged into the community and mentioning the wolf whistles and the effeminate demeanour that hung off him when he tried to give off an antidote in the shape of a macho appearance? A million stories went through Jim's head about what had caused this, but none of them changed the manifested reality. Perhaps it did not matter 'why' so much, but rather they key issue was simply that 'it was'.

Jim could not find a way to comfortably understand what had happened. The hatred seemed to flow from rumours about his sexual preferences; yet how could such issues elicit such immense venom?. Why would another be so concerned about Jim's personal direction, sexually or otherwise?

Whatever interpretation Jim leaned against, it had barbs and hedgehog like spikes, which thoroughly stung logically and emotionally. Human nature entails a business of striving to sustain a sense of oneself as important and good; surely Jim had reached bankruptcy in that sphere. For some sullied souls, self-promotion involves seeking to put others down and de-value the presence and contributions of animals from the same human species. Our Jim had perhaps reached a level of turmoil that for him, to be literally 'put down' would be the most merciful?

The masses embark on an implicit quest to artificially elevate the status of their internal representation of self. Blindly follow the pack in this regard and maybe side step much depression and angst. Sadly, a conscience held Jim back from joining. Simply, he was moved to breath-taking levels of avoidance.

Our Jim felt destroyed; taken to a level of deep sadness that outstripped what he had encountered earlier in his adulthood.

Chapter 14 – Jim's eager anxiety
readily attached to the residue of the
fateful night in the White Hart Inn,
encouraging him to stay on the run.

Mohammed Ali once suggested that "a man who views the world the same at fifty as he did at twenty has wasted thirty years of his life". After the interventions of Conrad and Mick on that difficult night at the White Hart Inn, Jim got stuck in a funk; not much changed for our Jim for several years. He shielded himself from the world for at least the next eight years.

The damage to Jim was done well before the events in the White Hart Inn. That said, the overtures from Conrad and Mick on that specific evening represented a sizeable negative shift in Jim. It marked a line in the sand; with surrounding grains concretised and our Jim not able to smooth it out. In particular, for several years after that evening onthe 13th May 1993, Jim hunkered down in as much of a comfort zone as he could create. Minutes, hours, days, weeks, months, and years, spent largely licking his wounds or maybe striving to avoid the possibility of further injury.

There was a morality to Jim, which often translated into his options being constrained. Jim's mind knew that a person should not be disadvantaged by their sexuality and it was wrong to put somebody down based on their sexuality. However, alongside this, Jim had long-since been carrying shame and self-hatred deep within his essence. His overdependence on what he believed people thought of him ran wholly through him and his life. He could not skillfully dodge the two-footed sliding tackles from stray bigots; Jim, more than encumbered.

The disgust, aggression, and hatred that our Jim had witnessed in that evening in the White Hart Inn left him more afraid and more ashamed. On a deeper level beyond logic, he felt that his village community despised him; his inner self-hatred and shame blossomed from this. The early work of the bigoted homophobic Braithwaites in his childhood had been dutifully continued by elements of his local community. Conrad had outed him without tender pomp and ceremony, and ahead of Jim's own awareness.

As a neurotic child fearing rabies and learning that fear of water may be a symptom, Jim would recurrently fill a sink to reassure himself that he was not afraid of the water. No less nonsensical, the sour taste of the specific persecution in the White Hart Inn stayed with Jim and he sought to rid himself of it. It left doubts about his sexuality and a ludicrous sense that he must convince himself and others that he was heterosexual.

Jim did not know which way to turn. He felt he had to convince others that he was not homosexual. But why? And how?

The more Jim tried to make his face look macho, the more it seemed to look effeminate in the internal image which he would generate in his mind. The angst of the dining hall of the Detention Centre spread like wild-fire to all situations when Jim was not alone. The more Jim tried to make his lips neither pout or push out in any way, the bigger and more fidgety they seemed. If he could not convince the world, then internal shame would thrive and the world would surely smite him.

Jim had the worry about someone like Conrad or Mick deciding to crystallise their aggression at his home, surely impacting his mother Kath in the process. His mind ever conscientious, felt guilt just in case he brought this trouble to the door of his mentally fragile mother.

Jim's sleep became more disturbed. Noises downstairs began

to yield a different meaning. Jim replayed the aggression from Conrad within his head; his early and premature warning system recurrently focussing on the possibility that Conrad or an attitudinal twin might settle on torching his home.

Jim rarely ventured out for several years after that difficult evening in the White Hart Inn. When he did go out, he would often glance back to see if anybody had painted offensive messages on the outside of the family home or left banners. On the rare occasions he braved the community, he occasionally saw blankets with painted messages celebrating people's milestone birthdays, such as:

'Joan – Happy 40th – Have a great day',

'John – Happy 50th – Life begins at 50!'.

After that night in the White Hart Inn, Jim would usually ensure that he got close enough to read every one of them. He checked that they were not hate messages pertaining to him and his sexuality. On very difficult days, he did not find the courage to check, just in case.

In his mind, everyone carried the belief that he was homosexual and everyone in the local community despised him for it. He could avoid others, but tragically he could not easily avoid himself. He was even plagued within his home.

Jim became increasingly self-conscious watching television at home when he was in Kath's eye gaze. A handsome man on the television and Jim's mind knew Kath was watching his every move. His facial expression surely under scrutiny and Kath judging at every turn.

Jim felt it. It was unmistakeable, though her outer shell never gave any clues. In his mind, his expression contorted such that it was saying to Kath as effectively as words, 'I am gay'. His vocal chords remained idle, but he felt her judgement.

Pathetically, the PR department that remained in Jim's mind was assigned overtime. It consciously and effortfully sought to give Kath the types of press releases which might cajole her towards the notion of his virile red-blooded masculinity. If he learned that one of his male friends was dating a woman or even found a woman attractive, then Kath must hear of it.

One day, Jim was delighted to hear that a distant male associate had been involved in a minor road traffic collision. In essence, a fence had interrupted the journey of this male associate, after he had been distracted by a pretty young female. Jim felt an urgency to recount this story to Kath. This distant male associate would remain wholly absent from Jim's life, but somehow he became a close friend of Jim's in an instant. The spin from Jim's busy internal PR department was dizzying. He was building a case, though never feeling fully convinced himself.

Chapter 15 – The lost years: part one.

Subsequent to being marked out irreversibly at the White Hart Inn, Jim hid. More precisely, prior to then he occasionally went out but always hid. For several years after, he stayed in and always hid. The hiding had the constancy of a great vast rock, in the face of a humble tide.

There may be some stretched parallels with the phrase '*you can take a kid off the streets, but you can't take the street out of the kid*'. In adult Jim's case: wherever he was placed, his propensity to hide and cower ran through him. Like the design on the circular inner of a stick of Blackpool rock. At times subtle, Jim sought to hide the hiding.

For eight years after that haunting night at the White Hart Inn, Jim largely ceased socialising. His leisure became boiled down to just a few games of golf during the year and several trips to a snooker club each year. Both of these very occasional tasks involved utilising venues several miles from his local area, by design; both were facilitated by his friend Spider.

The local area where he was not accepted felt too hazardous; Jim largely in avoidant mode. On rare ventures into the local community: there were several other men that he came across over the coming years that gave off an aggressive and unpleasant vibe to our Jim. Apparently, an army of Conrad and Micks roamed.

The other members of this crew took their position; wilfully ignoring Jim, even when he said hello. Such specimens would look at Jim with faces drenched in anger and disgust; sometimes seeming to mock with an effeminate voice. They would puff out their chest, demonstrating that they were not afflicted with Jim's 'disease'.

Each and every slight stung Jim; more drops funnelled into his great vat of shame. People who used to consistently say hello, suddenly afflicted with a very specific ocular deficiency; apparently no longer able to see our Jim. This ocular condition undoubtedly spreading; a raging pandemic, rife in his local community.

Jim retained some limited contact with Spider. Spider's car allowed him a small ration of time away from the community that closely surrounded the White Hart Inn. Like an individual trying to swim many lengths underwater, Jim would have the benefit of occasionally popping up for air and feeling a sense of being able to breathe, albeit slightly.

From the age of twenty five until the age of thirty three, the patterns in Jim's life were pretty repetitive. Like groundhog day, left lazily on constant repeat. Sleep, get up, watch TV, eat intermittently, and relatively freely use the toilet at home; then repeat over and over again. Whilst Jim's bladder celebrated wildly at the vacation, the routine was somewhat stagnant.

Eight years ticked by, with Jim only very rarely even venturing outside his home fortress. Jim had the regular benefit from Kath's wisdom, negativity, and disapproval. Very occasionally, Jim made a token application for a job. Typically, such folly was inspired by Kath's 'encouragement' reaching it's cyclical peak.

'You don't seem bothered about getting a job. All my friend's sons are out there working. You can't spend the rest of your life on the dole. What will people think? People will think you are lazy.' Kath urged.

Whilst Kath's advice was perhaps reasonable, Jim felt somewhat broken and burnt out. He sought escape from the world. It felt like Kath was seeking to remove Jim's life jacket; with Jim keen to just peacefully float, untroubled by interruption. Jim often intimidated by the sheer size of his mountain of fear; aware that well before he could reach the peak he would be in rarified air, struggling for breath.

An overt gesture of applying for a job seemed to assist Kath's harassment to decline, only to cyclically build up to another crescendo about four or five months later. The pattern not wholly dissimilar to a sound wave for a trumpet. Whilst Jim could sometimes lower the amplitude and the frequency, he could not snuff it into silence.

Jim's very occasional 'applications for jobs' were so close to 'pseudo-applications' that there was often less than a cigarette paper between them. Deep down, fear and insecurity were running the show. Jim did not really want the jobs that he applied for. He felt assured that he could not disentangle them from their inevitable attachments in the form of risk, danger, and the shadowy figure of failure ripe to jump out on him.

So, eight years passed with Jim hardly engaging in any work. The potential boosts to his CV were restricted to a couple of factory jobs in the neighbouring town. Both of these latter jobs slipped out of Jim's loose grasp within less than a calendar month.

Chapter 16 – The lost years: part two

The first job during the lost years was at a company called Parson's Packing Limited, with Jim aged twenty seven. The job role involved loading toiletries into boxes, as they came along a production line; over and over and over again. The closest Jim's experience had previously come to this task was probably the 'hook a duck' fairground stall as a young kid; yet on this factory paradigm, participants could use their hands and the rewards did not come till the end of the week.

Though perhaps not the job's only parallel, if one takes a historical trip down memory lane. In particular, moments of Jim's own life had travelled along the conveyor belt towards him for twenty seven years; our Jim unerringly seeming to grab each one and drop it into package after package of misery. The boxes of such spent moments stacked up to a vast height, intimidating Jim to the very core.

The repetitiveness of Jim's new factory job task was matched, or in fact perhaps even surpassed by the conversations in the three allotted daily breaks. The breaks that were dished out comprised of fifteen minutes in the morning and afternoon, and thirty minutes at lunch. The working week was Monday to Friday, and at each break the lady Margaret would hold court. Margaret undoubtedly held seniority amidst the team that fate's hand had decided to place Jim into.

Margaret was about forty five, just above medium height, and carrying a thoroughly lived in face. The other players were: three ladies aged in their early thirties, a lady that was aged around forty, a man aged about thirty five, and Jim (aged twenty seven). Margaret's pressure of speech left scant gaps for her congregation. Indeed, her non-verbal leakage suggested that quite often she did not welcome her monologue being broken.

Jim landing in this group, nested together by the overlap from navigating a shared occupational furrow. Margaret was the 'alpha' of troop. At the breaks, the team gathered about fifty yards from the production line, inside what seemed almost like an indoor bus shelter. Yet, despite him recurrently wishing for it, Jim's bus never arrived.

So, one might wonder what pivotal world issues were to be reviewed amidst this crew that were haphazardly thrown together? Jim found that conversations about the soap opera 'Coronation Street' were jam packed into each and every minute. It seemed that the specific oratory flow was quite probably a snug fit for the jaded assemblage. Horses for courses; neither right nor wrong in an absolute sense. A most topical solution; either consonant with the gathering or painstakingly tolerated.

The events of the break times took shape with an invariable rhythm, patterned and cyclical like the seasons. Just like the seconds hand of a clock, going round and round and round; with moment after moment left behind in its wake.

Monday, Margaret initially centred on what had happened in Coronation Street the previous Friday. As the day wore on, the focus switched to what might happen in the episode that Monday evening. It felt like the speculation was rubbery, and could likely be stretched to fill whatever breaks the work place might offer. Tuesday simply did not offer the fruits of another juicy episode on that evening, and so the breaks were focussed on opinionated coverage of what had happened in the prior evenings episode.

'I definitely think Sally Webster should leave Kevin. I mean, he's been having an affair and she just can't trust him. I know there are kids involved, but she'd be better off without him' Margaret might

offer during a typical Tuesday morning break.

'Mike Baldwin has a drink problem, as well......' and on it went.

Jim was struck by how the characters were spoken about as if they were real people; as if nobody dare mention *'the script writer'*. Wednesday breaks came, and more speculation about what might happen during the scheduled evening episode. Thursday devoid of the nirvana of another episode proceeded pretty much like Tuesday. Then Friday, offering opportunity for speculation as to the unfolding developments in that evening's serving. The end of another week, then soon back to Monday and we go again.

Sections of University common rooms might abundantly hum with in-depth analysis of major world issues. One might hear the odd fresh faced intellectual showboating with knowledge of some great thinker; debate and analysis rumbling on. Rest wholly assured, most certainly not on Margaret's watch.

No moments frittered away on such highbrow discourse. In this recurrent sanctuary from the drudgery of the production line, no words would be squandered on Nitsche, Darwin, Doestoyevsky, Martin Luther King, George Orwell, Plato, Einstein, Freud, or even Shakespeare. The breaktime bus shelter positively buzzed with heaven-sent names like: Vera and Jack Duckworth, Steve McDonald, Alf Roberts, Bet Lynch, and Ken Barlow. They simply rolled off the tongue; particularly Margaret's.

Important to realise, Jim was no intellectual snob. Indeed, whilst he occasionally read bits of a tabloid designed for the masses, that was pretty much the full extent of the literary specimens which had reeled in his interest. Even if he had been well read, his personality was such that he felt that people should be respected and allowed to find their very own innocuous best-fit solutions. Beyond that, Jim had so much shame-drenched focus on judging himself that he did not have sufficient unallocated neurons to notably judge others.

Jim's attention drawn relentlessly to threat; but for Jim the threat was other people judging him negatively. No real bite from general bla, bla, bla; blissfully the lense of his audience rarely strayed in his direction. Undoubtedly, the threat sensor in Jim's brain had dimmed down somewhat in this new work environment.

Blessings augmented with the factory being a few miles away from his local community. He did not know anybody within this work place. In terms of Coopers colour coding system for threat; in Jim's mind threat levels were typically reduced from the usual Code Red to probable Code Orange.

Jim was initially slightly curious about the breaktime patterns which were played out before him. It was almost as if he had entered a novel twilight zone that his mind was grappling to fully fathom. Of course, Jim was euphoric that he seemed to be amidst an innocuous ambience, in which the focus never seemed to be on him. A comforting level of anonymity, palliative for a psyche with hypersensitive allergies to interpersonal situations. Nevertheless, strangely, even this paradise began to wear slightly thinner after about three weeks.

On the job itself: variety was occasionally sprinkled sparingly by a divine gift, in the form of a machine malfunctioning such that the production line would have to stop. Then, Jim and his fellow line workers would feast their eyes on the chaos. Engineers and maintenance staff hurriedly rushed to the line. The fixers feverishly struggled to re-create what had previously been the monotonous status quo.

Occasionally, men in suits and ties would join the throng;

showing off their immaculate white shirts, whilst berating the lack of progress of the would-be fixers. The line workers, paused and transfixed. Endowed with what was almost akin to a snippet of a *'fly on the wall'* TV programme, yet 'live' and well before the future would dictate that a plethora of such shows would afflict the unsuspecting world. This gem standing even more beautiful, in the background of the grinding boredom which sat snugly next to it on both ends.

After four weeks of this job and Coronation Street dissected within an inch of its life, Jim was bestowed with an escape route. The exit arrived in the form of glandular fever, which opened up a legitimate path to sickness absence. The job at this factory had been through a recruitment agency. It took Jim several weeks to regain his strength, by which point another character had been cast as receiving the spoils.

Jim was free, in the sense of becoming unemployed. Many in that factory role continued to dance to the hypnotic beat of its drum for many years; sometimes for so long, they could no longer even hear the music. Days fade into weeks, fade into months, fade into years, fade into decades, and slip into the bulk of a lifetime.

For Jim within that role, his anxiety did not regularly reach the grating heights which wore him down in most situations in which he was around other people. Maybe this was a utopian slide, which could have relatively comfortably nursed our Jim into harmless obscurity? Better than a poke in the eye, but perhaps not quite as sweet as a back rub. Regardless, glandular fever stepped in.

Fresh from convalescing, our Jim did not have the inclination to try to break back in. As such, he was to forego the benefit of witnessing Margaret split every atom associated with Coronation Street. This interlude to Jim's occupational inaction had at least mixed well with the glandular fever, in that it was to yield a temporary cattle prod which would keep Kath's carping largely at bay for several months at least.

Chapter 17 – The lost years: part three.

Aged twenty eight and Jim found another source joining the queue, to give him a kicking. He would occasionally visit his widowed eighty year old grandmother (Norma, the mother of Patrick), perhaps once every couple of months. Norma's favourable pièce de résistance was that she made the most wonderful cakes. The regulars were tarts, cream cakes, and jam sponges. With these invitingly arranged on her cake stand, there seemed very little that could not be forgiven.

Physically, Norma stood just below medium height. She was slightly overweight. She had held onto quite thick curly grey hair, which had several stray companions located on her chin. Despite her advanced years, she retained an intensity and a bite. The very same spirit that did for a tough lad named Phil Holbrooke in Jim's school year around twenty years earlier; barely attenuated with the passing of the years.

Norma had lived through two world wars and had what we might kindly refer to as a long-lived and 'very traditional' window on the world. The panes having gone uncleaned for several decades. Norma's opinions did not have to be prized out of her. They were so well learned that they emerged with the snap of a highly strung mouse trap, as if unfettered by thinking. On this particular day, Jim's visit and the genre of conversation started pretty much like most of the others.

'That family at number sixty three, they've just got a brand new car. I can tell you for nothing it will be on tick' Norma declared, again finding herself somehow on the higher ground.

'Oh really' Jim reflected back, having long since learned not to enquire about the underpinning evidence. Due diligence not welcomed here.

'Oooh, and you won't believe it. Darkies have moved into number fifty seven' Norma revealed. Her tone, like a delusional alchemist that can turn irrelevant detail into something earth shattering. Her terminology and attitudes, surely untouched for nigh on a century.

'Have you got to know them, yet?' Jim asked

'No, I've not spoke to them' Norma responded abruptly, as if affronted by Jim's enquiry.

Jim chastened by a sense that Norma already knew this newly arrived family deep within her mind, without even collecting data. Authority trumping evidence, here. Then Norma's attention turned to Jim, with an unwavering eye contact. For some reason, Jim did not want to fully meet it.

With Jim's propensity for the path of least resistance, his wardrobe was largely filled with items which Kath's whims had set upon. Kath would intermittently return home with garments, freshly picked for Jim. It is possible that the clothes she bestowed on him were fashionable, in some obscure tribe somewhere in the dark recesses of the world.

Whilst Jim never uncovered such a location, he still diligently donned the offerings which Kath served up. On this day, he was wearing a light coloured floral shirt, with delicate blue flowers throughout. They were positively in bloom, on the white background.

'you've got flowers on your shirt' Norma declared.

Reality perhaps looks on, *'say what you see, Norma'.* The Roy Walker of catchphrase fame would be proud of you.

'*Yes. Do you like it?*' Jim asked, slightly nervously

'*Why have you got flowers on your shirt?*' Norma asked, with Jim slightly taken aback by the question. A slight pause ensued, as Jim strove to conjure a reply.

'*Are you gay? Oh my God, you are. You're gay*' Norma declared emotionally, putting her downwardly oriented head in her hands.

Norma's tone of voice mixed disgust with a real sense of tragedy. The level of the latter more befitting of learning that the whole of one's family had unexpectedly and suddenly met their end. Jim could feel her desperation.

It seemed that Norma had married the floral shirt with Jim being into his late twenties and not having had a girlfriend. The union clearly sat extremely uneasily with Norma. Through the soiled window through which she saw all this, the sight was likely horrendous to her.

Decency within Jim would tell him that individual difference is to be celebrated and a person's sexuality is never shameworthy. However, he was not unmoved by his experiences with society and Norma's powerful display. Jim did not have the skills to clean the grubby window through which Norma viewed the world. He was propelled into striving to appease and reassure Norma that he met her standard criteria for a red-blooded virile case. Perhaps even bordering on the Neanderthal, if that helped.

Things settled down with Norma. Jim continued to visit Norma, though typically wearing: dark jeans, black reebok trainers, a black top, and a manly leather jacket which Patrick had left behind. He also sported a bit of stubble. His new style seemed to sit better with Norma. On Jim's visits, Norma thankfully returned to the comfort of a default pastime of sniping at various neighbours.

Jim found himself unthinkingly dampening down the softer parts of his personality in Norma's presence. The floral shirt did not get another outing at Norma's. Indeed, he may perhaps have worn a mankini if he thought it would get the weight of Norma's judgements off his back. Jim's visits to Norma persisted, about every month or two. The delightful cakes were unremitting and Jim perhaps continued to sell out for a tart.

Chapter 18 – The lost years: part four

In addition to his brief stint at Parson's Packing Limited, Jim briefly snagged one other job during the eight year period from twenty five to thirty three. This particular short-lived endeavour began for Jim at the tender age twenty nine, working at Heales Engineering Limited. His job involved punching holes into metal pipes, for the entirety of the shifts.

Jim had to take two separate buses to reach his work place. However, if it got him further away from locals in his home community and he could avoid an unmistakable stench of stigma in his own nostrils, then he would probably have preferred to take seven buses. He needed a change of audience, as he did not consider that he had been well received by the ones that had gone before.

Strict rules abound in Heales engineering. It was an 8am start; don't be late. If an employee was late by even a minute on any day of the week, then they lost their weekly 20% bonus. The strange thing was that if a worker received the bonus, the job then paid close to what would now be classed as 'minimum wage' in the UK (adjusting for inflation).

When a worker arrived late, it perhaps provided some welcome drama and distraction to many of the employees. Like a blackbird, finding a juicy morsel: surely a welcome relief from the unending grind of digging for worms during the bitter chill of winter. What Coronation Street did for the congregation at Parson's Packing, a stray worker arriving at 8:02pm served up to the throng at Heale's engineering. Soap Opera substitute; assemblage surely surreptitiously entertained?

The spectacle would perhaps only have been intensified further if Jim Bowen of 'Bullseye' fame had been hired. More specifically, Mr Bowen could slickly prompt the pulling back a designated curtain like he did to reveal the star prize on Bullseye, whilst uttering to the dejected soul *'come and see what you would have won'*. In this instance, the coins and notes constituting the 20% of the worker's wages would be the well-presented 'sickener' lying in wait behind the cruel curtain.

When a colleague's arrival was deemed tardy, it felt that some workers perhaps bathed in the glory of being at that time unassailable regarding their achievement of the prerequisite markers of punctuality. Markers which by the end of the week would come together, to form the badge of honour, which the 'bonus' seemed to stand for. Jim was not completely immune to the thrill of having the higher ground, but he did feel some genuine upset for colleagues that were to fall foul of the bosses self-serving regulations.

Within this spell of just over three weeks at Heales Engineering, Jim suffered another blow to his fragile ego. A world that dangles great prizes, with one hand. But, alas then slaps you so fiercely with the other; before you can get near enough to reach the honey. For once, our Jim reached out; daring to dream that misery and abject failure might just be punctuated by a departure from the rut that engulfed him.

Within a few days in this new role, Jim was finding a greater sense of meditative calm; even though he was surrounded by other workers. Threat level orange was occasionally dropping down to threat level yellow. His bladder still almost exclusively disengaged and inevitably swelled, but he felt very slightly more oriented towards taking a step forward.

Jim's more settled state was perhaps fuelled by the repetitiveness and simplicity of his task, alongside constant movement. The latter providing a displacement vessel, ample to channel any nervous energy. Additionally, it was difficult to make a mistake. Place the metal tube in a pre-set position where it was just fed into a slot, move a specific lever down to make the hole, remove the pipe and put it in a box. Take a fresh pipe, repeat the process, and on we go.

To borrow from an old advert which was promient around that era, 'Findus – success on a plate for you'. It was difficult to go wrong. Jim, akin to a young toddler using an educational toy that lights up or gives off a noise when you press it. He felt a buzz from both the sight of the levels of completed pipes in his basket rising and the clunk noise that the machine made on the pipe when he pressed down the lever.

One of Jim's anxieties around people was often that he did not have a clear script in his mind, as to how he should act to avoid negative judgement. 'What should I say?'. 'What should I do?'.

For Jim, he was never enough in his own mind. He could not simply be; at every turn, reflexively striving to justify and legitimise himself. At Heale's, Jim was assisted by his job task providing him with a very clear and achievable script. His action legitimised him. He could justify himself more, particularly to the invisible audience within his head.

The whole day was further eased by a nearby radio constantly emanating pop music from Radio One. Jim found himself with the unaccustomed situation of intermittently becoming less self-conscious, even though there were 'people' at nearby work stations in the factory. His eyes had previously always tended to strongly focus inwards on himself in public, straining internally to see what other people were seeing of him. Grasping desperately to capture some of their internal judgements.

In this setting, his eyes began to slightly venture towards looking outwards at the world. Like a nervous young child, finding the courage to amble away from nearby parents and explore. For Jim, not so much bravery growing as anxiousness reducing.

When Jim turned to put the punctured metal pipe into its box, his eye gaze began to venture down the factory. He repeatedly noticed a young woman aged in her early twenties, working around sixty yards away. A truly numinous vision for Jim. Despite the distance, her large magnificent breasts stood out to Jim like a beacon. Like the welcome beam of a light house, breaking through an endless storm that stretched way back into his past.

This pure beauty in the distance typically wore quite tight faded jeans, deliciously blended with a figure hugging white tee shirt. Emotionally, Jim yearned to just disappear down her cleavage and unify with her, never to be seen again. In his head, it seemed the perfect fit. Emotion perhaps directing him; beckoned towards a means of mollifying his demons.

Then, it seemed, the world began to bequeath more than he could have ever dreamed. Heaven's magnus opus began to look in Jim's direction. She was simultaneously smiling and laughing.

Invariably in the past, Jim would have reflexively assumed that she was ridiculing him in some way; anxiety and defensiveness joining him in an instant. However, he brushed aside overgrown shielding, and took a different turn.

Perhaps intoxicated and mesmerised by what moved so poetically. Jim's head for once above the parapet, within an environment which had lulled him to slightly lower his guard. Jim's mind took off the hand brake and allowed him to actually wonder, maybe this precious jewel is radiating signals that she likes what she sees.

Jim's thoughts were perhaps moving to the possibility of a self-concept of maybe, just maybe, Mr Luvva Luvva? An unfulfilled sexual drive, perhaps crystallised into an emotion which was driving logic and thinking? Reality looked on; did it wonder if Jim was being steered towards bliss or an oncoming artic?

The injured soul of our Jim, perhaps craving to make peace and appease the perspectives of a plethora of bigots that had infected his grey matter, festering? The Gods would perhaps not let him wander woefully into the fourth decade of life, devoid of any sexual epoch. Maybe he would not land awkwardly into his thirties. Perhaps he would no longer clutch his virginity and suffer the fate of being pursued by the codeless clamouring homophobic bigots that peppered his local community?

He was twenty nine and there was still time. For a mind that rarely wandered far from contemplating everything that might go spectacularly wrong, he seemed to eye a clearing in which things could go well. In the context of what had gone and Jim's newly found deep lusting after happiness, the contrast was genuinely downright tear jerking.

One day, he heard somebody call his everything by the name of 'Rachel'. He had a name to integrate into the future that he playfully carved out in his mind. The glances and the smiles from Rachel grew frequent.

Jim was carrying both hope and fear. The power of his attraction to Rachel was something which left him feeling uneasy, like a fledgling jockey trying to control a wild stallion. This meant that his effortful attempts to return Rachel's smile were far from optimum; oozing more than an ounce of awkwardness. Jim's mind could not help sensing that his vain striving to match Rachel's smile likely belied his attempts at being nonchalant. A smile that his inner critic drew as looking somewhere in between geek and serial killer, but likely closer to the latter.

It was early on the Monday, on what would turn out to be Jim's final week at Heales Engineering Limited. At that point, Jim's impending departure was wholly unbeknownst to him. On one of his intermittent and perhaps slightly furtive glances towards Rachel, he noticed that she seemed to be looking at him and simultaneously talking to one of the men that works in Jim's section.

Specifically, Rachel was chatting with a man named Larry. Rachel was smiling and looking over in Jim's direction. He sensed that they were talking about him. Jim dared to wonder whether Rachel was opening up and discussing her interest in him.

As an aside, Jim had spoken with Larry, as they took the same bus from the main town centre to the factory (Jim's second bus in the morning, and his first bus when he returned home). In brief, Larry was aged about thirty five, with jet black hair and a bushy moustache to match. He was thick set, with a disproportionately large backside. Truly, a back-side sufficiently big that its solitary presence on the scales would likely make weight to face the ferocious heavyweight of that era, Mike Tyson.

Jim found Larry to be very opinionated and harsh. Larry was closest with a specific employee named Craig. The latter carried very visibly damaged facial skin, seeming to reflect severe scarring from what must surely have once been a plague of flourishing acne.

Craig was quite similar to Lance. He was a specimen that was again aged in his mid-thirties and seemed keen to create distraction, with a somewhat 'devil-may-care' attitude to any collateral damage to innocent beings. His propensity in this area was likely integral to his personality. Additionally, it possibly related to both keeping his own spirits up in the monotony of the factory shifts and perhaps seeking distraction from the horrendously pitted and pocked face that accompanied him everywhere.

Background aside, and back to the present moment that teasingly dangled in front of Jim. He noted Rachel chatting with Larry. Jim did not see Larry chatting with Rachel as any kind of a threat. For once, Jim's spider senses were not tingling, in that he did not foresee danger.

Jim sensed that Rachel liked him and he recognised that this could be a game changer. Aged twenty nine, Jim had not even had a romantic kiss. He began to fantasise.

At times during this brief period, the clairvoyant within him could virtually feel his virginity blissfully slipping away. Amidst the rhythmic hole punching routine and the upbeat tempo of the pop music, there was a sense of excitement and anticipation. His anticipation did not have to wait long.

Towards the beginning of his third week, the predictable morning break fell kindly upon the work force. The bell sounded to down tools. Now, Rachel had her break in a different canteen room, which took her in a path which was diametrically opposite to Jim's. Jim was just about to make his way to the canteen room, when he caught sight of Rachel walking in his direction.

The rush of excitement was elevated still further because her walk was combined with clear and direct eye contact with him. She also had that same smile that she had worn for him for many days. Wow, it was unmistakeable. Rachel was moments away from making contact with Jim. Her beautiful eyes fixed on him; magnificence even more prominent close up.

Rachel stopped very close to him and maintained the eye contact. She continued to smile, but she appeared slightly nervous. Jim sensed that she was about to ask him a question. For once, his mind did not browse through the compendium of a million possible problematic questions that could emerge. Instead, he fixed on just one.

The smiles, the looks, the walking up to him, the undeniable chemistry; surely, it could only be one question? He could feel it. Rachel was surely just about to ask him out and perhaps also bravely open up about her attraction to him.

Jim was nervous, excited, and determined not to blow it. Yes, he felt fear. However, he would accept her kind offer, when she bravely posed the question. The question from Rachel's mouth blurted out of her nervousness, and her smile returned again.

'*Are you gay?*' she asked, smiling.

In quick succession: managing to break through her apparent nervousness, deliver a somewhat intrusive blow, leave social etiquette in her wake, and then admire her work.

'*No*' Jim replied, the constructs and expectations which he had forged in his mind crashing down around him.

'*Oh*' she laughed.

'*Larry said that you were gay*' she finished. Rachel then turned and wandered back to her part of the factory, with a playful light-heartedness.

Jim was left in shock, dissociated somewhat, saturated in stinging emotion, and on auto-pilot. So, what did it mean to Jim to be called 'gay', at that time in history? It brought up a raft of angst, associated with: early learning from the homo-phobic Braithwaite family before his age had reached double figures, memories of that horrendous night at the White Hart Inn, fear of bigots inflicting negative consequences, and a sense that he had still not had any kind of sexual experience.

Jim also felt stigma. This stigma was not because Jim felt that there was anything wrong with being homosexual, but rather because deep down he still craved being liked and respected by others. He did not feel respected by Conrad, Mick, and other local bigots. He also recalled only too well the attitudinal dis-position of the bigoted Braithwaites.

More generally, within this era, negative comments about homosexuality swamped the tough Northern town that Jim grew up in. Indeed, it also crawled into coverage of such issues on television at that time. Perhaps, as Steve Maraboli suggests: *'if you hang out with chickens, you're going to cluck and if you hang out with eagles, you're going to fly'.*

Jim was not immune to the contemporary attitudes which pro-liferated his community and much of the broader world. It is a rare and outstanding beast that can step too far outside the prevailing societal attitude that infiltrates their era and their local tribe. Jim was neither rare, nor outstanding.

Back to Jim's personal world within his skull: defences which had been lowered to an unprecedented degree, raised and nailed in; in an instant. Electrified pulses travelling round the track of Jim's neural circuitry, but no platform for stop-ping at 'not caring'; wholly bypassed. Jim was left wonder-ing what prompted Rachel to ask this question, and trample the wonderful story that his desperate mind had conjured. It transpired over the next day or two, that Jim would solve this riddle.

Jim dared to ask Larry, 'hey mate, why did you tell Rachel I was gay?'. What followed from Lance was a complex sequence. Jim coupled this with a brief chat with another work colleague called Craig, to give greater clarity. He discovered most of the pieces of the jigsaw.

It turned out, Craig attended the same snooker club as Jim. In Jim's slightly more relaxed state, he had discussed some of his life with Craig and he had mentioned that he was a member of the Potters snooker club. By loosening his defensive grip, Jim let a cat out of the bag; wholly unaware that ultimately it would scratch him unforgivingly. The Potters snooker club was not too far from Heales Engineering. As it happened, word had recently spread in this snooker club that Jim was homosexual.

What would remain unbeknownst to Jim was that regulars at the White Hart Inn had actually used the same snooker club and had eyed Jim's name in the signing in book. They then gleefully shared their wisdom about Jim with the ever sociable boss, in the form of man named Andy. Craig knew Andy, and Andy knew how to share gossip.

Though we must also give Craig credit, he did his due diligence and enquired about whether Andy knew Jim. Craig could barely wait to share his findings with Larry. Larry then took it upon himself to share his wisdom with Rachel. Oh goodness, it's such a small world. Our Jim's world marching inwards crushingly, at pace; upon him. He was shrinking.

Subsequently, every time that Craig and Larry saw Jim, it seemed he drew out of them a sickening smile. Sickening in the sense that it etched into Jim's brain that their smugness was born of ridicule and negative judgement. Occasionally, the inaudible whispering and clear glances from Larry and

Craig reached the crescendo of harshly dissonant cackle.

Jim felt sure he had progressed to being simply a factory joke. It seemed the bigotry that came to pass in the White Hart Inn had followed Jim, tailing him to new pastures and now polluting his new work environment. Rare sprinkles of anger against others, rising up inside Jim. He would quickly push them down.

As mentioned earlier, there is value in Beveridge's position that *'people are prone to see what lies behind out eyes, rather than what appears before them'*. Prior to the latest set-back, Jim had dared to peep through a tiny hole into what was in the world outside his head. It had transiently allowed his eyes to feel the glow of a Rachel.

Now, he was back firmly looking behind his own eyes. Like the nervous young child that wandered from mum only to be bitten hard, the umbilical cord snaps back and the child retreats to within mum's shadow. Retreating to what he had come to know, Jim clung tighter to pathological defences.

Perhaps Jim should have chosen to just let it go and not be bothered by this minor incident in work? Just press a different switch in your mind Jim, one might say. But what if on the inside and in a place where Jim's strings are being pulled, there was typically but one jammed switch at this stage of his life?

Maybe to say to Jim, 'look at it differently' or 'react differently' is predicated on a delusion akin to magical thinking. Like asking a starving child to satisfy their hunger by looking at a vivid picture of what would be their favourite meal. Like an isolated man on the verge of dying of thirst in the middle of a desert, battered, disoriented, and hearing a clear voice in his head 'you need to drink'. To know what is needed or even be told what to do does not of itself solve conundrums; particularly when that solution is simply out of reach. Maybe the mountain to think and approach life differently had just become too great for Jim?

Jim quit the job at Heales engineering at the end of that third week. Fleeing from the scene, without the courtesy of a passing glance at the mental strength and possible growth opportunity he was leaving behind. Another mini chapter of Jim's life closing, unflatteringly.

Jim had dared to step out of his comfort zone; to walk into the jaws of this engineering firm. For their part, they had then bitten down harshly on him. Life had conscientiously chiseled out more residue from Jim's ego and his expectations of life. Surely, difficult not to admire its relentless work ethic?

Chapter 19 – Jim's life changes direction

Julius Caesar is quoted as saying, *'it is easier to find men who will volunteer to die, than to find those that are willing to endure pain with patience'.* Jim's pain perhaps not so much endured with patience, as endured by a man that knew no other route.

Jim was like a weary dog, in the worst phase of Seligman's explorations. It would take a Spider to bestow a game changing contribution upon our Jim; placing him in a new segment of the Gods' experimental chamber. A place where blessedly, he could take some shelter; shocked less intensely by the fresh paradigm of the Almighty.

Initially after leaving Heales, Jim retreated. He dedicated himself to the life of a hermit, stagnating and perhaps trapped in his own shell. A twenty nine year old Jim would make the journey to thirty three. Time passed without notable movement. Like an exhausted and shell shocked soldier suddenly realising that he was in the middle of a densely packed minefield, he was reluctant throughout this period.

Some of Jim's audience may just cling to the notion that this restricted lifestyle was simply *'self-inflicted'* adversity; our Jim wholly choosing this path. A wisdom perhaps fitting such audience like a convenient 'self-inflicted' soothing ointment; the inconsequential side-effect of this more than stinging to our Jim's being. Young Jim supposedly having all the cards; all the choices opened up fully for him. Certainly, our depleted Jim let fate wander and refused to grab it tightly by the throat. Go deeper if you may, but surely no vision comes without a lens?

Jim had ceased playing snooker and so his ventures out were restricted to a few trips to Castle Bridge golf course, with Spider. Even one of those proved hazardous, as he was met with the beaming smile of Andy (the boss at the snooker club) during one round. Andy mentioned that he had recently seen their mutual friend 'Craig' (from Heales engineering). Jim for his part, ineffectively tried to bluff out an unconcerned exterior. However, the situation did more than caress the hair trigger which activated Jim's mental representations of what an army of bigots thought of him.

Spider's life had moved on. He worked in a factory making bedding and was a team leader responsible for around fifteen women working on the machines. It was in this work environment that Spider was to find a partner (Cheryl), and they had recently had their second anniversary. Despite his life moving on, Spider continued to occasionally meet with Jim. He readily provided our Jim with support and encouragement.

With Jim aged thirty three and the outside world over a year on from crossing the threshold into a new millenium, Spider's philanthropic outreach programme again sprang into action. Spider made monthly visits to Jim's home, where they would chat for an hour or so. On a specific day with Jim's age resting wholly on the third rung of the eleven times table, they watched a TV programme which Jim had recorded on a video recorder machine. The programme was a psychological look at what influences people's behaviour.

The TV offering touched on the issue of whether a decent person exposed to merely the wrong chemical could commit extreme acts, totally out of character. There seemed a strong implication of the fragility of a human's 'free will'. For many, this might be a theme catalysing an imperative to look away; societal cement perhaps weakened by the laser beam of intense gazed contemplation on this deterministic leaning.

Yet, for our Jim such an idyllic impactful equaliser, seeming to land in the tenth minute of five minutes of injury time. Soothing the sting of social comparison. Stealing glory from the best and bestowing the parity of neutrality on the rest. Loosely, in an absolute sense: determinism = not my fault. Spider sensed that a speckle of interest flickered and broke through Jim's depression.

Several months earlier Spider had also noticed a book called the 'Murderers' Who's Who', at Jim's side. On questioning Jim about this, Jim had expressed an interest in *'why people do the things that they do?'*. Perhaps as an aside, Jim had also mentioned that he was struck by when people commit murder, there seems to be an initial outcry and then they kind of disappear away from society; often never seen again. The present of their crimes at once spectacular and falling firmly into past, giving way to a new present of eye gaze departed and expectations smoothed down.

A snug escape hatch, for the ill-fitting that hang untidily from this world? Either way, Jim shuddered at the thought of perpetrating atrocity without being awake and consciously moving one's rudder. Enormity striking particularly hard when it was revealed suddenly, from a hastily pulled covering blanket. Perhaps too much for the unsuspecting, jerkily teleported to a crash site, rather than meandering mindfully to such calamity; never far from the present. A deep part of our Jim yearned for control, and so much more.

Jim's interest in the book and then the TV programme planted a small seed, within the charitable soil that adorned our Spider's grey matter. Fast forward three weeks on, and Spider arrived again chez Jim. But this time, not alone.

More specifically, Spider was accompanied by a prospectus from the local college and an application form. He had circled a range of social science courses that he believed might be of interest to Jim. There was very little spark in Jim, but he did grace Spider with perfunctory gratitude for his endeavours.

Fast forward six weeks, Jim was settled in watching the fairly predictable sequence of daytime TV. Then, along came a Spider. Kath got the door, and led Spider through to the lounge at the back of their modest abode. Jim and Spider sat alone, aside from the accompanying contribution of the TV in the background. In the moments that followed, Spider moved from exploration to a more assertive pitch.

'How did you get on with the college forms, Jim?' Spider asked, altruism likely propping up his excited tone.

'Errrr. I've not got round to it yet mate, but I am looking to do it at some point.' Jim replied, after digging very deep, to mine the buried awareness that he had college forms.

'OK buddy, it's just that you only have two weeks left to apply, as the courses start next month' Spider added with a slight urgency.

Several minutes past, with daytime TV just continuing on in the background. Almost as if Spider had not arrived. It was then that Spider decided to put both hands on the steering wheel that was driving Jim's life, with Jim remaining inactive in the passenger seat.

'Get me a pen Jim, I'll fill the form in for you. If you get in you don't have to go – it just potentially might give you an option' Spider stated, in a tone which seemed lacking in doubt and firmly expecting that things would travel down the path that he was dictating.

'Cheers mate' replied Jim, as he went to get a pen. He knew that even if the application went in and he was accepted, he retained clear escape routes. If avoidance and escape became olympic sports, then barring a Devon Loch type capitulation

surely Jim would coast to the Gold.

Spider then dutifully completed the four page form, pausing occasionally to ask Jim any required information which he did not know. Without the need for Jim's clarity, Spider answered the *'further information'* section and the *'reasons for applying'* section. Spider seemingly enjoying the chance to be creative and resourceful. He decided that Jim was to study Psychology. Spider then took the form and posted it the very same day.

Fast forward just less than two weeks. At 11:43am, Jim was awoken by Kath's irksome voice, *'Jiiiiimmmm, you've got poooosttttt'*. With Jim having shed the responsibility of work, these vexing wake-up calls were thankfully rare.

'I'll grab it later, when I get up' Jim shouted down the stairs. His inertia not shifted by sensing Kath's disapproval of his resistance to engage with the day. Jim's depression pulled the covers over him and sought to submerge him painlessly in slumber.

There followed several spasmodic shouts from Kath, with incremental increases in volume. The shouts were not spread at even intervals. Jim's exposure to Kath's verbal lashes were most closely related to shifting events in her mind, rather than any clearly predictable sequence.

Jim surfaced at 12:49pm. He ate a mix of toast, cereal, and several cups of coffee. His mind intermittently engaging with whatever TV programme happened to be on.

After gradually waking up, it turned out that 2:07pm was the time of the big reveal. Jim opened the freshly arrived post. Spider's actions were not in vain; Jim had been accepted at the local Hampwood Hall College to study Psychology.

Jim felt nervous about taking on another challenge in the

outside world. However, he could not resist telling Kath that her only son had secured a small slice of success. When he released the news to Kath that he had been accepted into the local college to study psychology, he mentally sensed that he had unleashed expectations within her.

His loose lips brought chickens home to roost, in that it effectively increased the pressure he felt to break through his avoidance. Alongside this, even before the offer of a place in college, the status quo was not fitting beautifully with Jim. For many months, Kath's nagging and negativity was becoming progressively more bothersome, even with Jim's undoubted skill set at blocking the world out.

From within the uncertainty, Jim committed. He accepted the offer of a place at Hampwood Hall. This decision would change the direction of Jim's life.

Yet at this stage, surely hard to see how this educational track would ripen darkness within Jim? Already thirty three; wherein lie the seeds set to squeeze gross crimes from this creature more than brimming with inhibition? Perverse criminal deeds to a self, but no outward criminal tilt in sight.

Maybe something could flow from our Jim, with him moving away from loitering avoidantly in the shadows? Potential grist to the mill; perhaps that which for so long has lay latent and cocooned may be activated if rendered more exposed and raw? With Jim stepping out into a new arena, a shield lowered and cushioning removed; maybe something may pierce a reaction from the sorry specimen?

Unless criminal predisposition has been missed or so well hidden, the Gods would surely need to unleash a hurricane of a situational force to blow Jim to graze in such distant deviant pastures? Yet maybe much divine graft had already been done, unnoticed and behind the scenes? What if the Gods had stealthily carved out from the earliest beginnings, such that it no longer needed gale force intervention? Rather, if it was their current fancy, then maybe just waiting to deliver a critical ingredient of less than a gentle puff? Reality looks on silently, knowing but not defiled with words.

Jim's story continues. Thirty three and scheduled to begin his psychology studies in about four weeks. Inside, Jim considered that he now had two roles in life. Specifically, he considered that he was now both a 'loser' and a 'student'. Whilst he hoped that the latter would not be absorbed by the former, his expectations usually told him that it probably would.

Chapter 20 – Jim, the Hampwood Hall student.

Kath had a calendar hung on the wall, in the kitchen. She had a habit of crossing off all days that had elapsed. Striking them out; as if these prior days and their expired moments were in the bin of the past and could be let go. Ironically, Kath's mind did not take the message that the amended calendar offered. She would relentlessly and unhelpfully ruminate and fixate about negative elements of her past. In what seemed to be a self-defeating way, she would not let go of anything toxic.

Anyway, the days continued to pass and the crosses grew in number. When the crosses reached right up to (and including) the 16th September, it could only mean one thing. Specifically, the 17th September had arrived, as it had long since threatened to. Further, it was today that Jim commenced his psychology studies at Hampwood Hall.

On Jim's first day in college, he arrived clutching the demons that had stayed by his side since the early years. There may have been no pandemic back in Jim's college years, but he felt perceived threat from having other people close by. A life prior had suggested to Jim that the presence of people causes a most ghastly infection.

In particular, Jim readily acquired an infection of negative judgements about himself, quickly contaminating his mind. A threat to the mental more than the physical landscape of our Jim. No masks or hand sanitisers would begin to shield him. Too contagious.

Jim entered the classroom, striving to give off an air of confidence. He was wearing tight denim jeans, a black shirt, and a dark bomber jacket. He subtly looked around. Amongst the thirty or so students, there was a mix of ages. There were around half that looked in their late teens or early twenties. The remainder were scattered amongst most decades of later life.

The eldest student (Richard) tended to sit right at the back, with the grim reaper possibly stationed not too far away. All but four of the students were female. Gleefully, this meant that Jim would not stray much below fourth place in the 'alpha' hierarchy amongst the male students.

Jim's anxiety was partially appeased, due to him having an identity to cloak himself with (i.e., Jim was now 'a psychology student', with his presence somewhat justified). He could take cover behind this. Further, as the bulk of the time within his college involved focussing on a teacher releasing their wisdom, Jim was delighted that the attention of those surrounding him was channelled away from him.

Jim was further boosted by the soothing reassurance of an implicit script, in the form of *'sit there and listen to what is taught'.* Like in his days punching holes in pipes at Heales engineering, the script was clear and manageable. The other beautiful twist of fate came from the density of bigots being generally reduced within a group of mature students, relative to a random sample from the local community of a rough Northern town.

When Jim was last in education, he was juggling: neurosis, preoccupation, and avoidance. Attention, focus, and meaning were drained by the latter cohort. Still, he focussed in the latter years of high school. His exam passes were restricted to 5 GCSEs (for English, Maths, History, Chemistry, and French); 4 at grade 'C' and an 'A' at French.

The unfolding educational patterns at Hampwood Hall were very different. Jim found an obsession, which in turn chased off a bunch of his negative thinking. For so long, suspended in a vacuum. Jim wanted to compensate in some small way, for all that he was within his own mind.

Beyond that, he was more than interested in psychology. Though he did not know it in these early stages at college, he needed it. Like a faded junky reaches for the needle.

Studying psychology provided a not insignificant healing remedy for Jim. Since before he even entered adulthood, Jim's mind had raced with what he considered to be negative judgements that others were making about him. His levels of shame and self-hatred started as being immense, but had grown to a point which was likely off the scale. Deep within his own mind, Jim knew that he fell horrendously short; in just about every way.

Jim's shame-based secret regarding his neurotic bladder and its life choices was something that he had never shared with anybody. The secrecy around this provided the perfect soil for his shame to grow, unencumbered. The occasional scrap of positive feedback was reflexively diluted by Jim's sense that *'it's only because they do not know about my shameful secret'*. An implicit mechanism that devalued the few crumbs of positive feedback that had landed on him. His secrecy largely closed off the harmonious path of mentally meaningful validation from others.

Most notably, prior to studying psychology: Jim had complete self-blame. His mind knew that not only was he the biggest and most embarrassing screw up in the world, but it was also *'all his fault'*. The self-blame was unfettered by consideration of context. Psychology adaptively broadened his focus.

Jim was five minutes into a lecture from James Stanworth, a social psychologist, hanging on his every utterance. Dr Stanworth paused briefly, then asked Jim's class:

"When we make sense of a person's behaviour, why does context matter?"

With the question met by silence, Dr Stanworth continued:

"Do nice people sometimes do things that are not nice?"

Jim so transfixed that he almost forgot the audience, and offered *"Yes"*

"Indeed they do, young man" Dr Stanford continued, perhaps encouraged by some form of response.

Dr Stanford continued, with:

"Let us imagine a hypothetical scenario. Say, within a supermarket, one observes a twenty five year old male, Simon, walking up to an elderly lady that he did not know and slapping the lady hard. Now, for most people, this would likely elicit negative judgements about Simon".

A pause from Dr Stanford whilst he surveyed the room, and then continued:

"Let us now imagine that we then have one extra piece of information about context, namely that a man outside the shop is holding a gun to a loved one of Simon and convincingly conveying that he will kill the loved one if Simon does not slap the first person he sees within the shop. The context may change how harshly we judge Simon.

Psychologically, this is essentially the idea that a person's behaviour is not just a product of their personality (i.e., who they are, in terms of character), but it can also relate to what could be broadly termed the force of the situation. Psychology teaches us that the situational influence can sometimes appear subtle and difficult to understand, but still be powerful. If we have the personification of a situation pushing and persuading a person towards an action, maybe they can be at least partially absolved of the blame. Sometimes, the force of the situation can be very strong and even propel people to do things which are out of character for them......"

Jim increasingly began looking outside himself to explain his screw ups. He studied psychology tirelessly, looking to bolster his ability to divert blame away from himself.

The blessings which psychology imparted on Jim went well beyond being able to say that when he fell short, it was partly because the co-occurring situational context had pushed him in that direction. He could also look back and 'explain' what things outside himself had caused him and his life to have evolved in such calamitous and unspectacular ways. The most attractive part of psychology to Jim was the notion that he could perhaps even be forgiven for his own character because perhaps it is carved by genetics (which he did not choose) and aspects of his prior history, particularly in childhood (which he largely did not choose).

Psychology offered Jim a path to justify himself, reduce self-blame, and begin to be able to look in the mirror. He could attribute *'blame'* for negative things in his life partly externally (on things outside him), rather than laying all the blame squarely on himself. He quickly had an unquenchable thirst to learn aspects of psychology which led him to the foreign lands of some threads of compassion towards himself.

Jim began forgiving himself more for his myriad of short-comings. Maybe they were not his shortcomings? Maybe it was the shortcomings of the world he had been given, simply manifesting through him? Like an innocent glass of water, being coloured by cordial. His mind began to boggle with previously unconsidered mitigation.

Jim's learning took some of the emotional heat out of so many situations. He became more compassionate with himself. He gradually saw meaningful reductions in the threat levels he experienced from situations, including ones that involved other people and potential negative judgements.

Perceived threat is like a funnel, into which so much of a person's attention and focus will flow. Jim read a book by the self-development guru Tony Robbins, coming across the notion that *often, we get what we focus on'*. Psychology taught Jim the power of focus. He recalls a teacher at college giving the following anecdotes:

'tell one hundred people in a waiting room the untruth: *there is a fatal and highly infectious disease sweeping the hospital and the way that you know you have got it is a slight tingling in your right hand, which means that you need medical treat immediately.* Guess what? Many of those people change their focus, and pick sensations up that they were not previously aware of. Tell those same people in the waiting room that there is a rampaging gunman in the hospital who is wearing a blue jacket, and guess what they reflexively scan for and notice more?'

Things began to make sense in a different and less upsetting way. With Jim's sense of threat declining, he began scanning slightly less for negative judgements from others. This meant he less frequently noticed 'evidence' for it. He also began looking outside his own eyes more, analysing others. This used up some of Jim's attentional fuel, which meant that there was less attention left to drive his prior excessive inward focus on trying to view himself through the eyes of others.

Chapter 21 – Behaviourism offers
Jim a more safe haven.

The course that Jim studied at Hampwood Hall had large amounts of what has been termed 'behaviourism'. It began on the first day, with discussion of some of the ideas of John B. Watson. Only just off the starting blocks and already Jim had precious themes that refracted a laser-like beam of blame partially away from his soul. The teacher put the following quote from Watson on the board, for the class to write down:

> *Give me a dozen healthy infants, well-formed, and my own specified world to bring them up in and I'll guarantee to take any one at random and train him to become any type of specialist I might select – doctor, lawyer, artist, merchant, chief, and yes, even beggar-man and thief – regardless of his talents, penchants, tendencies, abilities, vocations, and race of his ancestors'.*

There followed class discussion about the quote. Jim found solace from the idea that maybe it is the world that is given to an innocent infant that determines what they become. His case for the mitigation of his own perceived personal failings had begun, and it would grow like a large snow ball rolling down a never ending mountain of sticky snow. Jim pushed it from behind, as much as he could.

Jim's mind quickly developed an encyclopaedic knowledge of psychology. If the encyclopaedia of psychological knowledge had to have a name, it might be titled *'a million and one reasons why it is not my fault'*. He absorbed psychology like a sponge, always seeking to apply it to his own journey. Like the most committed defence barrister and yet working within his own mind; arguing with all that he could muster that the jury need to look elsewhere.

With an unquestioning acceptance, Jim took everything that psychology conveniently offered him. If a hungry beggar is given a wad of fifty pound notes, would the beggar simply take them gratefully or question from whence they came? Jim had an autistic respect and acceptance of all that psychology could teach. He needed it.

Society had given Jim glimpses of Watson's position in the earlier quote, exemplified in offerings such as the comedy film 'Trading Places'. However, these scant offerings in society had offered him little armour against the world within his mind. Jim felt that academia was a respected and definitive source, on which he could build a credible approach to life. A strong life line; categorically distinct from the worn cotton threads that were bandied about from the random blather that froths around general society.

At times, Jim even felt a sense of happiness in some of the classes. Despite nervousness, he occasionally offered views within the class discussions. Jim found it both fortuitous and strange that he was allowed to interact with beautiful young females; without them fleeing from him and without him being locked up.

Jim's desire to succeed meant that he did not just develop his psychology knowledge, he put hour after hour into developing his writing style such that it mirrored that of some of the most respected psychological books of that era. What happened was that the 'C' grade student that Jim was at school was transformed. He quickly became an 'A' grade student, at Hampwood Hall. Indeed, his overall grades were comfortably the best within his class.

Jim felt respected by his class mates, with many of the young students asking for his wisdom. Starved of validation prior to this course, Jim's grades meant that his levels of self-accept-ance and self-esteem had gone well beyond any previous peak. He was beginning to occasionally stray into territory which he was previously unfamiliar with. He could intermittently glance his reflection without blinding self-hatred.

Later in the behavioural course, Jim's case for outwardly di-verting blame for his short-comings grew astronomically. The latter arriving on the wings of the first lecture from a Mr Brian Tierney. Tierney was tall, thin, and highly intelligent.

'Today, we are going to study the work of B. F. Skinner' the lecturer Mr Tierney announced.

Jim learnt that Skinner was a pragmatic psychologist. Skinner focussed on how to use an environmental focus to assist in 'prediction' and 'control' of behaviour. However, what gelled with Jim even more was that Skinner proposed a philosophy of 'determinism'.

Ultimately, Skinner would suggest that even though our knowledge does not fully understand all the causes, the start-ing position is that in an absolute sense, 'everything we do and say is caused by things we are not responsible for'. Our psyche merely gives us an illusory feeling of having free will. Key elements of Skinner's 1971 'Beyond Freedom and Dignity' were a somewhat controversial and unpalatable philosophy for so many. Yet, they offered Jim a journey 'Beyond Extreme Hope-lessness and Severe Self-hatred'. As the saying goes, maybe 'one man's meat is another man's poison'.

For Jim, Skinner's teachings yielded a route to a world where, maybe, just maybe, who he was and what he did was perhaps not wholly his fault. Jim realised that through a Skinnerian lens: the notion that he was 'to blame' was wholly false. How can someone deserve blame if, as Skinner would have it, they have no free will. As guilty as a leaf, moving in the force of a strong wind. Blaming not deserved, but perhaps pragmatic if it had more benefits than costs.

Jim busily used the threads of Skinner's teachings to weave a safety net within his mind. The humanists tried to cut the strings by grasping at the idea that *'free will'* transcends causes and science. For Skinner, this attempt at a *'get out'* was merely an unsubstantiated and desperate attempt to sustain a convenient belief; grasping at straws. Like a baby reaching for its dummy, driven by a need for comfort and not with the cumbersome burden of logic.

Jim felt huge affinity for Mr Tierney, the lecturer that covered behaviourism at Hampwood Hall. A conspicuously intelligent man aged in his early forties, sporting a rat like face, large ears, and neatly gelled short hair. On this day, Tierney was in full flow. He seemed to love an audience and had an eye for the young ladies. Jim listened intently, absorbing every fragment. *'Right'*, Tierney continued:

> *"In layman speak, a person might be seen as making a choice and a person might feel like they are making a choice. However, they are like a very young child sat in the passenger seat of a car, feverishly engaging with a toy steering wheel stuck to the upper part of the passenger-side dashboard. We verbally label impulses carved elsewhere and we verbally label our behaviour post-hoc, in such a way that we hold on tightly to the illusion that we are wholly driving the vehicle which is ourselves. For B. F. Skinner, what we see as choice is ultimately just a constellation of causal forces outside illusory 'free will' that come together and produce that behaviour".*

A phone beeps within the classroom, and Jim notices that several of the younger members of the class are engaged with their phones. *'How could they?'* Jim briefly wonders. Tierney continues, enthusiasm undimmed:

> *"For Skinner, we are a mix of a past which we did not choose and genetics that we did not shop for. Though for pragmatic reasons, Skinner focussed firmly on the former. So, if one extends this, then punishment may be useful if it creates overall positive consequences. However, morally, if one adheres to Skinner's views then in an absolute sense the person being punished is not to blame and not responsible".*

Skinner offered Jim a route which took him light years closer to being more forgiving of himself. Jim snatched it with both hands and read everything that Skinner had written during his long career. The chains of justification, more than loosened.

Skinnerian philosophy akin to no ultimate personal blame and no ultimate personal credit. The former offering of dilution of blame presented huge mental relief for Jim. Alongside this, the loss of credit no threat to a man that perceived a total absence of any notal achievement within the entirety of his life.

Yet there was a side effect; not mentioned on any packet. B. F. Skinner, a skilful Doctor, had surgically extracted 'free will' from our Jim, ably assisted by Tierney. How Jim would respond to Skinner's surgery was, at this stage unknown.

Regardless let us not be too harsh on the late Skinner. Perhaps like a plastic surgeon whose clever hands create the perfect breasts for a fair maiden. How such assets are used, beyond the remit of their creator.

For our Jim: an over-officious conscience quelled; looking forwards, as well as backwards. An irony perhaps. That same language which had so hemmed in and constrained our Jim had offered a path to loosen the shackles. He could make choices in the new moments, potentially less encumbered with moral 'right' and 'wrong'.

Through a Skinnerian lens: if our Jim aimed a gun at his enemy then in an absolute sense, the trigger could only be pulled by the nasty world coalescing with a genetic handicap that we don't talk about? Our Jim, as innocent as a twig dutifully floating in rough seas? The themes liberated our Jim; not just to the point of statically peering through the bent bars of a cell, but moved, loose, roaming and less shackled.

Yet, which way were the scales tipping? On one side, the weight of moral conscience perhaps lightened by Tierney's teachings; a handbrake lowered. But on the other side, Jim was led to feeling more comfortable in his own skin; threat levels declining. The latter not a good recipe for squeezing foul deed from a specimen truly not elevated on psychopathy.

Poke a cornered kitty with a sharp stick, and hissing and scratching unfold. The stick which was poking Jim within his own mind being rounded and cushioned by this new learning. Surely no landscape for our Jim to break bad, hiss, and spit out horrendous venom? Adams cautions that *'time and experience alters all perspective'*. Yet, Jim holding a psyche surely not the platform for the type of trajectory to land as a patient in Broadmoor Special Hospital?

Jim's studying continued, at pace. Some beliefs driven heavily by a need to believe; though could anyone truly step outside this and see the mechanism? We stay within the matrix, snatching the blue pill from Morpheus's hand; perhaps only snatching the red pill within sweet vivid dreams?

Within a year, Jim could produce multiple psychological explanatory frameworks to account for any behaviour that he had ever manifested or indeed any behaviour that he might ever manifest. There was a welcome side effect of this latter richness. More specifically, over the coming two years our Jim attained the top 'A' grade in O' level Psychology and an 'A' grade in the A' level Psychology course.

One of Jim's lecturers named Joseph Duffy stated that even though the class had not attained professional qualifications, they could reasonably refer to themselves as 'Psychologists'. Alongside this, Jim basked in the glory of feeling respected amidst some of his audience of peers at Hampwood Hall college. Wholly unaccustomed to such a companion.

Chapter 22 – The impact of two years of psychological study on Jim's mind

Now, it is worth ending coverage of this epoch in Jim's life by putting these changes in Jim into some kind of proportion. On the plus side: the integration of psychology into Jim's mind was a powerful catalyst for increased compassion, increased self-esteem, and reduced inhibition. These initial college years were the first time in his existence that Jim's mind had seemed to find some green pasture to graze on.

It may be useful to briefly return to Jim's newly found friend, B. F. Skinner, to convey these changes. We return to one of the more technical lectures which Mr Tierney provided for Jim and his classmates. Tierney's vocalisation to his audience, included:

> "Quieten down at the back, please. I am not going to try to talk over you......Another prominent and controversial position of Skinner was that psychology should focus on observables, rather than speculating about what goes on in someone's mind. What was sometimes referred to as his 'black box' approach to psychology incorporated side-stepping issues such as thoughts, hypothesised drives, and emotions. Just focus on input (the person's environment, including consequences) and output (the person's observable behaviour), without speculating about what goes on in between. That is, don't speculate about what goes on within the opaque black box that represents the 'person's mind'".

If one used this 'black box' analogy and yet dared to talk about the 'black box', then much had been thrown into Jim's black box over his life. However, pre-college: the pattern of the relationship between the input to Jim (e.g., situations, experiences, and challenges) and the pitiful output (Jim's behavioural reactions) was fairly predictable and consistent. With

Jim studying psychology, it was as if something had been thrown into this black box which changed the input-output relations.

Jim was beginning to respond differently to situations, experiences, and challenges. Feelings that were held down, were beginning to be released more. Shackles and chains not wholly removed, but markedly slackened; allowing Jim more movement.

In truth, we have very blunt tools if we do not seek to give some sense of what is within this black box between Jin's ears. The change that the college years saw in Jim was significant, particularly with the contrast of a largely unchanging landscape in Jim's mind for many years prior. However, let us not overstate this. Yes, Jim's toxic inners were soothed. Yet, there was still significant unpleasant residue.

Jim became exceptionally skilled at using logic and applying psychology, to mitigate his being. Yet, much of Jim's pathology was mentally coded at an experiential and emotional level. Typically, logic does not fully penetrate at such a level; perhaps often just scratching the surface.

A rather flamboyant lecturer at Hampwood Hall named Hans Weinreich would don a cravat and explain such complexities. Weinreich was flamboyant, eccentric, and probably psychologically damaged on some deeper level. His moods visibly fluctuated across the term.

On one rainy Monday, Weinreich would strive to convey some key issues to the seated specimens, who varied greatly in their interest. Weinreich married psychology and philosophy, in an unusual way. His teachings were simultaneously: profound, departing from main stream, often reflecting originality in the way he expressed things, and difficult to follow.

Our Jim found what Weinreich conveyed to be a most beautiful and challenging puzzle to decode, though most of Jim's flock preferred to retreat into interacting with their mobile phones. *'Listen carefully'*, Weinreich urged, *'Some of this will likely be on the end of year exam'*. The noise levels reduced, and Weinreich continued:

> *"Imagine a therapist repeatedly explaining to an eager adult client with a severe dog phobia, that dogs are not dangerous. Let us suggest that this latter argument is made by the skilled therapist for weekly sessions which span over a decade, yet without the client having any exposure to dogs. Reality tells us that when the client encounters a dog for the first time over a decade later, then their fear will rise up and their emotion will tell them to escape.*

> *If we naively treat ourselves and others as if we fully run on logic, then we regularly open the door to outrage, exasperation, and confusion. Of course, some words and certain logic can help. Reality cannot pretend that 'self-talk' - what we say to ourselves and buy into, within our own mind - cannot sometimes be valuable or destructive; depending on its form. However, maybe we cannot fully cure with logic and words that which is coded mainly on an emotional and experiential level?*

> *Further, reality knows that convenient simplistic beliefs often err; certainly, when the gauge is 'truth value' and not benefit. Further, emotional and experiential coding are not only stood beside us when we enter that vast superstore in our mind to 'choose' self-talk, they typically hold the purse strings. Indeed, maybe they always hold the purse strings?*

Jim transfixed and mystified by how one class member was fighting to keep his eyes open. The latter clearly having to use much will, to repeatedly prod away a slumber. Weinreich noticing the weary battle of these pupils, and the wind visibly sucked out of him.

Despite his studies at Hampwood Hall, Jim did retain much of his problematic emotional reactions; typically anxiety. His psychological knowledge effectively gave him routes to improve his *self-talk*. So, he began to say more helpful things to himself in his own mind; improvements in how he interpreted: situations, his own thoughts, and his emotional reactions. Of course, this improved self-talk was helpful. However, Jim's neurotic bladder did not understand psychology.

Jim's ingrained behavioural patterns and tendencies towards avoidance were not suddenly chased wholly away by a constellation of psychology text books. His neurotic bladder largely stood firm. He also had extra angst that would perhaps not be unprecedented, regarding his status as a thirty-something virgin.

So, yes, the impact of psychological study on Jim's mind was huge. It changed the home which his mind provided, undoubtedly sprucing it up appreciably. However, it did not wholly evaporate all his woes. What it probably did is create some pliability, within an individual whose pathology had previously seemed to be hopelessly fixed, rigid, and unshiftable. At this stage, what this pliability would be bent and shaped into remained a mystery.

Chapter 23 – Jim's University years, and beyond

With exceptional references from his teachers at Hampwood Hall, Jim enrolled on an Open University Course in Psychology at the age of thirty five; the year 2003. The bulk of this course involved studying from home, which meant that Jim could continue to share an abode with his mother. Growing through learning, but still within a relative comfort zone outside his studies. Kath's negative world view still often hung heavily in the air, but Jim had much attention channelled elsewhere. Hence, there was less free attention in Jim's head; less space for Kath to dominate and infiltrate.

Within his home, Jim's bladder unchained and feeling relatively at ease. Jim's thirst for psychology continued unabated. The associated positive lift in life quality marched on, though perhaps showing signs of getting closer to plateauing after his early honeymoon period with his studies.

Jim's extreme pre-psychology difficulties in finding satisfactory answers to the questions which the world asked him had set the scene for his studies. This context likely lent itself to an autistic like retreat, into making sense of academia and science. At times, it shared elements with when he used to fully absorb himself in playing with his soldiers as a very young child; vehemently hankering to block everything out. Three years on, Jim had attained a First Class BSc (Hons) in Applied Psychology.

Aged thirty eight; we had Jim Butler, BSc (Hons). A totem of societally recognised achievement, standing alone but not wholly unproud. Appeasing some of the negative judgements from the internal world of Jim's 'representations of people's judgements of him', that inhabited the inside of his head.

Through his increasing ability to draw on self-talk, Jim could psychologically lessen the gravity of a million actions and more. Jim's ego felt less threatened by the world. The pliability of much of the architecture of Jim's psyche increased, and reductions in anxiety created space again within his mind. His suit of armour had been bolstered by him relentless squeezing psychological knowledge into his mind for five years, alongside working tirelessly to internally apply it in convenient ways to himself and his own life.

With the inner changes, Jim had started to step slightly outside his pre-psychology comfort zone more. Towards the end of his Psychology degree, Jim began having driving lessons. Jim's path to passing his test was not wholly smooth.

In the face of set-backs learning to drive, it was likely Jim's new psychological weapons that permitted him to refrain from downing tools. For once, not reflexively and invariably the short-termist avoiding the 'here and now' struggle. Jim, not unerringly following the immediacy of the path of least resistance.

As Jim had his provisional license (a license that allows you to drive accompanied, before you pass your test), Spider put him on his insurance for his black Ford XR3i. Spider would allow a somewhat nervous and reluctant Jim to drive his pride and joy, whilst he sat in the passenger seat giving out instructions. On one specific evening at around 8:30pm, Spider arrived on what had become his roughly fortnightly visits to Jim. After learning that Jim had never done any driving in the dark, Spider insisted that they venture out.

Spider explained the way the lights worked. Jim got a sense of switching them on and switching them off. Then, away they go, with the car giving off a deep powerful revving sound.

Spider directed Jim onto some unlit narrow winding country roads, with a sixty mile limit. The roads were quiet and Spider flicked the lights onto full beam. Jim was concentrating with everything he had, mainly on not crashing.

'Give it a bit of gas if you want' Spider invited, perhaps striving to sound as calm as possible to assist Jim's learning path.

With the molecule of residual attention that Jim had left and perhaps fortunately, he had no idea what that meant. So, he just kept driving and concentrating on keeping the car on the road. A few moments later, Spider noted an on-coming set of car head lights; somewhere in the distance and quite faraway.

'Kill your lights, Jimbo' Spider gently instructed. A suggestion which reality perhaps knew meant take your lights off full beam and onto the less dazzling setting.

Jim's lonely molecule of free attention was insufficient to critically evaluate the instruction. Jim somehow struggled and strained, trying to translate the instruction. *'It must mean execute the action of turning the lights off '* he reasoned. So, he killed the lights, completely! It was absolutely pitch black. Jim continued at around 40mph, on this narrow winding country road.

There was a microscopic moment when Jim was trying to remember the lay out of the road ahead just before the moment it went completely dark. For a microscopic moment, left briefly thinking something along the lines of *'wow, this driving at night is tough'* alongside admiring drivers whom manage this feat. Spider quickly dropped his gentle tone and let out a loud cry of alarm, reaching for the lights to turn them back on. Alas, the re-illumination was not quick enough to stop Jim's tyre touching a grass bank.

Jim's frantic attempts to solve the situation by breaking and jerking the steering wheel did little to rescue things. Instead, a trendy XR3i showed a mind of it's own. Like a passive rider on a stubborn wild horse, Jim was simply taken to the scene of the accident.

The car went through a hedge and connected with a brick wall, which fully ended their journey. As the wreckage remained stationary with steam coming from the engine, music broke through the silence as if it had just been switched on. As Coincidence would have it, Dusty Springfield singing a chorus which captured so much, as if finding the words that Jim could perhaps sing to the Gods.

> '........So Come on, come on, come on, come on,
> Take it,
> Take another little piece of my heart, now baby,
> Break it,
> Break another little bit of my heart, now honey,
> Have a,
> Have another little piece of my heart now, baby,
> You know you've got it if it makes you feel good...'

What followed along with the music was even more breathtaking, exceptional, and striking than the incident itself. In particular, Spider seemed calm. It is worth saying that again. Spider appeared calm.

'You OK, Jimbo?' Spider asked, with a normal level of volume.

'Yes, I am so sorry mate, I'll pay for any damage. Are you OK?' Jim replied, feeling truly gutted.

'I'm fine mate. No worries about the damage. I'm insured' Spider replied.

Jim was very close to tears, and indeed a couple did trickle down.

Spider offered *'its in the bin of the past. In life, the most precious thing you have is yourself and the people close. We have been blessed to come through this'*.

Whilst Jim didn't contemplate it, Spider had touched on a truth. If Jim had veered to the right in the darkness rather than left, then they would have met the lights of the different oncoming destiny. A different turn of the wheel, likely completing their journey on this planet.

Spider had recently bought himself a new mobile phone, a device still proliferating within the outer world and in it's relatively early stages. He had a very limited signal, but managed to call the breakdown firm that he was signed up to. Later that night, Jim arrived back home.

Jim's relationship with Spider continued on a similar path, appearing unchanged. Spider occasionally joked about the incident and that his words 'Kill your lights' could lead to Jim switching off the lights rather than dimming the full beam. Perhaps partly through Spider's special support and Jim's evolving mind, this crash did not de-rail Jim's attempts to learn to drive. The driving-based learning curve continued.

Chapter 24 – Don't give up, Jim.

Unfortunately, Jim's mishaps whilst learning to drive were sadly not restricted to the ordeal that he put Spider through. He had already had a brush with calamity, several months earlier. It all started one fine summers day, when he ventured out to the local lake with his mum, Kath.

Kath was driving her blue mini metro, which was only about four years old. The plan was park up and then walk round the lake, which would typically take about an hour walking at a slow amble. The ten minute car journey to the lake passed off without notable incident.

Kath brought her car to a halt at the far end of a relatively empty country car park, which stretched for probably around three hundred metres. The surface was a bit rough and unkempt, with occasional parts of overgrown grass and shrubbery. Kath joined the other cars, with all vehicles parked in a very small area at the far side. As Kath turned the engine off, she posed Jim a question.

'Have you done any reversing in your driving lessons yet?' she asked.

'So far, not much' Jim replied, keen to exit and have the distraction of the walk.

'Why don't you have a go now?' Kath asked, adding *'This large space is ideal'*.

'Thanks but I'd rather leave it for my lessons' Jim offered.

'Go on, Jim you will be fine' Kath urged.

Urging without awareness of an irony. Specifically, despite

having spent a life time urging Jim to contemplate everything that could go wrong, she was now casting herself in the role of promoter and optimist. Her own hand so instrumental in forging blinkers to Jim that precluded positive thinking; now, demanding Jim peep out, as if unencumbered.

It began to feel a bit like a dare to Jim. Further, Jim's delves into psychology had enabled him to construct rationales for overcoming avoidance and stepping outside restrictive comfort zones. Growth mind set, if you will. Whilst this often did not markedly reduce Jim's avoidance, he managed on this day to push past this initial inertia.

'OK, cheers mum' Jim agreed.

What followed was Jim and Kath swapping seats. Jim was struck by how much Kath seemed to be relishing her role as driving instructor. Kath, suddenly playing a new character.

Kath gave clear instructions. Jim pressed the clutch and managed to pop the gear into reverse. He then lifted the handbreak, gently depressed the accelerator and gently raised the clutch.

Within moments the car was moving backwards. To borrow from the old TV series of *'some mother's do ave em'*, it felt to Jim a bit like an *'oooh Betty, I'm flying'* moment. Jim, a reasonable Frank Spencer.

It felt strange to Jim, and he was focussing intently on keeping the car reversing in a straight line. He had one foot over the clutch (after having just gradually took his foot off the clutch) and one foot gently pressing the accelerator. This backward movement continued, in a fairly controlled manner. Then, things began to go alarmingly pear shaped.

After maybe around fifty yards travelling backwards, Kath spontaneously uttered the phrase *'both feet down'.* Now, Jim's mind already full with just reversing, fought internally to make a bit of space to process and execute this instruction.

Jim figured, OK, I have one foot over the clutch and one foot over the accelerator. Logic suggested that his mother would not want him to press the clutch because the clutch was for changing gear, and he was not changing gear. So, he kinda mixed logic and intuition and his mind found a path of *'feet need to be pressed down – it can't be the clutch and so I guess I am being told to push the accelerator'.* So, he did.

The accelerator seemed to increase not just the speed, but Jim's anxiety. It felt difficult to control the car travelling backwards at such speed. What followed inadvertently compounded the problem.

'BOTH FEET DOWN' Kath said, voice raised and Kath's own anxiety very much arriving at this party.

Jim was bamboozled, partly by his anxiety and also by his over-worked mind. He relied on the meaning he had derived earlier; of course, Kath wants me to accelerate more. In the recesses of Jim's mind, there lurked some dissonance.

When he is already positively flying backwards, why would his mum be asking him to speed up? This woman so typically fixated on what might go wrong and strikingly risk averse; so suddenly now an apparent adrenaline junky. Heavens to Betsy, it was as if she wanted to break the land speed record going backwards.

In his confusion, Jim pushed the accelerator closer to the floor. The car was making those awful screeching noises that are made when it is being asked to travel backwards at breakneck speed . Like the noise one might hear from the getaway car, after an armed robbery of a bank.

The screams from the passenger seat got louder, 'BOTH FEET DOWN'

Was this anxiety or excitement from his mother? If Jim had the spare attention to contemplate, then he would surely have concluded that the last grains of sanity had finally slipped fully through his Kaths very tenuous grasp. Jim's mind grew more flustered, in the face of this double-bind. His mind did not have a ready solution, but listening to the advice from his make-shift driving instructor did not seem to be settling his unease.

Jim reverted to his earlier de-coding of Kath's instruction by speeding up still further and striving with all he had to keep the car straight. As he had virtually travelled the three hundred meters of the car park, he had to turn the car round whilst travelling backwards. Amazingly, he executed this manoeuvre at a speed; potentially leaving many stunt drivers green with envy.

Jim was now travelling backwards at high speed, back towards the vehicles stationed at the far end of the car park. Onlookers at the far end of the car park must surely have concluded that they were witnessing a most extreme boy-racer, surely on the ragged edge? After another one hundred meters, the heavens looked down and dragged out a new phrase from Kath's frozen carcass.

'STOP, STOPPPP' Kath offered.

Jim understood this new command. However, before he was able to fully stop the vehicle, a hidden enemy emerged. Unfortunately the car collided with the residual base of a chopped down tree, which was hidden amongst tall grass reaching up around a metre. Kath's mini metro was pushed in significantly at the back bumper; alongside minor whiplash injuries for the occupants.

Again, Jim was gutted. Kath took over the driving and she was able to encourage the remnants of her car to limp over to what had been their original parking spot. Kath and Jim met with a select number of wide-eyed onlookers.

A post-mortem debate then followed, within the car. Kath incredulous that Jim did not stop. Jim incredulous about how Kath could expect him to understand this secret language of 'both feet down' if he had never been initiated in this. It turned out that Kath's driving instructor nearly forty years ago used the phrase 'both feet down' (i.e., press the break and clutch fully down, together) to mean do an emergency stop.

'I'm sorry mum, but I wasn't there in the lessons with you forty years ago and so I do not know the meaning of phrases or codes which you and your driving instructor used' Jim offered.

From there, Kath offered silence. The pair walked around the lake and barely a word was exchanged. After completing what had been their scheduled relaxing and de-stressing walk, they returned home. Within a couple of days, Kath did find her voice again. This escapade marked the first and final time that Jim ever drove his mother's car.

The driving lessons continued, though. Subsequent to failing his driving test the fourth time, Jim's driving instructor (Pete) uttered the inspirational line, 'you are never going to be a good driver, but we will eventually get you through this test'. Soon after delivering the latter blow, Pete's good-will evaporated in an instant, when Jim inadvertently steered hard into the curb at about thirty miles an hour.

'Needn't have bothered spending all the money on new tires last week, that's been wasted now' Pete said angrily, with a raised voice.

After nothing more than perfunctory directional instructions from Pete for many minutes after this collision with the curb, the atmosphere did thaw. Jim continued with the lessons; maybe God does love a trier? When Jim was at the wheel, Pete certainly earned his fees. Jim's bond with Pete grew closer, particularly towards the very end of the time they shared.

'So, Jim, you have studied psychology?' Pete asked, to confirm what Jim had conveyed much earlier in their contact.

Jim confirmed that this aspect of Pete's reality was veridical. What followed was Pete discussing in depth how his wife had engaged in an affair with his best friend, about two years prior. Jim having read extensively about Carl Rogers' approach, provided a combination of *'non-directional listening'* and *'unconditional positive regard'.*

This seemed to do the trick, with Pete opening up about his anger. Indeed, it hung in the air such that Jim's less polluted mind could find the space to almost taste it. Pete even briefly shed a few tears, in between two of Jim's emergency stops. Jim finding the counselling provision far easier than a three point turn.

A meandering journey with Pete over many lessons, ultimately landing at the targeted summit. Jim reached the promised land. He passed his driving test at the fifth time of asking, soon after completing his psychology degree and at the tender age of thirty nine.

The crescendo arrived in the form of Jim hearing the words from the lady that conducted his final driving test, *'Congratulations, I am pleased to inform you that you have passed your driving test'*. From out of the test car, a content male emerged: *Jim Butler, BSc (Hons), DRIVER!* Jim's life trajectory seemed to be just onwards and upwards; apparently, not a repugnant criminal act in sight.

Kath had then touchingly scraped out a sizeable proportion of her modest savings, and bought Jim an orange jalopy, in the form of a 'mini'. Jim was beyond grateful, as this presented another precious means of intermittent escape. No longer did he have to purely rely on submerging himself in a psychology text book.

After Jim had squeezed his six foot and three inch frame into this mini, he thoroughly enjoyed driving. The feel of driving the car reminded him slightly of sensations he felt on the couple of occasions that he had used go-karts, particularly when he swung it round a corner. He began venturing out slightly more, with his car enabling him to move beyond his local community.

Typically, he would go out with his friend Spider. His social anxiety remained, though dimmed down relative to the pre-psychology days. Sadly, there were no major changes to his neurotic bladder and the associated ingrained avoidance.

When you have walked the same unchanging path so many times, often your eyes and your soul pay scant attention. However, Jim felt less shame about his shortfalls since he had studied psychology. To his amazement, he had found that other people suffer with this neurotic bladder syndrome.

Jim had even come across nomenclature for his bladder issues, in forms such as 'bashful bladder syndrome' and 'psychogenic urinary retention syndrome'. Further, he unearthed an abundance of theories and explanations for why he suffered this condition. This meant he did not have to rely on the pre-psychology explanation of: he had this condition *because* he was the most inadequate, worthless, shame-worthy, and despicable human on the planet. Jim found he preferred his more recently woven psychological explanations, allowing him to feel less unease about his imperfections.

Jim continued to avoid using public toilets, particularly in local places or when he was with people he knew. Hence, when he was out in public his bladder continued to be under pressure. In this context, Jim felt the ticking of an invisible clock when he was out.

What had been a heap of merciful repression of a reality regarding Jim's toilet neurosis was rendered less necessary. An enhanced ability to attribute blame externally and increased compassion enabling Jim's eyes to glance more in the direction of this ailment. Jim had increased awareness of the inevitability that he would struggle to stay outside his home continuously for too long; denial holding him less tightly. He felt compelled to 'duck and dive', so as to facilitate returning home regularly. But he was more at peace, and surely safe distance from perpetrating any criminal atrocity?

Chapter 25 – More studying than you can shake a stick at.

Within Jim's frame, a slight longing began to percolate. Jim enjoyed the dynamic with Pete (his driving instructor), when he was essentially in counsellor mode and Pete was sharing his personal woes. He had also once listened to some of Spiders transient challenges, during a late night coffee at a quiet nearby service station. These tête-à-têtes had assisted the birth of a chrysalis, from whence a vision had emerged. Jim wanted to be a counsellor, helping people with problems.

Despite the psychological archive in his mind, Jim did not over-think why he had an affinity for this. Indeed, maybe sometimes if you truly enjoy something innocuous, then it is perhaps worth spending some time enjoying it? Perhaps better this, than merely pontificating about why it is enjoyable? Jim's mind was perhaps finding better avenues; experiential within the present moment occasionally trumping analytical.

Delving more deeply into Jim, the magnetic draw towards a counselling role had different underpinnings. Firstly, for a life which had been blighted by thinking excessively about himself and how others might see him, this counselling business turned the volume dial up on his focus on other people. He could partly drown himself out.

Secondly, Jim's self-esteem would collect stock from a sense that he might be helping someone and making a difference. Our Jim, much more of an altruist than a psychopath; not great seeds for criminal deeds. The threads of experience had interwoven with his genetics, and on an emotional level he was far from devoid of being upset by others suffering. He was most certainly not the street-wise psychopathic soul; not able to feast on the full gamut of options within situations; not unburdened by conscience.

Jim's life had led him by the hand, showing him emotional suffering, again and again. For those contrary souls who reach for a fitting life jacket of *'personal responsibility'*, maybe Jim simply chose to go there? Regardless, Jim's experiences had meant that *'emotional suffering'* was something which he perhaps *got;* on an experiential and logical level. In this sense, he could see himself as like, a kind crusader doing good. His self-esteem and his internal PR department would not shun this route.

Unbeknownst to Jim, there were other elements that were attracting him to being a therapist. If one looks back on Jim's path to this point, it is characterised by him feeling strong levels of helplessness. Simply not having the tools to carve out what he craved, within this largely uninterested world in which he evolved.

Now, to re-phrase this: Jim's journey to this point has been characterised by him feeling very powerless. The notion of him as a counsellor made him feel powerful, in some deep way. Imagine a starving waif; suddenly being given directions to a nearby free access all-you-can eat banquet. Deep down and many fathoms below his consciousness, the inners of Jim wanted to feast on power.

What followed was that Jim signed up to yet more education. Perhaps as Brian Adams might interject, *'gonna have to face it your addicted to...study'.* He pursued a two year counselling course, again via the Open University.

Jim could study and yet simultaneously continue living at home, with Kath. His life was progressive at one level, in that he was increasingly gathering crystallised grains of grey matter. Yet alongside this and at a different level, it was somewhat stagnant and avoidant. He was being protectively suspended within the ample bosom of a long-standing and restrictive comfort zone (i.e., home with Kath). Yet, maybe climbing a ladder should be done gently and perhaps not all avoidance is toxic?

Jim's pursuit of studying counselling augmented the psychological benefits that studying psychology had previously bequeathed upon him. He had that sense of meaning which was a partial antidote to the type of persistent blues, which were never too far away. Again, this latest endeavour diluted some long-time companions, such as social anxiety, shame, and self-blame. Pulling a pair of covering blankets back still further, to reveal that bit more of self-compassion and self-acceptance.

Again, as a side effect, the man that emerged from this two year course was: *Jim Butler, BSc (Hons), qualified driver, DIP COUNSELLING.* At the tender age of forty one, our Jim was a qualified counsellor. Through his life experience and his experience on the course, he managed to become a chartered counsellor with a professional body. Sweet Jesus, could he be more credible?

Surveying the recent years, Jim's path seems very much on an upwards trajectory; surely stability increasing. Our Jim seemingly travelling ever further from the type of downward spiral which might crush out unspeakable crime, and from such a kind and humble frame? Any latent vulnerabilities surely not even close to being activated?

Without a helping hand from Jim, the Gods would have to work much harder to catapult Jim to where he needs to be? Hard to fathom. Maybe ultimately a miscarriage of justice awaits; perhaps, our Jim will transpire to be an innocent man, found guilty?

Chapter 26 – Jim gets a job and moves out.

Two score year and one, Jim begins to scan the counselling bulletin for job opportunities. For perhaps the first time in his life, he is considering jobs which a part of him genuinely wants to be involved in. A square peg, possibly surveying a constellation of what appear to be square holes?

Jim eyes an opportunity to work for a private organisation, providing counselling to a range of individuals battling mental challenges. Cutting a long story short, the interview panel see enough in Jim to offer him the job. He gets his own office. The company organise clients for him to see, and essentially they take a 50% cut of the fees. There will also likely be some opportunities for over-time. Perhaps, finally, Jim's 'cup runneth over'?

The job is about eighty miles from where he lives with Kath. Hence, he leaves the home that has cocooned him for around four decades, landing in a small but neat flat. It is fully self-contained, having: an en-suite bathroom, a small office room, and a small combined kitchen lounge. An over-stretched bladder relieved and truly thankful of en-suite facilities, which have both good sound insulation and a blessed fan which activates with the light being switched on and masks noise.

Even when character is well formed, behavioural manifestations of a person (who they turn up as) is influenced by the situation in which they are in. Place an individual in a prison and we may get different behaviour than if that same person is placed as say: the CEO of a large company, an army soldier in a war zone, or a quadruple rollover jackpot lottery winner. Without going into the minutiae, Jim's occupational and residential move stood as the biggest situational change that had occurred throughout a pitifully stagnant adulthood; the biggest by a country mile. The mystery remained as to what acts his fresh milieu might loosen from his form.

In work, Jim quickly garnered a host of regular clients. Many probably befitting of the label, *'the worried well'*, with minor psychological suffering. Some were more severely depressed, but rarely close to the same league as Kath. Jim particularly enjoyed working with people suffering anxiety disorders; he felt at home.

The early months ticked by. Jim strove to help each and every client, to the best of his ability. Partly, it seemed that by *'doing good'* he was rendering himself more acceptable. There was perhaps a slight compensatory element to this drive, not wholly distinct from the function of a weekly confessional. Our vision of this Jim would likely be enhanced, if we ventured live into a couple of counselling sessions.

Firstly, Mr Tim Fowler. Jim collects Mr Fowler from the waiting room, and leads him into his neat office. Mr Fowler appears as a subdued man, aged in his mid-thirties, medium height, skinny, jet black hair receding slightly but brushed forward, wearing jeans and a tight and expensive looking leather jacket.

'Hi, do you prefer Tim or Mr Fowler?' Jim asked

'People call me Tinsy' Mr Fowler said,

Briefly Jim's inner mind whirled slightly. Our Jim committed, but perhaps he had limits. He felt slightly embarrassed about calling a man that he had only just met, 'Tinsy'.

A very small part of Jim's brain within the depths, fleetingly thought, *'Tinsy, Tinsy, I am not f***ing calling you Tinsy – what kind of tin-pot outfit do you think this? Are we back in f***ing kindergarten?'*. Uncharacteristic feelings of slight exasperation oriented outwards and not at himself. However, exasperation was pushed down by both his overriding compassion and his sense that he was to be paid £35 for the next hour.

Yes, he felt slightly strange referring to this newly made acquaintance as 'Tinsy'. However, if Tinsy is paying him £35 per hour, then he would call Tinsy whatever names his plagued mind's desires could muster. Further, beyond any money: Jim conspicuously wanted to help reduce the suffering of others. Altruism or ego? The latter likely ingredients which perhaps can't be fully disentangled or distilled pure.

'Right Tinsy' Jim said, pausing slightly to admire how smoothly he had run with this

'For the first session, I usually do an assessment to collect details and then this can be a platform to try to help with whatever challenges are around for you' Jim again paused slightly, before asking, *'does that sound OK, Tinsy?'*

At this point, Tinsy burst into tears.

'I've ruined my life. I can't go on' Tinsy declared, with difficulties getting the words out in between sobs.

Jim allowed a long compassionate pause, in commemoration of whatever was ailing Tinsy's mind. He produced a sombre, respectful, and compassionate expression. Given Jim's life and relentless inadvertent coaching from Kath, the sombre aspect was not difficult for his facial features to achieve.

'I wonder, Tinsy, could you tell me any more about that?' Jim asked very gently.

Jim genuinely felt for Tinsy. Also, there was probably some element of fascination regarding what out of the myriad of possibilities had so dejected this fragile Tinsy. What followed was Tinsy going into great detail about how: he was married with three children, he had engaged in an affair with a lady called Sheila for several months, his wife Kim had found out, and she had ended the relationship.

Tinsy had simply trod a path that creates problems for so many, specifically he had not behaved consistent with the things in his life that mattered the most to him. In essence, he had done what his emotions told him to do in a moment of lust, rather than what was most effective in creating the life he wanted. Now, he yearned to turn back time.

During the sessions, Tinsy cried rivers. Jim's contribution was mainly listening, alongside timely displays of that sombre face which came quite naturally. Tinsy's core situation remained the same. However, he perhaps mentally processed his plight better and the rivers of tears eventually ran dry.

Jim saw women that had followed similar paths. One day, a Mrs Jacky McIntyre walked through his door. A tall, slim lady; with model-like good looks. She had a husband (Geoff) of eight years, and they had a child (Millie) of two years. Unfortunately, Jacky was aware that Millie was probably conceived through an affair with Brad. Brad was a high-flyer from Jacky's work. Geoff and Brad were wholly in the dark, about the genetic riddle.

Whilst she had strayed, Jacky was not of psychopathic conscience; she was wracked with guilt. Jacky could not decide whether to reveal all, to Geoff or Brad or both. One of the few things Jacky did know is that she wanted to be with Geoff, but felt she did not deserve him. What would have been joyous moments of observing Geoff bonding with Millie were transformed into Jacky being tortured by her betrayal and the secret.

Jim listened and again there were lots of tears (from Jacky).

Our Jimbo augmented the listening with a type of problem-solving focus. Specifically, getting Jacky to generate all the possible options, and looking at what the costs and benefits would be of each path.

As a counsellor, Jim was not supposed to tell Jacky what to do. Rather, he had to create a space in which she could make sense of things and find her personal best-fit path. A plethora of technical and theoretical reasons behind this, perhaps most saliently: covering the counsellor's backside in case any advice was to backfire.

Ultimately, with Jacky's mind still very much in a state of flux, she broke off therapy early. Jim's mind would never have the benefit of scratching his itch of curiosity, regarding what unfolded. What did strike Jim's inners as more than strange was that a beautiful woman was staying in a room with him; indeed, choosing to. What rendered this even more mind-blowing to him was that it was *she* that was paying for the *'privilege'*.

Chapter 27 – Jim's counselling includes working with various criminals

Over the next twelve months, dozens of clients were to sit in the carefully chosen arm chair within Jim's bijou office. After twelve months, Jim started to become more involved in anger management work associated with the probation service. This introduced him to a raft of people with criminal histories, each of which he found intriguing. Jim, a creature so adept at a brutally inward focus, found tales that began to tempt his eyes to look outwards.

One day, Martin Mansell walked into Jim's office. Martin was aged thirty four, well over six foot, athletic, muscly, and with piercing blue eyes. Many of Jim's earlier clients were withdrawn, guarded, and less present. Martin seemed more connected to the now; more genuine and transparent.

Jim enjoyed communicating with Martin, and learning about his life. Not wholly dissimilar to a book that the reader just can't put down. Our Jim more than craved understanding Martin. Indeed, he wanted to live moments inside Martin's very mind, but with sufficient distance to as be shielded from the consequences.

Jim, a fascinated cuckoo; with perhaps some parasitical threads. Often sessions with Martin over-ran, beyond the allotted hour. The more our Jim could understand Martin, perhaps the more he could bring out a Martin in himself, when it was needed?

After the usual preamble, Jim was progressing through Martin's criminal history. Whilst his psychological brain could professionally justify pretty much any question that he asked a client, the truth was he was thoroughly fascinated by going over every fine detail of a client's criminal history. Martin had spent just over half of his adulthood in prison, and he began listing what he had been involved in.

'One thing I got away with for ages was selling fake Es' Martin revealed.

Jim clarified with Martin that 'Es' were ecstasy tablets, and then enquired lightly, *'OKKK, could you tell me how that went, Martin?'*.

'Yes, me and this other guy Crofty used to go round to big nightclub venues, in places like Blackpool, Manchester, and Liverpool' Martin began

'Yes' Jim said gently, nodding, wide eyed, interested, and his body language pleading for Martin to expand.

'So, we'd have big bags of maybe around a thousand tablets, the tablets would be somet cheap for stuff like headaches, blood pressure, diarrhoea, or whatever – but not real ecstasy tablets' Martin revealed, perhaps taken in by Jim's obvious non-judgemental enthrallment.

Martin continued, with Jim typically peppering Martin's contribution with regular snippets of an animated head nods or verbals such as: ah haa, hmmmm, okkk, really, sure, and ye. Hopefully, Jim being much more than just an organ grinder.

'We'd sell loads of them at £10 a go and make a fortune' Martin revealed, having opened Jim's eyes to another possibility within this vast world.

'I'm wondering though Martin, would people not come up to you and complain when the tablets did not produce the desired effect?' Jim asked, lacking shrewdness.

'*Usually not, mate. If they did come back to us after half an hour saying they weren't working then we would look surprised and just assure them 'it will kick in soon'. We might perhaps give them another tablet for free. When it was coming on top like that, we'd usually leave a few minutes after. Get back in the van, and disappear*' Martin clarified.

Jim's eyes were open. Part of him felt a buzz from such a powerful character calling him mate.

'*Did you ever have any serious trouble with unhappy customers?*' Jim asked, doing his due diligence on this business venture.

'*Not really, mate. I think there was one occasion where I had to give some guy a slap, but that was about it*', Martin stated

'*OK, so that generally went fairly smoothly*' Jim said, perhaps kind of complementing Martin on his success.

'*What other stuff have you been involved in mate?*' Jim asked, trying to replicate some of Martin's language to increase rapport. Perhaps grappling to get his hands on more of what seemed so seductively fascinating and raw?

'*Well, I got my three year sentence for a scam that me and my bird were pulling*' Martin said, introducing another goldmine.

Jim grabbed the nearest pick axe. '*OKKK, what was that mate?*' Jim asked, striving to keep the questions as open as possible such that no juicy details would slip outside the broad funnel.

'*Right, so we did this about five years ago. My girlfriend is absolutely gorgeous, and back then she was eighteen. She probably looked a bit younger, though. So, what she'd do is, come on to older guys, say between about forty and sixty. Most of them were mar-*

ried. She'd give them the come to bed eyes and be all over them, and then invite them up to her flat' Martin outlined the beginnings of the scheme, in a very matter-of-fact and relatively unemotional way.

Jim's verbal and non-verbal encouragement reached fever pitch and he was totally transfixed on this orator. It was probably beyond ironic that *he* was being paid when such palatable dishes were being served up.

'So, when she gets in the flat, she quickly slips off her clothes down to her bra and knickers. The guy then gets hands on.' Martin explained.

At this stage, Jim still cannot fathom the scam. His mind mainly transfixed, tries to think of how could this be a money making scheme? Suddenly, Martin helps him. In not much more than instant, the penny drops and it all makes sense.

'Right, at this point, I've been hiding in the next room with my ear to the door. I come in, all surprised and angry saying 'what the fuck, that's my fourteen year old sister'. I give the guy a few slaps and I take his wallet. Now, because the guy does not want to face charges of paedophilia or does not want his wife to find out, he disappears. Tail between his legs and never to be seen again' Martin imparted, revealing the full blue print of this particular business venture.

'OKKK, thanks for sharing that with me' Jim replied

After pausing slightly for breath and the vision of this scam bouncing around his mind, Jim had to enquire, *'Just wondering Martin, if you don't mind me asking, mate, how did you get caught?'*

'Hmmm, Martin said', pausing slightly as if having to focus on

an unpleasant memory.

Jim would hold the silence as long as it took to squeeze out these extra details. Jim sat innocuously, nodding his head gently, and allowing the silence. Who would blink first?

'OK, this one day, she got this taxi driver up to the flat. Everything went as normal, I bounced out of the spare room. Anyway, this particular guy fought back and we really got into it. I hurt him pretty badly, he was hospitalised for weeks, and he made a complaint to the police' Martin revealed.

'How do you feel now, here today, in this room, reviewing that and going back over it' Jim said, partly wondering if Martin had the burden of remorse.

'It's just one of them, mate. You know. It is what it is. It worked well for a while, but shit happens' Martin replied, summarising his philosophical take on the events. Such great gulf between perspectives of a victim, a psychopathic perpetrator, and an unattached oberver. The lens through which things are viewed, so close to everything; perhaps nobody immune?

Martin went on to discuss his burglaries. Jim, as in-depth as ever in his explorations.

'OKKK mate, you mentioned that you have done a lot of burglaries. Can you bring one to mind? Like, a specific example of one?' Jim asked.

'Yes, one I did on this posh estate' Martin generously offered

'OKKK, errmmm. Was it planned in the sense that you targeted that property? Or was it kinda impulsive, whereby you did not know you were going to do it till you got there?' Jim enquired

'Impulsive, mate. Ahhh,...I say that' and then a pause was followed with, *'I knew I was going to do a burglary on a house, but I was walking round scouting and looking for an opportunity'* Martin clarified, with a conscientious precision.

'OKKK, if you don't mind, errr, could you tell me what you see that draws you to that house?' Jim asked

'Well, it looked quiet, and not particularly overlooked from the back and, I know this is going to sound weird, but I prefer it when the outside gate is open' Martin stated

'OK, so what do you do next, buddy?' Jim asked

'Well, I walk up to the door and knock. There was no answer and so I walk round the back' Martin elaborated, with Jim watching a vivid a picture of this within his mind.

'How long do you leave it for the person to answer?' Jim asked, rewinding the image slightly

'Maybe a minute or so, not too long' Martin replied, with a calmness that suggested that he is most certainly not risk averse.

'OKKK, so I am wondering Martin, what would you do if someone came to the door?' Jim asked, at this stage unaware of the tactics.

'Just ask, 'is Fred in?' Or make up some name. Then, they say you have got the wrong house' Martin explained.

Jim's mind is whirling.

'has a person by the name you ask for ever lived in the house?' Jim asked, with a very slight smile.

Martin laughed, *'yes, to be honest mate, just once. I just pretended 'oh it's a different Fred, like I've got the wrong house'. People might sometimes think you are a bit suspicious, but they can't do owt'* he explained. It struck Jim, when you do not care about what others think, you have a certain freedom; chains loosened, unburdened from much.

'So, I was gonna ask if you don't mind, how much fear do you feel going up to the house and getting into the house?' Jim asked

'Pretty much no fear at all, I'm just desperate to get money for gear' Martin stated, explaining that the *'gear'* was essentially heroin and crack cocaine.

'So, sorry buddy, I interrupted. If nobody answers the door, you are at the back of the house. What happens next?' Jim asked.

'Just break in through a window and then get as much as I can' Martin revealed.

'Do you bring bags with you?' Jim asked

Martin laughed again. *'No mate, it would be pretty obvious if you turn up with empty swag bags. You get your bags inside'*. He slightly turned up the intensity of his tone with the latter five words, perhaps paralleling a maths genius responding to a student asking whether two plus two is five. This master so readily elucidated; educating the apprentice in the process. Martin gently laughing again after his explanation, perhaps reviewing Jim's naivety in his head

'I prefer to get money, but I also look for anything expensive that I can sell' Martin presented to his eager audience, readily delineating his preferences.

Some of Jim's other probation clients had expressed that they would never take items from a child's room in a burglary or never beat a father up in front of his own child. Perhaps in their mind, attaining a moral high ground over some more heartless criminals. However, on subtle exploration, it became apparent that Martin seemed unshackled from these specific moral restraints. For this Martin, a kid's piggy bank was more than fair game. With an apparent sense of pride, Martin recounted the total haul of £1400 cash from this specific posh house; adding that he even got over three hundred pounds from the kid's rooms.

'Thanks for sharing that, mate. How does it feel to review it here today, what thoughts or feelings does it bring up?' Jim asked.

'Nothing really, mate. It felt good at the time' Martin stated,

'Not bad money for about half an hours work. Bet that's more than what you are on?' Martin continued, allowing a broad smile and another laugh.

'Definitely more than I am on' Jim said, nodding and allowing a very slight and just perceptible smile.

'Errr, OKKK. I was going to ask, if you don't mind. Has anyone ever come home or been in, when you have broken in and what happened?' Jim enquired.

'Just once, mate. I managed to get out. If someone tried to stop me getting out, there's going to be a fight. Otherwise, I just leg it' Martin declared.

Jim was struck by how present *'in the moment'* and genuine Martin was. Clearly, not tied in knots within his own head; seemingly, nothing feigned. As if the censor department in

Martin's mind had been made redundant on mass; no policies related to political correctness, nor the burden of overconcern about offending others.

Within Martin's brain, neural pathways not wasted on PR or striving to tred the ever finer tripwire thread of political correctness (PC). PC detectors inactive, as if batteries taken out; PC breaches not even stimulating a stray neuron to fire. A purity of expression, surely akin to flow state; rendering powerful and real connection with other souls.

Was this specimen, a beautiful soul in an ugly world, or an ugly soul in a beautiful world? Perchance, as Barash advises, *'implications, like beauty or ugliness, are in the eyes of the beholder'.* Hard to side-step language and socialisation; surely no being wholly untouched by contingencies and reward schedules, polluted by lingual proliferation? For whatever reason, Jim was beguiled by Martin.

'Any other stuff you have been involved in, mate?' Jim asked gently, preferring not to specifically use the word 'criminal'.

'Shoplifting, quite a bit of that' Martin stated, with Jim beginning to wonder how Martin found time to fit all his work in.

'Errrr. What kind of stuff do you take, Martin' Jim asked.

'Meat almost always. Best steaks. I take a massive load of it and just walk out' Martin revealed

Jim felt sure that there must be some details missing from this masterplan. His mind wondering *'how the heck would this ever work?'.*

'Don't you get stopped?' Jim asked, with that fine balance of incredulous and open, probably erring towards the former.

'*No, usually not*' Martin expressed, with what felt like more than a small sense of pride. Then, he detailed his wisdom.

'*Firstly, I dress up very smart before I go into the supermarket. Then, when I take the meat and walk out, I act confident and not shifty. You just can't look nervous, mate. If you look nervous, it won't work*' Martin explained, almost as if he felt that Jim was going to give it a go that evening and he had been cast in the coaching role.

'*So, do you never get stopped?*' Jim asked, still trying to fully join the dots.

'*Hardly ever*' Martin said, with a matter of fact and deadpan delivery.

'*What do you do if you get stopped?*' Jim asked, wondering if this would precipitate violence against a security guard.

'*OK, mate. So, say store security or another staff member approach me, what do you think I should do?*' Martin asked, gently turning the tables on Jim; perhaps doing his own assessment of Jim and his competencies.

'*I don't know, mate. Would you run?*' Jim asked, not greatly trying to solve the conundrum but desperately trying to fast forward to the part where his curiosity is resolved.

'*No mate, you don't run*' Martin exclaimed, his tone sounding slightly pained at what he clearly perceived was a ridiculous offering.

After sighing slightly and gently shaking his head, Martin composed himself and continued, '*Right, think about it mate, if you ran then you are gonna give yourself problems - that's not gonna play out well'.* Jim sensed that Martin perhaps had a sense of pride in his street-wise criminal savvy.

Martin then left a slight pause before weaving his wisdom, 'OK, *if security are fronting me as I walk to the exit, then I'd say my wife has asked me to buy the steaks and so I am just taking them to her before I buy them, just to check I have the right ones. They then usually say, 'I am sorry sir, but you cannot leave the store with them - you will have to go and get your wife and get her to look at them in the shop'. I politely agree to go out and get my wife, looking a bit hurt and perhaps quietly mumbling something about 'there's no trust in the world', and then I disappear and avoid that supermarket for a while'* Martin explained.

'It is unusual, but if security insist on trying to stop me leaving, then they are gonna have a problem. I will snarl, threaten, and show my teeth. If that doesn't work very quickly, then I'm gonna fight my way out. For most security guards, it's just a job. They don't want to get hurt' Martin added, helping to cover all bases in Jim's mind.

'Once, I was grabbed by a have-a-go hero security guard in Safeways supermarket. He was built like a steroid addict who lives in the gym. This geezer had a vice-like grip and I couldn't shake him off'. Martin indicated; smiling slightly, as he recalled this predicament. *'So, with venom and aggression, I said to the geezer, 'I have HIV and hepatitis C, and I'm going to bite you'. He let go instantly, dropped me like a hot potato, mate. I legged it'* Martin revealed, with his smile broadening. *'Police caught up with me for that one a few days after, anyway'* Martin mentioned, concluding this chapter.

Martin went on to describe other scams. He mentioned doing some work previously with a colleague named 'Psycho Sikesy'. Apparently, Martin and Sikesy would intermittently travel round with a van and tow bar, to steal caravans. He recalled that on one occasion, they had transported a freshly stolen caravan on the motorway; from a caravan site in Blackpool towards a pre-agreed customer in Yorkshire. Forty miles into the journey and travelling just over fifty miles an hour, Martin observed that the curtains had been parted in the caravan. He looked closer and observed that the angry male owner was looking out, presumably having recently woken up to a most unexpected sight.

With some struggle, Martin apparently managed to somehow unhook the caravan (whilst moving) and fortunately it drifted towards the side of the motorway. Only by chance, the angry occupant of the caravan avoided a road traffic accident. Unfortunately, he would begin his day stuck near the hard shoulder of a busy motorway, some forty miles from the holiday park where he had expected to be enjoying his relaxing break.

Jim provided twelve sessions of counselling to Martin. The therapy focussed partly on anger management skills. Yet, Jim unable to subtly transplant a conscience into a psychopathic personality. During the sessions, Martin opened up to discuss aspects of his challenging childhood.

Towards the end of counselling, Martin came in looking slightly alarmed. It transpired that part of his recent money making scheme had involved 'taxing drug dealers'. Jim learnt that the word 'taxing' in this context means forcibly separating drug dealers from their stash of substances and money, either by threat or violence. Apparently, 'taxing' was both lucrative and often associated with a reduced life expectancy.

It turned out that one of Martin's targets was *'well connected'*. Hence, several members of a particularly vicious gang were seeking to make Martin's acquaintance. He had a close escape, the day before the session. It was within the final session that Martin revealed that he knew people in the criminal underworld, and one close friend whom he met in prison could readily get guns for the right price. Martin felt he now needed guns, to protect himself.

Jim was supportive to Martin. The sessions gave Martin a place to talk things through, with Jim a more than willing listener. Whilst Jim tried to assist Martin in leaning towards finding better solutions, the progress was limited.

Ultimately, despite Martin's apparent character flaws, Jim was disheartened that he could not assist him more. Saddened that he could not solve Martin's latest crisis. Beyond the conclusion of sessions, Jim did occasionally wonder how Martin had fared.

That said, the flow of new clients continued at pace. Jim, left with not too much space to ponder. Unbeknownst to our Jim at this stage, he would reach out to Martin again in the future; yet not in a formal work capacity.

Chapter 28 – Our Jim perhaps
starting to come off the rails

Psychologically and perhaps especially for the ill-fitting, as the well worn sayings go, *'we are who we associate with'* and just maybe *'attitudes are infectious'*. So, one might wonder whether Jim's criminal proclivities would burgeon alongside his regular in-depth counselling work with criminal offenders being rehabilitated. Overt criminality still nowhere to be seen from Jim, yet well hidden signs that our Jim and his life were beginning to unravel. Our Jim's fingers perhaps never straying too far from the eager self-destruct button.

Time marched on, and a forty three year old Jim sat in his office. Still, *Jim Butler, BSc (Hons), qualified driver, Dip Counselling*. Alas, Jim had become jaded.

Jim had explored a very cutely framed advert for online gambling around six months ago. From the seeds of Jim's exploration, there had grown a most unwholesome monster. In short, whilst Jim continued his work as a counsellor, he had developed a most ferocious addiction to playing fruit machines online. It largely dominated his existence.

The power of intermittent reinforcement well documented. Potency amplified when the outcome (e.g., a beautiful vision of a winning line, or a special feature) follows so closely after the response (the mouse click that spins the wheels). For some reason, inexorably drawn to these gambling websites; then, the parameters of this stimulation seemed to activate special sites in Jim's brain.

When these sweet spots in Jim's brain were triggered, it seemed to dissolve sensible self-control. Jim was relentless and with a zeal which mushroomed when he was 'loss chasing'. At times, surely beyond the fever of the haunted addict of

'Franklin', from the twilight zone.

A temporary autistic retreat, striving to control the uncontrollable. The gambling beyond seductive, yet with a reliable torurous hangover throbbing through a fuzzy cushioning within Jim's mind. Reality, an unwelcome guest, difficult to fully hush; arriving late and elbowing its way into the scant residue of the party.

At this stage, Jim's gambling addiction supported his dependency on being a therapist. Jim typically finished work around 9:15pm; seeing his last patient between about 8pm and 9pm, followed by hurried completion of patient notes. Then, the evening opened up and Jim was often temporarily lifted.

Jim had twelve hours before he would be returning to work. He rushed home from his work place to the solitude of his self-contained flat; ordinarily stopping on route to pick up some junk food. Mindlessly devouring, fish and chips, chocolate bars, crisps; washed down with sugary drinks. By 10pm, Jim found himself engaged in online gambling, typically playing the online slots.

With gambling, pleasure centres in Jim's brain stimulated. The tentacles of his pleasure centres increasingly sliding their hands onto the controller that operated Jim, in his mind. Subtly and imperceptible moving the fingers of logic off his inner controller device, with these redundant fingers just left moving and dangling in thin air. Possessed and perseverating, operating on a level of feelings; unable to see the perversity. Deafened by a short-term opiod like buzz. Huge Jackpots; just maybe, *it could be you!*.

Each press of the slot machine button, the quick opening of a present. Often empty, but sometimes great prizes lay in store. Games that offered Jim an alternate world; striving to win the features; immersing himself deeper and deeper. The ultimate switch off; a past evaporated, a future inconsequential, absorption in the '*now*'.

Often lured in by '*Gladiator*' slot and '*The fairest of them all*' slot. With the latter, a compelling universe, with a raft of animals around the reels within a country scene. The flapping of an owl's wings often meant treasure; the butterfly flying so gracefully, would it simply fly past or land on an outstretched hand of the maiden to bestow richness?; will the rabbit grab a carrot?; will the maiden reach into her basket and blow gold dust onto the reels?. All these feasts accompanied by an emergent music, that meant maybe, just maybe. Jim urged the music and willed these virtual characters into action, as their emergence so often led to golden prizes raining in.

Sometimes, Jim's mental urging seemed to work; intermittently finding the key. He yearned to travel into the mines with the dwarfs, watching them kindly mine riches just for him. Or the magic mirrors, gifting many a free spin.

In the short-term, what gleeful escape during this period of the spins. Our Jim was taken away, to a different world. Always aware that no matter how much he lost, it could all change with one spin.

One night, he attained £6,000 profit, though this slipped through his fingers during the next fortnight of gambling. The Progressive Jackpots which were advertised were life changing (often into seven figures); Jim often just missing out by a pixel from the wheel of fortune arrow pointing to an ultimate Jackpot. Maybe next time?

Jim would often begin the evening with 'one pound a spin', but regularly progress up to £30 per spin. The usual pattern was that by somewhere between about 3am and 6am, the gambling

Gods had typically extracted around £1000 from his personal bank account. On one occasion; he quickly rose up the stake ladder and experienced the buzz of £200 per spin, alongside the reality of £4000 worth of losses in fifty five minutes.

Jim stood in the rain, likely waiting for an outcome less probable than being hit with a treble lightning strike. Not sensibly tiring of what was likely a never ending holding pattern, never to land where he yearned. Excitement so often passing incoming rage and angst, as it left the site of Jim's latest downfall.

Whilst his nightly arrival at his exit point was met with a strange combination of numbness and despair, he had often experienced some short lived wins during the session. He had tasted the excitement and endorphins of the process. Almost invariably ending with loss, guilt, and an aching and throbbing mix of desolation and fury. Jim would then reluctantly emerge from bed after only two or three hours sleep, with a robotic readiness to drag himself to work and repeat the process. As was typified in his adulthood: his psyche did not allow himself the personal sanctuary of tears and a breakdown. Logic watched on open mouthed; wholly unable to break this cycle.

Another day beckoned with often eight to ten patients; each seen separately. The money which Jim would make from the day of work was usually dwarfed by what he had squandered the night before. Amidst his patterns, he was profoundly depressed and yet tried so hard to wear the mask of contentment.

Within the limits of his drained resources, our Jim strove to help every one of his patients. Often was the time when he was so sleep deprived that significant caffeine was insufficient to hold up his heavy eye-lids. Like a long-term heavy heroin user, trying on a sudden cessation: staying awake did not fit well with his being.

Through the fog and sleep deprivation, Jim recalled various sessions with a long-term patient when he wanted to close his eyes and go to sleep; the yearning was immense. Yet this did not jolt him from his later descensions into frenzied gambling. He was stuck; a record on repeat.

Often in sessions; he felt that his mind was so scrambled that he was at points close to a dream like state. Language ceased to have meaning. Once; in the choppy seas of exhaustion, Jim found a life boat in the form of a piping hot radiator next to his chair.

Jim repeatedly held his hand against the radiator during this one hour session, until he got a jolt from the subdued sensors within his shutting-down brain. Sacrifice in the line of duty. Perhaps akin to Mr Joshua holding out an arm towards the lit lighter of McAllister, though the sacrifice hidden and our Jim surely no lethal weapon.

Again and again; countless severe self-burning episodes for Jim within a one hour session. Session ten with this patient, Mrs Jean Shadwick, a plump lady in her mid-fifties. Jean had undoubtedly had a difficult life; held down by chains of depressive personality disorder.

Jean continued elaborating a narrative which Jim felt she had recounted so many times before. A lovely lady, but the reality was that she wove her web with a whining monotone; over and over. Like the *'to and fro'* of a pendulum that would hypnotise the most resistant subject.

Reapeatedly the lullaby dousing the flimsy embers of Jim's consciousness. Surely insufficient to have fingers firmly fasetned to radiators turned up full, in the depths of hell's furnace. Within his dream-like state; he felt an imperative to, 'ask a question' to show that you are still awake and to attempt to shake yourself from balancing so delicately on the precipis of full blown sleep. Like a jolt of lightning, he realised mid-way through expressing the question (as it played out in his head) that it did not apply in any form.

Jim was about to ask, 'how have you been since you got out of hospital?' As his conscious mind slightly kicked in, he realised that this patient had never been in hospital. He had begun, *'how have you been since.....'.* He paused and tried to look thoughtful, whilst giving one of the most extended mid-sentence silences of his life.

His mind raced to find the life boat of a plausible ending to the sentence. Whilst his ability to hide emotion was legendary, he noticed a look of concern on the patient's face and concluded that perhaps part of his panic had broken through. He turned up the volume on the *'I am in control, it's all going according to plan demeanour'* parameter. Trying to appear a swan, when the duck's feet were paddling frenziedly below the surface.

The seconds seemed to tick more loudly, but he rubbed his chin thoughtfully; perhaps partly to show that he was doing his job and partly to self-soothe. He then nodded his head with a wisdom, like he had found the holy grail and began the sentence again slightly differently *'how do you feel you have been, been coping since......'.* He was building it up as if it was the most profound question he had ever asked.

A little more silence. Then he repeated the sentence again; *'how have do you feel you have been coping since we started meeting for therapy?'.* A sense of relief, he had clambered out of a hole he had dug. His panic had probably jolted an awakening for at least another couple of minutes.

Jim increased his frequency of head nodding, perhaps mirroring the nodding dog decorations that sometimes adorn a car dashboard. If his questions were largely nonsensical, at least he could be encouraging and manifest a bit of positive body language. Like a fighter with a granite core repeatedly beaten to a pulp in the later rounds, he was holding on and giving everything to stay on his feet. It wasn't pretty. Sometimes maybe the fighter should just go down and mercifully be counted out.

The severe gambling problem continued for many months. When the heating system in the office intermittently broke down, Jim was like a rookie cop rushing into an armed robbery scene, *'I'm going in'*, only to look around and see no back-up. Fortunately, he had more than one string to his bow. Spittle surreptitiously rubbed onto the eyelids; recurrent sharp pinches to skin covered from the eyes of audience; he could re-peatedly prick himself from his would-be slumber. Conscious-ness prized out.

Chapter 29 – Nature's sweet beauty

The gambling addiction had gripped Jim with more tentacles than his mind could count. Resourceful in attaining loans, Jim had quickly amassed debts of just over £45,000. A man that had improved his life immeasurably, somehow finding a most efficaciously functioning self-destruct button.

Jim was on the cusp of reaching two score years and four. It seemed like there was nothing left. Our Jim, surely broken and finished.

Then, she walked in. Firstly, that persistent ring of the phone from reception; at this stage, as welcome as the buzzing of an angry wasp. Secondly, Jim wearily picks up the receiver. Thirdly, the secretary Jane again announcing to Jim *'your next patient is here'*. Nothing irregular, so far.

Fourthly, Jane continues, *'it's a new patient, Beth Holmes'*. Fifthly, a perfunctory reply falls reflexively out of Jim's jaded soul, *'thanks, I'll be out in a minute'*. Sixthly, Jim reluctantly opens the door.

Seventhly, Jim's eyes focus on the only person within the waiting room area; indeed, instantly, the only person in the world. Eighthly, it seems Jim's life is changed forever. Eyes that had long since let go of hope, instantly on stalks; awash with a new world beyond their contemplation.

Jim did not waste headspace wondering, how could such nothingness suddenly be teleported to everything? It defied the only reality that Jim had previously exchanged with. Surely rude to do anything other than purely experience this unfolding magnificence; words, so much less than unworthy.

Had the soothing ointment of recent years of psychology

dampened down Jim's angst sufficiently, yielding space in his mind for this petite enchantress to squeeze into? Had Jim's self-inflicted wounds over recent months created such soil of desperation, helping such beauty to bloom?

But, really, was our Jim truly so ripe to fix on something, such as: a cause of some kind, becoming a Hari Krishna perhaps, saving the whale, or falling in love? Or did this beauty squeeze that ripeness out of the most rotting, empty, dried up, finished entity that this universe had the misfortune to spawn? Jim beyond knew, it was the latter.

It was all beauty; he could not but be a passenger. For Jim, this beauty could more than waken the dead. He was in love; a wholly foreign land.

To borrow from Shakespeare, 'she doth teach the torches to burn bright!'. Everything around him became more salient and fulfilled with a different meaning, in an instant. Yet this Romeo, still blissfully unaware of where this path will meander.

The arrival of this belle leaving Jim's lens onto the world not merely cleansed, but wholly replaced. A bright and perfectly shaded light shone blessedly into the elements within the Kaleidoscope through which Jim viewed his life. Seemingly, gifting everything in Jim's world with a most beautiful hue.

Sore eyes transformed, so wanting to look again. Popper's black swan, falsifying all that came before it. No reference points through which to anchor this sweet beauty; prior meaning networks surely collecting their P45, on mass. Hence, all meaning changed in an instant, with a jaded lens taking leave; a new world. Blissful insanity?

'Hi. Beth?' Jim asked

'*Yes*' the beauty replied, with a voice that sung sweeter than a nightingale

Jim's mind had taken leave. Somehow they ended up in Jim's office, together. The attraction Jim felt to Beth made a mockery of all that had gone before.

She sat wonderfully, legs delicately crossed. Perfectly petite, with a slimness and a tenderness that cried out be cared for. A black dress, which rode magnificently up towards her waste. The most beautiful legs, that an inhibited Jim longed with his everything to touch.

The splendour of those breasts. Jim's eyes mindful to not get fully drawn in too much by the magnetic pull of these twins. Alas, he could not just silently stare and marvel at such beauty for the next hour. That said, the heat from the mere hint of this magnificence would be beyond a furnace for even a blindfolded Jim.

Debts of £45,000 instantly an irrelevance; mere seconds in these moments was worth more to Jim than all currency on this meagre planet. Jim was transformed by a glance at this wonder, taken to a place beyond emotion. Words dissolved into merely insignificant epiphenomena, more than subsumed by this everything. A mind overcome; never catching up with all the paradox. The mere presence of such beauty illuminates every single crevice of this insufficient world.

Jim was transfixed. He knew he did not deserve to be even close to the presence of what was so much more than exquisite. But he was blissfully paralysed by her presence.

Jim felt sure that being in the same room as Beth was more pleasurable than anything else that this planet could ever offer him. A treasure that he could hold forever without growing tired, but even a scant second may just count for everything. No need for self-scolding on the nearby radiator; surreptitious self-pinching surely surplus. Forever mesmerised by more than a tender pinch of beauty.

As the session with Beth progressed, she spoke casually, graphically, and extensively about sexual issues. Jim still and listening, but inside with a wanting that pumped round his body. The generations that had come before him, coming together within his mind; a drive to procreate that had been carved back through millions of years. A revolt against him denying them their birth-right for so long.

Then, an uprising. Jim crossed his legs and moved his hands to try to cover up what threated to be 'the big reveal' of his feelings and urges. Perhaps as his grandmother Norma might have interjected 'the devil's work'?

The rest of the session flowed so beautifully for Jim. Fully inebriated with amor. That one hour felt to count for so much more than the two score and four, that had come before.

Jim flicked through his session notes for hours after; re-living the session again and again. Jim did not need the session notes to remind him of anything that Beth had uttered, but he still read them. Almost as if he was trying to convince himself that even though what he experienced was better than a heavenly dream, it happened! Or perhaps yearning that the notes would somehow transport him back to those moments again? He contemplated every beautiful note that had come from those sweet luscious lips.

Feeling excited; yet surely, wholly unworthy. In reality, could paradise island truly welcome what by comparison was less special than a cesspit? Part of Jim's befuddled mind felt that she seemed to be perhaps doing just that. A fever-induced delusion?

Jim could not try to calculatedly make this his element coalesce with exquisiteness? Part of him wanted to uncharacteristically scheme, but it would be too rude; too disrespectful to nirvana. A beauty that should surely be left to just run free, and be. Yet, if in the magnificence of the freedom, beauty strayed in Jim's direction, then he could surely let it unfold? Indeed, could he resist such unfolding?

Chapter 30 – Beth.

Six sessions in and a jewel undimmed; just getting brighter and brighter. Of course, in Jim's mind: ill-fitting and inadequate to use words to discuss anything about Beth. Thankfully, not yet fully immersed in Jim's mind; scope for feasting on a few timely snippets from the assessment of this celestial gift.

Beth is a twenty three year old drama student, at a local University. The counselling sessions are paid for by her mother; of course, who could not love all that she is? Nocturnally, Beth tending to gracefully settle on a pillow located either within her room in the University halls of residence or back at home with her mother and current (third) step-father.

It seems Beth becomes cutely annoyed with people, very easily. Instinctively, Jim suppressed protrusions of self-expression. Bending dependably with the delectable breeze of Beth's whims. A most loyal lap dog, naturally following the owners every movement. Overjoyed to be able to instinctively dance between these heaven-sent raindrops.

Beth's dad left her mother for his male lover, when she was aged about seven. For a period in young childhood, she craved more attention from her father. Beth is unfulfilled within a two year ongoing relationship with a policeman (Brian) in his later forties.

Needless to say, there is nothing that Jim would not give to spend a few moments in Brian's avatar. Many children in the Western world spending what they have, to buy 'skins' which are then the frame which they populate in specific computer and console games. The child that is Jim would pay any price to spend moments in 'Brian's skin', within this new world.

Brian had left his wife and four children, purely for Beth. They spend a few passionate nights together every month, typically either in a hotel or occasionally in Beth's room in the University halls of residence. Beth wants to leave this man, whom she describes as narcissistic, domineering, and a bully. However, she readily conveys that the sex is sometimes so good that it is verging on some kind of mystical and spiritual nirvana. It bloody would be, with Brian, the bastard.

Beth describes how virtually every man she meets seems to fall in love with her. She expresses that when they don't, it frustrates and tortures her. However, she coyly indicated that she does not know what it is about her, but eventually all men seem to fall for her.

Car salesmen, mechanics, drug dealers, footballers, postmen, Doctors, factory workers, students; the spells she casts did not know how to discriminate. Beth cautioned that when she gets the scent of their inevitable arrival at being head over heels in love with her, her desire invariably turns to feeling an aversion and disgust towards them. A crescendo reversing her polarity, in barely an instant. A domineering conqueror, yet wholly unsatisfied so soon after victory arrives.

Beth mentioned that she is attracted to both men and women. She indicated that there is a particular older man (Harry) that she occasionally sleeps with, but it's purely platonic. Jim's mind struggled to even cope with the bliss that flowed from just thinking about sleeping next to Beth, without even a touch. Privately, he so yearned to fill in, when Harry went on holiday. Jim, ever careful that he did not inadvertently verbally air his inner thoughts.

Beth has occasionally earned extra money starring in pornographic movies, on several occasions since her eighteenth birthday. She mentioned sometimes sending sexual pictures of herself, in order to curry favours from certain men within her network. Whilst all the feedback the world gave her was overwhelmingly positive, Beth would frequently talk about hating the way she looked. It felt almost like she was seeking reassurance, but then the plentiful reassurance from others apparently seemed to quickly bounce off her. She oozed sexuality from every aspect of her being: every move, every facial flicker.

Beth conveyed that she has had various sexual partners, having disclosed a cast which had already reached double figures. Perhaps helpful that Jim's jealousy could be divided in many directions. In the course of Beth recounting extensive sexual history with a range of players and suggesting she thought she could acquire an STD, Jim gently touched on a thorny issue.

'I don't want to be intrusive, but if you don't mind me asking, do you use protection, Beth?' Jim asked.

Ever since his eyes had been first blessed, he loved the sound of that word 'Beth'. He could repeat it for several life times; never jaded.

'I hate condoms, they hurt. Kinda burn. So, I don't use them much, but I am on the pill. I am not bothered about catching something life threatening because I don't care if I die' Beth offered, leaving Jim saddened by her mental plight; if possible, drawn even more to this soul that was representing such desperation. If Beth was genuinely in a state of not being attached to living, maybe she was so much on the edge that she might even give Jim a second glance?

Beth had the ability to play an emotion-inducing tune to her audience, with an intuition. Too slick to be logically calculated. She just flowed.

There was a sea of emotions within her, which shifted. The audience could surely not be unmoved. Jim, adrift; ecstatically moving with the tide. Our Beth loved a drama; if this world would not gift her one at any time, then she would surely create it and so very gracefully.

Beth had beautiful complexity. Sometimes there was a grandiosity, alongside indignance if people did not show her respect. Yet, alongside this much of her magnificent output cried out that she had low self-esteem; intermittently yielding brutal self-deprecation. Jim yearned to save her; to reassure her. He implored the Gods to allow him to forever serve Beth, in whatever role might take her fancy.

There was at times a powerful kindness and sensitivity to Beth, which she occasionally shone at Jim. Yet, if she felt slighted or mistreated, a lion roared from her elfin frame; at such times, aggression seemed close to the surface. She could readily covet a million scourges upon those that she felt had offended against her. Still, so far Jim felt consistent harmony.

Beth had taken on various bouts of counselling during her life, including in childhood. She kindly proffered reassurance to Jim that he was unsurpassed in this professional regard. Beth showed a respect and kindness to Jim that he felt was well beyond his deserts, but still he found himself bathing in every drop.

Beth's knowledge of counselling was exceptional. At one point, she asserted *'I think I am probably elevated on the dark triad of personality traits'*. For the first time during his counselling career, Jim was adding to his inner psychological archives within a session. *'Forgive me, Beth. I am not fully sure what the dark triad of personality traits are'* Jim said gently, with his nonverbal accompaniment pleading to be educated. Beth obliged.

Whatever she did, it unerringly obliged our Jimbo.

The time came for Jim to write a letter to the GP summarising his assessment of Beth. If Jim was truly authentic, then he may have wrote something like:

> *'Infinitely ahead of perfect. Infinitely beyond nirvana. Words are hopeless messengers; vulgar to forward any representation faking to begin to capture this beauty'*

Whilst he knew his reality to his core, he retained enough insight to recognise that such honesty would not necessarily further his career. Of course, he sold out. He used some technical terms; once he began writing, he had to curb his drive to write several volumes about this entity that encased all that mattered in his world.

Beth described depression and anxiety, but what flowed from her was atypical. It was true that Beth was probably elevated on narcissistic personality traits. It was true that she was extremely elevated on Borderline Personality traits, probably to the point of meeting criteria for a diagnosis of Borderline Personality Disorder.

But really, how could Jim seek to place this word-defying majesty in any category? Whatever the category, it would be to try to shoehorn Shakespeare's Juliet, the 'snowy dove' into what can only be comparatively a group of rancid 'crows'. He did not categorise Juliet, but he used a collection of inevitably inadequate words to appease an unknowing audience. Maybe the ends justified the means? Jumping through a hoop to enable his raison d'être to continue.

Chapter 31 - Jim holds on tight, for six sessions.

Six sessions go by. Jim, inhibited and suppressing? Yes, most certainly. In some ways like a mouse, with an unaware predator nearby: still, reflexively frozen, alarmed that a foe may notice him. For Jim, the only foe was himself, staring back at him through his mind's made-up representation of the soul of this Beth.

Jim's threat? Express and uncloak himself and this angelic petal would surely be blown away from him, by his bluster. Jim, lurking in the shadows of his silence; listening, but with a body language which oozed acceptance and so much more.

Yet do not be fooled: Jim privately basks in the glory of his everything. He seeks to live each smidgeon of the hourly sessions, warming his soul with the afterglow. Yearning for Beth and his paltry being to be cloistered in these shared moments, with time standing wholly still outside their bubble; just for eternity.

Each single hour with this maiden wholly shone through Jim's existence. A clock within the therapy room, invariably running over allotted time. The sessions are interspersed mainly by Jim wondering about every turn of this beauty.

Never tiring of pulling out the wonderment of, 'what might she be doing now?'. Whilst longing to be part of that now, he is simultaneously bent to be overwhelmed; akin to a reticent young school boy who suddenly meets their hero. Even the fantasy feels almost too powerful for him.

An audience may wonder how will Jim ultimately react to this Beth? What determines behaviour? Behaviours that are squeezed out of a human frame are essentially the product of how a situation (in this case, beauty that defies words) meshes with a character.

The shaping of any character cannot be uninfluenced by the journey that a life's path takes that same human specimen. Jim's character includes inclinations to find some unusual and self-defeating solutions to the questions which the world asks of him. Often, character largely moulds and sculpts behaviour.

Yet on the rare occasions when a situation arrives like a tornado, it seems character is wholly lifted and moved to a completely different area. Sometimes the fingers of a situation crush a person so very tight, squeezing out a residue which is so very different than prior patterns. Jim more than loved the squeeze from the presence of his everything, dancing around tirelessly within his mind.

It is only on very seldom occasions in adulthood that our Jim had ventured out socially. On even rarer occasions, his avoidant eyes found a potential partner he dared to be attracted to. Within his nervousness, Jim used a consistent strategy in such circumstances: relentlessly give off extreme disinterest, particularly if approached.

The results were unchanging. Each evening ending in the same way. Like a resigned trawler fisherman, pulling the nets up again and again and each time met with vision of just the tight weave giving only the many holes of his net. No reward; nothing caught.

Our Jim dodging conscientiously, through a minefield of wisdom. Ducking reason. Perhaps detecting a thinly veiled trap somewhere within motivational phrases such as *'if you don't ask, you don't get'*; aping Tarzan in his prime, wholly swinging across that hazard.

Decades on, our Jimbo faithfully holding fast to a strategy. A strategy that experience had shown his logic over and over again was ineffective. Experience, surely tiring of her teachings unchangingly falling on deaf ears. Complexity might ask, was it truly ineffective?

Of all the drives and urges that bubbled inside the cauldron of Jim's mind, maybe 'defensive avoidance of living' was primary and above finding a mate? Regardless, the arrival of something so special as this Beth could not but shuffle the pack. With even the most stubborn unchanging character, there is likely a low probability event that represents such a mind-blowing 'force of situation' that new behaviours can be prized out of the most well-worn frame. Beth, that mega tsunami, and more.

Jim was hanging onto to this slippery slope of old habits and a defensive life of nothingness. If he lost his grip, he would surely fall inevitably into this abyss of living, positive feelings, things possibly going wrong, and the risk of loss. He hung on; fearing the splash that would marry him with a reality that his defences had long since encased in many layers of fluffy padding. Beth had more than oiled the slope. A mere flick of her hair or a glance from those eyes; a gradient at once transformed; a Jimbo barely hanging on to a slope rendered vertical.

How could Jim hold on for six sessions; still no whiff of confessing his undying love nor any breaches of normal counselling boundaries. An immense superego that any Freudian could not but marvel at. A disciplinary panel in Jim's head, fully appeased. There were shaky moments. Let us take you live into session five.

'I think I am infatuated with somebody and I think this person is attracted to me' Beth offered delicately.

The words marrying with a laser beam of sexual energy from Beth, reaching out from her eyes and boring into Jim's core. She slightly moved her facial expression and body language, increasing the volume of all that is angelic and turning up the magnetic pull. Jim virtually felt his chair moving.

'This person is so cute and he is so professional in his job' Beth continued.

'He wears the most beautiful blue suit and it makes him look so sexy' Beth said, increasing the specificity and giving what seemed like a deep and longing look to our Jimbo, who was again dressed in his traditional blue suit.

'I think he likes me, as well. But I am not sure' Beth continued, with a smile.

Jim felt himself slipping. Surely, his feelings, this beauty, this opening; it could but go only one way? Jim had perhaps dared to dream. Now, everything about his everything suggested that there may be an open door. What would our Jimbo do?

Before Jimbo had chance to fully process, he decided to stand in his own way. The words that flowed from his distorted core were:

'OKKK, Beth. I am wondering if you are talking about your GP?' he asked, whilst strongly striving to summon some sort of red herring.

Beth's face instantly gave a somewhat confused look, and in a slightly frustrated and exasperated tone, she replied: *'Nooo, I am not talking about my GP'*. The beauty undimmed, but temporarily the volume of her sexual energy was definitely turned down.

Jim spent the rest of the session akin to a frenzied game of wak-a-mole. Every time Beth moved things towards a theme which seemed to open the door to them getting closer, he sought to gently apply the mallet to somehow change the conversational flow. He propped up his strategy by a rationale of contemplating disapproval from the ethics committee. Jim wondering whether any non-professional comment or approach might damage this precious, delicate, petite, flower.

Of course, Jim's evasion not surprising for a man that had spent a life time running from his emotions. Consicentious cowardice, which always seemed to go above and beyond. The brew thickened by more than a pinch of low self-esteem and a generous helping of the genre of problematic doubt which is so often a bedfellow for the neurotic soul.

Jim's mental constructs struggling to squeeze in the the the notion of there being even a glimmer of interest in him; from a celestial beauty so incongruous with earthly realms. Interpretations of possible interest (in him) from Beth constantly switching to meta-cognition around him surely being delusional. He fluctuated between hope and despair, presented almost tachistoscopically to his inner eye; never firmly snagging which option was delusional.

Chapter 32 – Jim lets go from this elevated
spot, willing gravity to pull him down

Session seven with Beth beckons Jim, just minutes away. Fighting his way through irrelevance, to arrive at 8pm on Friday. Jim's life had begun with Beth. Such contrast with all that went before her presence; leaving Jim's pre-Beth history dulled, immaterial, and sub-rotten.

Jim had manoeuvred Beth's appointment to the end of his day. This left his mind free post-session to bask in this buzz from chemicals surely not of this planet, binding euphorically to every opioid receptor in his brain. Surely disrespectful to allow a further client to distract and interrupt this. Perhaps below Jim's awareness, he also wanted to unshackle some faint possibility that he and Beth could leave the session together, to begin their new life.

In Jim's mind, even the thought of Beth triggers an emotional wonderment, not totally incongruent with Tina Turner belting out, *'simply the best'* somewhere in the deep recesses of his mind. On this day, Beth just walked straight in. Not pausing to be met in the waiting room; not even knocking.

The greatest gift not even having to be encouraged, just coming at him. The rapturous rush of excitement elevating with every move that brought her closer. This Beth, dressed more seductively than Jim had ever been blessed to witness.

Donning threads that had no wish to hide her form. A feast, drizzled in delicately applied make-up. Though please, do not let latter folly lead your logic on any merry dance: no make-up could ever yield enhancement here.

Our Jim's eyes never previously wed with such short skirt; enviously figure hugging; covering that which the non-ethical part of our Jim so hungered for. Beth sits in her usual spot with greater vigour than has become customary, and she looks intently at Jim. The fiery spark in her eyes never lost, but today instantly accompanied by emergent tears.

'Brian and I have split up at the weekend. I finished it' Beth declared, haphazardly dropping verbal morsels which reflexively led to the grand opening of another fantasy in Jim's mind.

'OKKK, Beth. I can see that's tough for you' Jim reflected in a gentle tone. Of course, the truth was that he so much more than cared. His emotions told him he would sacrifice his life for this Beth, just to gift her succulent lips the shape of one brief smile.

'I have been on my own now for the last four days, what is it about me that it so repulsive?' Beth asked, pleadingly

A million forces were whirling around Jim's oral cavity, pulling and straining to tease out words that gave just a sense of what was in his soul. Did his unworthiness truly have the chance to make a difference to such unparalleled splendour? More than Aesop's fable, with our Jim less than a mouse, and Beth beyond the empress of the jungle.

More than ever, Jim wanted to stray into this foreign land of wholeheartedly owning what he felt. Yet, he knew what was ethical; he could still not release. Jim feeling increasing tremors all around; Mount Vesuvius breathtakingly close to discharging.

'I can see your really upset. I hear what you are saying, Beth. You have perhaps had the thought that some people think that you are repulsive. Though, when we have discussed things in session, you have mentioned that pretty much all men fall in love with you' Jim offered, feeling somewhat punch drunk from being struck by some many impulses

Beth moves to a different path.

'My mum said to me that I could not come out looking like this. She said I looked like a slut' Beth expressed, in between tears. The contorting of a crying face can perhaps often dim beauty, but here everything moved up; even beyond the impossible land.

Jim had a mix of conflicting impulses. Professional ethics had not gone on vacation, but they were perhaps getting more lost in the crowd. Jim perhaps dipped a toe in the water, though his ever cautions mind was still running a script about how he could justify what he said to the regulatory professional body.

'You look fine, Beth. Very smart' Jim said, nervously evading eye contact.

'Are you going somewhere afterwards?' Jim asked, unsure quite where this question came from.

Beth's tears dried slightly and she gave the most flirtatious look that Jim had ever felt in his life.

'No' She said, with the sweetest of seductive smiles alongside unwavering eye contact. Her facial elements had an unearthly way of synergestically coming together in a heart stopping symphony, littering the landscape with word-defying crescendos. Gestalt, at every turn.

Jim's mind was running backwards and forwards. Not graceful; perhaps like a chicken reared on amphetamine contaminated feed, pursued by a hungry farmer. A cocktail of excitement, confusion, and feeling flustered. Jim trying to remain soba; scrambling for a clearing.

Beth seemed to change track again; returning to an old tool.

'What is it about me that is so repulsive?' she asked, sounding desperate and at the same time subtly moving her hand on the desk closer to Jim's. The gap, probably a little shy of two inches. Tears were there; instantly this petite delicate gem, crying out to be loved and cared for.

A cry for help, maybe. A growing part of Jim yearned to give her help, and so much more. Jim's mind ached for physical connection with Beth; with all his being. He hungered to reach out and gently hold that hand; to enclose it softly with his ten electrified fingers. Her hand was there.

Jim wanted to make a difference; beyond overwhelmed that his forlorn carcass could possibly contribute to incomparable beauty. Jim yearned to be stuck fast, like two amorous dogs. Firm that being fixed forever like this would not yield Jim as a frightened dog clamouring for separation. His feelings antithetical to craving for society to throw cold water on the union. Still, maybe a reality beyond Jim's consciousness knew society's disposition.

Part of Jim's mind looking inwards; as if the disciplinary panel of his counselling regulatory body were sat in the room. But this panel could not prevent the arrival of new audience, gently activated in the darker areas of Jim's brain. In particular, Jim had representations of entities such as Conrad and Mick (from the White Hart Inn), the homophobic Braithwaites, and his grandmother Norma. Yet, did this 'new' audience ever really go away?

The prodigal son perhaps welcomed back into this foul fold, with their disgust appeased? Such a kind group, perhaps never giving up on him despite so many years of bitter exclusion. Could their reward ultimately be, our Jim picking up not just any old totem of his heterosexual inclination, but the most magnificent example any world would ever see? Perhaps a cleansing comeback story, to the eyes of the army pursuing Jim in his own mind, etched and locked in? Yet, Beth would be so much more than a handy trophy, with which to strike out at the internally represented bigots that blighted his being.

Outside Jim's mind, Beth's stray hand remained; charmingly and almost imperceptibly sliding ever closer. A million reasons in the distant recesses of Jim's neural circuity, straining to freeze any action. Beauty just melted each and every one of them to nothingness, in less than an instant. Something gave; maybe inevitability. Two undeserving hands collected Beth's petite foundling mitt; holding it for what it was. A priceless completion, elevating Jim an infinity beyond this skimpy mortal plane.

Now, perhaps at a different time and with a different audience, this may have unfolded with the recipient of Jim's expression pulling back a hand and angrily exclaiming 'what are you doing?'. Not here. No such recoil to block utopia's landing.

Jim like a Jackpot lotter winner, transformed in an instant from the jaded fantasist who had dutifully and unfailingly entered the weekly lottery without even catching a single number. As if the God's finally tiring of his torture. From their boredom at his unchanging misery, a great hand from the skies points benevolently at our Jim, and declares, 'it's you'.

In the therapy room, Beth moved her other hand over, to join this party. The hands gently ran over each other for the remaining thirty minutes of the session. Beth constantly beaming. For Jim, smiles recurrently broke through his nervousness. Some words long since bouncing round Jim's mind were finally ejaculated out, gliding inexorably to their target. Once released, he felt a great relief.

'*You are not repulsive, Beth*' Jim uttered with a sincerity, smiling and holding eye contact for longer than was his tradition,

'*you are more beautiful than anybody that I have ever seen*' he declared.

Jim continued to reciprocally hold the hands of this beauty so delicately. His touch repeatedly learning of every euphoria-inducing contour of these hands. His hands holding her like a precious bird; mindful not to crush or scare her but keen that she does not fly away; balancing blissfully and effortfully on a tightrope.

The session concluded with a pregnant pause. Beth was stood; Jim was mixed. Seated, yet upright. Beth effected hypnotic incremental approach; floating gracefully, with the ultimate zenith of Jim's first kiss.

All those years of kissing his reflection passionately on the glass pane of a mirror, not from self-love but from conscientious practice readying for this opening. The steam on the pain far less over much of the recent year. Now, living a moment that a weary part of Jim had almost forgot wondering about.

Beth's dainty delicate moist lips, with a taste to leave words floundering. Jim readily amalgamated with the ripe blosom, yielding the most exquisite explosion within his shuddered being. His senses not bitter from decades of exclusion.

Then, just before her departure, Beth reached into her pocket and put a piece of paper in Jim's hand, closing his fingers gently around it. Beth then confidently uttered, '*I have been feeling sooo lonely the last few days, please pleeease will you visit me later tonight? I've felt really desperate*'. She accompanied her verbal offering with a smile, a widening of eyes that could not look more innocent, and an air of elegant vulnerability.

Jim's lust and emotion had outgrown his thinking brain. *'Yes, that would be great. I'll probably come about 11pm'* Jim's vocal chords produced, his emotions fully operating his controller.

In the moment that followed, Beth smiled sexily and replied to Jim's prior utterance, *'Hey, don't be presumptuous'*.

Jim smiled back, the joke lost on him. Maybe they were operating largely beyond words. For perhaps the first time in Jim's adulthood, his feelings were running loose; Jim not tracking them. For once, our Jim perhaps unlike the impatient farmer straining to catch a loose chicken. Let it wander, where it will. The chicken felt free; surely he was?

Jim's verbal messengers, released and freed forever. What is said cannot be unsaid; what is done cannot literally be undone; time machines not ripened. With a touch of Beth's hand, a horse had long since bolted; running here, there, and Jim knew not fully where.

Yet, do not be fooled. Our Jim's core did not yearn for a rewind button. For once, not racing to regret. Not blocked from moving forward by anxiety soaked 'what ifs'; no wish to rewrite these recent moments. His only craving for a reversal of time, fuelled by longing to replay this everything over and over again; on repeat.

For once in his miserable existence, Jim had not hidden. He had stood metaphorically and literally, for something. Was his ecstasy mixed with his loyal companion fear? Most certainly. But, Regret? Bah humbug, not a trace; an alien in this landscape.

Jim watched his Beth vanish gracefully through the door, yet she remained wholly within him. He was left nursing the note, reading the beautiful handwriting that conveyed an address and room number 'E14' within the halls of residence, closed with a most beautiful cross. A cross that marked not yet another mis-step with Mrs Yardley's homework, but surely it could only stand for that kiss and their love?

Chapter 33 – Will Jim meet his destiny, in room E14?

Therapist Jim returns to his flat, arriving at 9:42pm. He has about fifty minutes to ready himself, for what the Gods have surely served up. He busies himself, trying to step round an ensuing approach-avoidance conflict.

Jim begins to feel nervous. Amidst the roaring flame of passion and partial vacation of his senses, threads of familiar self-doubt start to creep in.

Without effort, he visualised Beth sat on the bed, in her room; so far beyond perfect. Then, his mental image of Beth is joined by a contorted internal picture of himself. Beth beyond beauty placed so surely ill-fittingly next to the beast, rampant with ugliness. Jim, surely impertinent to even exist in the same Universe.

Jim tries on various clothes and none seem to fully hit the spot. He decides to hide behind a blue suit, with a smart black shirt. A helpless man, power dressing. Then, Jim busies himself making something of the remaining thick, theme-deficient, thatch that blights his crown. An increasing realisation that there would surely be no silk purses woven from this particular sow's ear?

Jim sighed heavily. He remained still for a while, mentally rotating the juxtaposition of Beth's immense beauty and the foul mess that stared at him in his self-reflection. Yet, no doubt he had been more than touched by the belle of all universes; diffusing his prior existence, with a partial cleansing.

Surely, Jim had to dance to this futile beat and visit Beth. The music was so feet-tappingly compelling. He had the note. He had the kiss. He had the freshly sculpted memories of the tactile taste of those precious hands. At 10:11pm, he again knew in his mind that the visitation would transpire.

Perhaps to fate and the Gods, his pursuit this night was merely old news? Why would Jim amble to the nearby halls? Buried deep within the causal chain and when the elevator descends to what is absolute, maybe there are answers which would humiliate the notion that pure Jim simply 'made a choice'? Perhaps the esteemed B. F. Skinner is waiting somewhere in the basement, chomping at the bit to utter 'I told you so'. Yet, maybe most frail humans would implode with the pressure of such depths. Stay near to the froth at the surface, and just breath.

Why does the same insult or gem from the Gods strike one being like a high velocity cannonball, and yet another soul feels but the brush of a gently flicked crumb? We dance to the tunes that society plays, such as 'it's all a choice'. Skinnerian philosophy provides a shout for the conscientious objector.

Language, an apparatus to clarify or conveniently obscure? When deep drives and emotions take on the magician role, maybe 'what is' can be vanished and a sight for sore eyes beckons? At times, a belief captured and not much more than 'a need to believe'.

In pursuing this beauty, it seemed that Jim was behaving hopelessly out of role. Yet perhaps in deep recesses, a fair slice of our Jim knew that his action was doomed. In this sense, was he really pursuing? Regardless, just prior to leaving his flat, Jim's mind briefly committed to action.

If indecision was an aircraft, Jim had nearly fully jumped out. Further introspection near the exit door, and it seemed he was unsure about his parachute. Quickly, Jim rushed to the bathroom to check whether he could find any comfort amidst the mirror image that lay in wait.

The picture that sprung out on him was surely a sorry offering for the gem that nestled in E14. Jim tried exhaustively to adjust his distance from the mirror, in desperate strivings to improve the offering. At maximum distance from the mirror, stood in the bath and with his back pushed against the wall, Jim could see from the waist upwards. It was this latter sad spectacle which was definitely the best reflection he could achieve.

Still, he continually swooped in and fixated on horrific close ups. Almost caressing the mirror like the good old days, he could see the foul contours of an acne pitted skin. Jim focussed on each mountainous formation which interrupted acceptability. Jim hypothesised that *'Students don't like bright lights in their rooms'*. He prayed for E14 manifesting as a dimly lit room or Beth having a fetish for wearing a blindfold.

Jim's stinging eyes grew tired. They wandered for relief, only to be jolted by an inpatient wrist watch. It was 10:26pm.

Jim knew he had to leave. He released as much as he could from his bladder, aware that it would be unlikely to serve him outside his solitary time within his flat. Hopelessly seeking ointment to sooth his wounds, Jim took one last look at himself from the maximum distance away from the mirror that he could achieve. Sadly, insufficient time to knock a wall through.

Jim knew roughly where Beth's halls were located, and he estimated it was a fifteen to twenty minute walk. Our Jim finally exited his flat at 10:31pm, his soul still very loosely secured to his body. He walked down the stairs, with an effort to portray a tasteful casualness. Almost as if our Jim was trying to convince Beth and the rest of the world that he was relaxed and bigger than 'this'. Maybe if he could satisfy the invisible audience within his mind, then he could persuade himself?

Opening the exit door, Jim received a welcome waft of fresh cold air. It anchored him slightly in the now, gently touching the brake pedal in a mind racing too fast and too far ahead. He eased himself into the distance, which at this point separated him from the focus of his beseeching addiction.

After a brisk walk, he emerged onto the University campus at 10:43pm and asked a helpful student where E block was within the Halls of residence. Following directions, Jim walks about three hundred yards across grass and concrete, pausing only momentarily to squeeze through several muffled conversations dotted around the campus. On reaching the female halls, he is slightly daunted by their vastness. Yet touched by being so close; he can feel Beth's presence; carnal desires excited to a slightly higher level.

Jim notices a side door open and he capitalised, like a pouncing gazelle. On entering, he observes a green felt scribble, boldly proclaiming 'F block' on the orange stone wall. He is quickly met by three options. Jim could pursue the nearby stairs in search of a higher level, wander left along the corridor he is on, or choose to go right. As if trying to convince his invisible audience of his legitimacy, he decides in an instant that he must go left.

Jim follows the path all the way through to the 'F20' door adjacent to his path. Then, a door meets him square and his hand renders it ajar, barely breaking stride. The odour of perfume unites with a beating heart; Jim's excitement pushing him through his nervousness. He pushes open a new door in his path and is met with excited voices and sharp laughter. The auditory sound waves too fierce; uncomfortably jolting his core.

Simultaneously, Jim is greeted by a jarring sight. Lay in wait, in the same green scribble that marked his entrance, he reads the word 'G block'. An unwelcome transfer from 'F block' to 'G block'. He is going up the alphabet, not down it. Jim's being bounces off this emblem like a coiled spring; retreating like a wounded, cornered animal, clawing for a way out. He retreats back from whence he came. Nervousness seemingly ratcheted up, but not a Yardley in sight.

Jim walks back along F block and reaches his original point of entry. The regulatory counselling ethics committee located in his head briefly pipes up, but feelings for Beth swiftly shoo them all away. He thinks for a split second that he could retreat and return to the safety and predictability of his flat. Yet, before he has even had chance to savour the possible merits of retreat, it seems an invisible push from Beth and his momentum quickly takes him through another two doors within his path. Inspired by a note and mentally noting a new sign, our Jim has entered E block.

Jim's breathing quickens and as if swayed, his heart beat increases in tempo. He feels being gripped by a fear that he usually avoids so skilfully. Yet, with fear comes something. From a prolonged nothingness, there are feelings dancing around in Jim's great cage of terror. He feels scared; part of him feels alive.

Near the start of E block, a fair beauty approaches; of course, well short of heavenly Beth. As this unknown girl gets closer, they pass at E20. Jim feels the futility of his attempts to exclude her perspective rearing up in his head.

Jim strenuously avoids looking at this stray female, in the external world. Yet as she passes, some trick of witchcraft leaves him with an image of her view of him. He can see himself through her eyes and feel her judgements of him. He feels a shudder from the reek of disapproval. A hair trigger is pressed; she waters the roots of guilt, growing quickly into a desperate need to justify.

Jim fears the world thinks he is here to attack and rape, and beads of sweat start to form. He is left with a slight urge to explain himself to each door in turn, but he simply rushes on. Yet again memories of pure beauty chase off some thoughts of escape. And of course, pure beauty would never think he'd rape?

Different views of Jim wrestle and duel within his mind. Perhaps the homophobic bigots of his Northern town nudge him to keep going, to prove that he meets their warped gauge? Maybe he can evaporate their disgust in one fowl swoop? Jim counts down the numbers which marked the upper centre of each door, E20, E19, E18, E17, E16.

As he progresses, some dull background noise flickeringly increases the pressure from Jim's invisible audience. Jim hears the sound of a pop song coming out of one of the early rooms on the corridor, *'Do you want to funk...won't you tell me now...if you want to funk, I can show you how, do you want to funk with me....'.*

Sylvester's tune leave Jim slightly embarrassed, as if his inners are being mocked by some dark force and everyone can read his mind. But then, he recalls Beth's flirtatious and seductive smile and it feels almost as if she is sexily singing the words to him. Excitement wins through, slightly.

Each door Jim passes seems more profound; his heart saluting each one by beating with an ever increasing rhythm. The felt markings that declared E16 were faded and there was a bold name badge which brazenly revealed 'SUE' to any old passerby. This slight distraction seemed to temporarily avert Jim's invis-

ible audience from gazing at him; the effect was mildly soothing until they quickly returned to their main task.

The more distant words of Sylvester's melody still reach Jim
and he is almost walking to the beat. A forty four year old, perhaps on the precipice of releasing something which had clung
to him always; like his unwelcome shadow. Still, his virginity
remained.

Predictably, E15 quickly became E14, and yet still he was jerked
by the sight. 'E14' jumps out at his fragile core and reveals
some raw fear. But yet again, beauty forwards some reassurance; as if she was near. Jim raises his hand, and beauty moves
it to a knock.

"*Yes*" the sweet maiden returns, without opening the door. Her
voice saturated by perfection. Nervousness and excitement
dance together for Jim, even more vigorously. Jim reveals his
name to the outside of the door.

Feeling flooded by the anxiety of having to justify himself to
the world that he could not even see. Then, the door to life
swung lightly open. Beth beamed such a full smile at Jim; nervousness diluted in an instant.

The beauty named Beth fully appeared in all her glory; seeming to yield the whole story. She floated, wearing the same perfect outfit from earlier. Beth implored Jim to enter; he crossed
a special threshold, into a chamber which comprised of a small
bedroom and an attached en-suite. All the items within the
room had a magnetic fascination for Jim; they were transformed into being sacred, purely by virtue of their owner.

Jim and Beth sat together on the bed. Beth had the most round
and angelic face; pure and flawless skin. Her face would have
fitted a girl much younger, and yet all of her 5ft 5 inch frame

was a woman and so much more. She shone all around her and Jim was wholly illuminated.

Beth had endless golden hair and eyes that soothed like never before. Jim's invisible audience which usually criticised him so dutifully were left spellbound by this vision; they had no time left for Jim. The internal focus of Jim's mind swung one hundred and eighty degrees in an instant; only able to see outwards; only able to see beauty.

Beth's CD player played a recent pop mix, at a level that served as quiet background noise. They were not troubled by the main light. Beth's bedside lamp on her nearby desk, seemingly knowing how to create the dimly lit ambience that our Jim had so hoped for.

Jim was struck by how relaxed Beth was as they sat on the bed. She increasingly draped herself over his frame. She constantly lent over for passionate kisses. Her speech and her movement seemed so free; so uninhibited; drenched with an incongruous combination of raw sexuality and an innocence.

Beth became increasingly tactile, exploring closer and closer to areas that pulsated. Jim was nervous when she brushed against the firming up of his lust, but tension released by Beth seeming beyond gleeful. Clearly tonight: this was not 'the devil's work' that his grandmother Norma had so powerfully dictated when he was a child, and perhaps even a welcome guest?

At 11:16pm, Beth ventured to the en-suite bathroom. Jim felt somewhat hypnotised and stared at the digital alarm clock on Beth's desk, taking several moments to decode it. He found the curiosity to briefly lift a picture that had been laid down, unexposed. A morsel of free attention lit up a suspicion that this might a picture of Beth with her ex-boyfriend (Brian, the policeman). On reviewing the confirmation, Brian looked every bit the stern and bullying character that Beth described him as.

Then, at 11:21pm, Beth emerged in the most erotic negligee. She sat astride on Jim's lap, moving up and down slightly and encouraging his hands to explore her perfect bosom. This immaculate pattern continued for many moments; Jim unable to refrain from basking in it's unspoiled magnificence.

Beth seamlessly unfastened Jim's trousers with a delightfully relaxed playfulness. She released what had been uncomfortably bulging; with the gentleness and altruism of one that has nursed an injured bird back to fitness, opening out their hands to free it back to nature. Her hands then gently moved around the centre of Jim's excitement; squeezing the firmness; feeling the throbbing; moving so sweetly up and down.

Beth placed Jim's grateful hands in areas that he had felt nervous to stray, but it seemed so smooth and readied. Then, Beth brought out lavender massage oil from the drawer next to the bed; sexily imploring Jim to massage every part of her perfect body. Our Jim; perhaps akin to the unaccustomed vagabond, offered temporary respite in an all-inclusive six star hotel? Yet when one moment counts for more than a lifetime, one cannot cheapen this everything by labelling the impermanence.

A body that so hypnotises; squeezing out all the irrelevance. There can be no past and no future; just the most perfect present. Jim was as a pre-lingual child, with his mind knowing only this now.

Soon, Beth sat on Jim's manhood, delightfully squeezing it in, and then moving playfully up and down. She smiled, laughed, and made sounds that pushed Jim to the brink of a crescendo. Jim watched her firm perky breasts bouncing up and down, in tune with her vigorous movements. The climax shuddered through Jim. He released noises, that he was unaware had ever been contained within him.

Overcome; warm feelings of euphoria danced over him. Rendering our Jim oriented towards crying, with tears crystallised from ecstasy and relief. Isolated moments stretched out into the next moment and without division, with 'Now' on repeat. Jim's mind in alien territory: stillness, not pursued by demons, not running, and safe. Surely, this could only be home?

Beth had bestowed Jim with what was surely beyond what the human soul can conjure. At one, with a euphoria that his mind floundered to fathom. Starved of intimacy for decades; yet now, suddenly by some trick of the Gods, he was intimately connected with the most beautiful woman that his eyes would ever greet.

Jim's neural circuitry did not need to flick through the catalogue of ladies that had crossed his pitiful plight. He knew to his core, what was in front of him was truly beyond compare. Enlightened and enchanted by this perfect enigma; perhaps marking the evaporation of a life-long stigma? The wonder of her form had introduced Jim to such warm pleasure never tasted. For a mere second of such experience, is a life every wasted?

Jim longed to remain inside Beth; for the rest of his time on the inadequate planet that surrounded them. Beth amorously woke Jim up several times during the night. Before sunrise, Beth had ensured that Jim had the delight of being inside her, in every way that his mind could ever wish for.

Jim was truly in love, with chemicals pinging round his brain infusing a soothing, satisfied feeling which simply completed him. Beth had broken him through to somewhere; the prior forty four years had given him no clues that such a place even existed. The grounded and battered ship loaded seemingly un-endingly with crate after crate of Jim's wasted life had finally sailed, docking at nirvana; cargo instantly transformed.

The mere thought of anything even vaguely linked to Beth yielded an immediate stirring down below. The letter 'A', next to B in the alphabet, 'B' starting the word Beth; connections were everywhere. Nothing was untouched. The beauty of it all; no longer what Norma had christened 'the Devils work' in Jim's childhood. No devils here, Norma; just an angel and surely heaven?

Chapter 34 – The best eight weeks of Jim's life, interrupted by more than a knock

Jim and Beth became a couple. They rotated sleeping at Jim's flat or Beth's room in the Halls of residence, with the occasional night apart. The physical intimacy was on most nights and sometimes several times each night. The sexual experience with Beth remained wholly undimmed for Jim, and somehow at times even more powerful. Jim's love deepened.

Reality knew more than Jim, that Beth was also in love. For Jim, a life beyond blissful. Yet, residue of insecurity within part of our Jim; perhaps not fully trusting that this world could be so philanthropic. For over forty years, the Gods had surely given him his worth? How could their whims now, so suddenly, transform?

A relentless haunted and tortured state that perhaps often envied the neutrality of nothingness, instantly giving way to an unearthly paradise. Why these Gods would suddenly tear up the rule book? Not just loosening the purse strings, but seeming to empty the whole pouch on our Jim's unworthy lap.

Had their watchful eyes just temporarily been distracted from his being? Perhaps only to imminently notice his ill-fitting fortune and then angrily or wantonly focussing their wrath, to stamp on his being with full force. Our Jim, a gangly ostrich that had suddenly taken heavenly flight, yearning to stay below the Gods' radar and not invite their smite.

The connection with Beth was so much more than sexual. Jim ached for her every word, her every glance, and her mere presence. The strings she plucked in his limbic system barely ever striking anything other than top note, even within the brief post-climactic refractory period.

Jim's bladder neurosis marginalised. A noisy ventilation fan within Beth's bathroom meant his bladder had auditory anonymity, and his bladder intermittently broke the previous picket lines. Thick doors in Jim's flat combined with a handy fan also enabled auditory privacy for a shy bladder; even Jim's neurosis unable to convince him that Beth could hear his stream. Moreover, there was a relaxation and completion that came from merging with Beth; soothing Jim's neuroses. In essence, a blushing bladder not suddenly rendered with ubiquitous confidence, but certainly less central and less restrictive.

Jim continued in his job as a counsellor. He had such a spring in his step; no longer relying on a hot radiator or a vicious pinch. He was awake; more awake than he had even been in his life.

Jim advised Beth to cease their counselling sessions. If ever she needed help, then he could help her outside his work place. He was aware of the trouble that he could get into if he was romantically involved with an ongoing client.

Jim recalled that he had once heard that sometimes a therapist can perhaps see a client romantically, provided the gap between therapy and the commencement of the romance is at least seven years. Jim struggled to be without Beth for seven minutes and so this route felt close to asking Jim not to breathe for seven years. Jim shuddered at the game-changing contrast between life before meeting Beth and life since meeting Beth.

Jim's life was largely pitiful and pathetic prior to Beth walking into his office. He felt that if Beth was not in his life, then it would quickly revert to what had predictably preceded her. More specifically, she was the ubiquitous damn holding back misery; no gaps. If she left Jim's life, then on her way out she would inevitably pass in-coming intense angst and desperation; readying itself to once again fuse with our Jim. As corny as it may sound, his mind knew beyond reasons that he was nothing without Beth.

Still, Jim did worry about whether he had 'trapped' Beth through what is sometimes called 'therapeutic transference'. He was aware that many would argue that he had abused the power which his counsellor role had bestowed upon him, and tricked a vulnerable young lady into a relationship. He loved Beth and he figured that such beauty should always be free and uncaged.

Yes, he was 'therapist', but surely not through some trixy con had he effectively placed space after 'the'? Beth was wholly consenting on this path, wasn't she? Jim was wholly uneasy of the notion that by some sleight of hand, he had diverted Beth onto a path that worsened her life. When he went along this theme in his mind, he was troubled by the question, 'if this amazing lady with unparalleled beauty had met him in normal circumstances (outside counselling), why in heavens name would she be even slightly interested in him?'. Human logic offered him no plausible answer.

Jim discussed these concerns with Beth. She simply gave him the fullest reassurance, combined with the bliss of tactile distraction. This beauty somehow cleansed much of the sullied and spoiled webs that Jim's emotion-driven logic might weave. All was better than well in Jim's world, for eight weeks.

Jim remembers an evening in the early weeks, at E14. Ingredients predictably blissful: our Jim and Beth in what felt like an endless hug, John Legend's 'all of me' playing on repeat. Completion in Jim's very soul radiating out to every atomic particle within him and beyond. Words inadequate; surely rude to ever return to them?

Time felt to stand still and a sense of moments merging with eternity. Alas, time did sneakily refuse to bow to heart-felt pleas for inertia. Jim's union with Beth continued, unaware that a menacing predator homed in on their celestial configuration.

On this particular night which is under the microscope, Beth and Jim are around eight weeks into their relationship. They had agreed to have a rare night apart. However, Jim expected Beth to drop in *'unexpectedly'*, very late, and very passionately. This latter pattern had become the norm, on their occasional nights apart. Jim was more than grateful for this trend.

On this night, he exchanged texts with Beth throughout the night. She regularly sent Jim some very sexy pictures, and this evening yielded still more. There was the daily combination of sexting and expressing their undying love for each other, with Jim congruent with every word. The gift of a mere incoming text from Beth rendering Jim reflexively upright; magic not needing the companion of volition.

From about 9:00pm, Jim noted that there was 'radio silence' for over an hour; this was highly unusual. Then, at around 10:15pm, there was a knock at Jim's door. Whilst he expected a gorgeous petite elfin, his mind could not help noticing that the knock was at least a couple of hours earlier than usual and it was many decibels louder.

Through the stained glass window our Jim could see a much taller figure than that which he craved for. He was struck heavily with a gross mis-match between his yearnings and reality. Reliably, Jim's autistic inners struggled with mis-matches and departures from predictability. Still, he opened the door.

The sight that greeted him was a tall man, in police uniform.

Jim did not need his psychological training to detect that there was more than a little anger, within the offering that this night had flung at him.

'Hi, I'm Brian. Beth's partner. I have had access to her phone and I know that you have been sexually involved with her. I also know that you are her counsellor' Brian declared, with a firm and slightly raised voice.

Jim was like a rabbit in headlights, stunned and watching his career slip through his fingers. Much more scary than anything, he feared losing Beth. He felt sure that Brian's reference to *'partner'* should actually be *'ex-partner'*. For Jim: another mis-match between his beliefs and what the world had cruely launched at him. He anxiously wondered where this new road would lead?

'I have spoken with her mum, and we are going to report you to your work place and to the regulating body for counsellors. We are going to ruin your life.' Brian asserted almost gleefully, perhaps lifted by feelings of power.

Jim did not want to betray Beth, by denying any aspect of what had lifted his pathetic life to dizzying heights. He remained somewhat dumbstruck. He could understand Brian's anger. To lose the love of Beth is a bigger loss than the strongest of men could even contemplate; of course, Brian will fight.

Brian's parting shot was *'by the way, I need to know whether you wore a condom because otherwise, I could have caught something from you'*

Jim remained silent, trying to work out a response that did not dig the hole any deeper. Before Jim broke the silence, Brian uttered, *'well I guess that answers that then, I need to get myself tested. You bastard'.*

Brian walked away and Jim gently closed his door. At 10:14pm, the landscape could not have been better. By 10:19pm, Jim was drowning in stomach curdling uncertainty. The utopian life that had somehow become carved itself into Jim's path, seemingly hanging by less than a tenuous thread.

The contrast crucified him. He yearned to re-unite fully with what had been the new norm, just five minutes earlier. If wishes could carve time machines, then our Jim would flee backwards, in less than an instant. He yearned to travel back just those few minutes, and then with all he had to try to strain and struggle, to hold forever steady the hands of time; remaining 10:14pm for eternity.

What followed came swiftly and with seismic impact. Brian (the policeman; Beth's ex) joined forces with Beth's mother, who had paid for Beth's counselling sessions. Of course, they both knew that all Beth's current psychological ailments were caused by the abuse she had suffered from her counsellor. The relevance of the prior twenty three years of mum's influence disappearing in a puff of smoke; absolved of all responsibility. It was all Jim's fault.

Brian and Beth's mother contacted Jim's work and hammered home their spin, the very next day after Brian's visit. Jim could hear the raised voices, with the walls of his office seeming to vibrate with the auditory fervour. Jim would have been suspended pending investigation, but Brian's boss Keith asked *'has anything sexual gone on between you and Beth?'*.

Jim suffered from a syndrome where he tended to answer direct questions as if he had consumed a most powerful truth drug. He responded with tears, *'yes, Keith. I am really sorry, but I have fallen in love with Beth'*. The transparency yielding an audience with widened eyes and lips pressed together; perhaps conveying the seriousness of the situation and representing a reluctance to inflict the inevitable.

'Then, I am sorry but I have no choice but to end your employment with us' Keith delivered in a voice which was barely above a whisper.

Jim packed up his belongings. His being already slipping back into that familiar avoidant style. He walked his way to the exit, for the last time. His frame was slumped and he looked like an empty shell, devoid of his recent animation. As he approached the outside door, one of the other counsellors directed him into their office.

'Hi, Carlos' Jim said, perhaps fearing that life would somehow find some untouched flesh to slap.

Carlos closed the door to his office and issued Jim with one of the most compassionate and caring looks that our Jimbo had ever witnessed.

'Jim' Carlos said softly, *'you can't help who you fall in love with, my good friend'*

'dude, you are a good man' he continued, *'don't worry about judgements. I mean what are they when we break it down, stray neurons firing in another brain. Not far from a random leaf blowing in the wind; inconsequential; meaning what we make it mean'*

'You may have made a mistake, like we all do. It does not make you a bad man. You are a good man that has perhaps made a mistake. If ever I can help, just let me know' Carlos concluded.

Yet when the chips were fully down, alas Jim would not reach out to Carlos. Rather, he would reach out to somebody else that he had met during his time working as a counsellor. At this stage, our Jim could not foresee the havoc, not too far over the horizon.

'Thanks, buddy. I appreciate it' Jim said.

Jim walked through the door of the counselling building for the last time. A sense of loss clawed at him; the unceremonious end of what had been more than an interesting era for Jim.

Chapter 35 – When it rains, it pours.

Early evening and just less than twenty four hours after the visit from Brian, Jim sat in his flat. Earlier in the day, he had lost his job. The latter much less than small fry, when juxtaposed next to an infusion of uncertainty about the status of his union with Beth. He had not been able to get a response from Beth, either via text or phone call. He was tortured by this.

What had happened to his recently arrived perfect life? What Jim did not know is that Brian had visited Beth at around 9:00pm the prior evening and discovered some of their sexting and declarations of undying love. Seeing the texts, Brian feared he had completely lost the most precious thing that he could ever contemplate.

Brian then on that very prior evening, enacted a very determined scheme. Specifically: he took possession of Beth's phone and then contacted Beth's mum and wilfully spun her up into a fury. Next, he arrived at Jim's flat and sought to poor ice cold water on Jim's connection with Beth. Then, Brian joined forces with Beth's mum and complained to both Jim's work and Jim's counselling regulatory body.

If Jim stacked up absolutely everything in his life prior to Beth, it was less than irrelevant placed next to his Beth. Jim was plucking up the courage to take on a trip to E14 later that evening. Yet, our Jim remained wholly unaware, that Brian had possession of Beth's phone. It was then that Jim received a text from 'Beth':

> *'Jim, I have thought about what has happened between us. I can now see that you have abused me, all along. If you contact me again then I will phone the police'*

Jim oblivious that this bomb had been released wholly by

Brian's fair hand, with not a trace of Beth within it. Of course, our Jim was a soul that had never struggled to believe the worst. He mistakenly took the text wholly as Beth's own words. Akin to the trusting soul following a pointing road sign which has been turned one hundred and eight degrees; the pointer taking him in the opposite direction to where he ought to go.

Jim had lived through some adversity before. Yet, rest fully assured, this text introduced our Jim to a level of pain and loss that more than outstripped the relative nothingness that dotted his past. He was truly destroyed, in that moment and on that very spot.

Brian very much keen on the belt and braces approach, phoned Jim later that night. His conversation was brief, and again Jim was largely dumbstruck.

> *'It's Brian. You've ruined Beth's life. We could sue you. If you are within one hundred yards of her again, then you will be arrested. Nobody wants you here and you need to leave town'*, Brian conveyed with the volume again turned up, but careful to enunciate each and every word clearly.

Thirty minutes later, and Brian had again managed to pull the strings of Beth's mum. She phoned Jim and consolidated Brian's message, almost like they had been reading from the same script and playing the very same role. It was all too much for Jim.

So recently, Jim had been inspired by the life that he perhaps had a hand in creating for himself. For those eight weeks, he had stood so grand above the pitiful and shameful fragments of the life that preceeded his eyes meeting Beth. He had felt like a magnificent phoenix, rising from the ugliest of ashes.

Overnight, it seemed that this all had to be *'recoded'* in his mind; he was a shameful abuser; immoral to the core; precious bright memories turned dark in an instant. Pushed to use a foul lens to view what had been by far the best moments of his life. His reality changed and shattered, with a few targeted swipes from Brian's determined blade.

Jim sold out, again. In his mind, he could not fight the inevitable. He returned home to Kath, that very day. It seemed fate had dictated that he would again bathe in the pervasive negativity that surrounded Kath, like a loyal swarm of hornets.

Beth was bombarded by the narrative of Jim as an abusive therapist; both Brian and her mother relentless. Still, Beth held onto hope that she and Jim would again unite. This hope was surely severed by Brian, with surgical precision.

Brian typed a hurtful and final goodbye letter 'to Beth' and supposedly 'from Jim', only a day or two after he had discovered the texts. The letter concluded with:

> *'You have cost me everything. I wish I had never met you. I do not want to see you again and so please do not attempt to contact me'.*

Reality knew that Jim would rather lose all his limbs than express such words to Beth. Brian was committed, though. He used the police computers to find Jim's address where he lived with Kath and he travelled to that specific town to post the letter, such that it had the valid postmark.

The dutiful Brian also bought Beth the most up-to-date mobile phone, which just happened to come with a new number. Brian had seemingly 'lost' Beth's old phone, along with its SIM card and all her old contacts. The old number which Jim held so precious, was no more.

Beth's forlorn hope had sufficiently walked; she felt that re-acquiring her old number would not be a bridge to lead her to Jim. Psychologically, Brian appeared to have covered all bases. A diligent arsonist indeed; surely no bridges left unburnt?

Jim wholly unaware of what had unfolded; never finding difficulty in believing a negative narrative. He would also forever remain unaware that a few weeks after he last feasted eyes on Beth, she discovered that she was pregnant. Tragically, she lost their baby through a miscarriage soon after. Beth became very depressed for many months, and she moved back fully under her mother's watchful eyes.

Yet, Beth never stopped thinking about Jim and she never stopped hoping that they would re-unite. Jim's path was a perfect replica; his soul ever praying for just one more moment together with his everything. Reality knew that all it would take to reignite this paradise would simply be for our Romeo and Juliet to lay sweet eyes upon each other.

All it would take would be for Jim to say *'let's make a go of it'*. Then, Beth would fling herself in again, *'all-in'* in the poker sense. They would then be a happy couple; Jim's journey transformed in a moment.

If fate could put these two together, nature would do the rest. But, would the path meander thus? What whims would their Gods play out?

Chapter 36 – Star-crossed lovers
or the stars aligned?

Seven months on; the truth of Beth's ongoing love for our Jim, still wholly obscured from him. He thinks about Beth every day. Re-living each word, each touch, each second that they spent together. The memories not chased away by the masses working hard to soil interpretations of the only interruption to Jim's otherwise fetid existence.

Jim's residual hope was less than paper thin. But when the dream is your everything, you can still sometimes muster movement. If there was a one in a billion chance of having a future with Beth or even a few more snatched moments with her, then Jim's emotion would stir him to roll the dice.

Jim yearned to plead his case, directly to Beth. Not knowing that no words were needed; merely meeting beauty would set everything right. The Gods stayed silent but surely knew that as weird, unusual, and damaged as Jim was, he had come upon a soul with whom his being just fitted.

Jim decided that if he travelled the eighty miles back to Beth's town, then he could possibly come upon her by 'chance', and then approach her and strive with his everything to make things right. The machinations of an avoidant, anxious, and somewhat autistic specimen. At best, subtle and indirect. Maybe gently nudging *fate* with the lightest of feather touches? If only our Jim could stamp down hard on the throat of the uncaring, fickle spirited, fair weather friend that fate surely proves to be, when allowed to roam free.

His plan, an indirect gesture towards his dreams. Not purely posturing and yet a distance from taking control. Not straining to move the hands of fate with all his being, more a gentle nervous flick. It could surely go unnoticed? Our Jim, as if with a sense that giving his everything for his everything, might perhaps be rude and vexatious to fate's fussy etiquette. His soul perhaps feeling wholly undeserving; a position bolstered by Brian's tireless, treacherous, travails.

Reality remained stingy and mean; keeping the truth about Beth's feelings in her grasp. Not offering Jim any hint that the mere meeting with his everything, would surely spark this utopian path. Jim largely in the passenger seat regarding the single most important issue in his destiny; less than a finger on the steering wheel; just hoping chance would serve him what he thought was the thinnest of threads of hope.

Eighty mile journey complete, tick. Jim arrived at mid-day, parked up, and made his way to a Nero coffee shop. It sat in the heart of Beth's town. The outer perimeter of the shop overlooked the town centre, and it was merely windowed from floor to roof. The perfect look-out spot.

Jim's confidence had waned, but not to the basement level of the pre-psychology days. Jim sat gazing out of a coffee shop window, right in the centre of Beth's home town. The smell of freshly baked croissants mixes well with the hustle and bustle.

It is 1pm, the sun illuminates a crowded place. Jim seated in Nero; waiting, as the patient fisherman patiently watching the float. Just maybe, just maybe on this fine day, Beth would walk past his look-out post?

Today seems to be a relatively normal Monday, in July. People come and go along the pavements of this high street, separately busying themselves on this shared stage. Partly distracted, but Jim's mind wanders.

Jim ventures back along the winding avenues of his plight, and from whence it came. Like a crash detective or the NTSB, painstakingly looking at where it all went wrong. Yet our Jim, more than one string to his bow; he did not just look back. As was customary, he also sought to map out possible problematic territory, in which he had not yet even trod.

Much had changed since Beth was within his world. Her departure from his life had dislodged him from an unaccustomed balancing on the soothing lily pad of the present moment. He was less than a frog, kissed by more than a princess.

Now, our Jim was submerged again; deep within the cess pool of rumination and worry. Rumination and worry dissolves into pure contemplation of a certain type of loss. A loss which seems to transcend all other aspects of himself and his experience.

It is several months since Jim has seen Beth. Do not be fooled. Jim thinks of Beth frequently, every day. He dreams about her relentlessly; awake or asleep. This coffee bar opens up possibility, maybe like a hungry dreamer spending their last coins on a lottery lucky dip. A dream, distant maybe; yet alive.

Jim yearns for once again laying his sore eyes on this beacon of everything glorious. Since they first met less than a year ago, Jim's mind continues to tell him that the solution to all is so neatly encapsulated in that beautiful vessel. For just this once, the by-product of his cognitive whirring has landed bang on the money. Perhaps as the phrase goes, *'for one night only'*, our Jim sensibly making sense of the platter that the world lay before him.

Life without Beth is like looking through to his world from locked within a damp, dark, icey box; everything painted black and experience so blunted; for Jim, back to normal. The more Jim's life goes wrong, the more he realises that she is everything. *'Beth, Beth, Beth'*....even saying the name in his head overwhelms him, with an opiate like rush. Balancing on a taut thread; pleasure of memories and crumbs of hope on one side and a most painful sense of loss on the other.

Some giggling young students draw Jim's attention back to the world outside the window of the coffee shop. After very close to forty five years of existence, Jim still finds threat from hearing the laughter of others. The laughter sounds off like a machine gun and in his mind, directed at him; ricocheting repetitively against his core of insecurity and self-loathing.

Maybe reality sniggers. It has been said that, *'something as small as the flutter of a butterfly's wings can ultimately cause a ty-phoon halfway around the world'.* Perhaps no end to how far we can take back the causal chain?

That very morning, a fourteen year old extrovert named Freddy Garside nearly forgot his school dinner money, only very faintly hearing his mother calling him back as he ran out of the door. Thank goodness he managed to have that appointment to extract some wax from his ears, only the previous week; squeezed in to an appointment that had been cancelled. Later that day (at 1:08pm and about an hour after our Jim arrived at Nero), Freddy's friend Barry Carter decided for the first time ever to eat his lunch on a specific bench within the local town. He was round a corner from Jim, but not much more than a hundred yards away; at this stage, less than subsidiary to our Jim.

Barry glanced up from the bench where he was eating his sandwich and thought he saw Freddy Garside approaching the taxi office. A taxi office just round the corner from the coffee shop were Jim was seated. Barry raced up behind Freddy and they playfully fought and rolled around the pavement. In their wrestling, Freddy unaware he dropped three silver coins out of his school dinner money.

Around one minute later (at 1:09pm), a tall obese man ambles along. He wears large jeans and a bright yellow tee-shirt stating 'relax, bro' in big black letters. As he reaches the taxi rank, he just catches sight the of three pieces of silver; each separated by about two feet. A discovery carried by an ambulatory quirk that this man tends to manifest. In particular, a pattern of alternating between slight upward and downward glances.

This gent's body creaks as it carefully reaches to pick up these three unexpected gifts; pocketing each one. In reaching for his new found wealth, he is slowed enough to notice and very briefly read a poster on the window of the taxi office, advertising for new drivers. He briefly glances around, slightly self-conscious that other eyes may have seen his apparent scavenging and checking the prior owner of the silver was nowhere to be seen. This slows the man's arrival in the clearing that Jim's window overlooks; yet only by maybe six or seven seconds.

The clock crawls onwards, to so nearly touching '1:10pm'. Several buildings away from Jim's window onto the world, beauty floats through the centre of the high street; close, but still out of sight. The Universe looks on as Beth approaches after many long months. Even this Universe must surely feel a wealth of emotion, as eyes long since impatient surely readied to set upon beauty in its purest form.

Jim's hungry eyes pointed wholly in her direction; yet, he does not see her. Completion not activated. As Beth passes the penultimate shop before appearing in Jim's view, the clock still arrives at 1:10pm and a tall obese man emerges in the same direction; blocking her form from Jim. A coincidence; beauty juxtaposed next to irrelevance.

Jim sees this man appear, unaware he is so rudely eclipsing Beth's form. This tall man, with the 'Relax, Bro' tee-shirt does not greatly register with Jim; there is simply a bright yellow tee-shirt and large jeans. The man unwaveringly gazes straight ahead, perpendicular to Jim's straight ahead gaze. Like a giant body guard, he shields Beth from any eye gaze coming from Jim's direction. She is fully covered.

Whilst social sensitivity typically buzzes round Jim like a cluster of angry wasps, he sees no threat. The Universe looks on, as this man unwittingly tracks Beth's movement; blocking Jim wholly from visual connection with pure beauty. Just after this man reaches half-way across Jim's world view; the Universe is witness to him slowing down ponderously, almost as if he realises the unfolding tragedy.

Of course, the Gods are intervening. They could surely never sanction such calamity; not on their watch; not on their watch! Beth will appear within Jim's vision.

Beth slips through this eclipse, appearing in her unmistakeable magnificence. Several milliseconds prior, Jim briefly gaze down at his half-eaten croissant and progresses to another bite. It crumbles onto his trousers and jumper. He meticulously brushes it away, as if readying himself for Beth.

Jim is then partially de-railed by laughter within the coffee shop. It pricks him, like a rusty pin. He turns to see two young adults insensitively laughing, in a manner as if they consider that they have discovered the answer to the meaning of life and stand on a platform above all others. Jim works hard to dilute the problem by mentally rehearsing well-worn strategies; striving to reassure himself that their laughter is not personal and they have not seen into his soul.

Jim looks up and returns to studying that which lies beyond his window. Tragically unaware; beauty has been, and fully gone. A large group of exuberant students stride down, whilst an elderly couple slowly amble up past the coffee shop. Several hours later, at 8:00pm, the coffee shop closes and Jim returns the eighty mile journey, back to his new old home. An un-eventful day passes.

Jim never knows how close he was. The Gods had casually, perhaps thoughtlessly, lit the blue touch paper which ran to-wards detonating a fulfilling future for Jim. Then, perhaps on a whim, they just snuffed it out prematurely.

The residue of a croissant stepping in between Jim and decades of relentless rapture; no crumbs of comfort. Our Jim perhaps trapped in a sliding doors moment. The higher powers allow-ing a door to close against him, forcefully trapping him for eternity and squeezing sweet potential irreversibly from his frame.

Our Jim had been flying on such a wonderful trajectory when coupling with his everything. Yet, maybe Jim's Universe not infinite? It seemed that mid-flight, his being had cataclysmic-ally struck an invisible wall, propelling him in a diametrically opposite path. He was going backwards, and perhaps begin-ning to spiral down.

Chapter 37 – More slings and arrows

Many more months run through Jim's fingers. Jim's gambling debts continue to chase him. He used to spend time talking within his counselling role. Recent months, he felt to be talking even more, but merely in attempts to fend off the clamour for him to pay money he did not have. Jim regularly making use of his mobile phone; almost exclusively in conversations with his new fiscal friends from several debt recovery organisations.

Jim has now used up nearly forty six years of his existence. Beth continues to echo within Jim's mind; surely mirroring the resonant frequency of his soul?

The days of yearning have largely passed by; hope packing up her tent and pitching somewhere unknown to Jim; leaving a messy residue of loss and regret. A body with wrinkles deepened, hair thinned, energy sapped; feeling so much further along the road to nothingness. Still, Jim manages to ache to the core with 'if only'. Still, it throbs and pulses within him.

Jim mentally cuts himself on every mirror; as it animates an implicit distinction between 'what is' and what a jaded self 'wishes was so'. Jim feels a deepening sense of hopelessness. He holds onto visions of Beth; but they ignite thoughts of *'what could have been'* and not *'what might be'.* Jim is retreating back to what was once familiar.

Then, another blow. Another tragedy. The unusual sound of the house phone ringing, chez Jim and Kath.

'Hiya, Jim speaking' Jim uttered with a tone that worked to convey casualness and contentment. Yet again, trying to portray an emotional state that was not even close to the inner reality.

'Hiya, it's Cheryl – Spider's wife' Jim heard, along with clear sobs.

'Spider has gone. He died in an accident at work' Cheryl announced.

'I am so sorry' Jim said, truly reflecting the gutted feeling within him. His being sinking down, as if Tyson Fury had landed his best punch squarely in Jim's stomach. More than a punch; surely enough to floor even much wilder men.

It turned out that Spider had been trying to do what he always did, help and support others. A huge machine had broken in the massive car making plant in which he had been working recently. In trying to be helpful, Spider had not waited for the busy designated engineers, but had gone in to try to fix it. Soon after he climbed into the jaws of this giant machine, it unexpectedly started.

Spider was crushed to death. Spider leaves behind his wife (Cheryl) and three year old twin girls. The funeral was heart wrenching for Jim, along with the many others whose lives had been touched by this Spider and his tireless altruism.

A few further weeks passed and Jim finally had the revised outcome of his disciplinary investigation from the regulatory counselling body. Various details of his experiences with Beth were already published online a few months ago, along with the *initial* outcome of: *'Mr James Butler'* receiving a *'one year suspension'* from counselling. What followed from various groups was an outcry about Jim's punishment being too lenient; ever obliging, the disciplinary panel soon upped the ante to:

'permanently struck off the register'.

How many times can the same person feel themselves licked by failure? Kath would also squeeze through the baying crowd, to swing a well timed foot at Jim's underbelly. *'What were you thinking, to do that?'* she asked, incredulous, disgusted, and all too keen to throw her two penn'orth in. Again, our Jim felt punch drunk and increasingly falling down.

Jim's limited options, or escape routes if you will, seemed to be closing down. It has once been said, *'beware the person that has nothing to lose'.* Still, Jim clung on.

Soon after the lifetime ban, Jim's curiosity took over and he explored his name on a google search. Perhaps as the good world knows, maybe google can tell us everything? Would the Butler name be in up in lights?

Jim discovered that insertion of his name into an internet search revealed a plethora of articles essentially conveying how he had abused an unnamed young patient (Beth). The eager audience could also readily glean that our Jim had been permanently struck off from the professional counselling register. No way back; a stain that apparently could never be washed away.

No sponge to easily wipe away traces of him from the world wide web. Snared; his name forever up in lights. Sweet Jesus, could he be any less credible?

Our friend google also yielding details of his sexual relationship with Beth, including that they were intimate. Moments they shared, not framed flatteringly. Words working hard to transform what was beyond beautiful into something so stained and shabby. This stung so much more than the loss of any professional credibility.

The most precious experience in our Jim's life by a distance, being re-written and trashed for all the world. For Jim, it would have been so much easier if the Gods had just killed him in whatever way was their whim. Rather this, than seeking to soil what for him had been the only thing of true magnificent beauty within a life that he construed as otherwise thoroughly rancid. Experiences with Beth that gifted a meaning for the whole of life, and yet then they wrangle and struggle to yank it from his grasp.

A further few weeks elapse, a forty six year old Jim feels he has nothing left. One day blends into another. He is unemployed and has a recurrent compulsion to just pull the bedcovers over him, to avoid the day. Jim is back surrounded by Kath's depressive world view and never far from Kath's disappointment. He has no social circle and no strong leisure interest. The former being crushed so harshly, within the car factory.

Despite the post-hoc onslaught in relation to his relationship with Beth, Jim still holds onto psychological ideas which enable him to dilute shame. He has found a way to be at least slightly more self-compassionate. Yet, whilst his psychological knowledge is vast, his bladder still remains shy and avoidant in public. He retains these toxic limits.

Jim's empty life leaves him space, which is sluggishly looking for something to fill it. His reduced shame translates into him not directing anger and disgust as much towards himself. Hence, if he does not direct such venom as unerringly to himself, then bits are starting to spill outwards. He is starting to experience more anger towards others. At this stage, perhaps just seeds, though maybe something is growing?

Chapter 38 – An apparent inertia
gives way, yielding movement.

A few further weeks on and something shifts slightly. Boredom and perhaps some 'je ne sais quoi' came together and mobilised Jim. At forty six, he was unemployed and had too much time to think.

Jim knew enough to suspect that if he could get a job of some kind, it would provide some soothing ointment which can come from distraction. This weapon of distraction would be sharpened still further if it could be meaningful distraction. Slight movement emerged.

Our Jim, still shy of the local bigots, remaining reluctant to venture out too near to his home. He decided to take a trip in his car to a town around eight miles from the local area. Jim took some job listings into a local general library and utilised the additional resource of their internet.

As Jim progressed with his job searches within the library, a middle aged-woman broke the silence by fixing on a newspaper which had been left out on a nearby table. She turned the pages without care, making noise without thought. There was no gentleness or subtlety; surely just a sense of entitlement. As if her greatness led inexorably to this being her Universe, and hers alone.

This irritant then quickly and disrespectfully threw the paper down, as if she was superior. Next, she moved gazelle like to pillage from another information source. It seemed that she indiscriminately made noise, at every opportunity. As if there was only her; perhaps philosophically solipsist or just plain common-or-garden selfish.

Like a pre-lingual child exploring items in a nursery – no need for subtlety or justification. For some reason: the unchecked curiosity which Jim found beautiful in a young innocent child, was vexatious in an aging inconsiderate hag. Jim was annoyed and close to using words to release the pressure valve.

Jim returned home early, frustrated and fed up. Reality watched on. It was clear that Jim was beginning to feel an anger towards a world outside his head; a well used handbrake straining. Something was perhaps shifting?

That evening, Jim decided to venture to a couple of pubs. He decided to take his car and drive away from the local area. Again using a formula which that horrendous night in the local White Hart Inn had forged into his spirit.

Jim reaches the Royal Oak public house; unsure what exactly had brought him here. He reaches the door alone, and a hand pushes it open. Jim enters the Royal Oak public house, noting a large crowd. None of them particularly notice our Jim. Yet once again something within him evaporates all doubt, crystallising it as pure certainty that 'they are watching me'. He can feel them watching; he can see what they are seeing. Their judgements weigh heavily on him.

Jim's body reacts, as a cat in a cage when it is prodded with a sharp stick. Aggression rears up inside him. Conflicted, wholly within. An overcontrolled specimen feeling intense emotions that it cannot understand; reflexive inhibition and pushing feelings down.

Social anxiety rears, and there are eyes all around him; each a mirror, which uneasily ratchets up self-consciousness. A deep dark part of our Jim craves to destroy every single person in this pub; perhaps only then can he possibly remove this definitive totem of his disgusting self. As the energy drains out of their eyes, surely each and every mirror to his soul shattered, blunted, and free of judgement. Jim hankering to be free, but the perspectives of live human beings lance him from all sides.

As Jim approaches the bar, the barman is waiting. As if, he knows. Our Jim clings on, struggling on this day.

'Can I help you, Sir?' the barman enquired with a perfunctory bending of his lips.

For Jim, this barman operated like a cheap second hand car salesman, trying to convince him to buy cheerfulness. His artificial tone mixed uneasily with our Jim's wounds from lifelong catastrophe. Yet, Jim felt caged by his tone; pressured by the expectancies to perpetuate this performance of politeness.

'Er, a double whiskey' Jim replied.

Prolonging the 'er' not to salute his companion uncertainty, but more to apologise to a guilt ridden core and a plethora of voices within him. Anger was bubbling in Jim, like never before. Within his inners, part of him still hung on.

Shame diluted, but part of him still told that his being had no right to feel emotion, least of all hate and anger. To hate something is often too close to guilt drenched acknowledgement of separateness and one's individuality. The whisky appeared, followed by a speedy payment.

Jim felt compelled to legitimise himself; a need to be doing, as his being is not enough. He finds himself putting coins on the side of the pool table, jiving with the *'winner stays on'* system. Soon, Jim finds himself playing against a muscular giant. The latter carrying an alpha demeanour, that speaks of a need to dominate. The game goes quickly, and ends with both parties on the black.

Our Jim shoots for a long shot on this black, which would win the game. The black wiggles mockingly in the jaws and comes to rest right over the pocket. Without mourning Jim's misfortune, this parasite ascends speedily. Like a vulture, he swoops in for an unmissable black.

Jim's disgust and anger rear again. Strange thing though, starting to buck a life-long trend of previously being directed inwards at himself. In Jim's mind, this man's sudden movement to take out the unmissable shot belies how superior this offering was, when put in the context of this inadequate specimen and the rest of his life. For Jim, his opponent had no class, no depth, and little skill. Yet the pool game did not register that, and this sat uneasily with Jim.

Jim glanced back as he walked towards a bar stool, and already someone was putting money in for another game. As our Jim reached the bar stool, just above the background noise he managed to hear the words *'You whipped his arse, Mikey'* emanating from the area of the pool table. It felt to Jim that these words were on a neon sign, for the whole pub to see.

Jim was struck by an uneasy mix of annoyance and anxiety, as he surveyed what part of him felt were a sorry crowd, gathered round the pool table. Escalating anger, lighting up specific stray thoughts, seeming to be running free and unchecked; so unusual for our Jim. He glanced at them again and instantly struck by a venomous thought, *'they run around, seized by their pathetic urges to transcend their nothingness existence; ever warming their hands around an illusion of superiority; freed by ignorance'.*

If a person seems to be reacting in a way that is out of proportion to the situation before them, then maybe they doth react to earlier elements that blighted their path. Unresolved issues were reverberating around our Jim's head, getting incrementally louder. Beginning to batter the bars that caged them; metal surely beginning to bend. The sound of groaning, almost audible; perhaps the bars close to accepting inevitability?

Anger bordering on rage, frantically scanning for a vessel into which it could be funnelled. A lifetime of holding back waste; oh the sweet relief to just discharge within a public place. Make no mistake: our Jim's thoughts were drifting back to his friends Conrad and Mick, from the White Hart Inn. Displaced demons, dragged from depths. Anger looking set to outgrow and dwarf more than a healthy portion of anxiety.

Jim remained on the bar stool for some time. As he sat doing nothing, he felt an increasingly heavier need to justify himself to the gathering within this pub. Though alongside this, increasingly conflicted.

A growing part of our Jim was feeling thoroughly sick and tired of trying to constantly please an invisible audience within his own mind; jaded of mental projections of surrounding people and their judgements, burning deep within his mind.. An audience that was so unrelenting, particularly in public. Decades of personal struggle, which was surely wholly invisible to other people and their sympathy.

Was our Jim on the precipice of a breakdown? Could he pull back? Even the great rocky cliffs that mark the boundaries of the sea are eventually changed by wave after wave after wave. Yet aside from a few spectacular weeks with Beth, Jim had largely tried to hold onto a way of living which was surely thoroughly unliveable. It seemed like each second of Jim's existence had represented yet another wave crashing heavily against his very soul.

Jim still holding tight; clinging on to a way of living that evolved early. Jim's main efforts had perhaps been directed at sustaining this type of life, at the long-term expense of himself. His existence was all that he knew and in this sense it was simply 'life' to our Jim. At least, thus far.

The loss of Beth had struck his core, largely returning him to his old groundhog day. From somewhere unbeknownst to Jim, he was beginning to feel hate and anger with a passion that dwarfed any negative emotion that had ever slipped through his overcontrolled exterior. Seconds had slipped into decades, and still the flood gates held back a volley of emotion which hammered their inner façade. But recent day, these flood gates were creaking like never before.

Amidst the inner turmoil, Jim moved calmly to the pool table. He placed a fifty pence piece on the side of the table, next to the two other coins which were already queueing for their masters. Jim then sat; watching the player that took his scalp, playing against a much older man.

The older man seems beyond retirement age; long white hair, interrupted by a very clear bald patch. His hair stood out, suggesting that a barber might blessedly release an ugly pretence; yet, each strand that was cut perhaps weakening the threads which held together a type of delusion. Perhaps sometimes it is graceful to let go, without fighting father time?

The younger man that earlier swooped in on the black against Jim remains, playing on. He is surrounded by a couple of male friends. One of the latter is draped over a very young woman, with facial features akin to a bull dog.

As the younger man bends down to take his shot, Jim is struck by his short cropped hair and the intimidating way it seems to mingle with a muscular frame which is well over six feet. He wears a tight pair of jeans and a tight sleeveless tee-shirt with

'PHIL's GYM' written across the centre. His feet are graced with black firm looking boots. Every aspect of his attire looks new, almost as if he is a man trying on a new image.

This putrid player in the sleeveless tee-shirt appears to be aged around his mid-thirties. Lines under his eyes seem to imply a wisdom and sensitivity, which is wholly inconsistent with his manner. Like an expensively wrapped gift containing thin air; perhaps not giving *'what it says on the tin'.* He move awkwardly around the pool table, fluidity lacking in these overdeveloped muscles. The play is interrupted by verbal interchange and occasional whispering between him and his crowd.

Jim can't hear everything that is said, but he feels that every utterance seems to be laced with lewdness and bigotry. The sleeveless wonder regularly accompanies his verbal offerings with a laugh which resembles an aggressive lions roar, and yet he uses his larynx to deliver it like a machine gun fiercely dispensing ammunition. The ferocity of this laughter seems to rise still further, every time an audible interchange degenerates into hushed whispers. Jim is trying to internally dodge this ammunition, but he feels distinctly uneasy.

Inside Jim, it seems that one tiny neuron has been allocated to watching this pool game; the rest fuelling a furnace which lights up his paranoia and angst. The old man seems to be concentrating hard on winning the game, but he has just missed another easy shot. This leaves his younger opponent with an open door, to finally put the game to rest.

A straight red and a black over the pocket are duly taken out, and another game goes to muscles. The disappearance of the black met with a loud, *'yesss, get in'* and more laughter. The old man leaves the scene, perhaps slightly crest fallen.

Jim afloat on an unprecedented sea of emotion; huge waves of anger and venom; striving to just swim on the spot. Decency, a barrier which had held back so much for decades; threatening to give way. An upsurge inside and a compulsion to insult Mr Muscles.

Jim more than slightly taken aback, a big part of him feeling like a spectator watching himself. At this stage, somewhat ego alien and not comfortably owned. Feeling increasing concerned that part of him would surely soon break free of his own reigns, he exited. Not waiting for the opportunity to have another game of pool.

Jim's frustration not far from spilling over into behaviour. But, a ship temporarily steadied. It would perhaps take something further to prize out the darker side of our Jim. Maybe the Gods watched on, unaware at that point what would be their whims?

Chapter 39 – A return to
the White Hart Inn

Several non-productive days pass. Jim settling into the dullest of retreats. Kath and Jim, kindred spirits. Commonalities which include: depression, avoidant tendencies, anxiety, and toilet neuroses.

Jim finds himself over-sleeping, partly using hibernation as a means of avoiding life. Television readily filling the limited moments left over. Not much left over.

As a young child, there were occasional moments when Jim's mind was filled with the antithesis of admiration for Kath's slavish adherence to passively watching the world, rather than doing and partaking. Not aware of the invisible weights of anxiety and depression, which poor Kath had to drag everywhere with her. When adulthood struck, our Jim seemed to have readily jumped into the very same furrow that Kath had rendered well trodden.

Jim's external nothingness enduring, but the recent arrival of anger remaining; close by. The television sometimes managed to pull some of Jim's attention kicking and screaming, away from negative contemplation; yet always readily yanked back. The only other intrusions to his misery landed in the form of Kath. Jim loved Kath with a loyalty, but for whatever reason the sound of her voice fell to him like a diving board. He was simply compelled to jump off, and plunge down, further into himself.

Jim spending too much time re-playing his life and his plight; stuck in some negative cognitive spirals. Wandering down the spiral stair case and plunging closer to the base of a never-ending pit, increased anguish for each level he descends. Stuck in the bin of the past; no time machine in sight.

Drawing on part of the masses of psychology he learned in his thirties, a part of Jim felt convinced that he needs to face his demons. Jim was very risk averse. However, when misery so diligently envelops, sometimes a sense of *'not much to lose'* can perhaps loiter. Largely avoiding his local community for over twenty years, he needs to walk back into the lion's den.

Hand in hand with fear, but the White Hart Inn beckons; despite or perhaps even because of the homophobic bigots that had persecuted him. Jim knows not fully why he needs to return to a such a scene, that he found so traumatic. Maybe a part of him yearns to feel something? Maybe at last, jaded by a failing strategy. After a lifetime of cowardly fleeing, he perhaps needs to stand?

The only thing that has ever really made him stand was his everything, Beth. Jim more than enjoyed those brief moments with Beth, as they fluttered by. Perhaps part of him again hankers to have rich powerful meaning; any meaning? He felt alive back then with Beth, albeit much too briefly.

Our Jim somewhere finds the courage to try to crush his form back into this ghastly hole, where his last visit concluded so tortuously. The patrons' decency towards him having started to topple like dominoes, precipitating his crest fallen escape. Over twenty years on; we go again.

The pointer on Jim's fear meter past maximum and threatening to break the instrument, he pushed the door open of the White Hart Inn. He walked to the bar, his eyes deciding to scan for Conrad and Mick. They would not have long to wait.

Amazingly, many years had passed but he eyed Conrad sat on a bar stool and Mick seated in the pool room. He also noted a couple of other characters that used to frequent this pub, back in the day. Décor had seen change within the twenty year interlude, alongside the arrival of a strong smell of pub food.

Jim sat further along the bar, trying to absorb some of his attention in the football game being shown on the 50 inch TV. Liverpool were taking on Manchester United, with the former not having won a league title since Jim last stepped foot in this den of iniquity. At first, Jim's arrival did not seem to precipitate much. Fifteen minutes in; maybe not St George slaying the dragon, but Jim did feel a slight sense of having conquered something.

Yet, as the saying goes; the fat lady had not sung. Jim saw a few congregating in the pool room, joined by Conrad. It seemed, something had pulled this Conradic shaped hunk of sleaze clean off his bar stool. Jim could hear whispers and laughter, and he was trying in vain to re-focus on the football game. Using his best psychological strategies to play whack-a-mole with a relentless paranoia that just kept re-surfacing.

Around twenty minutes passed and Jim's determination pushed him through nervous resistance, and into the same pool room. His plan was to sit in there or just have a couple of games of pool, if the opportunity presented. Maybe he wanted to break through something; maybe demonstrating lack of cowardice, or more likely just a flimsy representation. As he entered the pool room, an old dynamic replayed.

'Oooh, she's here' Conrad said in the most camp voice that he could find.

Mick was loving it, laughter fired out of him; again, like a scattergun to our Jim. Both his tormentors clearly older, yet not necessarily wiser; time had not been able to prize them apart from their bigotry. A couple of younger lads also managed to dig out a mockingly camp voice, with one of them urging, *'backs to the wall, lads'.* More laughter from this crowd.

Conrad still held on to that aggressive look, and he shone it right at our Jim; full beam. Conrad demonstrating with an ape like display that he was the alpha male; the lesser was subordinated in an instant. Yet a display of dominance so much more darker than that of the ape; Conrad, a lingual animal, surely allowing him concomitant self-consciousness and capacity for regulatory prowess?

Our Jim was hurt, as he had been previously. He felt fear rising up in him again. He did not engage, returning back to the bar area and pretending to watch the last fifteen minutes of the game. Then, on the outside, he uneventfully left the pub.

On the inside, he was breaking down. In between the White Hart Inn pub and the home he lived in with Kath, there lies a large gardened area which draws in many a dog walker. Instinct took him into there, hunkered behind a tree in the darkness. His eyes looked at 10:11pm on his illuminated digital watch, but his brain did not register this.

Jim was too upset to just return home; he needed time. Sat on wet grass behind this huge oak tree and high up in this park area, Jim started to cry. He tried to keep the noise of his sobs down, just in the very unlikely event that someone would be walking in the park so late. Always wary of other's judgements.

Jim cried more than he had ever cried within the whole of his adulthood; pain so typically only etched on the inside. The dynamics in the White Hart Inn had perhaps burst a dam, but some of the stream that followed came from a bit further upstream when he had lost his Beth. Many moments past, Jim wholly caught up in grief.

By 12:14pm, some new thoughts emerging, *'why did you even decide to kick that hornet's nest?'*, *'why didn't you fight back?'*, and *'why didn't you say something?'*. Anger arriving at this isolated festival of upset; yet much of it still turned inwards. The sensations of wet trousers united with soaked grass; a welcome distraction.

By 12:33pm (and around two and a half hours after leaving the White Hart Inn), our Jim arrives at the front door of his home. Key in the lock and door opening; a process that he had followed many hundreds of times during this lifetime. But then, something wholly new.

Kath collapsed on the floor, moving only slightly, faint groaning sound, and seeming to have tinges of a blue shade on her face. Jim instantly grabbed the house phone and requested an ambulance urgently. What followed was Kath being rushed to hospital, with Jim following behind.

Sadly, at hospital, Kath passed away. Jim sat with her, after all signs of life had exited. An immense yearning for her to open her eyes, and please give him just one last warning about what might go wrong. A concerned paramedic took Jim aside and gave him the tragic news:

> *'we did everything we could, but unfortunately your mother has died. It appears she has had a heart attack. It's so sad'.*

The paramedic observing Jim's tears, reflected *'I understand'*, whilst briefly placing an arm round his shoulders. From somewhere and by something, a final utterance was prized out of this concerned medic. It came in the form of:

> *'I am sorry for your loss. It's very sad.*
> *If we had got to her just a bit sooner, we might*

have been able to help her more'.

Kath's funeral went off uneventfully. She was cremated; hopefully at peace. Perhaps mercifully, the haunting ghost of neuroses may have been burnt irreversibly from her soul?

Our Jim reeling with the shock and the loss. Within only a few days, the shock and sense of loss had been largely elbowed out of the picture by a growing rage. Jim's vision clear; not clouded by even a bronze lining.

Initially, we very much had self-blame. Our Jim feeling furious with himself; *'if I would have come straight home, then my mum would still be alive'*. For our Jim in these early days, he was clear: *'it's all my fault – I've killed her'*.

Of course, this narrative fitted well with Jim's form, as he had made a life out of being down on himself. However, something strange and unprecedented happened. Within a meagre few days, Jim wholly let go of this self-blame. Anger towards himself, packing up it's tent and getting out of Dodge. One may wonder: this anger, where did it go?

All this blame and anger, where could it go? Under the carpet and suppressed deep down? No, not this time. In the outside bin? Nope, not a trace of it there. Outwards, wholly outwards? Yes, absolutely and *every* single drop of it. Over forty years it took, and Jim finally found the blessed switch that moves internal attribution for disaster, to an external attribution.

Something unbeknownst to us took up Jim's controller and he pulled up his initial anchors, which had been holding him so tightly adjacent to self-blame. His ship chartered a new course, joining the dots in a new way; arriving at the conclusion that this was the fault of Conrad, Mick, and their sidekicks; every single anchor on the ship then launched overboard. He was surely not moving again.

If these foul beasts had not returned to directing their homophobic bigotry in his direction, then he would surely have just
returned home. In Jim's mind, these extra couple of hours
would have undoubtedly saved his mother; a mother who
seemed to be growing more loved with each passing moment.
He knew: Conrad and Mick, by their actions, had killed his precious mother. His rage towards them was growing and close to
impressive; at this stage, Jim knew not what to do with it.

Chapter 40 – On the edge of a precipice

They had killed Kath. Loyalty roared up inside Jim. It felt that the Butler family name was on the line, along with so much more. The path of just leaving things unanswered, meandered to a never-ending corridor. Only a few steps after Kath's death, the walls closing in fast, such that nowhere left to go on this trail; reflexively and below awareness Jim branched off to avoid being wholly crushed.

Some tiny seeds had been scattered within Jim way back in his childhood and earlier adulthood, tirelessly waiting for the right moisture. The circumstances of Kath's death adding much to the soil. The blinding rays of Jim's anger now provided ample sunlight.

Yet, seeds still waiting for being cherished with the right level of moisture. The Gods perhaps wondered if the water would ever come? Perhaps a need to hold fire; maybe no need to commence construction on the ark?

Perhaps nobody yet knew that an Aussie named Mel Gibson would find himself holding an old worn watering can, which would leak so beautifully. From there, Jim clung on to a bean stalk that flew up, spiralling into the sky, and beyond the world which he had known. A fearless Jim only looking up from this skyscraper, readied for an adventure.

But the story rewinds, ever so slightly. Jim was to find this much needed moisture, with Kath's ashes still not blown far from their initial resting place. We home in; just about pre-bean stalk.

After Kath's funeral, Jim spent much of the next few weeks at home. His age crossed another barrier, reaching forty seven. Almost all his activity well captured under the headings of 'sleeping' and 'brooding'. The house increasingly smelt of old takeaways; awaiting the tender touch of a cleaner, which would never arrive. Curtains drawn not so much as part of respect for the departed, but more blocking out the world.

Jim loved Kath. Yes, her presence and manifestations often played some haunting and jarring tunes within his mind. Oft, he wanted an impenetrable cage, to block out being lanced by her presence. But, in many ways they were kindred spirits; they shared pain. Kath had inadvertently shared much, dating back to Jim's infancy.

Guided by psychology, Jim saw his mother as a person who had played the hand that she was dealt. Ironically, she was an influencer who wanted the best for Jim. Sadly the voice of this latter part was drowned out, by a plethora of competing screams within her tortured soul.

Like a molecule of cocaine mixed with a kilo of toxic contaminants; effects largely lost, but the former molecule of itself so very pure. Much more than anything, she was his mother. For our Jim, this meant something.

Jim plodded on, not working. Insufficient distraction, allowing his Achilles heel of over-thinking. A life lived, mainly inside his own head.

Yet, the Gods were witness to some shifts in Jim's precise state of mind. Fear had loosened her grip. Rage was squatting in the space that fear had previously populated so predictably. Fear struggling to squeeze back in, and perhaps neither fear nor rage currently keen to cohabit.

Psychology had diluted self-blame and introduced our Jim to self-compassion, yielding partial blocks to a lifelong habit of turning anger inwards. At last, the outside world beckoned.

When does the enemy within become the enemy without?

Other elements, added to the cauldron to increase the toxicity of this deadly potion. Jim increasingly felt that he had lost everything. Most achingly, Beth had vanished from his life. He had now lost his mother. There had been the crushing of his best friend, Spider. Not to mention the loss of: his career, his reputation, and around £50,000 on gambling.

A future that had perhaps once welcomed him, slamming a door very firmly in an overwhelmed face. Perhaps for so long weighed down by baggage from worries of loss, inexorably facilitating hesitancy and pondering within such a neurotic psyche. Jim now able to gallop, with a greater freedom? Perhaps, no obstacles to re-inventing himself.

Much of fear is often underpinned by fear of losing something. In his mind, Jim felt increasingly *a man with nothing to lose*. Strangely, the latter left him feeling liberated, unafraid, and much more powerful. A misery that mobilises, perhaps a most uncommon phenomena?

Prior meanings within his life lay in ruins. When a person feels they has lost everything and hope seems to have wandered out of sight, maybe one of two paths could be readily taken. Either spiral down in depressive lethargy, or 'act out' in ways unhindered by fear of loss. Jim's soul close to walking the latter route.

Perhaps in Jim's mind, how could the Gods take more from a man that considers he has nothing? Fear had followed Jim like a loyal canine through it all; suddenly it fled into the distance, over the hill and far away. Our, Jim neither gave chase nor grieved for its loss.

Jim, somewhat punch drunk from the smites that the Gods

had recently unleashed upon him. Rage, interspersed with some sense of emotional numbing and a sense that experientially things did not quite feel real. Our Jim, almost treading through a dream.

Jim was allowed to continue to stay in Kath's council house. Whilst Jim's debts from gambling had grown to around £50,000, he had inherited just over £60,000 from Kath. Due to so many significant non-material losses over recent years, the money felt close to insignificant to our Jim. Nevertheless with a few weeks of Kath transitioning from this world, Jim had channelled the bulk of Kath's life savings to pay off all his gambling debts. He had just over £10,000 remaining. Rest easy, he would surely find use for this residue.

During the nothingness of these early stages of Jim's post-Kath existence, there was a clear knock at the door. Three knocks, temporally close to equidistant from each other. Probably less than half a second between each knock.

Our Jim, mildly irked by the inconvenience. However, with his sense of duty rarely too far away, he was fairly quick to spring up and answer the door. Debts paid off, he was hopeful that bailiffs had been averted. Yet still Kath's son, he had some very slight foreboding.

To our Jim's surprise: it was Cheryl, the late Spider's wife. She was carrying a cardboard box. After briefly exchanging pleasantries, she mentioned that she had been sorting through Spider's things and had come across a box of DVDs.

She continued, *'I know that Archie was very fond of you. Now, I don't like films that contain violence and so I have gathered some of Archie's old DVDs together which I would not watch. I think he would want me to give these to you. He did not like wasting stuff or throwing things away'* Cheryl explained.

'*That's great, Cheryl. I appreciate your kindness*' Jim replied, taking the large cardboard box. Cheryl initiated a brief hug and Jim reciprocated; back in the days prior to any twenty first century pandemic, when such soothers were still a plenty. The hands of fate, perhaps gratefully nudged.

Chapter 41 – Film week

The box of DVDs sat for perhaps two or three days, before our Jim took it upon himself to explore the contents. Soon after he opened the box, he decided that he would try to watch each of the films. This thoroughness not just about an autistic sense of *'all or none'*. His decision was partly out of respect for his mate, Spider. Moreover, it also seemed like a way to just put something inside the vacuum which had become his life. Much of the days since Kath's death, he had mainly felt quite lifeless. Jim needed a focus and he needed a meaning.

On the Sunday evening after opening the box of DVDs, our Jim watched the film 'Gladiator', with Russel Crowe. With Jim's anger rising and a sense of vengeance not unappealing to him, something inside him connected with the film. Jim felt emotional when Maximus (Russel Crowe) delivered a line related to vengeance, and so convincingly:

> *'My name is Maximus Decimus Meridius, commander of the Armies of the North, General of the Felix Legions and loyal servant to the TRUE emperor, Marcus Aurelius.* **Father of a murdered son, husband to a murdered wife. And I will have my vengeance, in this life or the next'.**

Our Jim, losing his mother as a ripple which came from the bigotry of Conrad and Mick at the White Hart Inn; and in his mind, almost, *'son of a murdered mother'*. Maximus had lost everything, except the residual meaning of revenge. In the end, Maximus overcame the odds and killed his enemy. Bold Maximus exacted his revenge, found peace, and slipped off to an afterlife supposedly to be reunited with his murdered son and wife. For our Jim: what was there not to aspire to, in Maximus?

Maximus produced other gems which Jim clutched, such as:

'*Falling down is how we grow. Staying down is how we die*'. Perhaps as Maximus suggests, '*Death smiles at us all. All a man can do is smile back*'? Jim felt liberated by losses, with a sense that he was less scared of dying. He began to get a sense of himself growing; less shackled to fear and more galvanised by a sense of purpose.

Next, Jim watched the Film '*Heat*' with Al Pacino and Robert De Niro. He found himself admiring and rooting for the tough leader of a tight knit group of robbers, 'Neil McCauley' (Robert De Niro). Again, themes of revenge; Jim transfixed. Firstly Van Zant double-crosses Neil and is introduced to regret, just before prematurely departing this world (at Neil's hand). Some time prior to his termination, a phone call from Neil:

Neil: '*What am I doing? I'm talking to an empty telephone.....*'
Van Zant: '*I don't understand*'
Neil: '*Because there is a dead man on the other end of this fucking line*' (ends call).

Towards the end of the film, it appeared that Neil would not catch up with a man named '*Waingro*' that had tortured one of Neil's crew and informed on their planned bank robbery (resulting in members of Neil's team dying). It seemed perhaps, revenge not being served? Jim was most struck by the part right near the end of the film, when Neil was driving to the airport with the love of his life; ready to start a beautiful new life; assisted by the proceeds of his final bank robbery. As he approaches the airport, his fence and organiser (Nate) phones and tells Neil that all the arrangements are in place. Jim sat bolt upright in the armchair, listening intently to the end of the call:

Nate*: 'one other thing: you asked so I gotta tell you, the guy you wanted (Waingro) checked in to the hotel Marquis under the name Jameson, if you still give a shit which I figured you wouldn't*'

Neil: *'You figured right'*

Nate: *'So, so long brother. You take it easy. You're home free'*

Neil: *'Take it easy'*, ending the call.

Neil continues driving and battles with himself inside; perhaps an emotional desire for revenge battling a logical argument for letting go. He eventually spins the car around, drives to the hotel, takes his revenge against *'Waingro'* in a spectacular and powerful way, though ultimately pays with his life. Jim's hero in the film, not being able to let go of the need for retribution. He had a code; fear did not come close to diverting from that code.

Finally on that Sunday evening, Jim watched the film *'An Officer and A gentleman'*, with Richard Gere. A film that did not greatly touch our Jim's soul. However, he was struck with a part in the film where the drill instructor sergeant (Emil Foley) of the main character (Zachary Mayo) was threatening to throw him out of the training, and *'Mayo'* lets out an emotional primeval yelp and tearfully begs, *'don't you do it, don't, I got nowhere else to go'.*

Jim felt that to have that passion would be to feel alive and be capable of achieving special things. He wanted that passion about something, but in the absence of Beth he was struggling to conceive of a new meaning. Unbeknownst to him at this stage, he would soon taste passion, meaning, and drive. It was to become all he tasted.

Jim went to bed in the early hours of the Monday morning, and he slept well. He awoke at around 1pm, and ate breakfast. Then, our Jim stumbled on a find that accelerated his path. A path to single-handedly strive to create Armageddon, within a public house venue which he had stumbled through before.

It was a typical damp dreary Monday at 2:14pm, Jim picked the next DVD out of the cardboard box and inserted it into the DVD player. He noticed that his eyes were about to settle on 'Lethal Weapon' starring Mel Gibson and Danny Glover.

Jim quickly grabbed a coffee and rich tea biscuits from the dishevelled kitchen. Curtains were already drawn, lights turned off, and Jim settled down for another movie. A routine that had been played out so many times. Yet this gift transported his soul to the promised land.

Forty seven years stuck in this maze of life. Jim lost and fruitlessly struggling to reach the centre of the maze. Never fully reaching the treasures of shedding a hefty neurosis. Weighed down by avoidance in prior life, but still he wriggled, scrapped, and laboured. He tried so many different routes; constantly blocked. Aside from scant weeks with Beth, the maze hopelessly unsolvable. Then suddenly, this film played; a game changing wall simply fell down.

For the first time, a solution emerged. One minute feeling wholly lost and a million miles from the prize. Yet, he had been just one great wall from the centre of this maze; that wall had vanished when his eyes landed on the persona of 'Martin Riggs'.

A gift from the Gods? Perhaps finally growing jaded of his torture? Jim cared not why; he just plundered every last drop of this treasure. Merging with it; becoming one with it. A way of being that could fit into this slot called life.

What this film 'Lethal Weapon' provided was a handsome rugged hero, 'Martin Riggs' (Mel Gibson). Riggs was on the edge, suicidal. If a man is unafraid of death or loss at all, then truly what is left to fear? Even if Jim wasn't quite fully arrived at being wholly unafraid of death when the film commenced, Riggs seductively pulled him along; all the way.

Jim more than struck by Riggs' determination in the final fight scene. Over the subsequent months, our Jim surely came to increasingly feel that. Riggs occupied our Jim's vacant soul.

Riggs was fighting bad guys and injustice; Jim knew some *'bad guys'* locally. Riggs would not back down. In the end, Jim's *'Riggs'* was fired up beyond belief by revenge. In the powerless void that Jim had lived his life, revenge reached out to him with every tentacle. He was ensnared, to ensnare.

Jim marvelled at early scenes of Lethal Weapon. A drug dealer with a gun to Riggs' head and Riggs simply urging police colleagues to shoot the bad guy. A part of our Jim truly loved the bewildered look of the drug dealer.

The gun of this drug dealer had predictably rendered all an easy victim for his dominance, but his expectations underpinned by a lifetime shattered when Riggs was impervious to it. Jim knew a couple of individuals named Conrad and Mick, that had found an easy victim in him. How completely powerless they became against him, if he was not afraid of the ultimate terminus; how could they hurt him? He would surely have a surprise for his foes; never previously even close to being as keen to deliver a new present.

It hit Jim in an instant, though surely he had been led. How resistant to fear a man becomes if he is not scared of the ultimate demise, coming in the form of death. If death is not feared, then an escape route always open. The fight at the end of the film, Riggs would die rather than take the path of least resistance and let a 'bad guy' beat him.

Jim was so fed up, but his mind needed to turn it outwards.

He crystallised being grossly fed up and a conviction that he would never make his life work through conventional means; forming key elements to a most potent fuel. Jim's inners also contained ingredients which included: rage buried deep, righteousness, a meaningful cause, and now, a realisation that after forty seven years of this life, death held no fear. He drank ever drop of this cocktail.

Let go of your attachment to life and just watch fear walk off with it, hand in hand. The departure of companions that had previously been with him, at every turn. Marry that with rage at something, and we have a most meaningful and clear path. Enough, nay, more than enough for a man who had always looked inwards to focus wholly outwards; the direction of his pupils blissfully reversed in not much more than an instant.

Our Jim was fed up in the extreme, forty seven years trying to fit himself into a societal mould that his pathetic frame just could not satisfy. A switch was pressed; he had finally given up on the old life, with the old Jim. Jim as he knew it was dead; long-live Jim.

In our old Jim's mind, the time for remaining had gone; he had finally voted leave. Splinters had dug into a jaded rear after decades of suspension; nails that our Conrad and Mick had gleefully hammered into certain extremities, unendingly throbbed with ardour. Our Jim had been fixed on their cross, as his life slipped away; many a passer-by surely sneering and sniggering; perhaps powerless and pathetic to the masses. Enough; a beast inside him yanked flesh through the nails that had held him captive; like a butcher cutting dead meat. Our Jim, leapt down from his cross, joyously savouring each new breath. He would rise, in this life.

A cause resonated round his core, getting ever louder; the threads of a powerless man, finding immense power. The meaning from inflicting justice; fighting back against this world that forever smite him. A feeling of fearlessness for a man forever scared. He had his war; no need for the promise of seventy two virgins eagerly awaiting.

Jim's mind had gone round and round, looking at solutions that probably did not exist for him. Finally, he had stumbled upon the necessary mental re-route. The terminator had arrived; re-booted; ready.

Many of the masses may glance down, a perfunctory pearl of *'you should just rise above it'.* Jim had tried rising again and again, just relentlessly knocked down. He desperately craved to strike back.

Jim wanted to fully sink down to the level of an injured animal with rage, and nothing to lose. In a world rife with hypocrisy and covering up, there felt to be something pure in this expression. Our Jim felt more than justified; a crusader for himself and other downtrodden souls.

Jim's mind throbbed with intensity at the thought that he could enter the lair of Conrad and Mick, and show their solidified expectations a new reality; shattering them spectacularly. An unearthly climax; the frail unsuspecting wine glass, to the opera singer hitting top note. His bad intentions, his rage, and his intensity; his friends Conrad and Mick remained blissfully unaware of it all. They would surely just readily bully their easy victim, wholly ignorant of what was in store.

An academic might ponder Jim's watching of *'Lethal Weapon'*; where does it fit in terms of its influence of his path. *'The straw that broke the camel's back'* some may wonder? Of course, our Jim's life prior to watching that film had readied him; in many ways, so very ripe.

Barash might wisely interject with, in life my lingual friends, *'implications, like beauty or ugliness, are in the eyes of the beholder'*. Indeed so. Maybe the eyes of our Jim were increasingly pregnant for many months, pushing and straining to give birth to implications diverting our him towards revenge. But to describe the impact of this one film on our Jim as a *'straw'* seems to grossly understate its power; prior, Jim's path surely not quite pre-set?

This straw in the form of *'Martin Riggs'* did not so much break the camel's back. In a virtual instant, he obliterated the camel; surely leaving wholly in its place, the most committed beast of war. Prior to Martin Riggs; the Gods may have lazily wondered what path our Jim might follow; perhaps wondering where their whims might take him. After this one film, strings severed; surely they had no space left to ponder?

Chapter 42 – Preparations in full swing

Even before the end of watching the Lethal Weapon film, Jim's mission was taking shape and beginning to bounce around the inside of his mind. Clarity leaping forward; dissolving fully into Jim's being. Jim decided he was going to take spectacular revenge against Conrad, Mick, and anybody who chose to stand alongside them. He would kill them.

For a man whose life had been plentifully packed with half measures, it seemed he was suddenly primed to fully execute; not burdened by concerns of collateral damage. Over the next six months, Jim put his preparations into full swing. No need to feast eyes on further DVDs; the extraneous transformed into cumbersome folly.

Maybe in years to come, there would be DVDs about our Jim's path? For Jim, no such concerns. No contemplation of tangential themes; for once, not wondering about his audience's take on his actions; just burning intent. He was firmly and fantastically embedded in flow state.

The hunted becomes the hunter. Jim ached to execute; a big part of him wanted to fly immediately to the White Hart Inn and express his venom. However, he ached everywhere for *'successfully'* extinguishing his pray; he could not fail. His commitment was such that he would ensure he was readied. Too serious to risk going off half-cocked; they would see the full cock.

Jim had a timetable of readying himself within six months. It was Kath's birthday on the 23rd October (a Friday night), in just over six months. These creatures within the White Hart Inn had killed Kath, and Jim felt it fitting and respectful that they should be eliminated on that very date. Jim could execute, a few months shy of his forty eighth birthday. A magnus opus, fully crossed off before he was fifty.

Jim began eating well, rising early, and training his mind and body during each precious day. The more he put in, the more he was carried by his own momentum. From the beginning of this project: what he demonstrated to himself every day, fed into his self-concept and belief. A synergistic cycle, intensity ratcheted up at every turn.

Jim had some weights at home, which he regularly lifted. Jim supplemented this with daily trips to the gym. Bench pressing against weights that his modest arms should not move, but energised by imagining the face of his enemies one by one.

Our Jim drawing useful links in his mind: if I am not strong enough then I may be defeated, on this great eve of reckoning. Absolutely straining with every part of his body, but with the incongruity of a simultaneous smile at the thought of obliterating Conrad or Mick. One at a time though, savouring each moment.

Jim was not pushed to push by fear of injury or fear of death at the hands of his foes. His life, more than disposable. The only imperative for our Jim was obliterating the opposition. He trained to inflict damage and not to protect his life. The only tragedy of death would be that he would become devoid of the opportunity to further injure and terminate his fiendish tormentors.

Jim was more than committed. About three months into his preparations, he managed a conversation with Ted, a grossly over-sized specimen from the gym. What this man lacked in terms of deodorant, he more than made up for with his contacts. As the Gods would have it, big Teddy knew a man, that knew a man, that knew a drug dealer. He perhaps saw Jim's commitment, and revealed that he could get steroids, but only for his friends.

For the subsequent three months, Jim would have the benefit of a most potent steroid. The inconvenience of injections, but Jim would pay the price. He also had to pay the piper, which meant that just over one thousand pounds of his residual inheritance was channelled into this.

Jim's exercise regime at home was pretty fierce. Online purchases at the commence of his preparation meant that he managed to see off nearly another £1,000. It also meant that he would have the benefits of some additional weights and a 'boxing mannequin' early on. He never tired of hitting the latter, whilst imagining the scene of ploughing into his adversaries after they insulted him.

Amidst his intensity, there were times when he could virtually see Conrad or Mick's face on the boxing mannequin. He could smell their cheap aftershave. He could almost touch their over-washed hair. He felt the rage inside him, from his enemies presence. Intermittently venomously addressing these foes; far from sweet nothings.

There was a long mirror in the hall, and Jim would practice his aggressive face over and over again, along with blunt reference to what he was about to unleash. Tirelessly rehearsing an angry look and sinisterly delivered venomous words; hushed, with an intensity; directed into the mirror. The more he did it, the more he craved to repeat it.

Jim fed off his own face and felt the rage, whilst somehow simultaneously seeing his targets in another part of his mind. He felt powerful. When Jim stared into this mirror, the face staring back at him convinced him to his very core. He was more than a believer; he would execute his mission, as sure as darkness falls.

For perhaps the first time in his life, he did not feel doubt. He knew. To quote from Gladiator, *'imagine where you will be, and it will be so'*. His imagination so close to reality; no real bridge to cross.

Within the first two weeks of his preparation, Jim developed an *'exercise tape'*. The words and the beats were so carefully chosen; many signals to temporarily crank up the intensity of his punches to maximum. Our Jim's mind had travelled, reaching a destination where almost any lyric could yield a most fervent intensity; a crystallising point for his fury; a symbolic representation of his cause.

A rage switch close to jammed on; able to get riled up from the whistle of The Birdie Song right through to the words *'exterminate'* in *'Doctorin The Tardis'*. Fuel everywhere. Jim linked words and beats to destruction of his foes and revenge; images of his future work never far away. Increasingly, everything merged into a single melting pot; Jim effortlessly made it fit. All pointing in the same direction; cyclical incrementation in intensity at every turn; an irreversible inevitability surely leading to but one crescendo?

Jim shadow boxed every day, in front of the mirror. He coupled the latter with regular punching of the *'boxing punch dummy'*. He felt intensity oozing through every element of his being. Adrenaline fuelling ever increasing hand speed. He felt as if his punches could detach the heads of his enemies; repeatedly lifted by toppling the boxing mannequin.

Jim attained a uniform for his role. He would be wholly in black; straight legged dark jeans, black tee-shirt, and a long flat leather coat which reached to below his knees. Think Morpheus, from the Matrix.

With Jim's nervous energy driving his metabolism, he retained a relatively thin frame which reached upwards of six feet and three inches. With the work outs and the steroids, he was starting to fill out and gain muscular bulk at an impressive rate. He regularly checked out his reflection; he had mission, momentum, and meaning; along with a new pasture devoid of fear. Surely, unstoppable?

Chapter 43 – Jim decides to collaborate with a couple of friends

Jim clearly catapulted on a trajectory; set to ultimately enter the White Hart Inn, and take on several bigots. Specifically, a group which will likely consist of Conrad, Mick, any additional bigots attached to them, and any stray have-a-go heroes that may just seek to thwart him. Whilst Jim felt inside that his rage and his willingness to use whatever was to hand would carry him over the finish line, he knew he could not leave anything to chance.

Potentially, four or more against one would not be the most favourable situation. The completion of his work was non-negotiable; failure to fully execute was infinitely more bothersome to Jim than the possibility of his own death. The flavour of the unfolding could not be left as a hostage to fortune.

How could Jim solve this brain-teaser? Like a high powered computer running through every iteration; Jim's drive indefatigable, in running through possibilities and permutations. He could isolate his enemies one-by-one? This was not wholly unappealing to Jim, as it allowed savouring the process more fully.

Jim could place a bomb in the White Hart Inn? Effective in one sense. However, our Jim wanted to see himself as a righteous equaliser. Collateral damage if necessary, but not by design. His conscience was better than this.

It did not take Jim's mind long, to magic up the solution. He would enter the White Hart Inn with two friends. How can a man with no remaining close friends be convinced that two others would commit to such a path?

A riddle, indeed. However, these two friends would not be

fleshy or fickle. Yet, they would surely serve him.

Jim decided that his friends on this adventure would need to be two guns; if one jammed, he had the other. As luck would have it, our Jim had his old work diary from when he was a counsellor. He had the names and mobile telephone numbers of the clients whom he came across through the probation service, due to their criminal escapades.

Jim knew that his plan could get scuppered if the person he contacted had become fully reformed. What if the counselling he provided had actually helped these criminals to mend their ways? What if they were singing and dancing to a socially acceptable tune? Maybe even informing on those that stray from lawful paths? He could not even allow his mind to over-think such a horrific possibility, partly as it could scupper the execution of his grand plans.

Jim knew he had to tread very carefully. He decided to start with the character Martin Mansell. Martin had never strayed far from the path of deviating, in order to access funds. Jim uncertain whether Martin had survived the attentions of the vicious gang that were pursuing him, back when they had last spoke. Nevertheless, Jim picked up his mobile, adjusted the settings to 'callers number withheld', and took the plunge.

After five rings, the ringing ceased. Jim's hopes lifted. But then, a young female voice. It turned out that Martin had been sent to prison for six months for shoplifting, in the context of the catalogue of earlier offending. The steaks that got away, on this occasion.

Martin's girlfriend was answering his phone and could take a message. She was quite flirtatious on the phone. Jim already had an image of her in his mind, woven gleefully from Martin's colourful descriptions.

Rest assured though, Jim would definitely be reluctant to visit the flat. Martin, he recalled only too well, as a man very well versed in the honey trap. Jim felt unable to progress through this avenue. Yet the *'terminator'* not dissuaded from his goal; his mind re-strategizing in the face of any set-back. *'One mission, that's all he knows'*, *'that's all he does'*, and surely *'he won't stop'*?

Chapter 44 – When one door closes?

Martin's incarceration was very inconvenient to Jim; a dependable psychopath, perhaps a rare treasure? Jim decided to just return to his prior work diary, and work further down the list of potential criminals. They needed to fit two main criteria, firstly *'unlikely to snitch'* and secondly *'may be able to attain guns'*. Just over three months till the big day and Jim was down to number four on this initial list of ten names; time was ticking.

Number four was a gentleman named *'Fergus'*. Fergus was essentially a very posh creature that was aged in his early forties. He was breath-takingly articulate, often using words which had our Jim later reaching for the nearest dictionary. Fergus had a keen interest in the arts and various aspects of culture. His verbal output would often fit snugly within the common rooms of most University Faculties.

Fergus was average height, neat short brown hair, muscular and wiry in physique. Several years ago, Fergus had become a fourth Dan blackbelt in Tae Kwon Do. He had intense brown eyes. He always seemed groomed within an inch of his life and smelling of meticulously selected and carefully applied scents.

Fergus often wore a waste coat, expensive shirt, and very smart trousers. Perhaps most notably, his shoes. My goodness, those black shoes. They were polished beyond the pleasure of the most fussy army sergeant major.

More than once, the faint smell of shoe polish broke through the designated scents. In the absence of a mirror, these shoes would surely offer shiny reflection. He topped off his look with a full length black Crombie, which unbeknownst to our Jim was jaw-droppingly expensive.

From the counselling sessions which Jim provided to Fergus, he was struck by how meticulous Fergus was in his planning and organisation. Conscientious and thorough, to his very core. It had quickly become clear to Jim that in a criminal sense, Fergus was an all-round fixer.

People came to Fergus when they had problems, grievances, or had been threatened. Fergus dealt with the problems of family and friends with a conspicuous benevolence; nothing was too much trouble. Indeed, at times, Fergus was perhaps even over-zealous in his endeavour.

Fergus was a man that manifested exceptional manners, etiquette and politeness. He expected the same from others; probably implicitly demanding it. If they fell sufficiently short of what Fergus deemed proper, then it would outrage a sense of entitlement within him. Do not doubt for a second that Fergus had morals and principles; they were set in stone within his being.

Generally, Fergus had a refined delicately presented exterior, alongside a gentle manner and an adherence to social niceties and etiquette. What was most striking about Fergus was that this latter presentation and manner could change to a diametric opposite, with lightning speed. Jim and Fergus' decent rapport did not seem to have appreciably exited, at any point in the ten sessions they shared together. However, staying onside with Fergus required a careful balancing act; as if traversing the high wire.

Charm could turn to venom, if Fergus perceived that he had been slighted or wronged. In particular, Fergus was most triggered by *'perceived disrespect'*. That said, *'perceived unfairness'* was not too far behind. Fergus regularly used phrases such as, *'I could not leave that, it needed a conversation'*.

Through Jim's diligent explorations in their counselling sessions, he found that Fergus' euphemistically described *'conversations'* often involved smashing through someone's large lounge window, entering the house with colleagues through this newly formed entrance, and beating the life out of a targeted occupant. Surely, more than a great advert for double or even triple glazing? Fergus and his colleagues seemingly always keen to protect themselves from the chill, steadfastly remaining in their balaclavas throughout such *'conversations'.* At best, the targeted occupant's life was likely temporarily hanging by a thread, post-Fergus.

In the absence of Jim's gentle but relentless pursuit of meanings, Fergus would have likely not gone beyond the general descriptor of *'conversations'.* Often, not a word was spoken in these 'conversations'! Maybe as Tony Robbins suggests, body language more powerful than words; and Fergus certainly had his own brand of *'body language'.*

Perhaps, Fergus a believer in the old adage that actions speak louder than words? At times, under-stated in his words. Yet, when he deemed it necessary and proportionate, Fergus would not perpetuate the same folly with his actions.

Fergus had a wholly innocuous appearance and demeanour, which sat incongruously with repeated realities in his life; thereby serving as a most convincing camouflage. Rest assured; when wronged, our Fergus had a vicious streak. He once spoke to Jim about having stabbed several people in the buttocks over the years. Fergus laughed slightly when he recalled the noise that such victims apparently made when blade meets buttocks, describing it as a high pitched squeal not wholly dissimilar to a pig.

Aside from an isolated case of mistaken identity, Fergus wholly steadfast in his sense that his actions are always justified; no space left for remorse. The only time when Fergus' due diligence erred was when an innocent look-alike of a specific target was beaten to a pulp and restricted to hobbling with a permanent limp. Yet, it was the principled Fergus who waited the several months for this victim to be discharged from hospital and arranged for the injured party to receive flowers and an envelope with several thousand pounds in it.

Then, there was the informant who had inadvertently misled Fergus by assuring him that the look-alike was the target. When this same informant became aware of Fergus' wrath at their mistake, some believe they moved to an unknown location at the other side of the country. Certainly, they have not been seen or heard of since.

Fergus is thorough, organised, and professional; always prepared to address difficult tasks. Like a vet that needs to release a tortured animal that can't be saved, freeing it from the grips of never ending misery and pain. Like a nurse tasked with mercifully turning off the life support. Fergus was clear in his mind, he clinically carried out what needed to be done; with precision, diligence, and efficiency. Pride flowed from this, with Fergus looking down on the approach of most criminals as essentially 'amateur hour'.

What Fergus gave out, surely fed back nicely into his self-esteem. Fergus was an example of someone who had suffered maltreatment and felt powerless in childhood. The deficiency of power in the early years perhaps leading to an insatiable hunger for the same within the adulthood? Maybe, as Einstein suggests, *'for every action, there is a reaction'.* Gary Zukav in borrowing and extending from an Isaac Newton quote suggests:

'for every action, there is an equal and opposite reaction.

You receive from the world what you give to the world'.

Jim's mind had moved. Minds may differ about whether the latter part of the quote is best termed as helpful *or* flowery poppycock? For Jim, the latter and he did not want to be hand-cuffed by it. Too jaded to sit worshipping the wrong reciproca-tor? The world as the sheriff, dishing out Karma?

Jim jaded of the charlatan Karma, playing Lady Bountiful. How long do we passively sit back in our armchair turning the other cheek, waiting endlessly for this lazy specimen to play her hand? A growing part of Jim yearned to snatch the Sheriffs badge from an inefficient Karma; no longer waiting around.

How would it be to not wait for Karma to pop out of the never ending pipework, with turns at every turn? Just as his grand-mother Norma, firing slaps at a scared Phillip Holbrooke who ripped his coat; Jim increasingly felt it was time to become the new Sheriff in this town. In his mind, he had already collected the badge.

Certainly, for Fergus and increasingly for our Jim, maybe they were bent on giving back what the world had already given to them? No longer waiting for the world's tardy benevolence. Grasping bulls by horns, and striking back with hell's fury. Part of them deadened by a world that they no longer wor-shipped; not giving it the power to decide what they deserved; taking control, and giving back to the world what it deserved?

Back when Jim was providing counselling to Fergus, the latter did briefly infiltrate our Jim's being. Post-session and around a couple of years earlier, Jim found himself parking *legally* on a public road and adjacent to a specific house. Our Jim just needed to nip out to buy a loaf and some milk, from a nearby shop. As he exited the car, a similar aged man aggressively walked towards our Jim from the adjacent house. A Jim that had not fully shaken off the session with Fergus, that very same day.

'You can't park there, mate. It's right outside my house. We park here' the man instructed, clearly looking to dominate.

Anger rose within Jim; the bits of Fergus still inside him took over. *'So, which house do you live in?'* Jim asked, in a manly tone whilst stretching his height and his width as far as they could go. As he had already seen this man walk along a specific driveway, it seemed a rhetorical question?

'That one' the man said, vaguely signalling and perhaps picking up Jim's sinister tone. This home owner had sought to bully an 'unknown', whilst simultaneously revealing his dwelling. Jim tilted his head slightly in the direction of the man's house, eyes slightly widened, and asked *'that house?'.*

'Yes' the man replied, beginning to lose some of his aggression.

Jim gave the most menacing slow nod accompanied by slightly pursed lips and completed with a pregnant pause; as if a plan was hatching in his mind.

'OK' Jim said with a firm, calm sense of certainty, raising his head slightly on delivery. As if he had found a solution to something, Fergus still rising up, inside him. *'OK'* he repeated, building up the suspense.

The man intently waiting to hear, sensing what wasn't spoken. Jim had sought to leave a trail of crumbs, leading his opponent towards a sense of vulnerability. The power dynamic had shifted.

'Listen mate' Jim said, *'I am going to get a loaf and some milk and I will be gone in less than ten minutes'*

'OK', the man said, *'as long as you don't leave it there'.*

Jim met the latter face-saving finale from his audience, with a look. An intense brooding look bordering on a stare; feeling power pulsing through his every nerve and sinew. Too subtle to call, but too clear to miss.

It had put the wind up his newly made acquaintance. Perhaps the initial aggressor rendered to re-think, what had probably previously become a reflexive demonstration of his power and dominance to a plethora of unknowns. The man returned to his house, perhaps primed to ponder the next few times he heard a stray noise in the early hours.

Jim collected the items he needed. Our Jim felt powerful, because Fergus had shown him that he had choices. Attitudes are infectious, particularly when they tickle a need. But back then when our Jim worked as a counsellor, there was a handbrake never fully lowered. He used to feel that he had things to lose.

Fast-forward to our current forty seven year old Jim; something had more than shifted. Jim felt that Fergus had certain qualities. Hence, on this day, he decided that he might be able to achieve the necessary weapons through this avenue. Jim phoned Fergus; hoping he would be remembered fondly from their sessions.

Jim was hoping for a productive chat, rather than a *'conversation'.* Three rings, and Fergus picked up. They spoke like old friends, initially checking thoroughly on each other's welfare. Jim felt he could probably trust Fergus.

'I need to ask you a favour Fergus, in confidence. I have a big problem and I am hoping that you might be able to help me. Can we meet for a coffee?' Jim asked.

'*It would be a pleasure, I will do everything I can to help you*' Fergus said convincingly.

Jim was not being calculated and cunning in his interaction with Fergus. His presentation was pretty pure. He desperately needed help and his offering of respect to Fergus was not feigned. Of course, fear and respect are often bed partners; when fear jumps in bed, respect often finds an irresistible urge to snuggle in beside it. Jim was wary not to incur the wrath of Fergus.

Whilst Jim did not fully know it, the best way to get Fergus on-side was to both show him respect and play out dynamics where Fergus feels powerful. Fergus felt respected because Jim was clearly trusting him with a secret and asking for his help. He also felt powerful, as he was being put in a position where he could choose to assist the flailing Jimbo.

As is not unusual with the human condition, Fergus liked to have the sense that he was making a difference. Fergus once shared with Jim that one of his favourite films was '*It's a Wonderful Life*' with James Stewart. Sentimental, maybe. But our Fergus: a man who felt the need to make a difference, surely so?

The other aspect of Fergus which Jim suspected but did not know with certainty was that Fergus was absolutely committed to being truthful and genuine. He expected it of others, as well. For Fergus: stabbing a man in the buttocks or beating a man to a pulp was a reasonable and moral response to disrespect. However, lying was simply immoral and unacceptable. Jim had stumbled on a man that would perhaps rather die, than rat him out. Fergus definitely had principles and he had a code, though not fully mainstream.

Long story short: Fergus produced. He acquired for Jim, the

following: two Glock pistols, several boxes of ammunition, and a Keris Dagger. It only set our Jim back £7,200, leaving him just under £1,000 left out of Kath's savings. In his mind, he had used the money very wisely. He could not let Kath's death go unanswered; it was a matter of loyalty and respect.

Whilst Jim did not give Fergus all the specific details of his plans, he told him of the history with his targets and his plan. Fergus, more than on board. He offered to lend his hand and muster up a carefully chosen crew, free of charge. He also offered Jim some of the many samurai swords that he had adorning various walls, within his Northern mansion.

Jim managed to walk the tightrope of not getting Fergus more involved, whilst simultaneously verbally showering him with massive respect and gratitude. He also dangled the juicy morsel of: *'if I'm stuck, I will definitely come to you for help, as long as it would not be a burden'.* Fergus was quick to re-assure.

'No burden at all mate. Just great to catch up and I wish you all the best. Let me know if there is anything else I can do'.

'Thanks, Fergus' Jim replied.

'I am rooting for you' Fergus declared. He accompanied the declaration with that intense, piercing, unwavering eye contact; eyes perhaps given extra sparkle by the deeds of his history. In conventional prison, the most dangerous offenders are typically assigned *'Category A'* status. Fergus typically camouflaged his spikes so well, but surely his *'Cat A stare'* was a *'tell'*. Jim was energised; maybe we are who we associate with, perhaps particularly if we crave it to be so.

Fergus continued, *'Society should not have to tolerate such bigots. Moreover, their tone towards you, it insults you and your family'.* Fergus was an unparalleled orator, his emphases and his use of pauses were such that there was so much power in his spoken words. He paused, for dramatic effect, eye contact boring deep into Jim's soul, intensity of verbal tone turned up slightly, *'It cannot go unanswered'*. The odour of Fergus's aftershave looked on, yet somehow becoming fused with the experience.

'Make sure you punish em, mate. Make sure you punish them properly' Fergus urged. Every fibre of Fergus's body joined in unison, resonating wholly with the message; his being, willing Jim towards completion. In contrast to Jim's father Patrick's urgings just before that infamous egg and spoon race when Jim was nine, Fergus' words connected with hurricane force; surely propelling Jim to the undoing of his foes? More nudges not needed; the reels behind Jim's eyes broken and fixed on the winning line; yet, still Jim drank in everything that Fergus presented.

There followed a man hug, and they went their separate ways. Mission accomplished. Jim and *'his little friends'* ready. Three months to go and plenty of time to practice using the weapons. Jim felt some fulfilment and satisfaction. His plans were moving, as they should be; with an inevitability.

When he returned home, Jim put some of the songs on that fired up his anger and venom. Images, smells, and sounds of his targets; never far away. His mind could feel punches landing on their faces. Internal representations of his foes within his mind, jumping out; demanding to be struck down.

That evening, Jim discovered a new song, which he felt could almost have been written for him. In particular, Jim liked the brooding intensity of Leonard Cohen's, *'First We Take Manhattan'*. Quite soon and over the coming weeks, Jim heard and sang slightly different lyrics. Never previously singing with such a passion; owning every syllable; drawing on the karaoke instrumental version; completing it; again and again and again; ratcheting up the fevered frenzy inside, in an ever in-creasing *spiral:*

'*They sentenced me to 20 years of torture*
For trying to change the system from within
I'm coming now, I'm coming to reward them
First the explosion of resistance, then we obliterate the White
Hart Inn

....

I'm guided by a signal in the heavens (Guided, guided)
I'm guided by this pulsing, round my skin (I am guided by)
I'm guided by the beauty of my weapons (Ooh, ooh)
First, we hold position, then we take the White Hart Inn

....

I'd really like to stand against you, dickheads
I despise your body and your spirit and your clothes
But you see that figure moving through your venue
You're clueless, You're Clueless, You're Clueless, I am going
to win

....

Ah, you loved me as a loser, unaware I will soon win,
You know the way to stop me, but you don't have the discip-
line
How many nights I prayed for this, to let my work begin'
First we take their fucking hearts out, then we take the White
Hart Inn

....

I don't like your big-o-ter-y, mister
And I don't like this stress that's kept me thin
I don't like what happened to my mother
First we crush out retribution, then we take the White Hart
Inn

....

I'd really like to stand against you, dickheads
I despise your body and your spirit and your clothes
But you see that figure moving through your venue
You're clueless, You're Clueless, You're Clueless, I am going
to win

....

And I thank God for those items that Fergus sent me, ha ha
ha ha
I mean, the keris dagger and the glocks that complete my skin,

I've practiced every night, now I'm ready,
First we blow their brains out, then we take the White Hart
Inn

....

Remember me, I'm the easy victim,
Remember me, I brought your laughter in,
Well it's mother's anniversary and everybody's wounded,
First we take our birth right, then we take the White Hart
Inn

....

In his own mind, Jim had clarity. Yet, the fervour was escalating to unprecedented levels, with new highs emerging every day. At such an elevated spot, Jim's grasp on reality was becoming ever tenuous; his position likely difficult for those outside his head to connect with.

For Jim, maybe simply submerging into a new, exciting, and different reality? Enthusiastically grazing in a land which lay well outside the gates that encased the masses. It more than made sense in Jim's head; meaning, not madness?

Chapter 45 – The date of Kath's birthday
arrives and Jim reaches fever pitch

Jim did not let up in his preparations. He remembered a sweet conversation with his friend Spider, a couple of years prior. When he became the father to twin girls, Spider shared:

> 'there was a moment when I wondered because there is two of them, would my love be shared and halved. It bothered me. But I needn't have worried. Somehow my love inside me just doubled such that they both had the same love as if there had been one – I found more love'.

Jim found himself with a similar dilemma, because he had at least two targets (Conrad and Mick). He may have worried ,'would my hatred, rage, and venom be split between them and halved?'. Like Spider's experience with his twins, Jim need not have worried.

As Jim built up to the day of reckoning, his hatred, rage and venom more than doubled. Quadrupling and more; seemingly, doubling every day. He made his whole life about this; nothing spared from being put into these spittoon-like vessels.

If Jim could have inserted this mind-set into that little eleven year old Jim that wandered onto the playing fields to meet his foe Southworth, then a different fate. Jim would have obliterated young Derek, and with enough left over to wipe every trace of the remaining Southworth DNA from our fair planet. Still, grist to the mill; a failure that perhaps ultimately galvanised Jim's will.

Jim had enjoyed the journey over the recent months. He had felt so alive and so very present; as if a switch had been pressed and caught fast, at the commence of this operation. Joyous eyes, looking outwards.

Now, Jim had arrived late in the afternoon on the date of Kath's birthday. He felt a throbbing intensity in his mind. It throbbed with hatred and bile bubbling within; all towards his targets. It also throbbed gleefully with a sense of powerfulness and certainty. Everything simplified; to a man plagued with seeing the grey areas throughout his life, suddenly it was all clear; black and white; simply, good versus evil.

Jim's mind knew that he was unstoppable, on his path to the executions. Part of Jim wanted to re-live what was about to unfold, over and over again. A bigger part of Jim's inners just purely wanted to release everything, ejaculating every last drop of his emotions to render a most rare form of relief. He wanted completion.

Jim was rarely departing from a *'flow state'*. He was at one with his every action, which took him towards inevitability. Jim felt energised; adrenaline pumping round his arms, multiplying their strength.

All Jim's senses were heightened, to an impossible level. Only a couple of hours before he enters the White Hart Inn. Even the name of this pub now serves as a trigger for an intense and severe rage, shooting around his whole frame; pinging from nerve to sinew in an escalating upward spiral. He had found a switch in his mind that unleashed demons, ready on his whim to adminster justice. Possessed, he willed them in; with all that he was.

Skinner said that when we say that a person has learned, we are essentially saying that the person is a changed organism. The hills and valleys of Jim's avoidant adulthood had generally led to stagnation. Yet somehow, recent history had seen an organism radically transformed. Or, just maybe, the cross hares were closely trained on a wretched destiny long before Jim even reached adulthood?

Who is working Jim's controller. Is it the Gods? Is it the constellation of unchosen causal forces, in Skinner's environmental determinism? Fellow thinkers, please do not be kidded. Jim was awake; he was purposeful; he had enough intent for an army. Rest assured, he was calling the shots.

Never in Jim's whole existence had he ever felt to be holding more tightly the steering wheel that controlled his direction. That said, he was so well trained and programmed over the recent months, at this stage, he could surely take his hands off the wheel and wear a blindfold and yet still career towards the same beautiful crescendo. Parts of Jim's mind becomes a blur, more and more on autopilot.

Jim had worked for six months, tirelessly, to create this flow state. Not some meagre cold calculated psychopath. Our Jim was infused with so much more emotional fuel; strengthening his every sinew, sharpening his determination at every turn.

An autistic black and white clarity. His mental apparatus and his whole being, moving in one direction; totally cocooned by an impenetrable shield. The latter, not allowing even a particle of *what might others think?* or *possible negative consequences* to come close to penetrating this barrier. Intensity in his mind simply blocked this mental drivel, purity of flow such that all else vanished; it did not exist.

Every single element of his being 'knew' the path; he did not need recourse to any external audience, either internally in his mind or externally. Every proton, neutron, and electron within his form was dancing wholly in synchrony; never a stray foot out of place. He was the whole audience, with mental representations of others disapproval beyond evaporated by the heat of his intensity. For once on his path, it was only the mission; Jim, the instrument.

Surely, this was not madness? If it was madness, then Jim wanted to bathe in it; to play with it and harness everything from it. He wanted its energy to infuse his being. Not chased by this madness. He rode it all the way to the White Hart Inn; like one of Tolkien's Orcs, riding a rampant Warg.

Jim arrived at the White Hart Inn, it was around 8pm on the date of Kath's birthday. Jim, like a young excited child opening his main present at Christmas. He could not wait to break through, into the venue. Any nervousness, just adding further drops to a vast vessel of venom. Our Jim entered at 8:02pm. The air that was all around our Jim, took a deep breath.

Chapter 46 - Our Jim, back again
in the White Hart Inn

Jim entered uneventfully. Met with the sound of the chatter coming from some of the several dozen customers. Surrounded fully by smells of beer, aftershave, and perfume. Jim acquires a drink and takes a seat.

Our Jim sits, with the irrelevant prop of an apple juice. Keen that none of his senses will be subdued or compromised in any way by alcohol; he wants to feel it all; a need for perfect execution; he knows, it's coming. No sign of his targets yet, but he gratefully spends a few moments just drinking it all in.

Jim's resolve and confidence wholly unshakeable. He remained unmoved by the music, ill-befitting of the cut of his jib on this fine evening. Obviously a big fan of 'The Weather Girls' within the fold, with 'It's Raining Men' blaring out several times within Jim's initial hour.

No matter. Today, it felt more than good. Alone, very occasionally nodding his head very slightly, a face with an irony certainty. Never had confidence and power fired through his whole being like this before. A mountain of PCP could surely have just looked on, envious of what his mind could conjure. He felt beyond great, with an explosion of genuine expression, teetering on the cusp. The present and future separated by a cigarette paper; already ejaculatory inevitability long since reached?

Every single insult, hardship, and frustration coming together. As if he'd put them into a piggy bank for each and every miserable moment of existence; saving day after day. Today, he was cashing it all out; no worries about an overspend, paying all his real debts in what society may see as one fell swoop.

Is it partly the fervour of what Cus D'Amato suggested might flow from a 'scared fighter turned brave'? At a deeper and more technically precise level, this deadly intensity flows from 'the person that makes the journey from recurrent intense fear of something to genuine fearlessness of that same thing'. The transformation prone to render its subject, infused and animated; tonight, Jim did not need to look for a cause.

Jim's early journey in life, stagnantly fixed at 'what if'. A dominating sense of dread and a seemingly immovable barrier. Recently, so much movement; arriving at a devil-may-care 'so what if'; dread's departure. It felt beautiful. For Jim, the beauty and the passion were multiplied because he felt that he was righteous and justified. Meaning propelled Jim forward, like a V8 engine; with fury a most potent fuel.

Tonight, Jim is but a tool. His death would be a tragedy for one reason only in his mind, namely he could no longer torture and pummel the effigies of his rage. He was merely an instrument to administer consequences to his old friends Conrad and Mick.

Jim's attachment to his own plight beyond the latter was akin to the concerns that a gun or knife would have going into battle. The weapons have an endowed purpose; pain cannot be inflicted upon them. Jim was purely a weapon. No fear; such simplicity.

The time reached 8:43pm. Briefly, a very small part of Jim wondered if the co-stars in his show were simply going to be a no-show on this evening? It did not take the Universe long to answer his question.

Within a matter a few minutes, a most annoying group arrived at this public house. Their entry unmistakeable, and they were four in number. Laughing with an urgency, as if to communicate how big and in control they were. We had Conrad, Mick, and two younger males.

Swept in; all egos, bravado, and 'we are here'. Their foul smell not appeased by a drop of self-awareness. Like a baby needs their mother's breast; every fibre of them yearned to feast upon an easy victim, such that they could demonstrate their superiority. My friends, be careful what you wish for.

The two younger specimens were seen to masticate enthusiastically, as if to demonstrate that they were here to dominate. Their movements, over vigorous; akin to an ill synchronised war dance. Entitlement, sickeningly dripping off all four.

Jim heard Conrad and a younger member of the pack calling each other 'puff'. Jim felt instant shuddering echoes of the homophobic bigotry that had long-since been thrown at him, from Conrad and Mick. He did not need this trigger; a finger already close to reaching for another.

Jim was past caring and he had six bullets which he would readily magic into their destiny. For Jim, these four specimens were not cockroaches. If he saw a cockroach scuttling along the floor, he would not be inspired to liberate a single bullet.

The fully loaded guns in each of Jim's pocket made him feel powerful. He could administer a deeper justice that chance just did not take care of. He yearned to cause what he construed was justified consequences, raining down upon worthy vessels.

Jim's life was irrelevant to him, aside from being a necessary vehicle for the execution of his newly found mission. The gun was his friend because it could damage, where damage was sorely needed. Loss, simply not an option. He could not be dominated here. Jim shuddered at the way that him coming second would be absorbed into the meaning networks of this plague of sub-faecal wannabees.

The crowd went to the pool room, just at the side of the entrance. Jim followed soon after, residual apple juice in hand. Already a raging furnace inside; our Jim, craving for smoke. He sat as an isolated figure, subtending this army of four. To Jim's inner delight, the latter expressed. They replayed similar tunes, to the ones that used to so haunt him.

'Oooh, the pretty boy has joined us' Conrad said in his most camp voice. The aggressive stare from Conrad was not far behind. He looked at Jim sternly; as if our Jim was much less than the worst foul dropping, that had ever graced the underbelly of his adidas soul. Jim, himself readied to more than tread upon these foul residues.

Mick gave a whispered 'backs to the wall, lads', followed by a chorus of laughter from the rest of the pack. Jim was pleased that each of the quartet vented at least some mocking homophobic bigotry in his direction. Though to be truthful, tonight he did not need more reasons.

Jim sat for a few moments, on the outside relatively unmoved. Then, he began the departure from the expectations of his audience. This luvvie, about to rip up the well-worn 'easy victim script' that had so entertained this crowd in the past.

Now, Jim was not acting. The gist roared within him, but the precise specific manifestations were ad lib. For once, Jim did not hold the reigns on his eye contact particularly tight. Fairly quickly, one of this set began to demonstrate alpha status. It was the biggest and most objectionably loud creature within this collection. In particular, we had a Conrad: erect and stretching his height as far he could.

Jim's enemy cut an aggressive figure. This Conrad enquired at our Jim, *'what the fuck are you looking at? You got a problem, you knob?'* His pack readying themselves, aside him.

Jim stood. Without trying, he mustered the most disrespectful and aggressive tone to loudly advise the Conrad, *'Hey needle dick, why don't you shut the fuck up – you gormless dick head'*. Adrenaline rising in Jim, but it felt good.

Briefly, you could have heard the proverbial pin drop. Jim's hand was in his coat pocket, his finger was on the trigger, destiny was oriented as it should be. Strangely, the four initially took a couple of steps back into the newly created silence. The absence of doubt and fear in Jim's tone seemed to sit uneasily with them.

Yet, the inertia of the majority was transient. Jim suspected that their maths ability might lead them to realise that the number four was quite a bit bigger than one; he yearned for them to find their way to this insight. The recipient of Jim's guidance (Conrad) came back with, *'let's go outside and settle this, you knob – you're dead'*.

Jim's retort was fired quickly, *'why the fuck would I go outside with you four little boys. Jog on, dick head'* and the seething disrespect was not effortful. Those moments in front of the mirrors, not wasted. The foursome then began to very gently and almost imperceptibly close the distance, aggression etched on their faces. For Jim, their position was how dare you interfere with the farce of our ego-driven display of male dominance?

Just before Conrad was within an arm length, Jim ejected his revenge in advance. 'Bang'. With bullet coalesced, this big guy takes an extra step back. Conrad's second attempt to reach Jim was met with the same outcome. 'Bang'. That made two bullets, in the centre of his chest.

Conrad fell to the ground. His face blended shock, hurt, and weakness. The events had fallen well outside the bounds of his expectations. The red liquid within him, began to emerge. It came toward Jim, like a red carpet. He had briefly introduced the first casualty to regret, as a brief stage on a short journey which terminated at nothingness.

Jim felt an intravenous infusion of power and well-being. In that moment, he felt complete. However, there was still work to do.

The three other viral residue looked as if their mental constructs about the world were shattering. It had been four against one. Yet such a gold-plated opportunity to bully, abuse, and dominate had suddenly become a platform for their exit and ultimate defeat. Their terror tasting like honey, to Jim's palet.

With intense fear; one often finds people responding with: fight, flight, or freeze. Jim's gun was long since revealed and he quickly executed number two in the head. That was a reasonably definitive goodbye, to one of the two new members of the flock.

Then, big teethed Mick began to beg for his life, *'I have got kids, pleeeeease'*. Mick, no longer blissfully surfing on a communal tidal wave of venom towards Jim. No longer asking for bystanders to hold his chain, such that he could pummel this *'easy victim'*. Tonight, his lips had found new words.

'Look at me' Jim demanded. Mick nervously oriented his eye gaze towards Jim. Jim did not need to utter another word. A bullet to the centre of Mick's chest said absolutely everything else that Jim felt needed to be said. He watched the lights go

out in Mick's eyes, in an instant.

Number four had ducked down to nearly below table level and he was intently moving towards the door. Jim caught up to him when his hand was on the door. The target looked round, pale. He seemed to be donning the look of a man whose arrogance had drained out of him.

Jim fired the first shot to his back and in the stillness, he gave him a conclusion in the occipital lobe. No longer visions through this foe's ugly eyes; an occipital projector screen surely damaged beyond repair. Simultaneously, the glare from another light deep in Jim's mind dimmed, to the point it was close to switched off. Foul mental representations of his foes opinions of him, at once less bright.

Jim felt power and a type of euphoric relief, beyond the aftermath of any prior ejections. Yet, he had still not shed all his anger; still much in the tank. An animated and vigorous Jim went to each of the four and vigorously kicked them and announced to them all, 'fuck you'; managing to put immense feeling into the verbalisations.

Jim had also paid good money for his Keris dagger. Hence, the latter was unshackled from its sheath; allowing it a brief run out, on these lifeless corpses. Finally, he took his other gun out and treated each to an extra shot; belt and braces, as ever. They were perhaps convenient effigies of each and every blow and insult that this world had inflicted upon him.

Jim reloaded again, amidst the relative silence. At this point, it was as if his other senses suddenly returned. He detected the music from the jukebox, which by some wierd and fitting coincidence was playing the end of Queen's 'another one bites the dust'. The song filling the silence, almost as if to signal the approval of the Gods. Aromatic molecules of after-shave, perfume, and stale beer, suddenly starting to slowly circulate again; after surely being temporaily rendered frozen and open-mouthed by the intensity of what they had just witnessed.

Jim floated towards the door, departing this magnificence. Only at this point, he became aware of the residue of his audience, in the form of other people cowering within the pub. As it happened, over half of the pub had taken cover behind the bar.

The inertia of what remained of his audience surely much more than bystander effect. Jim walked out. He felt: immense, powerful, righteous, and justified. Echoes of something primeval shifted deep inside him, as an opioid to his soul.

In his own way; Jim felt to have changed the world. It seemed he had taken control. His emotions told him that in one solitary evening, he had shed the shackles of his whole pathetic powerless history.

Sometimes change occurs through verbal avenues which are oriented at changing thoughts and feelings. However; do not be fooled – the most powerful and deep change come when we behave differently. Jim was changed more in those moments than could be achieved by countless hours of therapy, re-framing, or working on thoughts. In his mind, he felt to have severed a festering feast of ugly growths, which prior time had relentlessly nurtured.

Chapter 47 – The genie is out of the bottle

After he left the White Hart Inn, Jim walked calmly to the nearby taxi rank. He utilised a taxi to a neighbouring town. He felt to have passed the point of *'no return'* or perhaps he simply sensed that he was on a roll. Maybe Kath's death had sealed his fate, long before this particular evening?

His mother's departure was probably a *'line in the sand'* moment. It represented the point when he perhaps finally shook off an inner preoccupation with Kath's judgements of him; an unforgiving cerebrally-based tail that had remained close behind all his prior movements. On her way out, Kath had passed on-coming traffic hurtling towards her son, in the form of a liberating anonymity perhaps akin to Plato's ring of Gyges? Finally, at least partially shielded from the glare of his mother's eyes.

Juxtaposed next to his firm approach to the opposition in the White Hart Inn, he was extremely polite in his communication with the taxi driver. Even ultimately over-generous with his tip, as if expecting that money may not serve him for much longer. Liberated, relaxed, unburdened, and more carefree.

Jim's troubled mind had evolved; busy dichotomizing members of the human species as either good or monstrously bad. After assigning the label, our Jim was a kind of Robin Hood figure. Not quite robbing the rich and giving to the poor. But rather, the path which a prolonged onslaught of life had revealed to him involved killing the 'bad' and being kind to the 'good'.

As the path lit up for him, Jim felt to have developed an amazing ability to unerringly categorise people in an instant. Suddenly, he could just spontaneously sense the flavour of a person's inner being. He felt righteous, strong, and the sheriff of all he encountered.

Playing the role of a powerless and pathetic man for so long. It was as if Jim had woke up, with a realisation that he had been so ill-fittingly typecast. He demanded a new role. If the world did not offer it, then he would simply seize it from its stingy grasp.

Jim's painfully resolute patience had finally worn out, and something had broken deep within him. In this moment, he felt unusually present. His focus aimed outwards, without the usual burden of that inward self-consciousness.

A couple of miles into the journey in the taxi, he caught site of a back street pub within a notoriously rough area. He settled on this. On entering, he purchased a large whiskey, carrying it to a quiet table next to the wall.

Today, Jim moved with a confidence. It was as if he was giving off some primeval vibe or pheromone. Jim found flirtatious eyes looking in his direction. Today, no threat from eye gaze.

Generally, the people busied themselves as usual, within this watering hole. All wholly unaware of what was in their midst. Jim quiet; still camouflaged.

Stealthily crouching, coiled, and committedly ready to pounce. To these uninitiated eyes, they were faced with something innocuous; he had a similar frame to an easy victim that he used to know. Tonight, Jim loved his billing as non-threatening, allowing cocky nastiness to flow to him so unencumbered.

The mental representations in his head had spent a lifetime telling him he fell short, by a vast gulf. Now, he knew something which the petty minds around him could not see. He did not fall short of others' judgements of him as powerless; he was so far beyond it. For once, he knew.

If the whim took him, Jim would demonstrate. He observed and monitored, unsure at this stage who were his targets and who were his audience. His emotions and his residual adrenaline settled, and no strong targets emerged. The rest of the night passed; even Jim's eager mind unable to find a target to be affronted by.

On this specific evening, Jim's forged master key not snugly fitting in the slot which this rough pub offered. It did not turn. A hair trigger trap, simply not activated by the players in this back street stage.

Jim returned home. He felt that he probably had the best night sleep that he had enjoyed in the life that had fallen before. It would take several months and much therapy for this euphoria to more fully settle, allowing a deeper insight and some threads of intermittent remorse.

For now, Jim basked in a sense of being powerful. In his mind: not just chasing off the demons of Conrad and Mick that had pursued him for over twenty years; not just briefly introducing such demons to regret; but obliterating them. No longer haunted by their mental representation, within his mind. They were owned, such that Jim clawed back some augmented ownership of his own mind. Jim, almost reborn.

It has been said that time and experience alter all perspectives, which often they do. But as Jim replayed this night in his head in the coming days, he was adamant in his position. Therapy would have to work hard to prise this perspective from his grasp.

One might wonder, if Jim was offered a time machine to travel back just before the murders, would he take it? Right now, he was complete; no need. Yet, rest assured: any early yearning to travel back to the point in time when these four would-be alpha males walked into the pub, likely born of a wish to re-live a similar script; for our Jim, no need for re-writes.

Early on, he suspected that he would never get bored of mentally re-living this night. In the idiosyncratic time-woven meaning networks which decorated the inners of Jim's brain, it seemed to symbolise something cardinally precious. In the early weeks, Jim was lifted.

Jim grinned when mentally replaying his exterminations. Not wistfully yearning to yank out those homicidal moments from the bin of the past. For now, this Cheshire cat wholly puffed up by the completion of his work.

In Jim's mind; he became a man that had not just paid lip service to *'how dare you?'*, he had more than lived it. Striking out against homophobes, and standing for all that have been blighted and haunted by their venom; striking out against those that would abuse what they saw as the 'easy victim'; striking out against those that would trample on the 'Butler' name and indeed, our 'Jim Butler'. Taking a stand for others; taking a stand for himself.

A sense of righteousness; a sense of 'I'll show you an easy victim'. The enemies' delusional sense of the power differential, absolutely exploded into a million insignificant specks. Jim positively leaping out from the long-worn disguise of an 'easy victim'.

A disguise Jim had worn so often and so plausibly, such that for most of his life he had more than convinced himself of its veracity. The bully's conviction that they are safely thrashing an easy victim, so suddenly yanked from their sweaty palms. Their rigid mental constructs disintegrating around them in an instant, leaving naked panic and terror, alongside pathetic attempts to cover up.

Travelling back from whence we came, to the beginning of our journey: maybe a riddle has been ever-present walking alongside us? Perhaps early threads of this biography lead many to suspect that murder was on the menu, yet maybe a trap in the form of *'parking curiosity too soon'*. A *'grotesque'* crime surely completed, but our Jim: the perpetrator or the victim?

Do we just stare hard at the cross-section in time which simply holds these fatal moments in the White Hart Inn? Or, perhaps, do we dare to offer more than a glance at the landscape that fell before this isolated momentary epoch, in Jim's prior journey? Perhaps, as Robbins might recount, 'we get what we focus on'?

Arriving here, curiosity might also ask: has a black and white resolution been bestowed? Are we looking inwards or outwards? Is a covering blanket on *'truth'* fully lifted? The Gods, perhaps reticent to permit such an unveiling.

Chapter 48 – Arrest and Broadmoor

In the context of Jim's long-standing avoidance of his local area, people in the White Hart Inn were initially unable to give police a definitive name or address for Jim. The day after the night before, Jim was able to awaken gently and within his own bed. However, by early afternoon, the long arm of the law sought to wrap itself around him.

Jim's endeavours of the previous night had built up an appetite within him. He decided to walk through his local community and attain fish and chips, from the local takeaway. He found himself, walking taller; head pointing slightly upward. Our Jim with a bit of a swagger, attention focussed outwards; within that same local community that he cowered from, for many a year. Much had changed, within the internal landscape between Jim's ears.

Jim smelt the fallout of the prior evening's demonstration. It was as if he knew that his local audience may be rendered somewhat taciturn in his presence; less keen to try to cast him as an easy victim. Perhaps inspired to be more frozen around his soul, stifling much; more hushed whispers than outright aggression.

Jim walked into the takeaway with a newly found confidence; many a demon chased away. Purchases in hand, Jim began his walk back home. Yet, he would never get to enjoy this specific delectable sustenance.

Almost as soon as he had exited the takeaway, the world changed again. A muscular man that appeared to be just walking past him, pounced and firmly grabbed his arm. Within a split second, another man had grabbed his other arm.

The grip of these new companions was steely tight. Jim

quickly realised that these individuals were police officers. The fight was perhaps squeezed out of our Jim by a plethora of variables, including: the catharsis of the previous night, the absence of a grudge, and the intensity of the grip. Handcuffs applied within a couple of seconds. The tallest of these two muscular specimens sought out Jim's eyes, and uttered:

> *'I am arresting you on suspicion of murder, contrary to common law. You do not have to say anything. But it may harm your defence if you do not mention when questioned something which you later rely on in court. Anything you do say may be given in evidence'.*

Jim was walked towards a nearby car. Blessedly, he no longer had a Kath to worry about. No pets to concern him. He had spectacularly completed his life's mission, and nobody could take that away.

At times, what a person says and does can neither be unsaid nor undone. On this day, Jim wished it no other way. He had avoided the ignominy of a failure to complete; wrongs had been made right, it felt.

As he travelled in the back of the unmarked police car, there was much to be grateful for. Jim felt better than a man should feel, in the shoes he currently donned within this world. His mind's analytical core gratefully jarred out of synch, by the jolt from events in his outer world.

The buzz of a reality which surrounded him, for once sufficiently loud to drown out the twitters of deeper thoughts. Thinking dimmed, our Jim did not begin to join the dots and develop reasons for feelings. He just felt.

There were variables which made his current plight less of an affront to his soul. Firstly, he had already reached 'mission complete', serving the causes which underpinned it. Secondly, a cathartic crescendo still infusing his system. Like a hit, not yet fully worn off.

Thirdly, our Jim had perhaps become closer to those characters in the movies that he had idealised; a lethal weapon or Jim Riggs-Butler if you will. A Jim whose life had been marked by caring too much about what others thought, committing an act that society would surely judge and condemn; there seemed irony that Jim's sense of self-acceptance had positively swelled. Self-analysis blissfully quietened.

Fourthly and perhaps most blissfully, Jim had managed to let his life slip down to a mere existence. He was not being yanked uncomfortably from commitment, success, extraneous bothersome meaning, or nirvana. Our Jim had evolved a platform which gave him close to the perfect launch pad for his new life. Failure and loss had loosened many a chain, allowing him to move forward along this new path unburdened.

On arriving at the police cell, Jim went through the standard protocol. He had occasionally seen arrested people being processed in the recently released *'fly-on-the-wall'* documentary *'24 hours in police custody'*. Yet to live this reality, animated the knowledge; with more of a feeling element in attendance.

Soon after landing in the custody suite, Jim was stripped of all his possessions and given a forensic suit to wear. It felt that along with his clothes, Jim's old identity was being stripped away. For a Jim that had spent most of his life drenched in self-hatred, this vague sense of self did not provide a particularly challenging contrast.

Many years ago, a prior colleague (Carlos) whom Jim met in his counselling job had told him that his tough life changed for the better when he had a re-birthing ceremony set up by a Shaman, as part of *'shadow work'*. In this re-birthing cere-mony Carlos was required to strip naked, buried wholly in sand at a nearby beach by the Shaman and five assistants, asked to hold his breath for around thirty seconds and then break out. When Carlos broke out from the sand, the seven of them danced round a camp fire, with Carolos remaining naked; vari-ous chants were sang by the group, and he was allegedly 're-born'. Symbolically, Carlos had shed all his old identity and his old wounds; he could re-start.

The Shaman also unburdened Carlos of just over £3,000; for Carlos, the best money he had ever spent. Whilst the police were not dancing round, chanting and celebrating Jim's re-birth; they were perhaps providing Jim with a similar service. His identity slipping, and he felt himself being eased into a wholly new chapter.

Jim was permitted to wear his trainers, but the laces were re-moved from them. Jim wondered if this was because it would be harder for him to *'do a runner'*. However, in fact, this was underpinned by striving to ensure that detainees did not use their laces as a ligature, to self-hang.

Over the following days, Jim was interviewed several times. In life he was skilled at being evasive, but not overtly dishonest. His deception in life was usually more about omission or se-lectivity driven by self-hatred, rather than speaking untruths. Within the interviews, he openly admitted everything.

The awkwardness arose when the police interviewers asked him *'why?'*. More specifically, *'why did you do it?'*. In Jim's head it made complete sense. Yet, when he had to try to explain it to this audience, they typically looked back somewhat blank.

Jim found it hard to put into words the *'why'* in a way that sat-isfied this audience and even perhaps such that he felt wholly satisfied. For one of the first times in his pitiful existence, Jim had acted on that fateful night in the White Hart Inn based on emotions more than thoughts. The *'reasons'* lay mainly in his feelings and not in logical thought.

It made absolute sense, on a level of feelings. On that rampage, Jim had *felt* the reasons, with a spectacular magnificence of emotional congruity between feelings and action. His emotions jaded and annoyed with their expression being distorted and diluted over many a year; perhaps dragging logical thought wholly off the steering wheel and flinging it into the back. From there, emotion gripped the wheel tightly; driving actions and thoughts, all the way. On the outside, Jim had let go.

Complexities aside, our Jim would not be released back into the community in the interim between being arrested and being place at Broadmoor nearly five months later. We return to our beginning; a forty eight year old Jim landing at Broadmoor Special Hospital. For Jim, perhaps a new start?

Chapter 49 – Why did our Jim choose to murder and was justice served?

Jim remained present, in his bedroom within the first day of his stay within Broadmoor. Several months earlier: snatched and arrested, unable to eat his fish and chips. Now, settled in his new home and readied to gleefully consume the latter, as part of this first tea time offering. Things perhaps being set right; historical insults perhaps corrected?

Towards the onset of our journey, Jim's new acquaintance (David) asked, *'What is your story mate?'* We took this as the starting line, on a journey to perhaps unpack *'why did our Jim choose to murder?'*. The direction of eye gaze may be everything; *'inwards or outwards?'*. Yet, perhaps flimsy dichotomies.

Elsewhere on this very day, the pontifications continue. Back in the same Hampwood Hall College that Jim overlearned many rudiments of psychology, a lecturer gives his version of lifting a lid on the mystery of Jim's crimes. The latter lecturer, Mr Ed Ingle, comes in the form of an uknempt, flamboyant, and gangly looking character. He specialises in psychology and philosophy, but leans more towards the latter.

Mr Ingle stands in front of a group of seated eager fresh-faced students. Most of his flock are aware of his excess penchant for consciousness altering drugs and his eccentricity. A legend amongst many students, partly because of his intermittent substance-induced unravelling within local student bars. Over the years, many a drama within a cohort from a fellow student allegedly having carnal adventures with his substance drenched form.

Today, he stands, ready to deliver. Ingle intermittently shakes his head, as his wiry long hair recurrently covers his eye; still an occasional black strand interrupts the grey mass. Facial twitches accompany him, with strong suspicion that they are the physiological trappings of a man that has consistently hammered a range of substances within his adulthood. He rocks and moves, like an overexcited child with ant in his pants. Undoubtedly, a man who loves an audience, particularly when they include pretty young women. He begins what is close to a soliloquy:

"I am guessing that many of you guys have seen some of the coverage of the crimes of Jim Butler within the news?". Ingle notices some of the head nods and verbal confirmations from the group, and continues:

"OK, for those of you that don't know, that same Jim Butler was once a student at Hampwood Hall. Yes, he may well have sat in the same seat that you are settled in, within this very lecture. In fact, maybe we have the next Jim Butler with us right here, today?".

Mr Ingle moves his face close to a young female sat at the front; alongside piercing eye contact, he offers, *"Is it you?".* The young lady clearly quite uncomfortable, but Ingle is rewarded by a few titters amongst his audience.

"So, why did Jim Butler commit murder? Was justice served? Let me help you with this guys. Sometimes our emotion is the shepherd and the sheep-dog, firmly leading our thoughts and behaviour. Errr, You know, perhaps only tenuous post-hoc rationalizations can look to prop up the notion that we are primarily logically driven? Often, Language perversely fuels the covering up of our main drivers; drivers which can surely precipitate extreme behaviour in us all.

So, it's kinda the case that all the magic of language does not truly alter nature, maybe just fencing with it. Nature's work goes on, whether we see her or not"

Ingle pulls a strange face, and extends a 'hmmmmm' for an eternity. In the context of his notorious exploits, this leads more than one of his audience to wonder if his brain has finally and spectacularly seized up. Then, he re-boots and offers:

"The wisdom of the monkeys untamed? Hear no evil, see no evil, speak no evil; what is this word 'evil'?" He raises his voice and draw out the word evil. Quite possibly, in some psychiatric ward somewhere, a poor soul may be being sectioned for similarly abstract ramblings. Ingle continues:

"You seeee. Just maybe, errr, one will find more truth in the being of an animal without language, than in the pomp and ceremony of the modern human animal. Language so readily dresses up and obscures what is naked and true. To borrow from recent parlance, if we put lipstick on a pig then maybe it is still a pig". Ingle intermittently markedly alters his voice in what seems like an almost comical way. This latter quirk perhaps aimed to keep the attention of the nearby ears or maybe just some leakage from poorly masked insanity. Either way, it did not render his ramblings more comprehensible to this somewhat dumbstruck congregation.

Undeterred by many a blank expression and insight likely long since dissolved, Ingle continued:

"The emotional underpinning of the human species and its behaviour may well be neither bad or good. Prior to being mixed with language, maybe they just are.

It's kinds like a sort of lingual tide crashing against what is, leaving reality covered by its froth; camouflaging not just to others, but to thine self. You see - our Jim; not transcending the human condition and perhaps not as wierd as we would like to think. Ok, errrr, to simplify, surely he had an emotional side, perhaps Steve

Peters' chimp, if you will; centred in a certain part of the brain. He also has a logical side, and a conscience. But, who operated the controls?

Ingle left a slight gap after the latter question, which contrasted sharply with his general rat-a-tat-tat approach to his monologues, words fired out with less gaps than one would detect in the output of an overzealous AK-47. Very animated throughout, three standard deviations above the mean in terms of vigorous arm movement. Two youths towards the back were fighting to hold up jaded eyelids, but Ingle continued:

"OK, lets put aside any unspecified idiosyncratic 'force of a situation' perhaps more than lighting the blue touch paper. Right, Now, let us imagine, the chimp of his brain as a huge ogre of a father. This ogre not formed purely from Jim's prior environment in this life, but combined with Jim's genetic heritage; stretching back for a myriad of generations before our Jim arrived, virtually ad infinitum.

On that special night at the White Hart Inn, this huge emotional ogre of a father standing beside logic and conscience as small and meek as a young toddler. In essence, the latter just simply dwarfed by the former. Now, how harsh should we treat this toddler for not neutralising great ogre? Errrr, You know, How guilty this toddler, for grasping the words that his father demanded he grasp?

"JUSTICE?" In vocalising this latter word, Ingle's voice rose 30 decibels higher than it had previously achieved. Sufficiently loud that the whole of his audience were awake, at least for a few moments. He continued, again:

"Maybe brain surgery, remove the 'guilty' part of the brain and strip its freedom? Leave the bulk - the bystander - left untouched, the freedom to die an innocent man? Or, errrr, maybe lump them

together and punish them both, 'joint enterprise'?

"It's kinda like, errr, for the masses, we see the product and we infer a wholehearted choice. Like a lake suffering the insult of some wanton boy flinging a stone upon it; fucking choosing to ripple because it is angry at such insult?" Ingle swearing and very opinionated for not the first time in his career.

"Now, I am also guessing that Jim struck lucky by getting into a Special Hospital, rather than a prison" Ingle speculated. He expanded:

"Errr, I would suspect that Jim was blessed with a very shrewd solicitor and a less than shrewd psychiatric expert. That is, errrrr, Jim's fate may have been befriended by a rather shoddy and superficial psychiatric analysis.

I am informed that the psychiatric analysis in this case was done by an elderly and very respected psychiatrist, WHO SHALL RE-MAIN NAMELESS. Yes, errrrr, this psychiatrist probably did what many do, and over-focussed on the crime, concluding that Jim's horrendous crimes and lack of remorse could only mean 'psychopathy'. Because, hhhh mmmm, only a psychopath would commit such a horrendous crime - NEVER YOU OR ME! Convenient self-soothing BS'

Still, Jim could take cover under the blanket of personality disorder. And, hey presto, he was not the common or garden criminal. And, errrrr, you know, Jim, supposedly a mentally disordered offender. Errrr, I think, probably prison and not hospital awaits for over 90% of 'Jimmies' with similar levels of forces working their controller to complete similar criminal legacies. But no such harsh landing for our Jim.

Yet, errrr, as I have suggested to you before: in it its simplest form, it is an unremarkable reality. Perhaps merely: sometimes we get more than we deserve; sometimes we get less than we deserve; sometimes we get what we deserve. An inexorable fabric of life, guys. You need to accept it, to survive in this world. Maybe to be outraged with such mirrors a man outraged at the sun rising; errrr, outraged at gravity pulling; and errrrr, outraged at leaves choosing to blow in the wind".

Mr Ingle's audience remained silent. On some level, Mr Ingle felt that the quicker he spoke and the more cryptic he got, the more intelligent he seemed. He was in full flow, and so he continued, but with the volume turned up on the cryptic nob

"Yes, so, guys, In the states, maybe a different fate. Perhaps pragmatism and maybe even what is self-serving will truly Trump meritocracy; an executioners axe lying in wait. Errrrrrrm, yes, Einstein spoke clearly, re-iterating 'you can't get an ought from an is'. But, errrrr, pragmatism requires a different type of justification, perhaps not so burdened with the weight of meritocracy and fairness. We need blame; yet goodness gracious don't forget to fucking dress it up so very nicely with language; never too many fucking layers?"

Mr Ingle glanced around the room, his pressure of speech finally gave way to a brief silence. As if, he was marvelling at his brilliance and waiting for a round of applause. A class dumbstruck. His silence, came back at him; as if echoing from the walls. He twitched nervously, and then concluded:

"Suuuperr. I've been Ed Ingle, You've been great. Same time, next week guys...."

Movement of chairs and various conversations started up, with several students stretching as if having only very recently awoken. Almost imperceptibly, a verbalisation came from the back of the room *"deeeeep, man"*. Another voice could be heard faintly whispering, *"did you understand any of that?"*. As a small lad exited the room, he offered, *"I think I need to smoke some of what he's been on to see any sense in that"*.

Intermittent laughter from several students, as they left the scene. Yet not troubling Mr Ingle, as he was intensely engaged with a young maiden that was describing how she was struggling with the essay assigment which had been set several weeks earlier. Ultimately, the 'me too movement' would stir a hornets nest of stubborn complaints against Mr Ingle; his career would consequently be ended prematurely, or for some perhaps, not a minute too soon.

Chapter 50 - The Broadmoor years –
Part 1: Adaptation to a new world

Jim's Broadmoor was akin to a new womb, for his blunted form. He was symbiotically connected to his host, through an invisible umbilical cord. Food, warmth, and comfort; flowing to him effortlessly from within this cocoon. No sharp edges; responsibility and expectation lifted.

Within our Jim's Broadmoor, there were around 350 male patients and about 150 female patients. Unbeknownst to Jim, he is treading boards that were once graced by the now departed soul of an infamous twin. The latter gangster launched into the surrounding abode by concluding a Cornell, in a public house.

Perhaps our late gangster, a troubled mind seeking solutions; rumoured unrepentant. Reportedly a feeling of release, triggered in the Blind Beggar Pub; with every single neural synapse drenched simultaneously with a heaven-sent cocktail of unearthly jubilation; allegedly humbling lingual expression, words not close. If fate had allowed their paths to cross, then our Jim would have perhaps connected well, with this Don Ron. Yet for some opaque reason, death had barged Ron off this path of potential union.

For a very short while, Jim would also pass by the live remaining embers of a notorious Yorkshireman. The latter meandering his way to Broadmoor through executing what he purported to have believed to have been 'God's work'. Our Jim met Peter on his third day, as his bloated figure approached one of the nurses to access his beard clipper. After a couple of brief conversations, neither gravitated towards the other. A debate raged about whether Peter was 'mad' or 'bad'. Just after Jim's arrival, Peter was transferred to prison. To the Aussie's, this man's handle may be a complement; yet in these shores, a meaning drenched with abhorrence. PS: Ripper.

On occasion decades before Jim's arrival, the latter very briefly breathed the same Broadmoor air as a sweet benevolent English Rose. The latter passing through as a Princess on the lesser known visit, briefly opening wings for the afflicted; blooming in March. Many a rose perhaps charmed up, by what some may see as foul, rotting, and with an ill stench. Many echoes, so gently whispering from these tall Victorian walls.

Jim did make some friends within Broadmoor, perhaps at fates hand. He met a similar aged man named Mark. Mark was five foot six inches, painfully thin, sporting shoulder length ginger hair, and an unfathomably long nose. His past was muddied with the murder of someone close.

Mark had carried through the latter deed at a tender age, in his mid-twenties. It turned out that Mark and Jim had trod on some very similar stepping stones in life. When feeling psychological comfortable, both Mark and Jim oozed kindness and sensitivity. Their early adulthood was particularly blighted by intense social self-consciousness and self-dislike; more than shy. In the community, they had both at times felt lanced by a mother's eye.

Mark and Jim shared interests in some similar areas of psychology and the philosophy of determinism, which had helped a part of them fly. They had both taken an interest in the work of B. F. Skinner and both had been struck by work questioning the notion of 'free will'. Within Broadmoor, Mark and Jim would share many a stimulating conversation.

All four fair hands had more than brushed many a page within books about notorious murderers. In both beings, more than small doses of autism and anxiety had been thrown into the melting pot. Within the murky depths and below consciousness, these tortured souls had been floundering for an escape hatch. Constantly feeling to fail at the game which their society provided; for one night, they would spectacularly shift to a different game, with different rules; their rules. From there, both launched into their current abode.

Yet, Mark and Jim far from twins. Many very similar stepping stones, but they crossed the river to murderous shores at different points on the stream. On the big night, our Jim premeditated for months, fixed on his targets, and bent wholly on revenge. For Mark, not so targeted. Perhaps, a drowning man flailing, swept downstream and using an innocent as a float; a victim struck so fiercely.

Nearly three decades earlier, a twenty five year old Mark moving uneasily. An act bubbling increasingly closer to the surface, but even the day before his becoming, unaware of where he was crossing to. Both Mark and Jim believed themselves conscious and awake, at the time of perpetration. But Mark's 'consciousness' seeing invisible enemies everywhere, projections of froth within his own mind; surely not Jim?

Mark, just lashing out blindly, hoping he would finish his unknown torturer. The irony that he would finish an undeserving easy victim; yet actions unleashing by-products everywhere, which ultimately ganged up and persuaded the haunting hounds that hunted him to largely stand down. Certain eyes instantly shut down on the outside, and at least dimmed within his own mind.

Within Broadmoor, the eyes that watched Mark within his own head grew more compassionate and less fierce. Another overlap, with our Jim's journey. Mark engaged for hour after hour in therapy; acquiring not just a crush on his therapist, but soothing ointment for his mind. Below his awareness, his inners had craved being re-parented; a re-birth, the ultimate escape from himself.

Our Jim also took on therapy. For the first time in his life, he gradually opened up about his feelings and his neuroses. When you have kept things to yourself that you feel ashamed of for many decades and have a psyche like our Jim, opening up for the first time can feel like a lower level of the Aron Lee Ralston dilemma. How do we begin?

In essence, Aron's arm was trapped by a boulder and he had to gradually saw off his own arm with a dull pocket knife, in order to survive. Believing severing will benefit through survival; yet, as soon as the knife touches the skin, it is surely excruciatingly difficult to bear down. At times, Jim had words on the tip of his tongue, but could not produce them. Eventually, he did. It changed him; demon's dwarfed.

As the therapist did not recoil with disgust when Jim opened up, something shifted inside Jim. He began to feel greater levels of self-acceptance and self-compassion; more than psychology alone could offer him. He reached a point at which he could allow himself to be flawed and imperfect, without self-hatred. Jim also found that the things that had bounced around purely inside the darkness of his own mind could be let out into the light, such that he could begin to view them with a more adaptive and less torturous clarity.

Jim began taking anti-depressant medication, which also dampened down his anxiety. Within his mind: this stilled, cooled, and purified what had been a boiling cess pit of neurochemical waste. Issues which pre-medication would create an intensity of fear of nine out of ten (where 0 is complete relaxation, and 10 is the most scared that our Jim had ever been), suddenly began to only generate maybe a three or four. Upsetting issues which pre-medication preoccupied our Jim for several hours and unrelentingly bounced round his head, were let go in minutes or even seconds.

Of course, our Jim's emotion could still be triggered; not wholly impervious to perceived disrespect, criticism, or unfairness. Yet, the spark rarely got beyond a few short lived small flames. Never reaching close to the roaring furnace that burned inside of him for many decades, ultimately gutting the inners of the White Hart Inn.

Within a mere twelve months of being at Broadmoor; our Jim was sufficiently improved that he needed a purpose. He had space for new things. For the first time: his wish for a focus was driven not so much by a need for distraction from what was inside him, but rather a more peaceful space of having free resources to invest. He probably did not so much need a focus, but rather he wanted it. Wholly unaccustomed to this platform.

Jim found a focus in two forms. Firstly, he provided warmth, support, and counselling to other patients. There were around five hundred patients within Broadmoor; men and women. Jim did not discriminate, he mixed with the patients and sought to sooth minds wherever he went. He knew about mental anguish; this knowing was part of the cocktail which propelled him to this kindness.

Secondly, Jim took to working and saving. Within prison and high security hospitals, you can do a job and earn around £15 per week, which can then be used at a shop which sells various items (e.g., toiletries, cigarettes, sweets, etc.,). Jim worked very hard, often doing two or three jobs every day; mainly cleaning jobs and occasional gardening jobs. Alongside this, he saved conscientiously. As a result of his endeavour, he was saving just over a thousand pounds each year, within his personal Special Hospital Bank Account.

Most of the patients within Broadmoor at that time did not save. Hence, often many could not afford the items they wished to purchase at the Hospital shop. Jim would intermittently help such people out, by buying items for them. This left him feeling that he was making a difference and it further increased his popularity.

In addition, news of his savings spread amongst the patient's and his money afforded him respect. He quickly became known as the patient within the hospital that had the most savings. He was akin to the Roman Abramovich figure, amidst this social group. Whilst within the confines of this environment, his standing paralleling a billionaire dotted in the society outside the walls. He sensed, an awareness and perhaps even a slight awe of him from other patients. Our Jim did not dislike this status.

Chapter 51 - The Broadmoor Years – Part 2: A special visit

Nudged by appreciable repetition, time ticked quickly. Three years, two months, and five days into his stay and our Jim had not been greeted with a single visitor, aside from what we could term *'professional visits'*. The latter essentially being a visitation by a person that is seeing Jim as part of their duties, within a specific professional role.

The reality of no informal visits was about to change. Jim observed nurse Frank Jenkins coming towards him. Frank, a small and very plump man that was never far from a smile. Frank was carrying some papers.

'Hiya Jim, how's it going?' Frank asked.

'Yes, pretty good, Frank. How are you?' Jim asked.

'Fair to middling young man, fair to middling' Frank replied casually.

'I am told that someone has made a request for a social visit, to come and see you?' Frank stated.

Jim was slightly unsettled by the potential thrust of an intrusion from an outside world in which he had previously so often felt plagued and tortured. Jim remained silent and awaiting clarity, whilst Frank glanced at his paperwork.

'Does the name 'Beth Holmes' mean anything to you, buddy?' Jim asked.

Boom. A rush of a thousand emotions fired off within our Jim, prior to Frank even completing his utterance. He had Jim at 'Beth'. Emotions which had been chained and tamed by antidepressants, unshackled and wild within an instant.

'*Yes*', Jim replied.

Not quite knowing what to say, he reached for '*Beth is an old friend*'. Seemingly preferring that to '*She is an incongruous and unparalleled jewel of pure beauty, mocking every other happening that this pitiful world has ever witnessed*'

'*OKKK, Jim. How would you feel about her visiting you next Thursday at 2:00pm?*' Frank asked.

'*Yes, that's fine*' were the noises that Jim's mouth formed.

For the subsequent days, this forthcoming epoch bounced around Jim's head; achieving every angle his mind could muster. He allowed his mind to contemplate that, maybe, just maybe, Beth had arrived at caring about him again. Perhaps, despite being previously de-railed, his Beth was back to even loving him.

In view of the press coverage that his case garnered, Jim knew he would likely remain within this institution for at least twenty years; possible never released. He loved Beth with all that he had. Even if Beth wished it so, he could not leave such beauty hanging in the wind for decades. Such beauty has to flow freely, unchained, dancing at will. She could not be tricked into aging alongside the wait for the final chorus from the never ending incarceration lament. The funeral song that played in respect of the death of Jim's freedom had to play for him, and him alone.

Beth arrived on-time. Impossibly, she was even more beautiful. Due to Jim having behaved more than impeccably for over three years, the visit was permitted in a comfortable side room. Jim and Beth together, alone. A nurse in a nearby office just wandered past every five minutes or so, glancing relatively unobtrusively through the glass panel within the door.

Beth and Jim held hands. For over ten minutes, they tenderly felt each other's hands, looked deeply into each other's eyes and simply cried. No words were spoken. Yet, Jim felt he had communicated and heard more in those ten minutes than throughout all of his remaining pitiful non-Beth existence. Words did eventually emerge, though typically separated by long meaningful silences and regular tears.

'I love you, and I have only ever loved you' Beth declared

'I love you more than my words could ever explain' Jim replied, after a long pause.

'I am going to wait for you, however long it takes' Beth said convincingly, though her emotion whilst pure was always very much in the moment.

That was just one other part of Beth's immense beauty. She was so present; always beautifully draping from the 'Now'. She perched, above it all and at one with each precious moment; seeming to simultaneously render moments all that they ever could be, and more. A Jim that wandered backwards and forwards unendingly, instantly transfixed and glued to the 'Now' by her very presence. For once, nothing to run from.

'Beth, you have to live your life. I will probably never be released. I love you with all that I am, but I don't want you to wait for a day that will probably never come' Jim implored

The ninety minute visit ended with twenty minutes of Beth and Jim tearful and in silence, their hands and their eyes continuously connected. They reached a common ground; mutual love and an acceptance that Beth had to carve a path separate from Jim. Emotionally, a grieving task still ahead for the pair.

So many *'what ifs'*, but maybe none of them worth their weight in wishes. If Jim would have found this *'self'* earlier, then surely his terminus so irrevocably changed? Though, maybe this self only lay waiting on this far and dark side of the murderous river. If Jim had opened up to a therapist within the community or taken medication, then his path would have been prone to meander from such a deadly course?

If Beth's ex-partner had not been so destructive and cunning, then maybe? If Jim had been more assertive in his pursuit of Beth after being sacked, then the road forks to pastures new? Unbeknownst to them both: if the guy in the yellow tee-shirt had not been delayed by several seconds and Beth would have been available to Jim's eyes as she glided down the high street, then surely? Likewise, if young Freddy Garside had not been offered the cancellation appointment to have some wax extracted from his ears?

Elements of tragedy, echoed within 'Romeo' and 'Juliet'? Our Juliet; at once magnificent and yet surely incongruent with Jim's world. Not of his world. A bizarre juxtaposition; a weary world alongside such beauty. Perhaps inevitable that the two would struggle to be married.

In Broadmoor, the visit of our Juliet brought many a feeling to the surface. It would be several months before the ripples of this interlude settled down, but settle down they did. The icy touch of reality, freezing *'what might have been'* into hibernation. Jim continued his journey in Broadmoor, separate from all that was outside the institution. More than touched, but not irrevocably derailed from the path that preceded his one and only social visit.

Chapter 52 - The Broadmoor Years – Part 3

Jim continued along the same path. His being increasingly forged through helping others and saving money. Days flew by at light speed. Weeks seemed to pass in an eye blink; months were readily converted into years; years began to stack up into decades. Very occasionally, a fellow patient was discharged or a new patient arrived; yet, the landscape largely unchanging. Jim's routine and living situation was relatively fixed for around thirty years.

We re-join Jim in his late seventies. There were never any institutional romances for Jim. He stayed wholly loyal to the memory of Beth. After such beauty, respected and treasured memories more than outstripped anything that a new reality could ever offer.

After thirty years, Jim remained within the comfort of his Broadmoor. For several years, there had been talk of possibly releasing a seventy odd year old Jim. However, the upper segments of the hierarchy struggled to squeeze him out of their gates.

At this point, Jim's relentless work ethic had catalysed an ever-rising bank balance which had hit the heights of just over £35,000. His status amongst patients elevated markedly by this figure; respect and hushed whispers when he entered many a room. Music to Jim's ears.

Jim had seemed to generally age well, but recently he had begun feeling more fatigued. Several months prior, he had reduced from working around twelve hours each day, to a mere six hour shift on week days, as a cleaner on the sycamores unit (the old, D block). Still, his money gently grew.

The way the Broadmoor system worked meant that officially,

Jim would not be released until he was deemed no longer a significant risk to the public. Jim's case was complicated because with the media coverage of his case, there could be a public outcry if our Jim was released. The latter concerns were largely an unofficial reality, likely placing more doors between our Jim and the outside world. Of course, the unspoken does not just permeate the outside world.

The driving force behind a patient being released was the recommendations of their 'responsible medical officer (RMO)', typically a psychiatrist. The easy route for the RMO was to keep the patient within the confines of Broadmoor; never to be proven spectacularly wrong. Keep Jim in Broadmoor and less need for his RMO to battle anxiety whenever new atrocious unsolved crimes were mentioned on the national news. Further, in our Jim, the RMO had an easy patient to manage. A patient that consistently created no hassle; no headaches.

Yet, the RMO in Jim's case (a psychiatrist, Dr Patrick McGinty) was prepared to take the risk of releasing Jim, though aware that it could bite him on the backside if Jim re-offended. Dr McGinty had been recommending that Jim be released for just over four years. Presumably, he felt that Jim was no longer a significant danger and ready for release into the community. However, Jim had repeatedly refused to be released and perhaps tried to suggest that he was not mentally ready for release. Our Jim perhaps more rounded, succumbing to sometimes moulding his truths to fit his purpose.

Partly, being aged in his seventies and coping with a specific world for around thirty years, our Jim was apprehensive about having to adapt to a new and less shielded world. Alongside this, his drives for exploration and adventure were waning. Jim cocooned within a comfort zone; seeming content to remain, gently slipping towards an end point.

Moreover, Jim did not want to be released because it seemed his life's work would close to vanish; with just a few waves of a DWP wand. Jim learnt that if he was released, then the rules relating to social security benefits would mean that he would *not* get key benefits until he had spent virtually all of his £35,000 savings (on rent, food, clothes, and living expenses). This latter reality translated into discharge from Broadmoor meaning: everything that our Jim had spent over thirty years working massively hard for, dwindling to virtually nothing within a couple of years.

Over thirty years toiling in line with a certain meaning; it would all begin to quickly slip through his fingers as the outside gate clanked shut on his departure. Waving goodbye not to just to Broadmoor, but to: everything he had built and amassed, the propping up of his self-esteem, and a purpose that had become etched into his soul. His flailing resolve could not consent to the excision of such valued chunks of his current reality. A burden too unwieldy to withstand, even within his mental contemplation of deviating beyond the Broadmoor gates, to the harshness of a less shielded and less caring milieu.

For Jim, he anticipated staying put, until the point that they changed the benefits system such that he could get benefits *and* keep all the money he had accrued. Within the special hospital environments, he had a situation whereby: rent, food, and other living expenses were free. Also, through the work he did in the hospital, his savings were very gradually increasing. Things wholly at an impasse, such that it seemed that Jim would likely never be released to spend and enjoy the money he had saved.

Jim would quite likely ultimately die with money that he had earned from several decades of work remaining in his account, just a figure and unused. Almost like he was constantly saving for tomorrow, but in the end the *tomorrow* never came. One is left with the riddle of whether this part of Jim's tale is a sad story or a happy story?

Let us not get too clogged up with ill-fitting pathos. Our Jim enjoyed many more moments in Broadmoor than he did within the earlier part of his adulthood within the community. In particular, he found a formula that for him meant that he savoured much of his time; his day to day journey improved.

Jim's path of saving gave off various psychological benefits, including: a sense of achievement, pride, higher confidence, feeling special, a sense of power (e.g., people regularly asking him if he could help them out with some money or a loan), and meaning. Deep within, he also enjoyed the recognition and respect from other patients. He found a good solution. The latter enabled him to experience appreciably more positive moments during the latter thirty years that he was in the Broadmoor environment, relative to the vast bulk of the almost half century which came before.

It is perhaps not a tragedy: if we strive, enjoy the journey, but ultimately perhaps do not reach our ultimate goal? Within a potentially difficult environment, Jim had managed to find a path such that he got some pleasure, pride, and purpose. The glory of the latter perhaps not hugely dimmed by the reality that he may never reach the destination of spending his riches.

Alas, Jim did not need to resist release for much longer. Unbeknownst to our Jim; whilst he grafted and saved in his outer world, something sinister worked and grew inside of him over many months. The outside manifestations began with regular heart burn, weight loss, breathlessness, and fatigue. Fairly quickly, it spread.

Various scans and tests at the local hospital and fairly soon, an appointment to receive the results. Jim never fully lost his ability to sniff out negative possibilities. Our Jim nervously entered an office, guided by a helpful nurse. He noted that the door offered a dark sign, holding a white indented impression of '*Dr Jenny Griffiths*'.

A serious looking young female Doctor, managed slight eye contact. The bookcase and a couple of pictures in frames gave clues that this was Dr Griffiths' own designated office. The smallness of the room blended with the humble rather cheap looking chairs, perhaps suggesting that this lady was not at the very summit of the hospital hierarchy. The room, filled with a smell of overused detergents and bleach.

Jim feeling somewhat helpless and out of control; at the mercy of whatever words happened to flow from the amply qualified maiden. A male assistant sat passively, taking it all in.

'There is no easy way to tell you this, Jim, but I am afraid it is not good news. The results from our investigations show that you have cancer which has spread to various sites, including the oesophagus, the stomach, the liver, the kidneys, and the lungs. Unfortunately, we cannot cure the cancer, but we will do everything to make things as comfortable as we can', Dr Griffiths delivered, with the respect of marrying it with a serious and sombre expression.

For the messenger, a far from unusual element of her standard working week. Desensitized through repeated exposure; thoughts of Jim's demise occasionally giving way to the mundane, regarding contemplation of dinner plans and issues at home. For our Jim, her words hit him with the force of a speeding HGV to a frail frame. The form of her sounds, surely signalling a shuddering swansong.

'*Are you OK, you look a bit anxious*' the Doctor asked

'*Yes, thanks. I'm Just taking it in*' Jim replied.

'*Could I ask how long you think I might have left?*' Jim asked

'*It's very difficult to be precise, for various technical reasons. However, if I had to estimate then I would suggest between about six and twelve months*' the female Doctor offered. Again, the calmness of her demeanour suggested that she had already played out this dynamic a plethora of times, within her young history.

Whilst this broadside initially hit our Jim firm, his mind was not devoid of defences. Soon the external reality was surrounded by several cushions of inner fog; fuzzy, edges rounded, and quite deep down within his mind. Oh, the merciful power of repression. In addition, our Jim's physical condition left him jaded; his resources worn down and less able to fuel intense fear. Jim returned to Broadmoor, but soon his physical health deteriorated to the point that he needed to be transferred to an outside hospital. Perhaps the grim reaper, perfunctorily and unemotionally sharpening his scythe?

Chapter 53 - The end is nigh

Jim landed in a bed, within an outside hospital. He had his own room, starched white sheets, and even a window looking out to a lifeless quadrangle. The stench of death and bodily residue hung heavily, not fully masked by strong disinfectant.

Cancer had spread quickly around Jim's body. This evolving companion seemed to somehow eke out pain, from every nook and cranny in his frame. Pain in places where Jim had previously just taken the silence and nothingness for granted, without even noticing. With the scant and depleted energy which had remained loyal, he recently yearned for this prior silence and nothingness. Intermittent blessings came with opioid pain relief, mercifully blocking some of the bodily reality.

Throughout much of Jim's life, his pain used to so often relate closely to words and meaning. Words and meaning which his mind seemed to frivolously scatter, in ways that damaged and blocked him. His history was dominated by an emotional pain which his neurosis kindled, with a touching relentlessness. Now, his pain no longer needed such tireless support from his meaning system. It was much more raw; seeming to have the foreign quality of being married to a tangible reality.

This vessel which Jim used to transport his soul around in, thoroughly ravaged. He looked tragically close to a skeleton which was barely covered by a pale thread-bare clinging throw, starting to develop faint tinges of blue. The sands of time had done their work.

The grains of energy in the upper segment of the sand glass were once so aplenty; now a mere couple of grains from being rendered empty. Reality flowed, with the inevitability of gravity. A rotting shell, surely close to liberating Jim's soul.

Jim's final fate on this planet is but not his sole companion; ubiquitously lying in wait for superstars, billionaires, great presidents, and the rest. The glory days finite; bound to pass by, contracted with reality to be lost. Shed not surprise with great contrast between the picture of the hopeful cheeky toddler that was once young Jim, placed alongside the unforgiving exit shot as that same toddler eventually departs their mortal coil in the final form. Time does its work, unremitting.

Mortality runs through all being, interrupted only briefly by life. The photographer Robert Frank suggests, *'things move on, time passes, people go away, and sometimes they don't come back'*, and maybe just the pictures remain: *'photographs that immediately make everything old'.* Yet, has our Jim made his mark; after vanishing into nothingness would he take comfort from a legacy? Amidst the flatline, will it matter to that mind?

Our Jim had kept the powder dry, in so many ways. An almost unending drought, throughout his history. Our Jim not cleverly awaiting prime opportunity; not focussed on immaculately timed swoops. More, diligently standing in his own way, at every turn.

Generally a lonely existence, particularly before nuzzling into the bosom of Broadmoor. Jim had not managed to spread the Butler seeds around this planet. No future generations, to perhaps follow in father's footsteps.

As he clung on, the only aspect of Jim that remained untouched was the steadily incrementing bank balance. This upwardly ticking figure had formed his raison d'etre for the past thirty years. A nest egg that would ultimately be swallowed up; governmental money very soon, perhaps not long after warmth had slipped from our Jim. The legacy of Jim and the product of thirty years of hard graft: destination, unknown.

Maybe, Jim's thirty years of labour would fund a few months wages for some major fat cat within the civil service? Or, perhaps making up a small fraction of some golden handshake bestowed upon an achiever within the upper echelons of the governmental hierarchy? From there, tabloids would have us consider that it may not be inconceivable that it would be channelled into avenues such as high class hookers, gambling, and booze. Then, maybe as the late George Best might suggest, the rest would be just wasted. Possibilities limitless. Though, their relevance maybe not central to our Jim, as he seems to be taking what may be the final gasps of this journey.

Yet for so many years, the figures which Jim saw in his bank statements used to sing sweet songs for him. Particularly sweet, alongside social comparison with fellow prisoners who so coveted such funds. Amongst his group of peers within Broadmoor, his savings had given him a status and a standing that had eluded him for the vast bulk of his life before his incarceration.

For decades in Broadmoor Special Hospital, his money had bought him more than it ever could if he had readily spent a penny. As his money grew, the offshoots were a level of self-esteem and self-acceptance; helping to abate some of the fierce backlash which self-consciousness had previously unleased. His money had been a most efficacious panacea for much of his residual mental ailments, positively shifting the hue of his journey. He would surely not be buried with his money and it was unlikely to grieve for him. However, it had afforded him ample despite, or perhaps rather mainly because he frugally held onto it and watched it grow.

If we flick back to the present, it was clear that Jim's time left on this earth was quickly ebbing away. The close approach of the end of an era might be a time of reflection. On the face of it,

Jim's journey does not seem integral to any significant epoch.

Looking down from a higher plane, Jim has the gaze of a not unfamiliar philosophy and psychology lecturer that has long since departed. The latter Mr Ingle had long since succumbed to the side effects of his life of hedonism; passing on to the journey that Jim is on the very precipis of. If this Ingle was generating one of his rambling and largely unfathomable philosophical takes on Jim and his life to offer fellow departed souls, he might offer:

"We have seen much of our Jim; maybe too much. Perhaps as the proverb cautions, 'no man is a hero to their valet'. Individuals that litter Jim's society would likely typically consider themselves the antithesis of Jim. They would feel their presence on such higher ground they might strain to see Jim; perhaps equipped with handy difficulties seeing any similarities.

The reality is that Jim shared a condition of being a human. This latter condition translates into carrying genetically carved propensities and trying to make our life work within the world in which we are presented. Often flawed; often making mistakes; often taking wrong turns. Jim's vulnerability perhaps never more easily discerned than observing the final moments of his life: laboured breathing, barely moving and pain etched into his being.

In Jim's life, he chose neither his genetic predispositions, nor the world in which he would land. Prior to his arrival, he did not visit a superstore in the ether and make these latter choices; rather they landed forcefully on him, from above. Yet, self-blame and other's opinions hung heavily in our Jim's mind for so many years, lingering like a determined noxious odour.

Was Jim akin to an uncertain roulette gambler being forced to put all his being on a colour and opting red, only to be met squarely with the vision of black eight? Self-blaming, yet ironically perhaps without the resources to effectively predict or control the outcome. Was Jim, like a child born with a significant invisible handicap? Unless we look very closely and shed convenient myths, perhaps some handicaps are much more visible than others?

Compassion and caring would ooze from an audience met with the vision of a particular beautiful young baby, which was at once wide eyed, innocent, and afflicted with the burden of significant deformity or handicap. But what if the baby was born with a marked deformity that was inside the head; within the brain and yet invisible to the audience? The manifestations of this deformity may be just as burdensome in terms of the overt behaviour that flows from it. However, the compassion of the audience would often be readily swapped with disgust and animosity, perhaps fuelled by an illusory notion that the creature that grows from this baby wholly chooses their path and their behaviour.

Maybe nobody hears the silent whispers of an invisible inner deformity. An inner deformity that likely has some unchecked influence on the output of the specimen to which it has attached, uninvited. Like a novice and over-zealous toddler gaming with a PS controller, under their elder brother's name. The remote audience attribute control to the latter, yet outcomes at the mercy of the former.

So much is unknown, but perhaps society often works best with the over-simplified views of many of its integral elements? Voltaire takes issue with such over-simplicity, suggesting 'whilst doubt is an unpleasant condition, certainty is an absurd one'. Yet, a world awash with busy brains that can't let things just be. Judgements littered like rabbit droppings, inevitable waste from the unstoppable whirring of a normal lingual brain.

Maybe we are left with a sense that the window into Jim's life needed cleaning more diligently. Perhaps then, we could better warm our hands around a glowing illusion of understanding. In truth, in a land before complex language, no judgements could land. A human species picks up this magnifying glass called complex language and it never endingly sticks to the lens; seemingly no longer aware that a vision so sullied by such a soiled tool.

How can we have sought to tell a story about Jim, but often reveal so little about the characters that trod the boards of his stage? A teaser, indeed. Yet maybe the truth knows that the main characters that populated Jim's life were not the actual flotsam and jetsam that passed around him, but rather their representation within his troubled mind.

Language weaves an ineffective barometer for measuring how close to Solipsism our 'reality' lies. To borrow from Neo's matrix, can we ever step outside what our mind is plugged into? Maybe those that do step outside the matrix are akin to a dreamer who dreams that he is awoken; yet beneath awareness, this new reality still lies deep in their inexorable slumber. So, do you really see Jim Butler? "

We again return to Beveridge, and this position that 'we are prone to see what lies behind our eyes, rather than what appears before them'. Jim excelled in his focus on the former; surely top of any class. Not alien to the normal human mind within present day society, ultimately so much of what bothers Jim flows from the reflexive spin that his mind puts on it. If only he could have better tamed this wild stallion, which bolted to a million negative meanings and more.

Maybe Jim's path also touched by a perverse habit of often nailing his colours more to positions of bald truth than the buffered positions of shaggy benefit? Photographer Robert Frank perhaps enlightens with the notion that, 'it's easier to show the darkness than the joy of life', though perhaps more than one lens through which he viewed his matter. Reality will probably dictate that the epitaph that truly captures Jim's journey is to remain unwritten."

Perhaps the Gods continue their vigil? Meanwhile, in Jim's present: a couple of nurses briefly check on him. Fate has dished up the benefit of nurse Grayson and nurse Holt. Nurse Grayson, a senior male nurse in his late fifties. He carries a heavy frame and facial lines which could suggest that he may have known struggle; yet, there remains some sparkle in his eyes. A man that has perhaps not been fully worn down into wholly ceasing striving.

Alongside this, it is possible that his sparky demeanour was not totally uninfluenced by the presence of a recently qualified nurse Holt. The catalyst of nurse Holt came in the form of a youthful, impressionable, and stunningly beautiful female nurse. Two nurses together; relative power and beauty, transacting opaquely.

The ugly stench of nearby death increasingly filling the air; Jim readied for the union. For many hours, Jim has not appeared conscious to the outside world. Alongside this, it is believed by many that the last sense to depart during the dying process is the ability to hear. These two nurses gather round the lifeless manikin and provide cursory and perfunctory checks on the attached equipment.

'He has definitely not got long left' nurse Grayson announces

'Do you know what he did?' nurse Grayson whisperingly asked his female colleague.

'No, what do you mean?' nurse Holt replies, with an enthusiasm which provided the very stage that nurse Grayson hungered for.

What followed was nurse Grayson's hushed voice forwarding his slant on the events that led to Jim being incarcerated.

'*Uuuugh...That's evil*' nurse Holt declared, clearly animated by this morsel of juicy gossip.

'*Well, he ain't gonna hurt anyone else*' nurse Grayson pronounced, positively lifted by his relatively powerful position; surely only one alpha in this room.

Perhaps an irony that our Jim spent a life so often plagued by what where primarily internally generated false representations of how others were judging him. Now, with a final curtain twitching and readied, real negative judgements simply bounced off him; less than insignificant. Maybe an escape hatch opening?

This dutiful pair of nurses would then leave Jim's room, chatting about the developments in a reality TV show which they both shared an interest in. Nurse Holt perhaps not fully aware that for many months, this senior male colleague had conjured up and treasured fantasies about intimately merging with her. Jim is left alone on the final stage which this tiny hospital room represents; no resources for a final soliloquy.

Minutes pass and Jim remains unaccompanied; drifting closer to the peace of complete nothingness. The nearby radio played out Jim's last few moments on this earth, with Terry Jacks assisting his departure. Jim had slipped well beyond the point that he connected with words, but the vibe of the song just seemed to fit.

On a level which words could not explain, the song that surrounded him felt to capture so much. The hypnotic melody seeming to soothingly wash away the final threads of Jim's journey:

'Goodbye to you, my trusted friend

We've known each other since we were nine or ten
Together we've climbed hills and trees
Learned of love and ABCs
Skinned our hearts and skinned our knees
Goodbye my friend, it's hard to die
When all the birds are singing in the sky
Now that the spring is in the air
Pretty girls are everywhere
Think of me and I'll be there
We had joy, we had fun
We had seasons in the sun
But the hills that we climbed
Were just seasons out of time

Goodbye papa, please pray for me
I was the black sheep of the family
You tried to teach me right from wrong
Too much wine and too much song
Wonder how I got along
Goodbye papa, it's hard to die
When all the birds are singing in the sky
Now that the spring is in the air
Little children everywhere
When you see them, I'll be there
We had joy, we had fun
We had seasons in the sun
But the wine and the song
Like the seasons, have all gone

Goodbye Beth, my little one,
You gave me love and helped me find the sun
And every time that I was down........

It is said that in a person's final moments, their life flashes before them. Our Jim, close to floating above it all, observing snatches of his very own childhood. Memories flicked through

341

his mind in seconds; time almost standing still......

Chapter 54 – A mind travels back;
allowed some final glimpses.

Jim drifting; so close to departure; still lay in the hospital bed which will very soon become the last scene of his attempts at a life. The dying embers of his mind float back to the beginning, deep within his own mind. Distant reality, flying through his mind at breakneck speed.

Memories of childhood are often snatches of visions, viewed through the eyes of a child and re-interpreted by older eyes. Jim's childhood has always been a bit of a blur to him. Yet, to seek to truly accompany Jim on his whole journey, a need to shine a light on the dark corners of his childhood journey.

Perhaps as Watson would have us suspect, a man is so often close to a reflection of that which his childhood inflicts. The ghost of times past, at once haunting and ironically Scrooge-like with reality. Found tightly clutching the purse strings; surely afraid that one of her secrets might just spill out, shared. We need to travel with this spirited companion; hoping that this stingy mite could just unthinkingly loosen and drop a few morsels of the reality that has littered our Jim's path. Perhaps a need to be frugal, spending any meagre offering very wisely.

Jim's final moments allow more than a playful peek at small pieces of the gigantic jigsaw, which is Jim's childhood; more than a few fragments. With many pieces placed on the table unconnected, a platform can emerge to start to join pieces and glean the deeper picture. To understand Jim, outstretched is a journey of toiling through Jim's childhood; getting closer to a place where Jim's adulthood can be retrospectively feasted on with perhaps greater wisdom.

In the absence of these clouded glimpses of a childhood, an audience surely drawn even more magnetically to an explanatory framework that draws on convenient 'truths'. Without the burden of reality, what is grey can readily be glossed over as pure black or white. We find our own way.

An audience typically scans the meagre tip of an iceberg; so much left hidden. Jim sunken like the Titanic, with thin strands of his glowing epitaph clinging tightly to their craft; the ending inevitable? How very few dive deep into murky waters, struggling to get close to what is icy and bitter. Who cares to strain, to see and feel more clearly the gravity and magnificence of what truly sank our Jim? Why would they?

Let us not walk past this God sent sunset, with barely a glance. Pray sit, open every sense to drink in this beauty; let it unfold. At this stage, an audience watching a magician making something disappear behind a curtain. Left wondering, how did that happen? In Jim's case: why did he commit such an atrocious crime? Maybe clues in childhood?

How did that seed of life grow and become catapulted on such a trajectory? A trajectory that culminated in such a bitter collision with societal norms, after so long outwardly seeming to be within reasonable limits. Touching on elements of Jim's childhood; taking some of the audience behind the magician's curtain and perhaps allowing a partial tachistoscopic viewing. From here, we may have more of a sense of how the magic of Jim and his actions have manifest.

We wind the path back, meandering through the landscape of Jim Butler's childhood. There begins with a vision of a child, born into his world; many years ago. Jim Butler is born. At once, innocent in this life and with an in-built structure relentlessly oriented to learn.

The yelling of pain from Jim's mother (Kath) marks a beginning, which gives way to Jim's introduction and triumphant declarations of how beautiful Jim is. The dice of genetics have been rolled, and Jim has emerged. Perhaps the hinges of Pandora's box creak, ever so gently?

This small bundle breathes. His heart beats. In the same inescapable way, he learns.

To ask a child not to learn is like asking the sun not to rise. Nature imposes itself, with an inevitability. Never far from the watchful eyes of young Kath, twenty eight and filled with demons.

With our Jim still in his first year, Kath would meet with an old wily psychiatrist. She was soon to be diagnosed with agitated clinical depression, with some obsessional elements. Later, things would lean towards a diagnosis of what, back then, was often termed 'manic depression'. So, what did this constellation of mental ailments mean?

Well, Jim had the blessing of some degree of unpredictability and a sense of walking on shifting sands. Indeed, it is often said that variety is the spice of life. In which case, rest easy, our Jim had plentiful spice. In essence, Jim did not have pure consistent sadness from those dark eyes that bore down on him.

Intermittently, there would be days when our Kath would have a bee in her bonnet. On the wrong day, Kath's mind visibly stung by insults such as a very young Jim behaving like a child when the family went out for a meal. Alternatively, her wrath may spill over if our Jim left things very untidy when he played. If the wind was blowing in the wrong direction, six year old Jim might hear a passionate speech flowing from Kath's lips. Echoes deep within his mind, reverberating:

'I'm fed up with your room being untidy. Its a tip. I'm going to set fire to the lot of it. You are absolutely spoiled. You get every mortal

thing you want and you can't even keep your room tidy' on repeat, on some days. The *'every mortal thing you want'* was hammered, by rhythmical equally spaced enunciating; stretching out each of these five words; using each bullet in the chamber. Kath's feelings painstakingly wrapped around every word.

Once Kath became annoyed or anxious about something, she was like a kettle with a faulty switch; able to switch on, but seemingly unable to switch off regardless of how much steam. A pressure cooker, without the release valve. Steam pouring out, but the pressure inside not appearing to abate for many hours and sometimes days.

Think Kathy Bates in the film Misery, but with a fierce commitment to amphetamines. Patrick (Jim's father), as we will learn, was an unsafe vessel for Kath's outpourings. So, our young Jim would gain more than his share. Interspersed, Kath was subdued and sometimes very loving towards our Jim.

In Jim's broader world and within a world long before the internet, the masses tweet and twitter. The noises conveniently dance in tune with the illusion that a person simply chooses their path. The beams of nurture readily impact, striking hard on a genetic prism. Perhaps, the consequences can only unfold? Like the ripples of a stone, launched aimlessly into a pond.

Baby Jim is built to eagerly learn from the world with which he is presented. His world is not your world. Let us not be fooled. The world which Jim is given comprises of the complex interaction of the experiences to which *he* is exposed.

The early years of learning from his world accumulate and invisibly forge the architecture of his personality. A society fervently grasps at pretending to understand this process. Often, perhaps it barely scratches the surface of compassionate understanding?

Many years on, Jim arrived in adulthood. By then, Jim was perhaps bound in a form, tightly woven by his earlier childhood world. He did not choose his childhood world. Hence, perhaps the adult Jim did not fully choose the cumbersome personality which he carries around during his adult years?

Within his early world; Jim's ability to use language evolves quickly, defending him against living. As time goes by, he increasingly invests his moments dwelling on past events or worrying about the future. More than most, he finds it difficult to fully land in the recurrent gift of the present moments.

Jim's self-consciousness grows. Pure pleasure seeking is overtaken by a drive to appease *his* mental representations of others and what he perceives *they* might think of him. Jim's Freudian superego swells unendingly.

Unable to fathom or control his outer world, Jim looks more and more inwards. He becomes an expert in mining the inner world, that lies behind his eyes. Mining tirelessly; releasing emotionally rich mental representations, which so often speak of negative judgements from others. He creates huge holes and craters, in which to hide; locked in to digging deeper, in his forlorn efforts to get out of these holes. Increasingly losing his ability to be in the present moment; his experience grossly blunted.

Baby Jim is propelled towards what is referred to as 'life'. Guided by parental limits; Jim is distilled through apparatus of: language, experience, and society. Perhaps much of the product seems pre-set?

Blinkers aside, the societal sausage machine can often squeeze much waste from the raw products. We may vaguely know what goes into the apparatus (fresh, innocent, baby Jimbo). We may readily and often even gleefully 'label' what comes out (an adult Jim with murderous deeds). We work hard to obscure the reality that we do not know what happens inside the machine. This ride may be bumpy, maybe cling on tight to societal illusions.

Chapter 55 - The early years
– A mother's love

Jim's early world comprises largely of his parents, particularly his mother (Kath). On the outside, Kath is five feet four inches, permed dark brown hair, dark eyes, and never far from a frown. Several years ago, she married a tall man named Patrick.

Patrick was thirty three when Jim was born; having manged five more years on this planet than Kath. He stood at six foot three, with only the early beginning of an inflated belly. Patrick's hair was dark, but lightened appreciably when it had a season in the sun.

Patrick carried the Butler bald patch over the crown, which had blighted the thatches of a long-line of earlier generations. As he aged, he began to bare slight resemblance to an amalgamation of the later versions of the actor Clint Eastwood and the politician Tony Blair. He had quite striking blue eyes, that often found themselves winking at the ladies.

Our Jim born back in a time that Patrick's regular references to young ladies as 'love' or 'darling' was largely tolerated. If there had been a 'me too' movement at that time, it would sadly have been mainly uttered by the male office workers queueing up to pat the harassed rear of the nearest female secretary. Our Patrick had many affairs during his marriage to Kath, working part of Jim's childhood as a travelling salesman.

Of course, Patrick was an influence on Jim. However, whilst Jim will never be able to verbalise much of the complexity, the bulk of what this bundle of joy (Jim) will learn, will be from his mother. Kath more than loves Jim, she needs him.

Baby Jim serves as ointment to provide Kath with snatches

of respite and distraction from her inner turmoil. Her inadvertent motions are everywhere. They will weigh heavily on sculpting the product which becomes Jim. Kath has spent much of her adulthood in the grip of clinically significant agitated depression, with obsessional features. After Jim's birth, this worsens.

Kath later referred to repetitively holding on tight to Jim's pram, to avoid flinging herself in front of passing cars. She had bouts of ECT at this time, but she was not hospitalised. Jim could then enjoy the full benefits of having his mother around in these crucial formative years. Baby Jim did not need logic; when angst took hold of Kath, he could see dark shark-like eyes and her inner turmoil screamed out.

Jim plucked portions of early memories of his mum crying, in all kinds of everyday situations. His young mind could not understand it. An inbuilt yearning for some control over this crazy world manifests in Jim trying to work out what it is about *him* or *his* behaviour that is leaving his mum so distraught.

If it isn't him, then perhaps the reality becomes even more frightening. If he is not the cause of his mother's desperation, then the illusion of control evaporates. His sense of control walks out of the door, passing helplessness on its way in. It *must* be him. It has to be his fault.

Jim remembers being ushered away when his mum was in floods of tears at the bottom of the stairs. She was receiving some traditional '*pull yourself together*' type comfort from Jim's dutiful gran (Norma). Old school, you might say.

Jim recalls the desperation in those loud cries and screams from the floored Kath, as if the world had ended. As hard as he strained to see, four-year old Jim could not see the end of the world. However, he emotionally knew it must be coming. He would spend his life increasingly looking for it.

Though his vocabulary could not articulate it, his mind intuitively knew that these signals meant danger and trauma. He did not know at the time that the crisis and these yowls of inner pain were linked to Kath being expected to prepare a meal for the in-laws. It would take Kath more time to implicitly coach Jim, in such a way that he could increasingly learn to be able to see the world through the eyes of Kath's injured soul.

In his own mind, Jim would never be far from the tireless laser beams that emanated from Kath's eyes. Diffusing and refracting in whatever direction Jim took, even when the virtual Kath was miles away. Our Jim moving this way and that, trying with his everything to contort his way in between these beams. Opinionated judgements activated with hair trigger sensitivity. Jim, ever yearning to not activate Kath's disapproval deep within him. The ugly dance continued; bearing down.

Jim flailed and struggled to lift the weight of his early childhood. Aged around five, he began having nightmares. He would often see an image of a witches face on his curtain, typically just as he awoke. It terrified him.

Jim decided that his house must be haunted. Just before Jim had fully learnt to bury everything, he shared the problem with his mum. What followed was one of the few moments when he saw a smile on his mother's face. Jim stumbled upon a most rare find, namely: something which did not appear to worry or trouble his mother.

'Our house is haunted' Jim blurted out anxiously, with tears beginning to roll down his smooth rounded cheeks

'Don't be daft – it is not haunted' Kath said, alongside what seemed like a real laugh.

For many children, this would likely have eased the fear. For Jim, it intensified it. Already Jim's brain did not resonate with light-heartedness. His mind did not mirror such folly. His brain reasoned, *'Not only is the house haunted – I can't get my mum to accept that it is. I am going to have to face this one alone'*.

Mercifully, within a couple of years, Jim had largely let go of this idea that the house was haunted. He would soon find new things to concern him.

Chapter 56 – The early years: Toilet training that went way beyond the functional and spanned Jim's childhood

Outside school; at a very young age, little Jim learns some very influential lessons. Kath, once an innocent cherub had suffered her own journey; blighted by so much unchosen. Yet, in order to better elaborate the lessons or lesions served upon our young Jim, we have to delve further into the neuroses which afflicted Kath. Compassion in hand or perhaps even a Skinnerian deterministic neutrality; if a leaf blows 'the wrong way' does it deserve our wrath and blame?

A central part of Kath's anxiety centred on her worrying about having an accident with her bowels in public. That is, she is terrified of: not being able to reach the toilet in time and the bowels releasing their product in an unconventional public place, with eye gaze and judgement from other people. Her fear, avoidance, leakage, and compensatory behaviours in this area are beyond monstrous.

Kath is no criminal. Do not doubt, this poor lady suffers; at once love and kindness in her heart and neurosis riddling her very soul. This latter cancer often spreads, recklessly.

It seems Jim chose to learn dutifully in his early years. Whilst Jim developed a merciful defence of withdrawal, there was also residual striving to pick up on the emotional state of his mother. If this young mind struggles to fathom the sources of his mother crying, then he clearly needs to attend more carefully to the meanings of his mother's world.

In a world for Jim in which his primary caregiver's mood and emotional state is both important and unpredictable, his brain is reflexively prone to attending to that. A reflex not far from breathing; not much effort needed.

With his child brain, he seeks order and patterns amidst the apparent chaos. Jim needs to learn what he needs to fear. At birth, we far from fully know the answer to this riddle of *'what do we need to fear?'.* We need help, to learn.

One of Jim's earliest memories is as a very young pre-school child emerging from a very hot bath and crouching on a rug next to the fire. The heat from the bath had rendered his mind in an even fuzzier state. He recalls subsequently having a minor accident with his bowels, whereby he unthinkingly relaxed his sphincter muscles; relaxation yielding a tiny creation.

Jim has vivid memories of Kath coming across the small product of this latter process on the rug. An inadvertent present for Kath. Her reaction was to say, *'Jim'* with a level of disgust such that even the memory echoes still leave Jim shuddering. The researcher Davey may make reference to some inbuilt 'disgust' response to other's biological waste, perhaps weaved with evolutionary threads of 'survival value'. However, the staggeringly ginormous intensity of Kath's augmented response probably teleported her to a different galaxy.

Much flowed from a reality that Kath was beyond terrified of having an incident in which her bowels gave way in a public place, prior to reaching the toilet. Jim would repeatedly pick up on his mother manifesting negative emotional shifts in response to words relating to toilets or normal bodily functions of excreting waste. Reminders, verbal or otherwise, lit the shortest of touch paper inside Kath's skull, leading inexorably to the most toxic fear exploding inside Kath. Kath tried to cocoon and mask what may have seemed a nonsensical explosion deep inside, but the vibrations at the surface were unmistakeable. Nonverbals in Kath speaking perhaps more loudly than any words ever could; Kath visibly pricked by a reminder.

Of course, when a threat is sufficiently seismic to a being, it seems almost that all roads lead to Rome. Do not doubt, our Jim would more than pick up on his mother's anxiety around toilets and using the toilets. Blessed sensitivity; when Kath was kicked hard by this, Jim learned to limp along with her.

When Kath entered a building outside the home, it was a 'code red' and she invariably had to initially locate the toilet. There was then a cardinal need to sit in a position within the building where she could visibly see the toilet area. Reassurance, if you will.

If Kath did not know the location of a toilet before entering a building, then Kath's anxiety was deafening for her. The internal chaos in her mind manifested in a type of 'shut-down' in her being, with the power source to her soul killed in an instant as a safety measure. On the outside: with the power outage, we had large unresponsive eyes, shark like.

Jim found these eyes, again and again. At such times, Kath was not present. Her body appeared to the outside world as an empty shell, and 99% of her resources were inside her own head and firmly tangled up with her fears.

Within Kath's neurosis: home was safe. Outside the home was dangerous and scary. In the context of her neurosis: Kath's meaning networks evolved such that mention of 'toilet' or words associated with bodily functions could serve as a reminder of her fear and disgust, with associated negative emotional shifts.

Sometimes the reminders were situational and without words. Sometimes, reminders seemed to perhaps just flow from a frenzied pinball richocheting inside Kath's mind, lighting up an almost unavoidable buffer that seemed to almost wholly encircle Kath's brain. Emotion gripping tightly on the steering wheel that drove Kath, cruelly elbowing logic well beyond arms length away.

The fear was cranked up way higher if such words were heartlessly shot in her direction when she was outside the home. At such times, Jim could smell and taste his mother's fear and emotional upset; perhaps far more putrid than the waste she so feared? The words pricked his mother like a sharp needle and Jim was able to learn a rotten dysfunctional meaning, which would become woven into a trap beyond his resources.

When the family were outside the home: it was as if when Jim asked to go to the toilet, his mother reacted momentarily as if stung. Outwardly and to the untrained eye, she perhaps showed little. Her language was typically designed with an imperative to mask and deny this problem, rather than transparently own it. Holding her cards tightly, like a poker player keeping them safe from possible prying glances. But sadly, Kath had an inability to suppress the tells.

Something massive internally within Kath gave way to those unmistakeable ripples at the surface. The leakage was foul. Young Jim could not verbally label or understand it, but he felt it. He was very moved by it.

For the creature Kath, outside the home anything that took her mind to the theme of 'toilet' touched off an internal fear structure around having an accident; at a time when she was in the line of fire, due to the gazing eyes. An irony beyond Kath that the eyes that so troubled her, were within her own head. If Jim went to the toilet at home, Kath seemed more comfortable with that. If Jim mentioned wanting to use the toilet in public, Kath's core shuddered. A switch was pressed.

Jim had a sensitivity born of living in a world in which a

relaxed state was an endangered species. The odour of Kath's fear struck him hard. Ultimately, it followed him like the most loyal canine, rarely leaving his side. It would increasingly come to follow him, in his own mind.

Chapter 57 - The early years – the benefits of a male role model

Jim's father (Patrick) staggered as he attempted to arise from his arm chair. He seemed to catch a brief glimpse of Jim's injured eyes. Aged seven and already Jim's eyes were becoming more and more weary. They had seen too much.

'*I have not been drinking*' Patrick said. The stale stench of alcohol spoke of his lies, without needing to say a word. Jim followed suit.

To show this man a mirror of reality was akin to poking a ferocious trapped animal with a sharp stick. The anger of Jim's father was always near to the surface. Jim buried himself in a defensive mental fog, providing a partial screen between him and reality. He progressed to a point that he virtually never tasted the sweet embrace of the present moment.

Whilst he couldn't articulate it, Jim knew on a deeper level that there was no point in raising the contradictions and lies of his father. We only put our hand in the fire so many times, even if other meaning structures were suggesting we should continue. The bitter accumulation of prior experiences had taught Jim that honesty with this man does not lead to any positive break through, merely defensive lashing out (verbally and physically) and more insincerity.

Several hours later, after several trips to the shed for more 'work', Patrick's restraint had dissolved within some neat spirit. Jim had long since fled to his room. Later, he would hear the unrelenting chorus of screams from his mother. The beat goes on.

The courage of venturing from his room and investigating the screams had long since walked. He remained in his room, pulling bed covers tightly over a shaking body and squeezing the predictable cuddly toy for comfort. Just Jim and his small grey fluffy rabbit, clinging on to the raft of each other for comfort. Buffeted amidst an unforgiving sea of fear and uncertainty. They remained still, but many fathoms from being unmoved.

As this young child, Jim had learned on a non-verbal level that his father's well woven character neither permitted his father to be real nor take adult responsibility. Jim couldn't verbalise this dynamic. Nevertheless, our Jim dutifully danced to this dastardly ditty. Beyond the point of daring to stray out of step; a beat sure to catch the wanderer.

The experiential learning which Jim endured around his father was mentally coded on an emotional level. He *felt* it. Fear quickly gave way to submission.

The path little Jim needed lit up for him, like a beacon. The emotion dwarfed, overpowered, and trumped any type of logical system. Logic retreated to such a safe distance that it could no longer begin to make out the hypocrisy and lies.

Young children can learn to believe in Father Christmas and the Tooth Fairy. However, with the stability of his father's toxic failings, Jim's hope had long since walked. In this world, Patrick's personality transplant was likely long since lost in the post.

In these early years, how do you make sense of random beatings interspersed with occasional warmth? The predictability of these beatings was beyond Jim, but still he tried. With this inhumane conundrum wantonly etching disease, deeper and deeper into his soul.

Jim was like a desperate well-worn gambler, looking for a pattern, Trying to work out the formula to beat roulette. Staying hour after hour, in a downward spiral, seemingly devoid of the capacity to leave the game. At times, even developing superstitious ways to try to control that which a hushed part of his mind suspected he could never master or grasp.

If I touch my nose twice, the roulette wheel seems to land on a red number. When I press the slot machine button three times in quick succession, I seem to win more. When I clench my teeth and look up wide eyed, the beatings are usually not as bad. If I stay still, it ends quicker. At this tender age of seven, Jim was still trying.

Chapter 58 – The soothing ointment
of play for a 'lucky little Jim'

When circumstances permitted, Jim's nirvana like escape was solitary play in his room. It was like the soft petals of a sweet smelling rose, amidst the thorns of his life. He had some cheap soldier like figures, about two inches high. They had a value beyond words.

Within snatched moments of these early years, Jim organised his figures and ran his own world. His time with them was a slither of control and predictability, surrounded by life. Within this world of play, he worked through some of the myriad of issues which troubled him.

Young Jim focussed so intently on these soldiers that he got respite from life. He played as hard as he could, driven by a need to block out the rest of his world. Pacified, within a comfort zone which verged on the autistic.

Any intrusion was harsh. He hated the voice of his mother and father or having to leave this world of his figures. It punctured him to the very core.

Distraction from this play was like bringing him back to a world, in which he felt not to fit. It brought the flood of a sudden intensity of poisonous feelings. Like an unwelcome prick from a long sharp needle, boring into his soul.

The outer world was knocking on his door, again. It never stopped. Despite his mental detachment and his avoidance of looking at his world, it still kept getting through. Ugly, painful, and intrusive. With the predictability of breathing, it just kept coming back. He could not hold his breath for long enough.

Jim yearned for a life of constantly being embedded within his own world, controlling his army of toy soldiers. Somewhere, perhaps in the skies; the Gods maybe playfully moved the figure of our Jim on their whim, alongside shifting each integral figure within the population? Around once a month, Jim's grandmother Norma visited. She did not engage much with him, but he did recall her repeatedly letting him know how lucky he was.

'You are so lucky, little Jim' his grandmother declared, searching hard for the eye contact of six year old Jim.

'Not all children have the benefits of both a mother and a father, at home' Norma emphasised. She was kindly orienting Jim's gaze to how fortune had smiled on him. He was clearly getting so much more than he deserved.

'With being an only child, you also get all the attention to yourself!' she continued.

She ended this monologue with, *'oooh, you get everything, you do. You are spoiled'*, alongside a knowing and contented smile and a playful pinch of Jim's cheek.

Hmmm, *'you are spoiled'*. Maybe the scattergun verbal *'rat a tat tat'* from this blindfolded oik would uncommonly just let off an isolated stray bullet, which might graze the tale of that evasive beast named *'accuracy'*. Perhaps leaving accuracy to momentarily pause; still, stunned, and licking its' wounds.

Jim's outer shell felt some kind of obligation to return Norma's smile. Within his withdrawal, young Jim typically fled from the meaning of words. They were largely unwelcome sounds, intruding on him. Buzzing round like hornets, intent on stinging. They pierced painfully into his withdrawal.

Squeezing meaning out of words typically left a foul residue for our little Jim, partly because it involved engaging with the world and the presence of others. Connecting with others seemed to hold a mirror up to him, oozing shame. Even by the age of six, Jim was running from shame.

Peddling in words also rendered Jim flailing to squeeze them into gaps which were left by emotion, hypocrisy, and lies. They did not fit. A tiny Jim; around so many players that used words to mislead, posture, represent, hide, and justify.

Words oriented him towards torturous riddles, which his mind simply could not solve. He was punished for straying into shining an overt light on the contradictions and hypocrisy of his outer audience; wholly unwelcome. If he did not pick these words up, then he could partly sidestep this painful futility.

Reminding Jim of how lucky he was did not represent the only contribution from his grandmother Norma. Whenever she visited and Jim went to the toilet to relieve his bowels, she insisted on accompanying him and wiping his rear. She was very diligent, wiping it with both toilet tissue and perhaps somewhat alarmingly following this up by wiping it with the damp facecloth next to the sink. Belt and braces, I guess we might say.

By the age of about seven or eight, Jim found it within himself to float the idea that it would be fine for him to fully take on this process, independent of Norma's kindness. However, his grandmother's forceful altruism was undimmed and they continued to share these moments. Most awkwardly, on a couple of occasions, amplitude and rhythmical commitment from his grandmother precipitated a physiological knee jerk type reaction in our Jim.

In particular, Jim's weenie stood up slightly, and extended.

Norma readily served up a meaning which sat uneasily with Jim on some deeper level; laying largely dormant in the childhood years, but sure to be activated later. In particular, Norma declared with more than slight alarm, *'that's the devils work'.*

Chapter 59 - The early years –
Educational opportunity

At age five; Jim went to school. He had long since learnt to bury himself deep into his shell, which perhaps blunted the puzzles which his world presented. Of course, some part of him still learnt. There remained a part of him that still sought to understand his world, as five year olds do. He was not yet fully worn into hopelessness.

In the days of Jim's schooling, playgrounds were not well monitored. Jim was quiet and unsure of himself. This appeared to draw in a specific bully named Peter Thomas, with an almost magnetic force. Our Jim, would have the benefit of more than making Peter's acquaintance. For the early months, Peter would repetitively kick and punch Jim at playtime.

Jim recalled that one day, Peter's punch resulted in his lip bleeding and this was noticed by a specific teacher, Mrs Roberts. She asked Jim, *'how have you done that?'.* Jim replied *'I was hit by Peter Thomas'.* What was perhaps striking was that in Jim's tone, there was no sense of feeling wronged or indignant. His utterance was matter of fact and reflected that by now he accepted his world.

It was as if in Jim's mind, *'this must be what school is about'.* Perhaps tutored and readied by his father Patrick, regarding the somewhat random nature of violence. His acceptance was perhaps fuelled still further by withdrawal and guilt that something about him must be making his mum cry repeatedly at home.

The puzzle which the bullying presented was dwarfed by the enigmas which he experienced within his home environment. To her credit, the teacher sought to address this issue with our friend, Peter Thomas. Jim subsequently suffered less bullying from this specific foe during primary school.

Jim's mother continued to manifests severe depression and severe anxiety. Jim noticed the manifestations and his child-like mind sought to account for it, as best he could. He was learning about the world.

Unbeknownst to Jim, his mother was called in by a concerned teacher. The teacher looked intently at Kath and expressed concern that our shy little six year old Jim had summoned the courage to approach her (his teacher) in school and ask:

'why does my mum always cry when she makes the toast?'.

This tiny meaning-making vessel named Jim struggled to make sense of this sequence and it troubled him. Why could he not make his mother happy? Guilt surrounded him. After all, his mother was crying when she was making toast for him. He was always there and being, at the time when his mother was upset.

Jim often managed to somehow make a fuzzy mental link between his mother's upset and him and his behaviour. Not versed in complexities of causality. If two things occur to-gether, then one is the cause of the other?

It seemed to make sense. It allowed him to retain perhaps some thin illusory sense of understanding within his unpre-dictable and nonsensical world. This understanding was ex-pensive and he would pay in full though guilt, lowered self-esteem, and a sense that him and his needs were in some way not right, or fell short.

Still, understanding did not properly find the companion of control. He did not know how to stem the tide of his mother's tears. Hence, there was still some sense of helplessness and reflexive withdrawal.

Among less central experiences; Jim recalls at the age of about seven, he was a fussy eater. Perhaps not such a major affliction for today's pampered poppets, but such silliness not endured so patiently back in the seventies. Jim recalled that he did not want to eat the school's pink custard. However, the dinner lady (Mrs Broad) barked, *'you are not wasting good food - I will stand over you until you have finished that'*.

It was a struggle, but Jim felt fenced in. The result was that through the endeavour of his relentless coach, Jim finished the pink custard. Soon after, he repeatedly vomited in the classroom just after lunch.

Kath was phoned and told of the development. Not long after, he had the blessing of his mother sending him to school with sandwiches. He could side-step the land mine of school meals.

Rewind a couple of months before the saga of the pink custard; Jim brushed his feet on another landmine within the dining hall. Our seven year old Jim walked up to the serving hatch, and he must have been shuffling his feet along the floor. A large dinner lady shouted angrily, *'pick your feet up when you walk!'*. Jim carried on moving, with a lack of understanding born of the combination of his withdrawal, mental fog, and a paralysis of fear.

The instruction then repeated with even more annoyance: 'PICK UP YOUR FEET, WHEN YOU WALK!'. The volume had been raised by several notches; everything around our Jim seeming to freeze with silent anticipation. Perhaps Freud's 'angst vor etwas'. Our Jim on red alert, but unsure what was unfolding.

Jim knew the anger of this substantial dinner lady was growing and he had to take some action. What did she want? Unfamiliar with the expression, Jim made sense of it as best he could and literally lifted his feet with his hands when he walked.

This precipitated the dinner lady bellowing 'YOU CHEEKY BUGGER', followed by a firm slap. This platform dished out extra helpings of anxiety for Jim, within the dining area and beyond. Jim's brain struggled. Increased anger seemed to follow compliance with angry requests. The escape hatches in this world seemed very well hidden.

The early school reports reflect that Jim was constantly day-dreaming. Many teachers clearly saw it as a volitional character flaw and he was at times struck and shouted at for 'choosing' to day-dream. His reflexive attempts to withdraw from the sharpness of the world included the evolution of an infusion of mental fog. This was to elicit further wrath, from the Gods.

Chapter 60 - The early years – the benefits of an eager teacher?

Little Jim sought to hide, through being mentally barely present. It numbed some of the pain. He was placed in special remedial classes during his primary school journey.

Young Jim was very nervous about speaking in front of the whole class. All those eyes and all that judgement. Alongside his deep-seated sense that he was not good enough, there resonated the worries such as, *'What if I get it wrong?'*, *'What if I fall short?'*, *'What if I upset or anger people?'''*.

The world seemed scary to our Jim; barren of safety-nets. Kath's lense was already beginning to step firmly in the gap between his gaze and reality. A twisted template through which to view the world, with gaps increasingly restricting focus to *'all that might go spectacularly wrong'*. Often, much emotion sat behind, pushing his vision through these doomsday slots.

School day begins with registration. At age eight, Jim was repeatedly presented with a challenge of responding to two registers on a specific week day: terrifying Thursday. One register was for the teacher to mark down who was attending the swimming baths - to which Jim needed to say *'Yes, miss'* when his name was read out. The other register was for school meals - to which Jim needed to say *'No miss, I have brought sandwiches'*.

On the Thursdays, with these dual demands: Jim spent much of his morning from waking up, worrying about responding to the latter registers. He particularly worried about the school meals register, which required him to say more words.

In Jim's mind, the difference between the classroom demands of two words (*'Yes, Miss'*) and six words (*'No Miss, I have brought sandwiches'*) was a chasm. The number of syllables in *'sand-wiches'* seemed nothing short of mockingly cruel. Jim also found anxiety around using the word *'No'*.

On this particular Thursday, Jim practiced and practiced in his head, barely present in his broader surroundings. He did not want to fall short. Our Jim did not want to let the teacher down when he responded to the register.

His big moment came; his name was read out by Mrs Yardley. The classroom heard a sequence of: *'Mark Anthony,....Yes Miss, Phillip Bostock....Yes Miss,........**James Butler'**.

Like his mother when she needed to cook a meal for the in-laws, he was very nervous. It felt like the whole world rested squarely on his frail and tiny shoulders. He managed to nervously utter the words that had ricocheted and rebounded inside his head for the past hour, *'errrr, No miss, I have brought sandwiches'.* Executed like a true professional; by Jove, he'd done it!

An instant later, things didn't feel right – but then, they rarely did when he self-expressed. At that point, Mrs Yardley roared loudly, *'BUTLER, GET HERE NOWWWW!'.* He made his way towards the front of the class, drenched in fear and guilt. He did not understand why Mrs Yardley was angry and yet he felt sure it was all his fault.

Mrs Yardley and her companion anger could not wait for his arrival. As he got half way towards the front of the class, she rushed towards him from her lectern. Her hands grabbed into his jumper, gripped him tightly, and shook him vigorously in front of the class. He moved from side to side, like a rag doll.

As her grip released, she struck him firmly on the back of

the head and boomed fiercely, 'CONCENTRATE BOY! ARE YOU GOING TO EAT YOUR SANDWICHES IN THE SWIMMING POOL? She managed to catch Jim's expression, which combined a rabbit in headlights with a gormless lack of understanding.

Again she shouted, *'YOU ANSWERED TO THE SCHOOL MEAL REGISTER WHEN I WAS READING OUT THE SWIMMING REGISTER'*.

This conscientious teacher had attentively sniffed out a learning opportunity for Jim. The teacher teaches and the child learns: a most beautiful and basic cornerstone of civilised society. Jim had a sensitivity and he learned quickly from his world.

Sometimes we learn more than that which is explicitly taught. By this point in his childhood, Jim was perhaps too damaged to regularly cry. He would increasingly learn to withdraw. He sought an uncontroversial way of being that allowed him to exist, without being as often shaken by this world.

Chapter 61 – Time with Patrick;
the best bits.

Jim's young mind was jaded; yet, he still moved within the maze which engulfed him and a part of his mind still sought to identify patterns. One of the challenges for our very young Jim was that very occasionally Patrick behaved outside the character role in which he had been cast. Patrick's 'bad cop' character seemed to occasionally stray from the over-used script; most definitely drifting into a rare appearance as the 'good cop'. Surely, sufficiently off-piste to leave the director confused and frustrated.

The probability of an altruistic emergence correlated negatively with the amount of alcohol that Patrick had consumed; a dance so synchronised that they were so rarely out of step. At times, a rare abstinence perhaps launching young Jim to flap his waxy wings too close to a large fiery ball of hope. Not yet fully worn down.

With young Jim aged about nine, his father surely did receive the long awaited personality transplant formula in the post. Alas, only to apparently send it back after test-driving it for just over four weeks. Why these brief glory days? Reality knows more than Jim, and perhaps it might give up some clues.

The causal chain seems to begin with Patrick finding it within himself to deliver another unremarkable beating of Kath and young nine year old Jim. This had not stood out of the landscape that fell behind them, for many years. However, the setting conditions of the beating slightly tweaked.

In particular, Kath had seen something empowering on television of the *'sisters taking a stand'* genre. Far rarer to see such content back in that day; swimming against the tide and well before Oprah had navigated the Atlantic. Kath had daringly dived from the platform that the programme provided, and given stern Patrick a post-beating ultimatum.

'Quit the booze or we are finished' Kath had been able to release, in between sobs.

Now, typically such folly would quickly and progressively stretch an elastic band in Patrick's mind; it would surely very soon only snap, which signalled a violent procession. For reasons which perhaps reality herself does not fully know, the trend was bucked. A perfect storm came to pass and Jim ceased alcohol for about one month. Paradise Island, the only blot on an endless rough ocean; the family would not stay ashore for too long.

Within this glory month, Patrick took our Jim to a couple of football matches at the ground of the local team. We were back in the nineteen seventies. Our Paddy found his place, as ever behind the goal amidst the most fervent *'football fans'*.

A crowd of several thousand. Early on, many songs abound, sang by this tight congregation. All would-be alphas, singing about how they could beat up the opposition fans or bragging about their virility.

> *'Rovers boys we are here, whooo, whooo, Rovers boys we are here, whooo, whooo, Rovers boys we are here, shag the women and drink the beer, whooo, whooo'.*

Clearly aspirational, but perhaps not at the pinnacle of Maslow's hierarchy; not pinging the bell of enlightened nirvana. Now, rest assured, nine year old Jim was not living this latter life of beer and ladies which was flagged up in the lyrics. However, for some strange reason he joined in the song.

Sadly, the choir had more than one string to their bow. Additionally, vile abuse directed at black players, including what have been referred to as 'monkey chants' whenever a particular Afro-Caribbean player touched the ball. Our young Jim could not escape noticing that virtually everyone behind the goals joined in; mainly men in their twenties, thirties, forties, fifties, and even beyond. Sentiment that should be beyond the pale, given airing.

Civilised reality surely knows such venom as decency-defying. Akin to the notion of persecuting people because of their eye colour or the tone of their voice. A genetic characteristic not chosen; a futile barometer of a soul. But, the pack were unrelenting.

Perhaps people are simply people, valuable in terms of their own merits; uninfluenced by any visual characteristics. Very often, the ugliest of human nature just does not work like that. Lip service often paid; words to mask.

Jim was perhaps akin to a young nine year old in a church, with all around him singing hymns. Jim's taste buds sufficiently green that he could not fully discern the foul flavour of this flock. Patrick, singing with all his heart.

A fuller smile, Jim had perhaps never seen on his father's lips. Clearly, this was ticking some boxes in Patrick's inners. Seemingly the fullness of Patrick's smile perhaps in direct proportion to the level of vitriol directed towards a minority group, which were numerically less.

Egged on by Patrick, nine year old Jim unthinkingly joined in some of the *'songs'*. *'Monkey chants'* echoing and reverberating around the ground, like some gross war cry. Our Jim then recalls a moment of seeing a father of Afro-Caribbean descent donning a home team shirt, with a son that was similar age to our Jim. Sadness and anguish etched on to the father's face.

Even then, a nine year old Jim felt awkward enough for his chants to quickly reduce in volume and cease. He would blessedly shed such rancid racist themes from his core well before adulthood. Within our Jim's being, there was a caring centre. Albeit often having to filter through many layers of anxiety and torment, in order to break through at the surface.

Indeed, in young adulthood, Jim would look back and remorsefully contemplate the fate of this father. A father adjacent to his son; both surrounded by something beyond horrific. Likely as many fathers, working with all that was within his core to create a wonderful life and a beautiful future for his young son; finding himself in a world whose elements often worked so hard to deny this. No other world to choose from; heart breaking. Wanting so much more for his son. Though tragically, one man, surely unable to hold back the tide of that time.

Likely carving out what he could for his family, with his everything. Yet, at times akin to a parent on a pavement helplessly watching their kin suffer a horrendous car crash; again and again and again. Pale society just keeping wilfully, mockingly, steering into their kin. As an adult, our Jim could be rendered tearful if he truly contemplated this; his form not numbed to the suffering of others; leaning more towards altruism than psychopathy.

The choir sings on at this football game, each element seemingly feeding off the others; justification, belonging, and security in numbers. The era looks the other way. Many years later, our Jim would hear about psychological underpinnings of such venom from a flamboyant lecturer.

Just before our Jim was born, Erik Erikson spoke of man's ingrained tendency towards 'pseudospeciation', striving for distinctions to enable an in-group that we are in and an out-group that we are not in, followed by relentless pillorying of the latter.

As a 'regular' UK prisoner to a 'rule 43' with deviant sexual proclivities; as fan of one team, to their rivals; more isms than we could shake a stick at; surely *'me too'*? Our humanity mixed with language, so often a cocktail that leaves a hangover of *'needing to hate'* and *'needing to be better than them'*. A cheap way to boost our self-esteem, provided the potion is left devoid of decency, wisdom, and insight.

We see it everywhere, we squash one form and it just comes out somewhere else. The foul underpinnings and gross products manifest, at times dressed cleverly in flawed logic or subtle disguise by some sly old fox. Unbeknownst to our Jim at this nine year old stage, he will himself live to directly taste the rotting breath of such discrimination, prejudice, and hatred; fired firmly at his adult self, repeatedly. The White Hart Inn awaits; at this stage, hidden.

Jim returned home from the football matches, back to the bosom of his family home. Quality time with Patrick ticked off. Time marched on slightly, but we still find ourselves in Patrick's month of sobriety.

Chapter 62 – For one month only, kick one Butler and they all limp: a family united

Another day; another collection of slings and arrows colliding with a nine year old Jim. However, this time, ammunition not fired by Patrick. Indeed, Patrick a definite ally. If it was a film, perhaps 'The Equaliser' starring Patrick Butler.

A walk from his school to his home would see Jim grabbed by a youth several years older, and pulled into a ginnel. This youth had what seemed to our Jim to be Goliath like stature, but Jim surely no David? Two girls watched on giggling, as Goliath punched Jim square in the face. A most unsolicited offering.

Jim's head banged against the wall, inflicting a double whammy. Jim instantly terrified and tearful, with his generous audience allowing his departure. The girls seeming gleeful, as what may have been some type of northern courtship ritual played out.

Jim meandered his way back home, occasional sobbing, and constantly looking round furtively.   An unlikely saviour emerged. A car pulled up at the side of him, with Jim's initial anxiety giving way to the realisation that this was his father, Patrick.

Patrick arriving in the chariot, in the form of the family's rusty brown Ford Cortina. This vehicle could still wearily plod from A to B. Indeed, it often gave extra, in the form of an impersonation of the sounds of an old singer sewing machine whenever the accelerator pedal was pressed.

'Hey buddy, hop in. Why are you crying?' Patrick asked, sounding genuinely concerned

Jim recounted the tale, and felt the warmth of Patrick's concern. What Jim would never know is that Patrick himself suffered horrendous bullying and teasing for much of his childhood. The echoes deep within Patrick's hollow shell were perhaps fainter, but definitely not silenced.

'OK, bud. I need to nip to this electric shop to get a couple of bulbs. Then, I'm going to take you to the sweet shop in the precinct and you can have whatever you want' Patrick declared.

Reality knew the latter benevolence were blessings from not just abstinence, but from residual money from a recent and extremely rare win on the horses. As it happened, one of the ladies which Patrick was having an affair with was a nurse named Jean Medhurst that worked nights, yielding Patrick to be inspired to put the bulk of the family money for that week on a horse called 'Night Nurse'; the latter romping home. Jim, unaware, but simply grateful.

Bulbs on board, Patrick pulled up in a parking spot next to the sweet shop. In essence, this area contained two main shops, a sweet shop and a traditional chippy. Arrival here was usually a signal of a very welcome treat. There was a small concreted court yard leading to the shops, where youngsters often congregated. The youths perhaps magnetically drawn to feasts worthy of meeting their salivation and truly dancing along their eager taste buds.

On arrival, Patrick exited. Soon, he noticed that his young companion had not followed. He looked back and saw Jim was cowering; refusing to exit. Patrick approached the door and noted Jim's alarm increasing when he pulled it ajar.

'Hey, what's the matter?' Patrick asked, sensitively.

'That boy' Jim said, very slightly moving his eyes nervously in the direction of Goliath. *'He's the one that hit me'* Jim whis-

pered.

'The one in the grey jacket?' Patrick confirmed, identifying a Goliath that was still accompanied by his two female fans.

Jim nodded nervously, his eyes widening appreciably and his lips pursed and disappearing. Jim felt it; Patrick's anger for once on the side of his own family.

'Come on buddy, he ain't gonna touch you' Patrick said, with conviction.

Patrick held a comforting arm around Jim's shoulder and shepherded him towards his fear. Only at this point did Goliath become aware of Jim and his father. He visibly jumped slightly.

'LOOK AT THE SIZE OF YOU AND LOOK AT THE SIZE OF HIM', Patrick bellowed fiercely, at this would-be bully.

'CAN'T YOU FIND ANYONE YOUR OWN SIZE TO PICK ON?' Patrick asked.

To the untrained eye, every ounce of body language that leaked from Patrick spoke loudly that he was about to physically attack this youth. Maybe he was?

'I'm really sorry' Goliath uttered, with tone and demeanour changed in an instant. A feral specimen probably remained, but temporarily shackled by changed situation parameters.

'GET DOWN ON YOUR KNEES' Patrick demanded, with his volume drawing in a small crowd.

Goliath followed the command, seamlessly.

'NOW BEG FOR FORGIVENESS' Patrick boomed.

Goliath initially began begging Patrick for forgiveness, but he was quickly re-directed to beg little Jim for his forgiveness.

'I'm really sorry, please forgive me' Goliath pleaded, with tears beginning to flow.

Patrick conclude the interchange by saying, *'RIGHT, NOW, GET OUT OF MY SIGHT AND IF I SEE YOU ROUND HERE AGAIN I WILL HURT YOU'.*

The two girls no longer stuck to Goliath's shadow, static and visibly crestfallen. The awe drained out of these maidens; going south. Patrick perhaps pouring cold water on the titillating fantasies which may have been built around the earlier alpha male display which Goliath had put on; the northern courtship ritual interrupted. Their ferocious fearless alpha fizzling out before their very eyes; slipped from his lofty perch.

As Goliath wearily ambled about twenty yards away, his tears had begun to flood. He shouted back defiantly at Patrick, perhaps trying to salvage grains of his ego, *'I'm coming back with my dad and he'll kill you'.*

Patrick boomed back in an instant, almost overlapping Goliath's words, 'BRING YOU DAD, GRANDAD, AND YOUR WHOLE BLOODY FAMILY. I CAN TELL THEM WHAT A BULLY YOU ARE AND I'LL DEAL WITH THE LOT OF THEM'.

Goliath vanished. Patrick, a big fan of Charles Bronson in the *'Death Wish'* films. In these triumphant moments, he had perhaps had chance to act out the vigilante role.

Jim saw no sign of bluff in his father. In the face of his youthful kin, Patrick's words seemed to contain a rare resonance with his body, behaviour, and being. A few scattered moments where Jim marvelled at the cut of his father's jib. Simultaneously, treasured and impactful for our Jim.

What followed was Patrick slightly impatient with Jim in the shop, hurrying him along to get his sweets. They then moved swiftly from the scene and were able to return home; more than victorious. Unbeknownst to little Jim: reality knew that whilst Patrick was genuine in those moments, the visual stimulus of angry adult kin of Goliath would surely have seen him take flight, and run to the hills?

Jim could not but be lifted by the sense of power that he felt, when he saw fear in a bended Goliath's eyes. These feelings tasted even sweeter than the candy, albeit that Goliath's fear was not directly of Jim, but of a Patrick-shaped weapon that he unleashed. Something moved and shifted, inside our Jim.

Patrick had a certain 'side' to him. Rest assured, Patrick's anger sometimes really took hold. Jim witnessed an altercation Patrick had with a small shopkeeper. A punch from Patrick landing squarely on a foreign hooter, readily producing claret. Jim's eyes also fell upon an argument between Patrick and an effeminate manager of a bar. Patrick reaching out to the latter, and dragging him over the bar.

When Jim was aged about twelve, he would experience the challenge of his family house being burglarised. For months after, Patrick kept menacingly saying *'I'd love to find out who broke in. Just give me five minutes with them in a room'*. Reality knew this particular verbalisation may have had more than a little ruse within it. Nevertheless, this *'let me at them'* or *'hold me back'* type war cry was often spewed from our Patrick.

Patrick often appeared like a drowning man struggling to swim on the spot, always craving the temporary relief of a life jacket in the form of a vessel into which he could put all his anger. He stumbled from one grievance to the next, struggling hugely in between. If there was nothing worthwhile to get angry about, he'd have to work harder to get angry about something that was not worthwhile.

Our little Jim did not greatly comprehend why Patrick would wish to spend his time with the rascals that burglarised their home. But, know this: more seeds were being scattered in Jim's mind. Most seeds lay dormant, perhaps never spectacularly activated.

The genetic dice long since rolled, perhaps generations before Jim's arrival. Yet these seeds would still need so much more to flourish. They awaited the right soil, the sun, and the right amount of water.

Would future conditions gently nurture these fragile dependent threads? Time retained her secrets back then, but ultimately time would surely tell.

Chapter 63 – Patrick's brief project
to make Jim a winner

Important to give a more complete picture of this fine figure of a Patrick. When Patrick was not dissolved in ethanol, there were more than a couple of strands of decency. During this month of sobriety when Jim was aged about nine, Patrick gave so much more.

Now, the Butler family had never excelled at anything that society deems credit-worthy. No victories, no medals, and no commendations. An exceptional craving to be winners; yet hunger left wholly unsatisfied. Such harsh and ungiving reality, that had unrelentingly surrounded them.

Jim had competed in the compulsory three events at Sports day for three previous years. He was nil more than an *'also ran'*, in each of the nine confirmations as a Butler. The three events comprised: sprint race, obstacle race, and potato and spoon race.

Jim once had a rare playdate with William Rogers last year, the superstar of the year. He briefly ventured into William's upstairs bedroom and was left open-mouthed at the plethora of trophies and medals. There seemed scant room left for little Willy.

Surely nothing short of a structural masterpiece that the creaking floorboards could somehow carry such silverware. No such stress at Jim's residence. Rogers had won all nine of the prior nine Sports day races, without even the generosity to drop a crumb for his thwarted class mates.

Whilst Patrick had only attended the "*silliness*" of Sports day once, something grew in him during this month off the booze. He would change the course of the Butler trajectory; he would coach Jim to win a race! Patrick had recently watched a documentary about a coach who used carefully designed strategy and *'sports psychology'* to catapult an athlete to greatness.

Jim would become Patrick's project. The residual energy which Patrick had left over from his multiple affairs, he would channel it to make Jim a winner. Patrick pursued this dream; as if it would chase off all the unchanging losses that had filled up his own lifetime.

Now, Patrick knew that Jim could never win a straight running race. In the absence of tripping other runners, two weeks training would not open up a path for a relative tortoise to pip the Usain Bolt of the year. Neither did Jim have the speed and agility to win the obstacle course. However, Patrick eyed an opening in the potato and spoon race.

Last year, Patrick attended Sports day for the first time and he observed the spectacle of the potato and spoon race. He saw children running at full pelt and dropping the potato several times, then having to stop, fumble around, and then gradually build up speed. Patrick felt that if Jim just learnt to balance the potato for the full race and moved at a steady pace, then it may just be enough.

What followed was two weeks of heavy training from Patrick, evenings and weekends. They spent more quality time together for those two weeks than they had probably shared in the prior nine years. Likely a relatively lonely jewel, in Patrick's fatherhood crown.

Patrick remembered a quote from the documentary, *'if you think you can or you think you can't, you are right'*. He tried hard to instil a belief and confidence in Jim. However, even by age nine: Jim accepted this pressure-sell on the surface, but his deeper self-concept was unmoved. The potency was akin to trying to feed a starving child through providing pictures of food; Jim was just unable to digest it on a deeper level.

Then, the big day arrived. It was a sunny day and a large turn-out. William Rogers romped home in the first two races.

In these initial two races, our enthusiastic Jim was near the back of the eager pack. Patrick coped with these not unex-pected showings. He pulled Jim aside just prior to the final spectacle of the potato and spoon race, breaching the etiquette of parents on one side and children on the other.

'Come on Jim, you can do this, it's all on this' Patrick said, with an uncomfortable intensity. His eye contact piercing, striving to magically fill Jim up with extra energy and vigour.

Jim lined up alongside eleven class-mates, excited to the point that he had perhaps slightly left his own body. Not a major problem, as Patrick had him so well trained that he could prob-ably vacate his body and still execute the technique. Patrick met Jim's adrenaline and raised it, and part of Jim could still feel his father's eyes.

'three,....two,....one, GO'.

A gaggle of about five lads ran well ahead of Jim. But then, to Patrick's delight, it began to unfold. All but Jim were con-stantly blighted by dropping their potato.

Jim cut through the pack, like a hot knife through butter. About ten strides to go and he was clearly ahead. Glory was waiting for Jim; he could feel the warmth of her arms out-stretched and ready to embrace him.

It was then that Patrick let out a primeval roar that must have been heard in the deepest darkest depths of Peru, "DON'T DROP IT!". Now Patrick's vocal chords have never been shy, but Jim had never heard him make such a noise before; it felt like the whole air vibrated.

Jim visibly jumped and gravity took firm control on the potato. He re-gathered himself, but just got pipped into third place by William Rogers and a rather surprised Billy Jackson. Strange thing, William Rogers slipped from perfection for the first time. He tasted second. Jim was not displeased for Billy Jackson because he was a nice lad who never really did well in anything sporty and he often got teased for being a bit podgy.

In all races, the first three had the glory of several seconds on a podium, whilst family snaps were eagerly taken. Jim had got onto the podium, for the first and as it happened, last time. As Jim stood on the third place step, Billy Jackson beamed at the top and William Rogers sobbed. Patrick looked on with an intensity; a spectacle enough to make a soba man drink?

Jim could sense that whilst Patrick was not shedding tears, his disappointed dwarfed that of young Rogers. Soon within his childhood, a part of Jim's inner depth whirred with the notions that *'if I had been better, maybe my dad would not have drank?, maybe my parents would have had a better relationship?, maybe my dad would have been less violent? maybe Kath would not have suffered such severe depression?'*. Reality held her secrets close; Jim surmised.

In truth; Jim was lifted by this third place finish. Somehow able to partly step outside Patrick's disappointment; Jim felt it was a treasure which bestowed upon him some real glory. A triumph which felt well beyond anything that had befallen him on his earlier path. In his mind, it stood for something so much better than him.

In Jim's school, there were no medals for third place; just a small circular red sticker which stated 'Third Place' and showed a small picture of a trophy. Jim's hankering to amount to something perhaps captured by that third place sticker stuck firmly on his clothes wardrobe. It still remained several years later, with edges crinkled and scuffed.

Chapter 64 - Patrick: the gift that keeps on giving (for a month at least)

This soba month rolled on, with neat Patrick offering yet more rewards. Still aged nine, Jim is met with sight of Patrick and Kath entering his room. No raised voices on this day, but still the intrusion upon his withdrawal feels ill-fitting. He notices that Patrick is carrying a large bag; bulging, with something bulky inside.

Patrick gives him the bag, with a smile. It feels soft and Jim's mind initially thinks it must be bedding, like a big quilt. Yet, his mind struggles to match bedding with the expectant smiles of these parental creatures. As Jim starts to pull out the item, he is dazzled by the brightest orange that has ever been inflicted on his defenceless retinas. If ever a colour required sun glasses, he had just found it.

Fear surrounds young Jim, but he is unsure why. For a split second, his mind conjures with the remote notion that this could be clothing. He tries to reassure himself, urging in his mind, '*it can only be bedding.....for the love of God, it can only be bedding*'. Whilst slowed down, he pulls it further.

Jim feels a depth of padding which would surely be sufficient to give safe landing to people jumping from the top of eighty storey buildings. He feels assured that he will be feverishly warm with this bedding. Surely, readied for the depths of winter.

Keen to get this ritual completed and return to his soldiers, he completed the reveal. It is then that Jim has the realisation, it is a coat! Or to be more precise; a bright fluorescent orange coat that would quadruple his width in an instant.

Inside, little Jim is left thinking, '*I would kinda look like a bright orange bubble in that coat'.* Before Jim gets chance to weep, he manages to catch Patrick and Kath's excited expressions, followed up by *'your dad has spent a fortune on this designer coat, with real goose feathers'.*

After a brief moment of perhaps praying that there is a goose inside the coat which will take flight, Jim glances up again and catches the smug self-satisfied smiles of Kath and Patrick. It seems their minds believe that they have given him the greatest gift that could ever grace this fair planet. Jim not only withdrawn, but feeling hemmed in by their expectations. Reluctant to shatter their delusional world view. This coat albeit sent with love, perhaps also a totem of Jim's separateness.

Jim remains cornered for a few moments and from somewhere, he manages to stutter *'it's grr, grr, great, thanks'.* Nine years old, Jim's main way of coping with the world was trying not to stand out. So, why would he not want to look like a fluorescent orange version of the Michelin man?

'I told you he'd love it' said Patrick, looking at Kath. A family back on track, for now at least. Patrick then looked at Jim intently; triumphantly uttering, *'your mum thought you might want to choose your own coat, but I knew this one was just right. Sometimes you just know'.* Yes, sometimes you just know!

Reality knew that Patrick had delved into a second hand shop earlier that day and seen what was actually an expensive designer coat from America, going for a song. This coat happened to be washed up there, a few years after a very wealthy American tourist had been robbed for the coat and their valuables. Hopefully, it might bequeath better fortune for young Jim?

'He's going to be the smartest boy in School' Kath declared. Triggering further misery setting into Jim's soul – he realised

that he was expected to wear this at school! Expectations surrounded Jim, like the bars of a cage. He could not see any escape; he was going to have to wear this *'bully magnet'* within his school.

As the orange coat docked in Jim's wardrobe, this ship had well and truly sailed. Too much for this young waif to own. Jim hated eyes settling on him. Like a young child thoughtlessly playing with a magnifying glass to concentrate the sun's rays on a confused insect, Patrick had found a way to focus and magnify the eye gaze of peers upon our Jim.

Soon after, a coated Jim returns to school. He finds himself wearing the orange monstrosity, self-consciousness ratcheted up to new heights. It has so much padding that one might question whether the world is still graced with a feathered goose.

For a Jim that wants to blend in and not stick out, he feels that the coat will reach out to the bullies like a bright beacon. He feels that it would be less risky to simply wear a tee-shirt that says *'Please bully me'* in big letters. For once, Jim's radar is not fully off.

Jim quickly gets the nickname 'tango', though this is short-lived and will be followed in later years by much more hurtful names. Additionally, within the first few days of going to school in the coat, a boy called Phillip Holbrooke homes in on him. Phillip's creativity manifests in him finding a new break-time entertainment, involving swinging this orange bubble round by the hood of his coat.

Several dizzying break-times come and go. But then, something gives. In particular, the hood of Jim's coat is ripped off and the coat torn untidily at the top. Jim, suddenly separated from the bridle; free.

Our young Phillip is left holding a detached hood in his hands, as Jim is flung to the ground with a thud. Machine gun laughter is rattled off by Phillip and several onlookers; aimed wholly in Jim's direction. Phillip finds the good grace to say, *'I'm sorry, Tango'* and he hands Jim back his hood.

As school ended that day, Jim was met with sight of his grandmother Norma. Whilst he was unaware, Kath's depression had reared up viciously and Norma had stepped in for the pick-up. In an instant, Norma noticed the torn hood in Jim's hands.

'What happened there?' Norma demanded, crossly.

Jim recounted the tale with his usual veracity. They walked on the pavement just outside the school grounds, towards the car. It was then that Jim eyed Phillip Holbrooke, walking along the playground along the side of the school; separated from them by just the green iron fence that marked part of the school perimeter. Without thinking, Jim gave more richness to the tale by sharing with the obviously interested Norma that, *'the boy over there is Phillip Holbrooke, the boy that spun me round'.*

'Wait there' Norma demanded. Jim had inadvertently released his pit bull; wholly unaware of what he had set in motion. He observed Norma entering the school grounds by the nearest means, and ushering Phillip into a corner. They were clearly conversing.

Soon after, Jim saw Norma's hand lifted up and brought down heavily on young Phillip. She targeted a cheek and then the top of his head. Norma, with the grace of a skilful boxer; finding the gaps in Phillip's makeshift attempts at defence; picking her shots so very well.

It seemed that there was a new sheriff in town. Then a barrage of three of four quick slaps. God had gifted this sixty eight year old lady with a blinding hand speed, that wholly defied her age.

With just a few blows, Norma left a tearful Phillip; probably introducing him to regret. Norma squeezing out retribution, with actions probably not too far from the bounds of appropriateness within this earlier era. Legislation to curb such urges not yet effectively manifest. Our Jim, quietly impressed with the power of his Norma, effortlessly dominating perhaps the toughest boy in his year.

The show went largely unnoticed, aside from drawing in Jim's peepers and the stray eyes of one of the posh looking tall and stick-thin mothers. The latter reacted akin to a standard on-watcher, when a fierce gunslinger enters the saloon; no resistance and wide berth. A scene befitting of some of that haunting music from the spaghetti westerns of Sergio Leone; perhaps '*The Good, The Bad, and the Ugly*'. Maybe at different times, Norma would befit each of those labels?

Chapter 65 – Have I got rabies?

Just before high school, a cloak of helplessness and withdrawal had all but enveloped Jim.   With a level of encouragement surpassing the enthusiastic Patrick prior to Jim's potato and spoon bronze, little Jim's world seemed to be beckoning him to slip further and further down the rabbit hole within his mind. He was more than obliging.

The great magicians make what they cloak disappear.   After the vanishing, transfixed eyes might be greeted with a beautiful substitute. Maybe a snowy white dove or the cuteness of an innocent rabbit.

The magician that was Jim's world seemed to be making him progressively disappear, deep within a cloak woven of helplessness, avoidance and withdrawal. Yet, eventually, the product of the big reveal may not be so kind to any awaiting peepers. What was hidden, would ultimately appear. Perhaps, increasingly gross and distorted?

Perhaps a world wore away what could have been? Maybe Jim's world was an entitled cuckoo; nay but a foul usurper? Or maybe, just reality.

Jim's mind became like a magnet, drawn to fear. Jim's mother Kath wanted her son's life to go well, but the yearning squeezed Jim through the template of her plagued soul. When one combines a mother's wish for her son to have a good life with a mother's affliction of severe anxiety and depression, one has the ingredients for the development of a most officious early warning system.

Whenever an excited young Jim arrived to tell Kath of a new possibility in his life, Kath was like a coiled spring reflexively warning about what could go wrong. The heat of Kath's words readily evaporated enthusiasm and joy. Jim's mind settled increasingly on *'what could go spectacularly wrong'*. Well before adulthood, *'what could go spectacularly well'* was a contemplation which was a foreign land to Jim. A land that he would very rarely look to visit in adulthood.

Jim's focus became unerringly focussed down the barrel of disaster, drawing him to it. Living it relentlessly in his mind. His energy had found a home.

Aged nine, young Jim had learned that there was a condition known as *'rabies'* which could be fatal. His mind then managed to wander to an anxiety-drenched *'what if I have rabies?'*. Jim needed a way to get reassurance. He could not live with this weight.

Our young Jim no longer trusted the outer world. This was too big to share, with anyone. So, he was alone. He had to find his own solutions to this conundrum of whether he had been afflicted with rabies.

Young Jim's world back then saw technology in a relative infancy. No internet in sight. No option to confide in Google. Hence, Jim's path to find the treasure of reassurance took him to reading about *'rabies'* in one of the few books within his family home, a medical encyclopedia.

Jim went through the well-worn pages, which had so often had the company of his mother's mitts. He learnt that another name for rabies is *'hydrophobia'* which literally means *'fear of water'*. He discovered that this *'fear of water'* reportedly can be a symptom of the disease of *'rabies'*.

Jim's fear not acquiesced by this research. Yet, the yielding of an avenue to perhaps reach the reassurance that his troubled mind sought. Jim reasoned that he could fill up a sink with water and check in with himself, to see if he was afraid of it. If he was not afraid of the water, then perhaps he could consider that he probably did not have rabies?

Now, young Jim decided that he was probably not afraid of the water he invited into the sink. However, his over-scanning of his soul left a sense that he probably did not especially like the water. In this sense, maybe it was a mild fear. Hence, maybe he had rabies?

As he walked away from the sink, doubt and an intrusive thought, 'what if I missed something', surely better to check again. On some days, it was as if he was connected to the sink by a strong elastic band, snapped back again. Belt and braces maybe, but how many fucking belts and braces did his needy and torturous emotion demand? Never enough.

For more than a year, he was involved in a dance. Several times each day: filling up sinks, checking in with himself to see how he felt about the water, and being left with perhaps brief partial reassurance. Still, there was always the reek of doubt and anxiety. Kath's training had been thorough, '*what if*' catastrophising was like an eager wasp constantly buzzing within Jim's mind.

Filling the sink over and over and over, countless times. Yet, for many months, the reservoir of fear simply refused to run dry. Ultimately, the reservoir remained full, but it would be diverted through other channels. The fear of rabies passed before our Jim reached his teens.

Chapter 66 - In bigots we trust?

Within his mental files of his childhood, Jim recalls spending some of his childhood with the Braithwaite family. They lived on the same cul-de-sac on which Jim's own family residence lay. The Braithwaite family were opinionated, judgemental, and heavily bigoted against homosexuals. The latter no stranger to that era. For this family, their opinions were fired off reflexively and without a trace of contrition; akin to an overzealous gunslinger with an itchy trigger finger.

The Braithwaite family voiced their defensive judgements; in a way that could only mean that they had the sole franchise on what was acceptable. They had a swagger that can flow from relentlessly defining people different from themselves as wholly inadequate. Defining all that they themselves are as the gold standard.

Unbeknownst to Jim, the matriarch of this tribe would judge against his mother; firmly deciding that her depression simply meant that she was *'weak'*. Their lack of doubt and the frequency of *'shots fired'* gave them an aura of power to our young Jim. He found himself anxious that his being should ever stray into a place in which they shot their wanton venom.

Aged eleven, Jim heard the Braithwaites make very negative comments about a famous male singer that was *"gay"*. The domineering and tough mother of this family shared her wisdom, *"he is still not married at forty and so he must be gay....he's a shirt lifter"*.

It was not just the words of the Braithwaite's regarding *'homosexuals'*, but the feeling that young Jim picked up behind it. There was unmistakeable mockery, aggression, and disgust. They were like a pack of wolves, and the hatred in their tone was difficult to ignore. Sadly, their attitudes were not conspicuous during that era, especially within the harsh northern town in which Jim was reared.

The Braithwaite's desire to feel superior seemed to crush any sense of decency, self-awareness, and logic. Young Jim was overpowered and he had to follow suit. He experienced the Braithwaite's teachings on homosexuality on several occasions between the ages of about seven and eleven years of age.

Even by age eleven, Jim was unable to make sense of this with any adult logic. Still, he *'learnt'.* If his mind did not think along with the Braithwaites, then surely he would be firmly within the crosshares of these ultimate arbiters of *'what is acceptable'* and *'what is abhorrent'.*

For the Braithwaites, the line between the latter dichotomous positions seemed less than thin. The obvious hatred of this respected and powerful family must mean that being homosexual is really bad, Jim's child-like mind thought. At such tender age, it dare not think against them.

With that, Jim's mind had found something else to fear. He had found something else that could go wrong. More specifically, maybe he was *'gay'*? Living within a harsh northern city drenched with bigots, in the seventies, eighties, and nineties: he spent countless years worrying about *'maybe deep down, I am gay?'.*

How could a civilised society begin to leave people so troubled by such wondering? Perhaps, as Bob Dylan sang, answers *'blowing in the wind'.* Regardless, young Jim perhaps only had the society which he had been given.

A big ask for a young mind to be uninfluenced by the society which they find themselves in. Surely, perhaps close to asking a person without an umbrella to venture outside of shelter in torrential rain without getting wet? Jim not drenched, but certainly dampened by his context.

Jim learned quickly. The toxic teachings of the Braithwaite's stood between him and the sanctuary of an attitudinal position of decency and reasonableness regarding sexuality. His young mind could not break through the barrier.

Soon after being touched by the obscene distortions of the Braithwaites, Jim's worries took off. He was minding a two year old neighbour, whilst he and a friend played football on a nearby school yard. The two year old boy was crying. To Jim's mind, the crying felt like sharp finger nails dragged on a chalk board. Instinctively Jim briefly kissed the young boy, striving to comfort the child and cease the crying.

The two year old child instantly stopped crying, though looking slightly confused. Suddenly, the gravity of the situation hit home. In the far distance was the residence of the Braithwaite's. They overlooked the yard.

In an instant, Jim knew that the whole Braithwaite family had seen him kiss this young boy. They knew he was homosexual. The remnants which were left of his soul sunk, even deeper inside.

His fear blocked logic. The Braithwaite residence was around three hundred yards away, and only just perceptible through a couple of trees. There was a truth that knew that in order to even begin to see Jim from the three hundred yards away, the Braithwaite's would need very high power binoculars which could almost see round corners. Even then, they would likely be unable to see the momentary peck which Jim instinctively gave to comfort this young boy.

Jim's truth knew only one thing – the Braithwaite's saw him.

He *felt* it. Their judgements weighed heavily on him and they would not be readily shaken off. He knew what homosexuality meant. He had learnt from the very powerful Braithwaite family. Too meek to question.

Young Jim would later also ruminate about having, through the brief kiss, diverted this innocent young boy to an inevitable path of homosexuality. Fresh from Braithwaite logic, he was tortured by the notion that he had ruined this innocent soul. Through clumsy words, he spent hours trying to repair the *'damage'* for several years. Trying to amend his impact on this young boy's life path. He felt responsible.

Jim's mind had evolved to be able to find an endless supply of dangers to worry about. His world became increasingly polluted by negative possibility.

The risk assessment department in Jim's mind grew ever bigger, increasingly taking up the space of the other sections. Fear infiltrating every division. Working neurons flocking to join the risk assessment specialty within Jim's brain; packed tighter than sardines, with overzealous emotions squeezing more than a few red herrings in.

Alongside this, let us note that fear does not invariably lead to shrinkage and compliance. Imagine even the domesticated cat, cornered in a cage and prodded firmly and repeatedly with a stick. A paradigm to yield a creature feeling threatened. Not surprising if such a tender pet would soon reflexively hiss and scratch; aggression and spite from little kitty. Threat can yield aggression and lashing out. Of course, our Jim carried the weight of language and associated regulative prowess, but still we might have wondered: how many prods will our Jim passively take from this world?

Would Jim's rage at his world stay forever buried, under tremendous debris of fear? If our Jim arrived at a place where he conceived that he had nothing left to lose, what products may manifest? Yet, at that stage, maybe fate still wondered if there would ever be such a game changing liberator akin to Plato's ring of Gyges? Perhaps the Gods unaware of their future whims; which pieces would they arbitrarily move, in their pursuit of passing time?

Chapter 67 – A tragedy in the neighbourhood

Even by age eleven, it seemed that Jim's mind had evolved such that it did not even really need significant events to create neurotic fixations. Jim had so much anxiety inside that it could not be prevented from squirting out and landing on something. Like water forced through a tube that is frequently pocked with large holes, there is an inevitability that it will leak out and dampen the outside world.

Alongside this, at the age of eleven, Jim did stumble on a real tragedy. The evening ended like many others. Jim went to bed. On this night, he was sufficiently relaxed and fatigued to effortlessly drift off to sleep. Consciousness quickly floating away.

When Jim had difficulties sleeping, he sometimes used to imagine that he was a spy like James Bond and he was shooting maybe fifteen to twenty enemy operatives. In the process, he imagined having been hit by about ten bullets, but he was so strong that he just managed to shoot the last one of the enemy and complete the mission. At which point, he was wounded and drifting out of consciousness and it was unclear if he would die. He felt himself drifting off. Then, he fell asleep. Reliably, his strength was such that he always managed to survive, with his imaginary wounds healed; awakening amidst another morning.

On this particular night, Jim had managed to fall off to sleep without the need for taking bullets. A few hours into his slumber and in the early hours of the morning, he had begun to hear lots of loud voices from downstairs. Sleep had such a hold of him that he managed to convince his mind that his parents were having a party downstairs and he could just get back to sleep. However, the noise continued and loudened; eventually he was shaken from his sleep.

For some unknown reason and in a dazed state: Jim partly opened the curtains on the window next to his bed, pushed his head against the window, and glanced up along the row of houses. He was greeted with the sight of huge angry flames, flicking outwards and upwards from the residence which housed a friend named Martin. The meaty flames aggressively cavorted. Their orange tips moving in all directions, like the menacing lashes of a devils long tail.

The vision which met his eyes teleported him deep into panic. Jim did not notice the fire engine, which was already trying to tame this ferocious adversary. He ran downstairs, reflexively knowing that the people in the party must be made aware of this unfolding catastrophe. Jim expected a group of adults with drinks in hand, talking, and that customary smell of over-used perfume. Before he had got to the bottom of the stairs, his panicked being announced *'next door but one is on fire'.*

'We know' Patrick said. *'Go and have a sit in the lounge with Kelly'* he continued in his broad Lancashire accent. Kelly was the teenage girl from the house in between Jim's house and the house that was on fire. She was perhaps sheltering in Jim's house in case the fire spread across to hers.

Later, Jim would realize that there had never been a party on this evening and the noise that had surrounded him related to the repercussions of the fire. As Jim walked through the kitchen on his way to the lounge, Jim saw the slightly charred and animated figure of Dierdre. Dierdre was the mother who lived in the house that was in flames. She sounded hysterical and kept repeating, *'I've killed Emma, I've killed Emma'*, volume raised and more than saturated in torturous emotion. A paramedic, someone Jim did not recognise, and his parents were all nearby trying to reassure and support Dierdre.

It transpired that Dierdre had argued with her husband, got drunk and fell asleep on the sofa with a lit cigarette in her hand. The cigarette had dropped onto the carpet, which was close to the wooden stairs. When Dierdre awoke, the wooden stairs were already fiercely alight.

Furious flames taken over; dominant, spreading without conscience, and unreachable by any human plea. On awakening, Dierdre was already travelling irrevocably and with a sense of helplessness to the site of her tragedy. Many of her future moments would be eaten up, willing the Gods to turn back time.

Dierdre's nine year old daughter Emma perished in the fire. Emma, a fun-loving young girl that our Jim regularly spent time with. It was not lost on Jim that by chance, any poor soul could be ended at any time by unforeseen tragedy.

From that point forwards, Jim became afraid of his family house burning down. He would develop obsessional checking in relation to the cooker, the plug sockets, and the appliances. He might check that something was off, but then go back as many as a dozen times to ensure that it was off. It was as if he did not trust his own eyes; often he needed to also touch the appliance with his hands, to appease his doubting peepers.

No matter how many times he checked, he would still have to walk away with some grating uncertainty left over. He never found a specific number of checking attempts which would fully chase away this unease. The puzzle remained unsolved.

Sometimes Jim would return home just to check the cooker was not switched on. Hundreds of checks, all revealed that it was never left on accidentally. Hence, one might think that Jim's logic would learn that he did not need to keep repeating his checks. Instead, his emotion learned that this repeated checking strategy worked. Jim kept over-checking and there was never a house fire at his childhood home; so the emotion felt that the strategy of over-checking was working and remained necessary.

The emotion barked, *'why change a winning formula'*. Sometimes, his emotion implored, *'if checking ten times keeps us safe, just imagine how safe we would be if I checked twenty times'*. The checking worsened.

The fire did not really create a neurosis. Rather, the fire provided an outlet for neurotic predispositions which had long since been close to bursting little Jim's seams. These latter predispositions were carved deep into Jim's core; long before Dierdre had even lit the fateful cigarette. Jim's soul searched tirelessly for new things to worry about and mitigate against; in life, we tend to get what we focus on.

Jim's neurotic tendencies could surely not but limit his life path? Maybe no need for a crystal ball to foresee that such strong propensities would litter Jim's path with more than his share of misery and failure? Yet, at this stage: the remainder of a sweet mystery regarding whether Jim would ultimately burn himself out and quietly fade, turning frustration inwards? Maybe the Gods had yet to decide back then, would he extinguish with an imperceptible whimper or would our Jim go out with a bang?

Soon after, young Jim's checking also spread to locking the outside door. There became an elaborate process of locking the house, triggered when Jim ventured out at times that there was nobody else at home. He would follow a sequence of: lock the door, move the door handle backwards and forwards trying to open the door several times, before moving away and then typically returning to check again later. Similarly at night time, Jim sneaked down to check if his parents had locked the two doors and closed the windows.

Jim was often somewhat tortured by 'what if I make a mistake and the house burns down or we get robbed'? Jim's inners creaked uneasily if he felt there was risk or doubt. His compulsions were underpinned by a sense that checking reduces risk and lowers doubt.

Despite his vigilance, there would be one break-in at Jim's house when all the family were out. A somewhat heartless act, as it was within weeks of Christmas. Jim was aged about twelve at the time and perhaps spurred by following verbal crumbs placed by Patrick, he imagined two young delinquents having climbed in through a specific kitchen window.

Jim remembers Patrick saying, 'I wish I had come home when they were in my house'. Whilst the burglars took money and jewellery, it was fortunate that Patrick had recently taken out insurance on 'home contents'. Jim would never learn that the money and jewellery were actually taken by somebody he knew well; very, very well.

Reality can help clear this one up. In fact, temptation had been too much for a man named Patrick. He had realised that he could take his own things and then claim for them on his recently arranged insurance. He could also play John Wayne, by bragging about how he could bravely and single handedly deal with what he must have known were 'imaginary burglars'. The latter not wholly dissimilar to his moral conscience, in that reality knew they were less than tenuous.

Jim did some joining of many disparate childhood dots in his adulthood. However, his ignorance of this deceptive insurance scam would ensure that this would be one of many things that would never be married up with external reality. Jim retained his notion of a couple of youths breaking into his childhood home, and Patrick yearning to catch up with them. Patrick's self-serving spin, feeding his own ego and his own pocket. Also, the bluffy bravado perhaps enabling Jim to see his father as more powerful and protective. Perhaps a lot to live up to?

Chapter 68 – Early stages of High school – Jim takes the worst beating he can imagine; yet his opponent does not lay a glove on him.

In early high school, young Jim's mind sought escape. His low self-esteem meant that other people were an unpleasant reminder of himself. Being around people set off self-consciousness; other people were his mirror. As if seeing himself through the eyes of others; within his own mind he created distorted and gross visions of himself on these mirrors.

Jim craved the predictability of playing with his soldiers. When it was just him and his soldiers, he was within a world in which he had complete control. Crucially, his soldiers did not judge. A fragile self-esteem sought safe haven.

By age eleven, Jim fairly suddenly developed a hypersensitivity to normal peer banter; a complete inability to laugh at himself or his shortcomings. He saw slights and perceived 'shots fired', when peers that actually liked him engaged in mere playful quips. Defensively, he had to be beyond even a hint of reproach.

Jim moved round with an internal imperative of others respecting him at all times. An affliction which manifested with an autistic rigidity. If the imperative was breached, then his inners told him that he had just sustained an immovable stain on his being; it had to be defended with all that he had.

Within an unsettled milieu of high school, Jim developed a very brief 'acting out' coping strategy. He became aggressive in demeanour, if her perceived that any of his peers had come even close to putting him down. He reacted as a cornered animal, under threat. Fight, flight, or freeze? For a very brief period, Jim's emotions pushed him to the former option of aggressing.

In a school play-ground, being able to bark loudly can give some status. For the first two or three months of high school (with Jim aged eleven), he roared at peers when his mind detected even a hint of disdain. He felt powerful and seemed to be squashing some of the negativity.

Jim felt lifted by this new approach to the world, such that his threshold for disrespect was falling ridiculously low. For a few months, ever keen to demonstrate. A low and frail self-esteem deep on the inside, but outward manifestations not wholly inconsistent with grandiosity and entitlement. Tragically, Jim was not served for long by what was essentially flimsy attempts to dominate and prop up his self-esteem.

After about two or three months, he received a minor insult from Derek Southworth in Chemistry. Now, through a normal lens: it was nay but normal peer banter. However, it seemed Jim's lens saw Southworth's minor utterance as a huge immovable stain, eclipsing all reason. Or maybe Jim had just become addicted to the early effects of barking, achieving some sense of power and dominance. A power which was highly seductive; with its draw amplified by a history which had been truly drenched with helplessness.

Jim had seen films on television, where characters like his namesake *'James* Bond' fought the bad guys. It seemed painless. For the film characters Jim identified with, a fight seemed like a prelude to the glory of winning. Winning arrived with what seemed like an almost painless inevitability.

Almost before Southworth had completed his banter, Jim's mouth convincingly declared: *'I'M GOING TO BEAT YOU UP AFTER SCHOOL'.*

Now, the much bigger Southworth smelt the lack of doubt in Jim's presentation. Southworth was rendered nervous, in the face of the cut of Jim's jib. However, Southworth felt somehow trapped into not fleeing from the challenge.

'Fine' Southworth said. The word content did not seem to have companions in his tone and broader body language. Even with his breadth and height, the leakage of Southworth's anxiety was there to be sensed. It leaked from his every pore; filtering into the air.

The clock ticked, building up to a crescendo. Chemistry was the last lesson of the day. Twenty minutes later and the bell rang. A group of around seven boys walked with Jim and Southworth, progressing to the school field.

Every few steps, it seemed that a new person got stuck to the ever increasing group. Like a large snowball rolling down a snow covered hill, the crowd seemed to constantly grow as it moved. Strangely, Jim felt energised by the increasing eyes that moved along with him. In his mind, pressure was temporarily bumped aside by the sense of an 'opportunity to demonstrate his power to a keen audience'.

Adrenaline pumped through Jim. His excitement and frustration broke through his kindness. On the way to the school field, Jim began swinging punches at the frame of this threat to his self-esteem. The punches did not come close to troubling Southworth's superior physique. Within seconds, Southworth had Jim in a head-lock. His vice-like grip neutralising the once eager Jim.

In what seemed like an instant, a new reality broke through to Jim. He was stuck. Worst still, Southworth was clearly much stronger than him.

It seemed, a cat was surely on the cusp of leaping fully out of the bag. He felt crushed between his pride and reality; increasingly hemmed in, like two walls moving inescapably in on him. There seemed no way out.

'Let me go' Jim tried to aggressively urge Southworth. Difficult to sound intimidating in a stooped position, with your adversary firmly holding your head pinned to his side. But Jim reflexively tried.

'No' Southworth retorted, like someone who was coming to terms with suddenly having all the cards. Perhaps akin to a pessimistic poker player coming to terms with hitting a one-outer on the river, to reach the nuts.

'If I let you go, you'll attack me' Southworth stated

'I won't. Just let me go' Jim urged. He was pathetically trying to conjure up an aggressive voice, to ward off the aura of helplessness. The futility did not fully escape part of his core.

Eventually Southworth released his catch.

What followed was Jim's weasel-worded attempts to put the fight off till the next day. Fear was operating the controller that moved Jim. Suddenly, he was searching for an escape.

'Lets fight tomorrow, there seems to be a lot of teachers around' Jim suggested, pointing back towards a school building.

Jim had seen a life raft, in the form of a teacher an uncomfortably long way in the distance. Southworth straining his eyes, could perhaps just about make out a tiny figure in the distance.

Jim was attempting to make the world stand still, just till tomorrow. It was as if Jim didn't know that the next day would arrive. He was akin to a washed-up salesman, striving to survive by peddling garbage.

Largely, Southworth's anxiety had long since walked. That said, he was still partly coming to terms with his newly found dominance. Southworth agreed to leave the fight till lunch time on the next day.

The consequences were that for the subsequent evening and morning, Jim was terrified. He felt his whole reputation was about to fold. It felt as if his life would cease.

As if the stars were mocking him, Jim recalls hearing the number one song on that solitary evening, *'Everyone considered him the coward of the county...'.* Kenny Rogers may have been singing the song, but it was as though everybody that knew Jim was joining in the words. It felt like the world would know, tomorrow. Jim could not stop time and his heart increasingly ached, as time demonstrated this.

The next morning, Jim trudged back into school. Southworth and his entourage could feel a shift. Southworth was showboating. Perhaps another epitome of what the great American boxing trainer Cus D'Amato referred to as the danger of *'a scared fighter, turned brave'.* A theme which, unbeknownst to Jim, may just leap out on him in later years.

Southworth suggested to Jim in the morning that maybe they should shake hands and forget about the fight at lunch time. When Jim showed a strong interest in this path, Southworth smugly declared that he had only been joking. He surely sensed Jim's fear and was mocking him. The fight would go ahead, at lunch time.

Jim went home for his lunch, with his home only a couple of

minutes walk from the high school grounds. He felt his world was about to end and he knew no way to stop it. He left home and walked towards the school field at the designated time. His legs knew no other way.

Jim walked in with a good friend at that time, Jonny. The anguish inside him was off the scale, but he did not even mention the dilemma to Jonny. They parted company and Jim walked the hundred yards or so, onto the school field.

A huge crowd had gathered. As he got closer, he could see the figure of Southworth. Southworth looked ready, with his bulk oozing confidence. Jim had no plan, no solution, and a sense of being hopelessly trapped.

Southworth was stronger and Jim's attempt to act tough were about to come crumbling down. His early high school reputation as being tough was about to vanish, without a trace. He could not sustain the illusion.

What happened next surprised everyone, including Jim. As Jim got closer to Southworth and the group encircled them, something broke inside of Jim. Tears flowed down Jim's face, in an emotional outpouring.

In between sobs, Jim announced *'I don't want to fight you'*. The crowd watched on. There was much laughter. Southworth surveyed his crushed prey. The mockery ensued.

From that moment, Jim began apologising for himself. He shed his aggressive demeanour. For the next three or four years, Jim armed himself with nothing but appeasement gestures, self-deprecating diatribe, sickly excessive praising of others, and deferring to all others. The emotional pain would not subside for years.

To the outside world, maybe not markedly earth-shattering. Yet to Jim's inner world, an emotional scar that would linger; perhaps not even shed before the dam broke several decades on, in the White Hart Inn. Even by eleven, Jim's mind could muster a staggering intensity of pain from an injured pride. The latter was a vulnerability that could potentially yield withdrawal or outwardly focussed destruction; at this stage, our Jim firmly chose the former.

Jim was an avoidant soul. The irony is that the pain which he inflicted upon himself consequent on this perceived humiliating capitulation ridiculously dwarfed the pain that a hundred angry Southworth's could have visited upon him that day. If he had been armed with a crystal ball and been able to grasp the magnitude of the long-serving internal repercussions of tearful pleas for mercy, then he would have fought Southworth like his life depended on it. If this was a sliding doors moment, maybe his life did depend on it?

Chapter 69 – Early stages of High school – Life after Southworth

The ripples of Jim's demise were far reaching, in his own world. Soon after, Jim would hear himself being mocked by the creatures that he had labelled as friends. Any minor argument might hear, *'oooh, what are you going to do about it Jim, burst into tears?'*, or *'don't cry, mate'*.

Sometimes, the put-downs involved Jim being offered a tissue or a handkerchief, if he seemed to or even might disapprove of anything. The respect which fear had afforded him, quickly replaced by ridicule. Children often very clever and unrelenting in creatively sculpting teasing banter. The latter, all the more humerous by the obvious impact of their work on Jim. Certainly not an operant extinction schedule; the slights amounted to everything in Jim's world, and consequently they endured.

Jim became a magnet to bullying and teasing. Undoubtedly, Jim's inability to laugh at himself was a vulnerability; within childhood and beyond. Some beasts were drawn in, by his reputation, albeit brief, as being tough; sat alongside the open goal that his capitualtion suggested. Many now saw an opportunity to dominate Jim and a queue formed; he became someone that others sought to step on to elevate themselves.

Within weeks and in the face of relentless persecution from Jack Houghton, he tried to stand up for himself. His head was slammed repeatedly onto the concrete surface of the school yard. His temples were swollen in the extreme.

Despite clear disbelief of teachers, Jim insisted to the PE teacher that his opponent Jack did not deserve severe punishment as he had only punched him. Jim's support for his assailant was not representative of lying to protect him, but rather it flowed from some loss of consciousness.

The first three years post-Southworth also afforded Jim the opportunity to become very familiar with a youngster named Howard Rothwell. Jim had grown up being double-jointed in both hips. This ailment had contributed to Jim's feet pointing inwards appreciably, whenever he walked or ran. This reality was a catalyst to Rothwell invariably greeting Jim with the label 'Spaz', alongside Rothwell's energetic portrayal of what he envisaged was representative of a person with severe spasticity. Hands bent down at the wrists and the emission of a most injurous grunt. The scorn repeatedly injured Jim, intrusively lancing into his being.

Howard followed this ritual humiliation up with an incident during PE. The PE lesson involved a game of football, in the third year of high school. Jim was aged thirteen.

Rothwell lacked athleticism and manifested a striking absence of even a whiff of football talent. However, he found a way to entertain himself on this particular day by kicking Jim very firmly in the private parts. Just to eliminate any possibility of this being accidental, he executed this when the ball was about forty yards away from both him and his prey. His intermittent laughter and smirks were only interrupted by an isolated and wholly insincere apology.

One of the ways that Jim sought to cope with his perceived loss of status amongst peers was through striving to achieve more with his school work. He learnt that he could learn. Achieving academically began to very slightly reduce the strength of his self-hatred.

Jim seemed to have found a way to exist. The autistic focus which provided retreat with his soldiers could be applied to school work. The newly found intense focus on school work was a comforting way to block other things out.

Well before his teens, Jim's world was grossly distorted by the internal apparatus of what had gradually become his mind. By the time reality reached a teenage Jim's level of experience, it had been distorted beyond the capacity of a tandem of funhouse mirrors. The product was far removed and yet: pure reality, for Jim. The adjective 'unpalatable' does not begin to convey the flavour of this wildly contorted reality, as it pogoed on the idiosyncratic taste buds of Jim's soul.

Chapter 70 – Outside school: Jim's spirit briefly and regretfully rises in defiance, against a couple of bullies

Perhaps a digression. Or, maybe a sense that at age thirteen, there was life in the old Jim yet. When Jim reached high school age, one of his heavenly escapes was to cycle to the local lake with his good friend Jonny. On one particular day, a thirteen year old Jim and Jonny had the misfortune of inadvertently crossing paths with a couple of local bullies. They came in the form of Jason Proctor and Alan Capper, and back in good old 1981.

Capper and Proctor gleefully came upon Jim and his friend Jonny. They took it upon themselves to call Jonny and a thirteen year old Jim a collection of names, with each one appearing to convey the antithesis of admiration. Wisdom alongside, both Jim and Jonny rolled with all these punches. They left each and every insult, wholly unanswered.

Jim wrestled with his injured pride. He would then make the mistake of shouting something slightly cheeky back, at a point when he believed that his foes were well out of earshot.

'Bye, beanpoles' Jim shouted, as the enemy moved in the opposite direction. The shot that he fired, referring cheekily to their ectomorphic physique.

Jim looked on horrified, as this pair of bullies oriented towards him. Two heads turning, in synchrony. It was as if his words had pressed a switch, and mobilised these monsters.

Young Jim flabbergasted and horrified, in equal measure. He had attempted to pitch the volume at a level that even the 'sonic ear toy' of that era would have been unable to detect. Jim and Jonny were only around forty yards from uniting with the angered antisocial duo and yet well over a mile from the sanctuary of Jonny's residence.

What followed was a long, long, bike chase. The gap between the parties did widen briefly. However, Proctor and Capper were not about to let such a *'glorious opportunity to demonstrate dominance'* pass them by lightly. They had the vessel they needed to vent whatever upset and frustration life had dared to blight them with.

Indeed, if Proctor and Capper were to catch up with their targets, perhaps it may leave some other poor soul in the clear; perhaps the backside of their cat blissfully unfettered; perhaps the wings of a fly not wantonly torn. Morsels for reality to digest, but surely no silver-lining for our Jim. Jim uneasy with himself for sloppily releasing this verbal shot across the bows of such aggressive, antisocial animals.

Fear peddled hard, along a road which was surrounded by largely countryside. There was what seemed like an endless straight section, where Jim's glances back were readily met with a vision of his pursuers. Alas, Jim's mind was increasingly creating pictures of a future which was perhaps not yet written.

Jim's mind increasingly saw Proctor and Capper catch him, with doom enveloping him with both arms. They were still a good thirty yards behind, but Jim decided to turn into a large commercial property on his right hand side. He reasoned that there might be someone around, which might curb the enthusiasm of the chasing duo. Jonny was slightly ahead, and he scooted off into the distance towards his home.

Proctor and Capper followed the path of Jim, like guided missiles. The commercial property was deserted. Jim put his bike down, and stood next to a mountain-shaped pile of small stones around twice his height.

Jim remained, his captors right in front of him. Fear oozed out of him, in the form of the most extreme deferential apologies. People who have slaughtered small villages would struggle to muster up such remorse.

Capper was a year older than Jim and over a foot taller. He had the mercy of angels, to allow Proctor alone to execute the aggression. Proctor simply walked up to Jim, and punched him hard in the face. Jim was not even close to retaliating. Anger was nowhere to be seen for Jim, but fear was everywhere. Proctor got Jim to verbally agree to being several of the worst insults that Proctor's limited mind could muster.

'You are a coward, aren't you?' Proctor asked rhetorically

'Yes, I am mate' Jim replied with a wide eyes submissiveness.

The dance continued for several insults. Proctor then gave a parting shot, of another firm punch to Jim's face. The laughter from Capper boomed almost constantly throughout the interchange between Jim and Proctor. The audience appeared to be clearly entertained by the spectacle.

Then, they left. Initially, the fulfilled Proctor and Capper cycled gleefully into the distance. Then, a few minutes after, the departure of our Jim and what measly remnants were left of his pride.

Strange thing, though. In the face of fear, Jim was previously firmly wired to be the most resourceful in paying any price to avoid the immediate danger. Fear activated short-termism in Jim, such that he was purely driven to avert the short-term danger almost regardless of the long-term cost. We look back to Southworth, and crying seemed to be the ultimate appeasement gesture. However, in this situation with Capper and Proctor, he did not come close to using tears. Maybe, just maybe, something was changing?

Chapter 71 – The later stages
of high school

Towards the end of high school, Jim had shed some of the emotional residue which had seemed to never endingly weep from the wounds of the Southworth fight. It had taken three or four years, but his mind was less busy squeezing toxic implications from the fight that never was. Nevertheless, Jim retained scars from his earlier childhood; self-acceptance levels were low.

In this context, Jim again lashed out in the final year of high school in response to peer banter. He had still not found a path to learn the potential benefits of being able to laugh at yourself. He remained hypersensitive to others, as their view of him seemed to hold up a sullied mirror to his soul; not knowing that the reflection was not veridical, but merely distorted output from his own rotten depth.

A group of peers were discussing where they would be going for their summer holidays, in the school common room. At which point, Paul Cross turned to Jim and dryly said *'I don't need to ask you where you are going on holiday this year Butler, you'll be away with MenCap again'.*

Jim was aware that MenCap was an organisation for the handicapped. In his mind, Jim linked the comments of Cross to the years of relentless *'Spaz'* name-calling which Howard Rothwell had unleashed due to Jim's feet turning in. Jim almost reflexively lashed out at Cross in the form of a punch, a fight broke out between them, and it was agreed that there would be a fight the next day.

Jim was bigger and he believed physically stronger than Paul Cross. However, perhaps driven partly by fear, Paul would show a level of nastiness which Jim was wholly unequipped for. Paul's work would educate Jim towards a realisation in later years. In particular, Jim would learn that in conflict, nastiness will typically inflict more damage than strength.

The fight with Paul arrived, the next day. It took place on a muddy field next to a stream, over the dinner hour. Around a dozen lads gathered for the spectacle, chomping at the bit. It began with wrestling and Jim was on top. He pinned Paul down, but then our Jim did not really know what he was supposed to do next.

After what felt like a long period of inaction and Paul pinned to the floor, a new pattern emerged. Jim lost and without a script and Paul eventually managed to get an arm free. This loose arm then fixated, purely on trying to remove Jim's eye balls from their sockets. His hands relentless scratching out at the eye balls, working hard to dig in. Paul managed to arise.

The fight moved randomly across the field. After managing to keep possession of his eyeballs despite several determined scrapes from Paul, Jim was worn down. The stakes felt too high. At a point that Jim was on his knees on the muddied grass, he conceded the fight. Paul delivered a parting shot of kicking Jim's head as if it were a football. It seemed that Jim had created another humiliation, in his pitiful existence.

Yet perhaps to return to the old proverb, perhaps *all is grist to the mill'*. Pain, insults, maltreatment not wholly needed, but perhaps often bedfellows of later serious crimes. Certainly, if anger was to underpin a perpetrated atrocity then maybe difficult to get off the runway if life was simply too blissful. Maybe Cross, Rothwell, Southworth were lending helping hands, nudging Jim towards his becoming?

A small silver lining did fall at the end of Jim's schooling, aged sixteen. Specifically, he had focussed sufficiently on school work to attain five 'O' levels. This fell beyond the expectations of a Jim that was beneath humble.

So, our Jim emerged from high school. Aged sixteen, he found himself armed with a raft of facets, including: qualifications, social anxiety, various other neuroses, a pitifully low self-esteem, and an ever present obstacle of a bashful bladder (i.e., an inability to urinate in front of others). Jim had more vulnerabilities than one could shake a stick at. A mind finely tuned at picking up what might go wrong, and avoidant tendencies which were off the scale.

More broadly, Jim left school with a mind-set and ingrained habits which were wildly unsuited for carving out good life quality and success in adulthood. Like an entry for the sack race fully immersed in sack, mistakenly lining up in the elite sprinters final; Jim felt ill-equipped to make his life truly work. Necessity perhaps the mother of invention; in his teens, Jim often reached for short-termist hiding, bluffing, and faking. The bull ran free, Jim not even close to it's horns.

Chapter 72 – Toilet training continues throughout childhood

Long before his teens, Jim had an established and ingrained bashful bladder. Jim was progressively bombarded by learning opportunities around toilets and those dastradly bodily functions. Throughout Jim's childhood, Kath taught our Jim volumes about bodily functions and toilets. What she said with words, wholly incongruent with messages that her indiscrete non-verbal offerings relentlessly betrayed. The non-verbal competitor more powerful; arguing the case so much more persuasively.

A young Jim opening a door of a toilet in public would surely see himself swept in by a record breaking tsunami wave of pure shame. Avoidance, the panacea. Dancing to the tunes his mind could detect. He felt the beat, with words and logic hushed to less than a whisper.

If we swim, we get wet. If an arm is cut deeply, it bleeds. If a human creature is placed into a world, it learns.

Within the limits of an individual child, it seeks to adapt. Jim continues to reflexively seek to squeeze out useful paths, from the learning opportunities which Kath and his world unknowingly provides. A tortured and confused mind, seduced by short-termism and striving to settle on soothing solutions.

Jim recalls an occasion when he was out with his family at the age of about five and he wanted to use the toilet. The place where the toilet was situated was a bit run down. Jim recalls his mother, Kath, saying, *'he's not going to that toilet, it is 'dirty'*. He recalls Kath venting the word *'dirty'* such that it was beyond saturated by disgust.

Jim's dad, Patrick, tried to reason with Kath and say *'it's OK, he'll be fine'.* At which point, Jim's mother became emotionally more agitated. Unleashed inner demons, so often grossly pushed down.

In his soba state, Jim's father managed to keep his anger in check. Patrick turned to Jim and asked something like, *'can you hold it for twenty minutes or so, till we get home?'.* Whilst Jim really wanted to go to the toilet, he recalled saying something like, *'yes, I guess so'.*

At which point, he was enthusiastically praised by his mother. It was as if he had solved a big part of humanities problems. He continued to learn, from his world.

Time marched on, barely a cursory glance at Jim's plight. Jim has a vivid memory of visiting the home of a camp middle-aged hairdresser, who lived with his elderly mother. He was having his haircut. A simple process, but Jim's world never stops teaching.

On arriving with Kath, little Jim (aged seven) felt a strong urge to urinate. Soon after arriving, the urge was powerful; to the point of precipitating the strategy of asking the mother of the hairdresser, *'please could I use the toilet?'.* Kath instantly responded with strong disapproval, *'JIM, WE HAVE ONLY JUST GOT HERE!'.*

Her words followed so closely behind Jim's that they seemed to merge as one. The mother of the hairdresser joined in the dance, saying *'I know what it's like at that age, you are just curious and want to see other people's toilets'.* Little Jim felt fenced in.

A part of Jim really wanted to say, *'I just want to use the toilet – what is so difficult to deal with about that'.* Alongside this, he kinda knew that adults are the brokers of reality. For a seven year old Jim, they have the unofficial franchise on what constitutes truth.

Jim did not fight their reality. Instead, he sheepishly attempted to go to the toilet, with a strong sense that he was being told that he should have held it in. Jim felt that what he had done must be so wrong and flawed that the hairdresser's mother was pretending that he did not actually want to go to the toilet. Somehow, in this world: this pretence was more palatable and socially acceptable than the reality that his body was telling him he needed to use the toilet.

Jim learnt that using the toilet outside the home was in some way wrong. If he reflects back on his primary school and secondary school, then he can recall the whole layout of the buildings. However, in his mind, he is unable to locate the toilets or visualise inside a school toilet.

Very notably, Jim able to recall that there was an occasion when he was aged about ten when he desperately wanted to use the toilet for most of the afternoon. His solution was to hold it in all afternoon and then at home time, rush home the mile from the primary school to his home.

On arrival at home, Kath asked him why he was rushing. He replied that he had rushed home from school to use the toilet. The irony is that Kath then (with Jim aged ten) gave the advice that there is nothing wrong with using the toilet in school and that it is nothing to be embarrassed about. At this point, Jim vividly remembers thinking that he absolutely *knew* what his mother really thought and that she was pretending her beliefs were different.

Jim knew somewhere in his mind: by rushing home, he had behaved in line with his mother's feelings. He knew that using the toilet in public was in some way wrong and shameful. He had paid attention to his mother and long since learned from the world he had been gifted. Already attitudes towards toilets and producing human waste were etched into his neural circuitry, deep within his young brain. His core knew that his mother was superficially paying lip service in a way that he knew was phoney.

By then, Jim could not verbalise it, but it just was. When you step out into the rain, you get wet. To feel this, you do not need to be armed with words.

Jim also knew at the level of feeling and instinct that his mother was riddled with festering inconsistency. Words offered young Jim no route to cut through this. He just continued to join in the ironic dance, as best he could. Naked truth and adaptive reality fully cloaked; our Jim only able to see the emperor's new clothes, at this stage hanging unchangingly from Kath's frame.

Of course, Jim also knew that his mother loved him that much that she could tolerate his intermittent need to use the toilet. Whilst Jim did not logically label it this way, it was as if family could somehow forgive him for engaging in this shameful natural process. He knew his mother didn't like it, but she could deal with it. He was blessed in this way.

Jim had squeezed learning from his world. The repercussions were that life presented a myriad a perverse self-defeating puzzles. These puzzles were woven of making sense of his world, alongside being drawn deeper and deeper into a dark chasm of avoidance.

Perhaps one of the biggest tragedies is that Jim did not engage in wholesale avoidance of life. He strives to exist as a normal adolescent, whilst simultaneously being a slave to the invisible master who dictates that he cannot use the toilet when he is with others that he knows. Learning, autistic traits, and anxiety come together; the path lights up for him. Still, he has not wholly given up on amounting to something, being respected, being succesful; being someone.

Kath was beyond skilled at arguing that *'what truly was'* in fact *'was not',* as if her life depended on it. If logic did not permit Kath to sustain what she held on to, or a mirror was held up to uncomfortable aspects of her being, then she would find emotionally driven display and action to keep it all at bay. Soon jaded by logic that often gave less than flimsy camouflage, Kath would reflexively venture to extreme measures if the audience did not respect the emperor's new clothes. On the few times our young Jim had sought to put apparent contradictions under the microscope, Kath always had one debate ending bullet in the barrel, namely:

> *'it is so, because I say so and I am the adult and you are the child, now go to your room'.*

Kath found a way to keep aloft, a most uneasily arranged stack of cards; with flimsy adhesion from ingrained avoidance and defences. Protecting it with an intensity. Like it was worth more than life.

But do not fooled, as not much coercion was needed. Typically, when we look at the prior behaviour of people that wilfully commit terrible crimes, we will often notice antisocial patterns which emerge well before the end of childhood. Yet, Jim's inner core in childhood is more contaminated with decency and kindness, than it is with cruelty and antisocial behaviour. He had a soul that reflexively cared about others.

Our Jim, no psychopath; he had been truly touched by a mother so often crying and releasing tortured howls in his early years. Blessed with a caring side and rarely more than stride from his guilt, he would work hard not to upset his dear Kath further. Dancing to Kath's tune seemed often as natural as breathing, for this little Jim.

Yet if time permitted, reality could surely show that Kath no less a victim than our Jim. If not, then maybe neither a victim. Maybe just a reality; just words.

Chapter 73 – A crystallised reality, under the microscope.

Jim attended secondary school and sixth form for a combined seven years, and he never used the toilet within secondary school or sixth form. Occasionally, his bladder decided to venture home early and miss the odd lesson. That said, his body had become so well trained; it very often largely shut off the sensations of needing to go to the toilet when he was outside his home or around people other than his family.

Rest assured though, teenage Jim was not volitionally pressing this switch. It was his body and his sub-conscious that had become top of the class, at this. Like Pavlov's dogs when they heard the dinner bell repeatedly signalling food; saliva just arrived as a necessary guest.

A sense of being around people came to instantly precipitate a switch being pressed within; a dominant part of Jim's mind came to reflexive fight hard to *NOT* allow sensations of needing the toilet to break through to his conscious mind. If it did, then he was merely left with what for him seemed an unsolvable puzzle drenched in fear. Stuck with a need thwarted, *'I need the toilet, but I cannot use a public toilet'*. The problem is that his automatic shut-down in this area led to more general shut-down in the presence of people. A catch twenty two, the latter collateral damage, to enable the short-term partial appeasement of fear and deeply buried guilt.

For the conventional human being: an ability to use the toilet in public is pretty central. The presence of people came to represent threat to Jim, an obstacle to an essential bodily function and a sense of needing to hide the reality of his being. This mixed uneasily with aspects of his personality which were definitely striving for connection. It would take time for these latter aspects of his personality to increasingly suffocate. An affinity for people could surely only wither.

The learning was to present puzzles for Jim to solve within his adulthood. Jim was propelled along the waves of shame and guilt. He put his resources into a firm and unrelenting path of avoidance; never speaking about this avoidance or its under-pinnings. Covering up does not prevent shame, it usually pro-vides the soil for it to grow like a cancer; beneath the surface.

With his sensitivity, Jim had learnt some core rules. He learnt that needing the toilet was shameful and to be hidden. Also, his emotions knew that he should avoid using public toilets.

Jim's genetics coalesced with the world that lie in wait. Or to phrase it in a different way, maybe our Jim simply made choices? Again; if a tree falls in the forest and there's no-one around to hear it, does it make a sound? Does the puppet truly move by itself when we do not see the strings being pulled?

Jim was left with the imperative of not using a toilet in public and not even making it known he needed the toilet in front of other people. It sat uneasily alongside the task of making his way in the world and enjoying the benefits of a normal life. He could not succeed at both, and he chose the path of avoidance and secrecy. If Kath could keep her stack of cards upright, maybe Jim could follow suit? His self-esteem was relentlessly worn away.

In his teens, sexual desire animated a desire for connection. But this drive, buffeted again and again upon the rocky cliffs of Jim's internal world which fully enclosed it. A small morsel rarely broke over the top, in some distorted and pitifully weak-ened form.

Still, our Jim continued to surreptitiously gyrate to a cardinal constraint of not going to the toilet when he was with others.

Apparently, a central platform on which to build his life. Akin to an engineer tirelessly striving to build a skyscraper, resting on the wave ridden surface of the deepest ocean. Ill-fitting foundations, attempts to progress just sinking; perhaps inevitability closer than Jim's shadow?

In world war two, pilots of enemy planes would bomb the runways of their opponents and drop mines into the craters which the exploding bombs created. To start to fill in the craters, the mines would have to be exploded, thereby yielding further damage. In Jim's case; exploding the mines was akin to admitting his problem (with all the integral shame) or striving to overcome the avoidance. Jim was either inadequately unable to face this task or so admirably committed to his avoidant mission that he simply stumbled round the crater.

He limped round this crater, year, after year, after year. His life slipped away, as if he was in a torturous hypnotic slumber. He held onto the waste, but time excreted it readily.

Jim perseverated with a perverse strategy, such that he did not have to hold up a mirror to his true being. Some clear eyes staring into this very same mirrored reflection might have merely seen an innocuous flaw of Jim's being, perhaps not yielding the unearthly levels of disgust that surrounded him. However, at this stage: the reflection that Jim ran from was a warped sense of the eyes and judgements of others, somewhere deep inside the perimeter of his own skull. Avoidance constantly shooed off an easier reality. The longer he walked down his path, the harder it seemed to do a U-turn.

In early childhood, the challenge was admitting to others he used the toilet by using public toilets when he was with others. He simply avoided using public toilets and avoided using toilets at other people's houses. His shame grew outwards to incorporate what seemed to be the bizarreness of his handicap.

Seemingly bereft of logic; how could he explain it? Shame stood between him and admitting to another person that he couldn't use the toilet when he was in public and with others. Secrecy often escorts shame to a place where it can grow and flourish; a land where praise and validation can be diluted and dismissed.

Fear was a powerful ingredient. If you've avoided something throughout life, then it must be a humongous threat. When we behave relentlessly in a given direction, it cannot but influence our attitudes, beliefs, and emotions. Surely, if you spend decades clucking, then you might start to feel more like a chicken?

If we constantly avoid something, then our mind is increasingly drawn to the notion *'I cannot cope with this'*. We are fundamentally demonstrating it to our mind, again and again. A mind that is always watching us; regardless of whether we verbally label what we see before us; regardless of whether we are watching it, watching us.

Our self-concept is of course partly evolved from observing ourselves behaving in certain ways, and then labelling our behaviour and labelling ourselves on that basis. However, Jim was not only hemmed in by fear, self-concept, or shame. The complete avoidance of using public toilets and avoidance of expressing an intent to use a toilet in front of others led to a type of physiological conditioning. Pavlov would have been proud of the demonstration.

Jim's urge to urinate or defecate emerging reliably in the setting condition of being at home; reflexively subdued when around the stimulus of other people outside his core family. A switch pressed, activating a well-oiled mechanism. This meant that even if he had ventured into a public toilet, he would have physiologically struggled to the point of being unable to release any product.

A resistance which would likely be impervious to an eccentric billionaire readily offering his riches for Jim to produce waste. Like offering inducement for a person to avoid producing any sweat within an hour encased in a sauna, with temperature elevated to the max. Surely beyond even a regal character; physiology takes over, then a form rendered slippery. His years of dedication had made a difference; beyond well trained?

Of course, intermittent pain and discomfort did break through from a body that did not want to obey its master. A body that strove to remain annoyingly committed to normal bodily functions of urination and defecation. Being around people started an invisible clock for Jim, as he could only stay around people for as long as the imperative of bodily functions could be subdued.

Jim rendered typically only able to flit in and out of public situations, in between draining his bladder back home. He perhaps gave off the impression of someone who *'ducked and dived'*. Amazing ingenuity pulling off a strategy which enabled him to almost live the unliveable; grossly marring his life in the process.

Jim succeeded in developing *'a way of being'* that he could force uncomfortably into the slot which the world provided, staying true to twisted prerequisites woven at least partly of childhood learning. The irony of this success was that it left Jim trapped and with an woeful and impoverished platform to carve out success in his actual life. Take a snap shot without the history and without recourse to emotional vectors; surely wholly illogical. Standing in his own way, at every turn. Some perversely sculpted warped emotional form appearing to effortlessly win its arm wrestle with logic.

Standing above it all: young Jim, seemingly stubbornly fixed on a harsh Northerly path with little protection from the elements. A decent future surely going South. Eventually, the being that Jim was became progressively worn down, increasingly paper thin. Surely, something had to give? Again, one may pause to wonder, had the whims of the Gods already fully fixed on where our Jim's path would meander?

Chapter 74 - An irrelevant part of the scenery, or a central determinant of Jim's life journey?

Complexity abounding and as the saying goes, *'plausibility proves nothing'.* Truth more than reticent to share all her secrets. Aged fifteen, Jim suffered an accident. This accident could be an irrelevant part of the scenery which passed within his history, or a central determinant of Jim's life journey. The secrets of reality, often remaining hidden. A grey area, which the human species often liberally transforms into something black or white.

On the 13th February 1983, a fifteen year old Jim took on a two mile bike ride to a local lake. He rode with his best friend Jonny and another friend nicknamed Kelvin monkey-face Grimes. A journey they had done dozens of time before, without major incident. Even within Jim's constant mental search for possible danger, this felt a relatively safe venture.

After minutes were passed wasting money in an amusement arcade at the nearby Lake Amusements, Jim was wholly skint. Playing fruit machines was a short-term panacea for Jim and perhaps his most effective way of escaping from awareness of himself. After the spinning of various fruit machine reels and Jim's money slipping quickly through his careless fingers, the trio then peddled their way back towards Jonny's residence. As Jim, Jonny, and Grimesy set off, it was 4:27pm.

About a third of the way through the mile and a half journey, Grimesy interjected: *'Let's go and see the haunted old house, Clegg Manor'.*

'Yes, why not' said Jonny, turning his gaze to Jim to confirm the plan.

'Nice one, I've never actually been to it' Jim added. As an aside, the truth that ultimately transpired was that Jim never would actually visit it, during the whole of his lifetime.

Jim had heard about Clegg Manor. He understood it to be an uninhabited, old, and run down mansion. Rumoured to be haunted.

In order to get to the old haunted house, the biked trio would need to traverse across the road. The turning was on the right. The road was a recently built road that tapered from two lanes going in their direction to one lane, just before the turning. It remained a 50mph limit, for all vehicles.

Grimesy went to the point of the white broken lines at the middle of the road, with his hand stuck out signalling that he was turning right. Now, Jim could see that there was no on-coming traffic on the opposite lane and so his expectation was that Grimesy would just continue, across the road. However, Grimesy stopped in the middle of the road, perhaps waiting for Jonny to catch up.

Even as Grimesy saw Jim approaching just next to his bike, he stayed motionless in the middle of the road. Jim remembered feeling slightly irked because it was awkward for him to stop, as his bike was slightly too big for him. When Jim was sat on his bike, the tips of his toes only just reached the ground.

As it happened and unbeknownst to Jim, the bike which he had been given for Christmas was stolen from a nearby town by his father Patrick. It was chosen based on opportunity, rather than size. Jim's bike wobbled, and he was temporarily unable to see a solution to the puzzle which Grimesy's inertia presented.

Grimesy was blocking our Jim's path. In a brief instant, Jim decided to return back to the curb where Jonny was catching up. That is Jim's last memory, for many minutes. His mind temporarily left him.

Jonny saw the whole thing and so we need to borrow his lens. Jonny observed a car speeding past him well beyond stipulated legal limits, without slowing down. As it approached Jim, he noticed that Jim turned his wobbling bike slightly and diverted it into the path of this metal monster.

Somehow, the bike went under the car and Jim was propelled into the air. Jonny looked on in horror, as Jim went up into the air and looked like a rag doll. He seemed to rise as high as fifteen feet, and came down wholly on the top of his head.

In that moment, Jonny firmly believed that his friend had died. He went over to the motionless body. He was surprised to see Jim looking back at him, and asking '*am I going to die?*'.

Jonny reasoned that if Jim was well enough to ask that question, then he would surely survive. Hence, Jonny replied, '*No Jim, you are going to be OK?*'.

Now, in childhood, if Jonny or Jim wanted to know whether the other was kidding, they would ask, '*do you swear?*'. This was an abbreviation for '*do you swear on your mother's life*', which Jim took to mean that his mother might die if he lied at such a time. It was used as a means of increasing confidence that the other party was telling the truth. Hence, at the scene, Jim followed Jonny's reassurance with 'do you swear that I am not going to die?'. Again, Jonny served up reassurance.

Jim appeared conscious from immediately after the accident. However, he has absolutely no memory of the first forty minutes following the head injury. Our Jim lived a whole life devoid of any memories of these early minutes; temporarily in a type of consciousness that he was responsive, but not able to form any new memories. His brain starts to be able to create new stable memories from a point that he was travelling within an ambulance, and just about to reach hospital.

He is in the back of the ambulance, with a paramedic as his only audience. Jim's first memory is asking the paramedic in the ambulance that same million dollar question that Jonny had heard at the scene. Specifically, Jim asked the paramedic *'Am I going to die?'*.

The paramedic seemed to conscientiously over-apply some aspect of his training with the response, *'we will be at the hospital soon'*. In Jim's mind, this was as close as it got to answering *'Yes, you may well be about to die'*. The paramedic perhaps reasoning that if Jim died, then the patient could potentially rise from the dead and sue him for giving shoddy reassurance.

Strangely though, Jim felt reassured within a couple of hours. Kath had arrived at the hospital and he had been briefly checked out and reassured by medical staff. Kath was clearly relieved that he appeared fine.

Jim was discharged the same day. In this accident, he could have gone under the car. He could have died. He could have landed differently.

The timing of it all slightly altered, and our Jim and his legacy stopped short. However, as chance would have it, he survived. The fickle and frivolous fingers of destiny raised a thumb upwards and not downwards, on that particular day.

The police took a statement from Jim, in which he conveyed that he had no recollection beyond slightly turning his handlebars in the middle of the road. He suggested that his friend saw everything and they would get a better picture from him. The policeman chose not to interview Jonny, and fed back to Jim and his mother that the driver had been very upset and had been through enough already.

That seemed to be the end, aside from somewhat typical peer banter when he returned to school the next week. Grimesy had taken it upon himself to detail the incident to anybody within school that would listen. The upshot was that several lads spent a few days mockingly saying to Jim, *'Butler you fanny, am I going to die, oooohhhh, tell me please, am I going die?'.*

The shock of the incident seemed to at least temporarily dampen down Jim's inner reactivity to perceived disrespect. For once, less defensive than usual and almost letting it go. The humour within Jim's school could be quite brutal. Nobody was safe!

On occasion, Grimesy himself was at the sharp end of peer humour. When Grimesy was aged about fourteen, his older brother Mark suffered an accident in which he caught fire, suffering terrible and potential life changing injury. When Grimesy entered school soon after the incident, his class mate named Paul Cross referred to the incident.

Sympathy and compassion, you might think? Not a bit of it. Paul Cross instantly and enthusiastically shouted across at Grimesy the words from a well-known song, *'Goodness gracious, great balls of fire'.*

Leaving tangential details aside, the incident in which Jim was knocked off his bike may seem like nothing of great significance in his journey. However, within weeks of Jim's assessment in Broadmoor Special Hospital and after *'criminal insanity'* was asserted (in Jim's adulthood), a specialist neuropsychologist documented in a report:

> *'Jim reportedly suffered several head traumas in childhood. He may have suffered a significant traumatic brain injury in childhood, as a consequence of a specific road traffic accident. It is noteworthy that he suffered a period of anterograde amnesia, which he estimates to have been around forty minutes. Additionally, there are significant discrepancies between his verbal IQ (136) and his performance IQ (102).* **Given this pattern, there needs to be further investigation of potential brain injury and its potential relevance in his very serious criminal offences'.**

Jim settled in Broadmoor, creating no waves and barely an unpleasant ripple. The latter investigations never manifested. Metaphorically, the jury is out. Many of the masses may be unconvinced by what they perhaps see as a frivolous sideshow. Familiar companions of ambiguity and uncertainty, never too far away.

Returning to Voltaire, Mr Ingle might throw in, *'whilst doubt is an unpleasant condition, certainty is an absurd one'*. The human brain so often seeks simplicity. Do we use language to find the truth or obscure it?

Homing in on post-crime discussions of Jim's case in society, and so often there lies a black and white dichotomy. Like the babbled conjecture on the Yorkshire Ripper, 'Is he mad or is he bad?'. 'Is he pure evil, or is he insane?'.

Such foci will not just emerge within a pub of inebriated souls. It will occur throughout. In households, in offices, in hair salons, in nail bars, and amongst mental health professionals. In Jim's case, as in life: we are left with ambiguity to resolve.

Several decades after Jim is long since transformed into ashes, this Broadmoor report and other documentation related to Jim have been shredded and incinerated by a specialist confidential disposal company. Perhaps the final testimony to Jim's existence, up in smoke. The last remnants of our Jim, slipped away several years after his terminus.

Chapter 75 - The very last grain of sand slips from the hour glass.

The scene returns to Jim, aged in his seventies; dying. A childhood flashed before him, as if time stood still. He remains, within his hospital room. The radio continues to blessedly play Jim out, with Terry Jacks continuing the soothing melody.

Faint echoes of the touch of Beth's hand are replayed, deep in Jim's mind. The final flickers; a soft twitch cocooned by nothingness. In the next few moments, Jim slipped away from this life. The song continued with a respectful resonance.

.........it's hard to die
When all the birds are singing in the sky
Now that the spring is in the air
With the flowers everywhere
I wish that we could both be there
We had joy, we had fun
We had seasons in the sun
But the stars we could reach
Were just starfish on the beach
We had joy, we had fun
We had seasons in the sun
But the stars we could reach
Were just starfish on the beach
We had joy, we had fun
We had seasons in the sun
But the wine and the song
Like the seasons, have all gone
All our lives we had fun
We had seasons in the sun
But the hills that we climbed
Were just seasons out of time.......

DAVID NIGHTINGALE

....

Printed in Great Britain
by Amazon